vILLAGE
ON THE HILL

AN EPIC COLLISION OF FAMILY LIFE
AND GLOBAL DISASTER

ANNIE DOYLE

LITTLECROFT
PUBLISHING

For all those who have fought
for our freedoms.

ACKNOWLEDGEMENTS

Publishing my debut novel was a dream come true. The inspiration for *The Cocoa Girls* and *The Village on the Hill*, came from family history research. The women I discovered in my mam's family continue to inspire me and I hope my stories do credit to their incredible legacy.

Writing can be a lonely business and I must thank my ever-faithful support at home for not complaining when I disappear into the loft for days on end. So many ideas arrive and plot holes are solved when I'm out with best dog Alfie. Authors would be nothing without readers. To anyone who has read my debut novel, thank you. To anyone who has reviewed it, thank you. To anyone who has attended any of my talks, thank you. My family and friends; thank you for your constant support. Thanks to: Jacky Collins, aka Dr. Noir, dear friend, powerhouse of all things fiction, editor extraordinaire and provider of wise words; my lovely, constructively critical beta readers Astrid and Dawn; Rob Barnes for typesetting, fantastic cover design and illustrations and being a hilarious human; Valerie Speed for my wonderful author photographs; Sam Myers and my Rockbox and Ribby ladies for space to punch and star jump my frustrations away without hurting anyone; Kelly Lacey for fabulous publicity and book tours; Glenda Young, friend, constant supporter and author of powerful historical sagas and cosy crimes; Fiona Veitch Smith, friend, supporter and author of *The Miss Clara Vale Mysteries* and *The Poppy Denby Investigates* series; Shelley Day, friend, supporter and author of *The Confession of Stella Moon* and *What Are You Like*; David Turton, friend, supporter and author of *The Malaise* and *The Psychic of Sachsenhausen*; terrific local independent book shops for taking a chance on a debut author – Helen, James and the team at Forum Books, the bound and The Accidental Bookshop, Nicole and Stephanie at Featherbed Books in Houghton le Spring and Emma at Collected in Durham; everyone at Gateshead Libraries and Gateshead Archive for collecting and maintaining such a valuable local resource. Many others helped along the way.

Thanks to each and every one of you.

FICTIONAL CHARACTERS
IN ORDER OF APPEARANCE

Ena Leighton/Evie Brown – 12 years old when our story begins.

Ivy Dinah Jane Leighton/Primavesi/Dinah Jane Brown - Ena's aunt.

Jack Todd – Ena's friend in Gateshead.

John Todd – Jack's uncle.

Mona Leighton/Margaret Brown – Ena's mother.

Elizabeth Ann Brown/Lizzie – Ena's nemesis. Ivy and Mona's cousin.

Peggy Willow – English dancer and actress. Mona's friend.

Marvin Marvel/Marv – American director at the Paradise Theatre in New York City.

Clara – Mrs Newbold's maid at Parkview guest house in London. Suffrage supporter.

Mrs Newbold – owner of Parkview guest house.

Nancy Glover – Ena's friend in Gateshead (deceased).

Agatha Brown – Lizzie's mother and Ivy and Mona's aunt.

Herbert Joseph Primavesi (Bertie) – Ivy's fiancé.

Louis Levy – Ena's father.

Vernon Revill – steward on RMS *Titanic*.

Walter Hampson – Lord Hampson's (of Hampson Hall) elder son.

Grace Opal – opera singer and actress. Walter Hampson's wife.

Mr Newbold – Mrs Newbold's husband (deceased).

Lena Primavesi – Bertie's 27-year-old sister.

Isabel Primavesi – Bertie's 26-year-old sister.

Gertrude Primavesi - Bertie's 24-year-old sister.

Leo Primavesi - Bertie's 22-year-old brother.

Theodosia Brown – Ena's grandmother (deceased).

Miss Kinghorn – Ena's teacher at South Street Infants School in Gateshead.

Isabella Holliday (Bella) – wealthy American travelling on RMS *Titanic*.

Hilda Tilley – cook at the Primavesi home on Lansdowne Road in Bournemouth.

Gladys Upward – maid at the Primavesi home on Lansdowne Road in Bournemouth.

Catherine Primavesi – Bertie's mother.

Giulio Cesare Primavesi – Bertie's father.

Rachel Leaman – Ena's friend.

Ruby Rogers – scullery maid at Hampson Hall. Ivy's friend.

Mrs Jackson – housekeeper at Hampson Hall. Ruby's nemesis.

Edwin Leaman – Rachel's father.

Meta Leaman – Rachel's mother.

Cyril Leaman – Rachel's elder brother.

Donovan Leaman – Rachel's younger brother.

Bessie Bentley – stage actress.

Harold Barnes – music hall performer.

Lawrence and Celia Stratton – husband and wife trick cyclists.

Monsieur le Grand – director at the West London Theatre.

Maud Quick – librarian.

Seymour Love – Rachel's piano teacher.

William Love – Mr Love's son and Rachel's beau.

Dr Porter – Ivy's doctor.

Madeleine Proctor – Ivy's midwife.

Miss Rix – Ena's arithmetic teacher.

Olga Curwen – Queen's Needlework Guild organiser, volunteer at Endell Street, Ivy's friend.

Victoria Burdon – Voluntary Aid Detachment (VAD) nurse at Endell Street, Ivy's friend.

Johnny Johnson – Donovan's friend at the Western Front.

George Scott-Smith – Ivy's second husband.

Albert Revill – Vernon's brother.

Alice Reeves – solicitor and Ena's employer in Bournemouth.

Irene Revill – Vernon's mother.

HISTORICAL CHARACTERS

Edward J. Smith – Captain of RMS *Titanic* (1850 – 1912).

Joseph Boxhall – 4th Officer on RMS *Titanic* (1884 – 1967).

Karl Behr – tennis player and banker. Passenger on RMS *Titanic* (1885 – 1949).

Helen Monypeny Newsom – love interest and later wife of Karl Behr. Passenger on RMS *Titanic* (1892 – 1965).

Thomas Andrews – British businessman and shipbuilder, RMS *Titanic*'s architect. (1873 – 1912).

Elsie Bowerman – British lawyer, suffragette, political activist. Passenger on RMS *Titanic* (1889 – 1973).

Emmeline Pankhurst – British political activist and founder of the Women's Social and Political Union (1858 – 1928).

Joseph Bruce Ismay – Managing Director and Chairman of the White Star Line (1862 – 1937).

Louisa Garrett Anderson – medical pioneer, member of the Women's Social and Political Union, suffragette and social reformer. Co-founder of Endell Street Military Hospital. (1873 – 1943).

Flora Murray – Scottish medical pioneer, member of the Women's Social and Political Union and suffragette. Co-founder of Endell Street Military Hospital. (1869 – 1923).

Ethel Smyth – English composer, member of the women's suffrage movement (1858 – 1944).

Lewis Harcourt – British Liberal Party politician and avowed anti-suffragist (1863 – 1922).

Thomas Beecham – English conductor and impresario (1879 – 1961).

Emily Wilding Davison – English suffragette (1872 – 1913).

John George Phillips – senior wireless officer on RMS *Titanic* (1887 – 1912).

Harold Sydney Bride – junior wireless officer on RMS *Titanic* (1890 – 1956).

Colonel John Jacob Astor – American business magnate, real estate developer, investor and writer (1864 – 1912).

Mrs Madeleine Talmage Astor – American socialite and wife of

John Jacob Astor (1893 – 1940).

Sir Cosmo Edmund Duff-Gordon – prominent Englishman and sportsman (1862 – 1931).

Lucy, Lady Duff-Gordon – leading British fashion designer and wife of Edmund Duff-Gordon (1863 – 1935).

Charles Herbert Lightoller – 2nd Officer on RMS *Titanic* (1874 – 1952).

Edward Pomeroy Colley – Irish civil engineer. Passenger on RMS *Titanic* (1875 – 1912).

Helen Candee – American author, journalist, interior decorator, feminist, and geographer. Passenger on RMS *Titanic* (1858 – 1949).

William Murdoch – 1st Officer on RMS *Titanic* (1873 –1912).

Millicent Fawcett – English politician, writer and activist. Louisa Garrett Anderson's aunt. (1897 – 1919).

Elizabeth Garrett Anderson – English physician and suffragist. Louisa's mother. (1836 – 1917).

Edith Amelia née Ward, Lady Wolverton – keen follower of politics and political gossip (1872-1956).

Sir Alfred Keogh – Director General of the Army Medical Services (1857 – 1936).

Lord Kitchener – senior British Army officer and colonial administrator (1850 – 1916).

Elizabeth Robins – actress, playwright, novelist, and suffragette (1862 – (1952).

Beatrice Harraden – influential feminist writer and suffragette (1864 – 1936).

Jane Crow – schoolfriend of Elizabeth Garrett Anderson (c. 1834 – c. 1914).

Annie Austin née Crow – schoolfriend of Elizabeth Garrett Anderson and 3rd mistress of Girton College, Cambridge (1835 – 1901).

Emily Davies – English feminist and suffragist, pioneering campaigner for women's rights to university access and 4th mistress of Girton College, Cambridge (1830–1921).

Barbara Bodichon – English educationalist and artist, a leading mid-19th-century feminist and women's rights activist (1827 – 1891).
David Lloyd-George – Prime Minister of the United Kingdom from 1916 to 1922 (1863 – 1945).
Christabel Pankhurst – British suffragette (1880 – 1938).

MUSIC

'The March of the Women' – music composed by Ethel Smyth, words by Cicely Hamilton (1910).

'Jack Be Nimble' – the rhyme is first recorded in a manuscript and was collected by James Orchard Halliwell in the mid-nineteenth century (c.1815).

'One Fine Day' – aria from Madame Butterfly by Giacomo Puccini, an opera in three parts based on the short story *'Madame Butterfly'* by John Luther Long (1898).

'The Village Maiden' – composed by Stephen Foster (1855).

'All That I Ask Of You Is Love' – written by Edgar Selden and Herbert Ingraham, performed by Helen Clark (1910).

'The Mosquitoes Parade' – composed by Howard Whitney Swope (c. 1899).

'Vision of Salome' – composed by Archibald Joyce (1908).

'Trumpet Voluntary' – composed by Jeremiah Clarke (1700).

'Wedding March' – composed by Felix Mendelssohn (1842).

'Put Your Arms Around Me Honey (Hold Me Tight)' – words by Junie McCree, music by Albert Von Tilzer (1910).

'Songe d'Automne' – composed by Archibald Joyce (1908).

'Nearer My God to Thee' – composed by Lowell Mason, sung by John McCormack (1913).

'A Bird in a Gilded Cage' – composed by Arthur J. Lamb and Harry von Tilzer, sung by Hamilton Hill (1900).

'Clair de Lune' – composed by Claude Debussy (1905).

'Spring from The Four Seasons' – composed by Antonio Vivaldi (between 1720 and 1723).

'Home Sweet Home' – composed by Henry Bishop, words by John Howard Payne (1823).

'In the Good Old Summertime' – words by Ren Shields, music by George Evans (1902).

'Alexander's Ragtime Band' – composed by Irving Berlin, sung by Collins and Harlan (1911).

THE VILLAGE ON THE HILL

PROLOGUE

Prologue

Bournemouth – May 1912

Ena

Ena Leighton shook her head to try and shift the unwanted memories. They had crept in under her bedroom door while she slept. She looked around at her pretty, comfortable room. She took a deep breath. She was safe, the people in her dreams couldn't reach her here, they couldn't hurt her anymore. She walked to the window. Her aunt's garden glistened with early morning dew and a solitary blackbird greeted the new day with his lyrical notes. She tiptoed to the bathroom to wash her face and brush her teeth then back to her bedroom to get dressed. Barefoot, she made her way downstairs and out into the back garden. A shiver shot through her when she stepped onto the wet lawn. Grass squelched up through her toes and a picture of dirty, smelly mud filled her mind. She looked down to check. She managed a tight smile. She was in Bournemouth, not filthy Pipewellgate. She owned shoes now, ones that fitted her properly. She could go inside and put them on, if she wanted to. She rubbed the stem of a plant with her thumb and forefinger and lifted her hand to her nose. Aunt Ivy had called it lavender. Ena sniffed and the sweet, floral scent drifted up her nose. She stared at the plant next to the lavender. Delicate lines of silver thread hung between the blooms. In the middle of the spider's web, a black fly struggled in the sticky trap. Ena watched the spider bite the fly then quickly wrap it in silk. She turned and looked at Aunt Ivy's house. A home, not somewhere she was trapped like the fly. Somewhere she could be happy. Why then, did she feel something tugging at her, as if she was on elastic? Something pulling her back.

Her aunt had said this was her new home and Ena wanted to believe it, but she worried it could all be whisked away. Her dreams were a constant reminder of other times. Times when hunger gnawed at her insides and the threat of violence was never far away. She wanted to fit in but was conscious of her Geordie accent, a jarring sound amidst the gentle lilt of her aunt's husband's family and friends. They had welcomed her with open arms and she was fortunate to be here. She would be 13 next week and her aunt was arranging a picnic for her. Aunt Ivy, the only mother Ena had ever known. Aunt Ivy rescued her from a life of hell, gave her security and for the first time she could remember, love. The sun started to warm the air around her and Ena breathed deeply. She looked up into the cloudless sky. She sighed; would she ever find somewhere that felt like home? Somewhere she belonged. She started life in Gateshead in the North East of England, but wasn't sure she could think of it as home after everything she suffered there. She knew there were better parts of Gateshead, better homes than the one she was forced to endure. There were girls and boys at her school whose clothes were clean, whose families gave them food to eat in the playground at dinnertime. She pictured her friend Jack Todd. Jack's parents died when he was a baby but his aunt and uncle took him in. Jack's aunt died soon after, but his uncle never considered not keeping him. Unlike Ena, he was well cared for, given enough to eat and a warm, comfortable bed to sleep in. Ena's lip trembled, that was how family should be. She lived with her mother's cousin Lizzie, a woman as far from Jack's uncle as it was possible to be. Her mother left her to rot in a slum with a cruel, spiteful drunk for a guardian. All Ena's mother ever gave her was a handkerchief and a picture. She didn't even sign the picture as being from her mother, it was signed 'To my little girlie, with fond thoughts, yours lovingly, Mona'. Ena didn't know who Mona was, but Jack's uncle confirmed it was her

3

mother. Jack helped her to escape from Lizzie and she stayed with him and his uncle the night before Aunt Ivy came to collect her.

She closed her eyes and imagined a pretty village and a little house with a garden and friends living nearby. She shook her head, the village only existed as a picture in her mind. She was homesick for an imaginary place. She opened her eyes and squared her shoulders, she had to believe life could be better, that things could change. After all, she never imagined she would live in Bournemouth. She never imagined she would have a different name.

ACT ONE

Chapter 1

Southampton - Wednesday 10th of April 1912

Mona

Mona Leighton walked along the path at the side of Southampton dock. She shielded her eyes against the warm spring sunshine. The majestic ship towered above her, waiting for its eager passengers to embark. Her stomach fluttered at the prospect of returning to New York City. The busy, thrilling city was full of the excitement and glamour her shallow soul craved.

'Mona! Wait for me!'

Mona turned at the excited voice behind her.

Peggy's short, blond curls bounced. 'Look at this magnificent ship! Isn't it fabulous?" Darling, we're going to have such fun!'

Mona's smile didn't reach her eyes. Since January, the friends had been performing in repertory theatre in English coastal towns until Mona's friend Peggy Willow, a sought-after actress, received an invitation to return to Broadway's Paradise Theatre from the renowned director Marvin ('call me Marv!') Marvel. Peggy said she would come if Marv found a position in his new production for Mona. Marv agreed, sealing the deal by sending them first class tickets for the voyage. Mona hesitated, saying she had responsibilities in England, responsibilities she had neglected for too long. She stared up at the ship and tried not to think about her daughter and sister. Her chance to be reunited with her family had gone. The lure of New York City's bright lights triumphed and here she was, the idea of home and the possibility of being part of a family, lost. Peggy touched her arm and Mona turned to her friend.

'Are you sure you don't want to go back to London? It's not too late.'

Mona pictured the Paradise and her mood lifted. 'No, I'm sure everything will be all right. Anyway, today is my 28th birthday, I deserve to do something spectacular!'

'Are you positive?'

Mona looked down and brushed her red wool skirt with a gloved hand. She and Peggy had visited an exclusive London dressmaker to be measured for their travelling suits. They eschewed the fashion for pastels and instead chose bold, striking colours. The dressmaker incorporated slits in the ankle-length hemline of their hobble skirts to help them walk unrestricted. Mona tugged at the sleeves of her jacket then raised her piercing blue eyes, meeting her friend's elfin-like features with a smile. She smoothed her short, sleek brown hair and adjusted her red felt hat before answering.

'Yes! Let's leave this dreary country behind and sail off to a better place!'

Peggy smiled, a picture of petite elegance in her royal blue travelling suit and matching hat. 'Very well, Mona. We'll let the wind take us!'

*

Peggy laughed; her delight tempered by the shadows she knew would follow Mona wherever she went. Her own ghosts were with her on every voyage she took. She pushed the thoughts away; she and Mona were going to have a whale of a time. At the bottom of the gangplank, a member of the ship's crew recorded their names and a porter took their luggage. The women linked arms and the heels of their smart leather boots tapped up the gangplank onto the massive ocean liner waiting to return them to New York City.

Chapter 2

London - two months earlier

Ivy

Ivy Leighton looked up from writing her wedding invitations. She smiled, watching her niece's long auburn plaits bounce against her pink smock dress as she helped Clara clear the table. When Ivy brought her niece to London from Gateshead earlier that year, she was welcomed into Mrs Newbold's guest house. The young girl had spent the last nine years neglected and living in poverty and Ivy didn't know how she would react to the noisy house full of colourful, theatrical guests. She was delighted when her niece's confidence started to grow and gasped when she asked if she could change her name. Ivy explained she had changed her own name for her work on the stage. She couldn't argue against her niece following her example and she agreed, judging it a positive move away from the girl's dismal life in Gateshead.

'Seeing as I have parental responsibility for you and your mother left no forwarding address, I will ensure everything is carried out in accordance with the law.'

A solicitor friend of Ivy's fiancé agreed to arrange the necessary paperwork and with his help, Evie Brown put her miserable old life behind her and became Ena Leighton. When Ivy asked about her choice of name, her niece explained. Her name started with an E and the 'na' was for her friend Nancy. She wanted to take Ivy's current surname. Ivy never met Nancy but sometimes she heard Ena talking to herself and making strange movements with her hands, having a conversation with someone Ivy couldn't see. A few times Ivy thought she heard Ena say a girl's name.

Nancy. Ivy went to school with a girl who had no brothers or sisters. The girl conjured up an imaginary friend to combat her loneliness. Perhaps Ena had invented a similar friend during her time in Gateshead. Ivy trod carefully; she didn't know the full extent of Ena's life with Lizzie.

On the day she left her, Ivy had no choice. After their mother died, Ivy and Mona discovered she was deeply in debt to their vicious aunt. Aunt Agatha threatened to send her nieces to the debtor's prison and Ena to the workhouse. They had one bargaining chip; their mother's silver necklace. Aunt Agatha agreed to take it as a down-payment towards the debt, if Ivy and Mona took positions as scullery maids at Hampson Hall in Northumberland, repaying the debt from their wages. Ivy saw it as their only option but her flighty, irresponsible sister had other ideas and fled to London, abandoning her daughter without a second thought. Mona grabbed the necklace when she ran, leaving her sister and daughter to face Aunt Agatha's wrath. Ivy shook her head, how could Mona have abandoned Ena, not once but twice?

When Ena met Clara, she and Mrs Newbold's housemaid hit it off straightaway. Now Ena followed the young woman around the guest house, insisting on helping her. Clara kept her sleek dark hair short, the skilful cut reaching to the nape of her neck. Her smart maid's uniform was always spotless and she was never without a small pin on her bodice, the purple, white and green colours demonstrating her commitment to the suffrage movement. Since Ivy arrived at Mrs Newbold's two years earlier, she watched Clara work tirelessly to keep the guest house spick and span. She always managed to clear away all traces of the raucous parties Mrs Newbold encouraged when her residents returned from their work at the theatre. Clara had taught Ena the Women's Social and Political Union anthem and Ivy smiled, listening to Ena humming '*The March of the Women.*'

'Life, strife – these two are one,
Naught can ye win but by faith and daring.
On, on that ye have done,
But for the work of today preparing.'

During their years of enforced separation, Ivy and Ena dared to hope they would be reunited. Ivy tried her utmost to visit her niece, despite her hard-faced cousin Lizzie, the child's guardian, contriving to keep them apart. At Hampson Hall, Ivy saved as much as possible from her scullery maid's wages, determined to have enough to repay her mother's debt to Aunt Agatha and return to Gateshead for Ena. She also sent whatever she could to Lizzie, for Ena's upkeep. Ivy shuddered, remembering the sight of her niece when they were reunited. The image of the bruised, emaciated girl in a ragged dress would stay with her forever. When she came to London, Ivy continued saving her wages from the West London Theatre on Shaftesbury Avenue, but her financial situation improved beyond measure when she gained evidence of her aunt's pernicious money-lending scheme. When she threatened to engage a solicitor to uncover the extent of her criminal activities, her aunt removed her glasses and pinched the bridge of her nose with her fingers. She blanched before writing Ivy a cheque to repay the interest she had falsely demanded. Ivy watched the fight go out of her aunt, like a large popped balloon sagging into an unrecognisable shape.

Ivy studied the pretty invitation lying on her writing desk. She smiled, reading the words for the umpteenth time. She chose the theatrical Rococo design to reflect her late mother's French heritage. Her parents wouldn't be at her wedding, but Ivy imagined their joy at knowing their elder daughter had fallen in love with handsome, kind Herbert Joseph Primavesi. Picturing him, Bertie to his friends and family, she traced the words on the invitation with her long, elegant fingers.

MR AND MRS GIULIO CESARE PRIMAVESI
REQUEST THE HONOUR OF YOUR PRESENCE
AT THE MARRIAGE OF THEIR SON HERBERT JOSEPH
TO MISS IVY DINAH JANE LEIGHTON
FIFTEENTH OF APRIL
NINETEEN HUNDRED AND TWELVE
ONE O'CLOCK IN THE AFTERNOON
AT THE CHURCH OF THE SACRED HEART,
RICHMOND HILL, BOURNEMOUTH.

Ivy explained to Ena that after they were married, she would live with her and Bertie in Bournemouth, where Bertie grew up. Ever since her flighty sister abandoned her daughter, Ivy had taken responsibility for her niece. Mona showed a flash of maternal instinct when the sisters were reunited the previous month. She agreed to return to Gateshead with Ivy and bring Ena back to London with them. Then, true to form, Mona didn't turn up and Ivy travelled to Gateshead alone. Bertie didn't flinch when she explained her position. She wanted to marry him but there was a condition; he would have to agree to Ena living with them. Ivy closed her eyes, remembering the conversation. She would never forget Bertie's words; they allowed her to imagine a future for her and Ena.

'Of course your niece must live with us. I admire your compassion and fortitude in ensuring a steadfast influence in her life. I will love her as you do.'

Now they were preparing for the wedding and their new life together as a family. Ivy opened her eyes and looked at the invitation again. Her lip quivered. Her parents were dead and she didn't know where her sister was. There had been no word from Mona since January. She shook her head. She refused to chase after her anymore. She couldn't force her to understand the importance of being reconciled with her daughter, or make her feel the powerful maternal instinct that would have propelled her to rescue Ena from the danger she faced in Gateshead. Mona was on her own now.

Chapter 3

Mona

They boarded in good time and had an hour before the ship was due to sail. Peggy suggested they should find their cabin and make sure the porter had delivered their luggage, then make their way to the Promenade Deck for a view of the sea. They entered the ship through a large entrance hall. Mona gasped, taking in the elegance and splendour of what Peggy described as their 'floating hotel.' Looking around, she lost any sense of being on board a ship, *Titanic's* entrance hall was like one in a grand house. She pictured Ivy at Hampson Hall and shook herself to dislodge the unwelcome image, the memory serving as a reminder of her own disgraceful behaviour. Ivy was prepared to take the scullery maid's position at the large country house, to repay their late mother's debt to their spiteful aunt. Nine years later, shame still overwhelmed Mona when she brought her own response to mind. She fled, running away to London with Louis, her daughter's father. Worse, so much worse, she abandoned her daughter. She left her four-year-old daughter, alone and vulnerable, without so much as a backward glance.

'Come on Mona, we need to see our cabin!'

Peggy's excited shout cut through Mona's thoughts and she hurried to catch up with her friend. The demons of her past wrapped themselves around her like a dark, jagged shadow. They would follow and nip at her wherever she went. A steward approached them and asked if they knew their cabin number. Peggy flourished their tickets and he raised his eyebrows. Mona turned away; her face hot. Peggy's less than honest activities, which enabled their oft times lavish lifestyle, made her uncomfortable. The steward stared, unprepared for two young, unaccompanied women to be travelling first class. Mona watched Peggy stare back, challenging him to question her. The steward nodded and regained his composure before leading them towards the Grand Staircase. Walking ahead, he waxed lyrical about RMS *Titanic*, the 'unsinkable ship'.

'From her keel to the top of her funnels she's 175 feet tall, taller than the Statue of Liberty in New York Harbor. Have either of you ladies been to New York before?'

Mona and Peggy exchanged a glance and Mona gave a quick shake of her head. There were aspects of her previous visit to New York she wanted to forget. Peggy diverted the steward's attention by asking how many decks there were.

'There are ten decks, Miss. Or some people call them floors. From the top there's the Boat Deck, the Promenade Deck, then passenger decks B to G, Orlop Deck and the Tank Top. The Promenade Deck, also called A Deck, extends along her entire length, all 883 feet!'

Mona smiled, but the steward's question lingered. How would it be, returning to the city where fear kept her awake? She sighed; she had also been comfortable among New York's theatres and restaurants. Resolving to forget her fears, she concentrated on the steward's voice.

'This is the Grand Staircase. Look up ladies.'

Mona's eyes followed the steward's finger towards a large wrought iron and glass dome overhead. Shafts of daylight flooded in through the stained-glass skylight, casting a myriad of colours around them. Majestic oak panelling covered the walls, enhanced by ornate carved work. The steward explained the Grand Staircase, descending seven levels between the Boat Deck and E Deck, was the main connection between decks for first-class passengers and their point of entry to several public rooms.

'Alternatively, if you prefer, forward of the staircase and around the corner, you will find the three first-class elevators.'

Peggy tapped Mona on the shoulder. 'Do you remember the first time you used the elevator in my New York apartment building?'

Mona nodded. She remembered her rising panic as the noisy contraption clunked towards Peggy's tenth floor apartment. She became more confident about using it but her mind tended towards less favourable memories of her time in New York. She tried to concentrate on the small bronze cherub angel sitting at the base of the staircase, before tracing a gloved hand up the curved rail. The iron and bronze balustrade, supported by light scrollwork of intricately carved flowers and foliage, led them to a landing where a large carved panel contained a clock. On each side of the clock were female figures which the steward explained symbolised Honour and Glory, crowning Time.

'Which one are you, Mona? Honour or Glory?' Peggy laughed but Mona looked away. She considered herself neither honourable nor glorious.

The steward spoke led them along the landing. Mona walked carefully, not trusting her shaking legs. 'B Deck, or the Bridge Deck, is this way, ladies. And might I say, what an excellent choice of accommodation. You have use of the salt-water baths between ten and twelve each morning and the gymnasium and racquets court, should you wish to take physical exercise during your journey. The facilities are of the highest standard and you must avail yourselves of the A La Carte Restaurant. The Italian chef produces the finest menu imaginable. Breakfast is served from 8 o'clock until 10.00, luncheon from 1 o'clock until 2.30 and dinner from 7 o'clock until 8.15. You will be alerted to meals being served by the ship's bugler, who plays 'The Roast Beef of England' before each service. The delightful Café Parisien offers the best French haute cuisine, then there is the First-Class

Lounge and you must dance to the ship's orchestra after dinner!'

The steward continued chattering as they walked. Mona heard Peggy asking him questions but the noises in her head drowned out their conversation. She tried to concentrate on the here and now but the past was a formidable opponent and long-buried, unwanted memories triumphed. She didn't deserve to be embarking on the adventure of a lifetime on this magnificent ship when she had let people down, over and over again. If she belonged anywhere on board, it was steerage accommodation, not a first-class cabin on B Deck. A young girl skipped past, holding her mother's hand, laughing and jumping as she sang.

'Jack be nimble,
Jack be quick,
Jack jump over
The candlestick.'

'Walk properly now, Charlotte.'

Mona stopped and turned to watch Charlotte and her mother walking down the staircase. Her feet wouldn't move. The name, Charlotte. A different voyage not so long ago when she learnt about the underhand activities of a group of women known as 'The Charlottes'. Following the tragic sinking of a Thames pleasure cruiser named the 'Prince Charles', women masquerading as bereaved widows boarded ships with the intention of approaching well-to-do passengers. Regaling tales of woe, they claimed to have lost family members and livelihoods in the disaster. Mona recognised Peggy's suspicious behaviour as typical of this audacious act. Shamefully, at her most desperate point, she attempted to carry out the duplicity herself. She failed miserably and found herself poised on the ship's rail, staring into the unforgiving water below. A lucky wind blew her backwards, her miraculous survival only serving to increase her self-loathing.

Her lip trembled and she blinked hard to shift hot tears. Still the memories persisted. What had she achieved in her 28 years? What had she done for anyone other than herself? She shuddered, picturing Louis, her first love and the father of her little girl. He promised to make her dreams of living in London and dancing with the English Ballet Company a reality. She believed every word he said, travelled to London with him, a single woman, unchaperoned and naïve. Adding even more scandal to her already tarnished reputation. London was as far from her dreams as she could have imagined. Louis proved to be a coward, abandoning her to a sordid existence as an exotic dancer in a rundown music hall. She glanced down at the girl. She longed to see her own daughter and planned to accompany her sister to Gateshead. The opportunity to be reunited was there and she didn't take it. Instead, she was running away again. Her daughter would be 13 soon and nausea rose into Mona's throat when she realised she could no longer picture her.

'Ladies, this is your cabin. My name is Vernon Revill, please do not hesitate to ask for me, should you need anything. Or if you prefer, you may be attended by a female stewardess. There is an electric fire in your cabin. The weather is forecast to be calm in the coming days, but if it turns cold, please call and someone will come and switch it on. Alternatively, if you are too warm, you can unlock the porthole for fresh air. Coffee can be delivered to your cabin, along with fresh bath towels each day. If you place your day dresses on your bed they will be sponged and cleaned ready for the next day. I trust everything is in order?'

Mona watched Peggy thank Vernon, discreetly placing something into his gloved hand. Well-trained in the act of servitude he pocketed the gratuity, his expression unreadable. Mona knew Peggy's view; generosity was its own reward. Peggy threw the door to cabin B-58 open and they stood on the threshold, eyes wide at the sight before them. Vernon said their cabin was decorated in the Louis XVI style, with white and gold panelled walls. Mona took a tentative step onto the light green floor and tried to ignore the irony of the cabin's style. Would Louis follow her wherever she went? The door clicked shut with a satisfying clunk. Mona turned to see Peggy twirling around in the middle of the room.

'Our floating, first-class hotel room on the most magnificent ship ever built. We shall arrive into New York Harbor in the utmost style!'

Mona pushed her troubled thoughts away. 'Yes, we shall!' She stroked the soft, turquoise eiderdown on one of the two luxurious-looking beds. She lowered herself onto the elegant sofa, upholstered in a blue floral pattern. She sat with her hands in her lap, not daring to touch the polished armrests. Peggy bounced down at the other end of the sofa, running her fingers along the gilded wooden carvings.

'We can do whatever we like in here, Mona. It's all paid for!'

Mona stared at the colours streaming onto the table in the middle of the room. She looked up at the elaborate chandelier but Peggy gestured towards the blue, yellow and magenta stained-glass windows. Mona watched Peggy move around the cabin, pointing out the three-cornered drinks cabinet, the polished writing desk and the ornate grey sink and triple mirror vanity table with a matching upholstered stool. Peggy said they had their own bathroom, water closet and wardrobe. With echoes of Peggy's New York apartment, Mona forced herself to concentrate on the luxury of the cabin, rather than her time alone in Manhattan. Peggy's voice interrupted her thoughts.

'Come on. We need to freshen up then find the First-Class Lounge!'

Mona mustered a smile. Peggy removed her hat then picked up her silver-backed hairbrush. She brushed quickly, parting her blond curls neatly on one side and smoothing the short style over her ears and down her cheeks to her chin. Mona followed suit, drawing her short, sleek brown hair around her face in a similar fashion.

'Are you ready, Mona? Our first Manhattans of the voyage are waiting!'

Mona followed Peggy, thoughts of her daughter and her disgraceful past forgotten.

Chapter 4

Bournemouth - Wednesday 10th of April 1912

Ivy

The sun rose as Ivy and Ena left Mrs Newbold's. The muted rays cast pale orange and pink shadows along Chestnut Tree Avenue, the dawn promising spring sunshine later. Ivy smiled at the thought of seeing Bertie that evening. She was taking Ena to meet her fiancé's family before their wedding the following week. After the wedding, Ena would stay with Bertie's family while the newly married couple took a honeymoon a short distance along the coast in Boscombe. Ena looked down and Ivy saw her body stiffen. She held her niece's chin and looked into her large, dark-brown eyes.

'It's all right. The Primavesis are kind people. They welcomed me with open arms and I am sure they will adore you. You have the wedding then a new life in Bournemouth to look forward to.'

Ena nodded and Ivy relaxed. She recalled her first trip to the beautiful seaside town and her own introductions to Bertie's family. She was confident they would be happy living there after the wedding. The sea air would be good for Ena's health and she and Bertie would ensure Ena's life continued to improve. They said their goodbyes to Mrs Newbold and Clara the previous evening, knowing they would all meet again soon, at the wedding. Mrs Newbold promised to oversee the collection of their belongings for onward delivery to Bournemouth. Clara left them a small picnic to eat in the cab on their way to Waterloo station and Ivy watched Ena tuck in. She was still thin but had started to gain weight. Ivy smiled; everything was going to be all right.

Despite the early hour, Waterloo thronged with travellers. Ivy reached for Ena's hand and they made their way to the platform indicated for their train. A porter took their luggage and showed them to their carriage. The cheque from Aunt Agatha meant Ivy could afford a private first-class carriage. Ena hesitated at the door to the carriage. Ivy went ahead and sat on the padded seat to the left, gesturing towards the one opposite. She watched Ena gently trace her finger along the orange and green herringbone patterned seat before slowly lowering herself. Ena clasped her hands in her lap and crossed her ankles. Ivy pointed towards the cushions and Ena reached for one and placed it behind her back.

'No-one will disturb us apart from the train guard who will need to check our tickets. There is a lavatory along the corridor and when we start to feel hungry, we can visit the restaurant car. Are you comfortable?'

Ena nodded but jumped when the whistle shrieked to signal their departure. Ivy moved along her seat towards the window and signalled to Ena to do the same. 'Wave to someone on the platform, Ena!'

'Who? I don't know anyone there.'

'It doesn't matter, wave to anyone! It's a bit of fun!' Ivy laughed and waved at a middle-aged couple waiting on the platform.

Ena joined in, laughing and waving as the train chugged out of Waterloo. Ivy reached over and squeezed Ena's hands. Ena repositioned the cushion in the small of her back and removed a book from her travel bag. Ivy smiled; glad she had encouraged Ena to bring some books with her. Ena held Ivy's copy of 'Penny Whistles' by Robert Louis Stevenson. Before Ena's grandmother Theodosia died and their lives changed overnight, Theodosia read to Ena from the book of poems. Ena said she didn't remember being read to but told Ivy she had a favourite poem, 'The Swing.'

'Would you read *'The Swing'* to me, Ena?'

Ena's cheeks reddened but she nodded. She read slowly and quietly.

'How do you like to go up in a swing,
Up in the air so blue?
Oh, I do think it the pleasantest thing,
Ever a child can do!
Up in the air and over the wall,
Till I can see so wide,
Rivers and trees and cattle and all,
Over the countryside…'

'Thank you; you read very well now.'

Ena smiled. She told her aunt how much she enjoyed reading, since she got her spectacles. Ivy's anger towards Lizzie burned when she allowed herself to think of the neglect Ena suffered. The poem gave her an idea; they could get a swing for their garden in Bournemouth. She watched Ena's excitement grow as the train took them southwest from London. Ivy encouraged her to take in the view. 'If you look out of the window, you'll soon see Kingston-upon-Thames. It's a beautiful place, right next to the river.'

'Is the Thames like the River Tyne, Aunt Ivy?'

Ivy grimaced, picturing the oily, industrial river separating Newcastle and Gateshead. They were brought up a few streets away from the stench and pollution of the Tyne. 'No, it's not. People go boating on this part of the Thames. It's a very picturesque place, nothing like the Tyne. Kingston-upon-Thames used to be famous for its malting and brick-making industries, but this year there are plans to begin manufacturing aircraft here. Imagine Ena, it will be home to the first aircraft to be built in England!'

Ivy watched Ena turn to look out of the window. What grim memories resurfaced in her niece's mind by the mention of the

River Tyne? After some time, Ena turned back, her face impassive. Ivy noticed how Ena appeared to process recollections of her previous life. She said very little about living with Lizzie and nothing about the time before, when she was in the workhouse.

'Aunt Ivy, where did you meet Bertie?'

Ivy raised her eyebrows then smiled; she had been reluctant to meet him. When a piece of good fortune enabled her to leave Hampson Hall and travel to London to look for her sister, Ivy continued to place her niece's wellbeing above her own desires and ambitions. She accepted her responsibility to her niece more readily than the girl's own mother, knowing if Mona was never found, she would have to marry a very special man. One prepared to offer both her and her niece a home. When her friend Grace Opal and her fiancé Walter Hampson invited Ivy to dine with them and Walter's friend Bertie, she was flattered but concerned. She wanted to decline the invitation, thinking it wasn't the right time to have dinner with a potential suitor. She struggled with her decision, Walter and Grace were so kind in helping her get to London; they arranged her transport and accommodation at Mrs Newbold's. Grace even secured her an audition at the West London Theatre. She owed them a significant debt of gratitude but couldn't risk being rejected by a man because of her circumstances. She hatched a plan to 'forget' to take her evening gown to the theatre, hoping to make it impossible for her to accompany Walter and Grace. She smiled ruefully. Thanks to Mrs Newbold noticing she left without her gown and Clara bringing it to the theatre, she was now engaged to Mr Herbert Joseph Primavesi. Together they would give Ena the life she deserved.

'We met at a dinner at the Langham Hotel in London.'

Ena's face remained expressionless. Other than her three months at Mrs Newbold's, Ivy knew she had no experience of anywhere apart from Gateshead. Ena had never eaten in a hotel restaurant and Ivy suspected she spent years wondering where her next meal would come from. Ivy shook herself; her job now was to introduce Ena to the possibilities of a life away from the poverty of Gateshead. Her mother Theodosia insisted being born in Gateshead did not mean her daughters had to stay there. They didn't have to tread the usual path expected of women, they could be different, independent. She and Mona fought hard to achieve their independence and Ivy wanted the same for Ena. Her eyes sparkled when she remembered seeing Bertie for the first time. 'When I arrived at the hotel with my friend Grace, her fiancé Walter and Bertie were waiting to meet us. They were dressed for dinner, wearing immaculate white tie and tails.'

Ena looked blank.

'Do you remember the picture in the pretty frame that Mrs Newbold showed you? The one with her husband when they visited the theatre to see 'Madame Butterfly?''

Ena smiled. The picture showed Mrs Newbold, resplendent in a blue evening dress with feathers in her hair and her husband, smart and dashing in his dinner suit. She said she hadn't known it was called white tie and tails.

'Yes, I remember. Mrs Newbold looked happy.'

Ivy's heart broke for her niece. Happiness had been in short supply in Ena's life until recently. She and Bertie promised each other the young girl's future would be different. Ivy pictured Bertie. A tall, dark-haired man with deep blue eyes. Kind, compassionate eyes. The dinner was one of the best evenings in Ivy's life. Second only to closing nights at the theatre. She told Ena some of the details of the hotel's history and their dinner.

'The Langham had been open for 50 years when I visited. The Prince of Wales and much of Victorian high society attended the spectacular opening ceremony. It was the favourite venue for royalty, artists and musicians from around the world, and I never expected to set foot inside such a grand building.'

Ena's eyes were wide when Ivy described the delicious dishes she enjoyed. She told her niece she silently thanked her mother when she opened the menu.

'Why?'

'When I looked around the room, I knew she wanted this for me and your mother. For us to rise above the low place of our birth and escape to situations such as dinner at the Langham Hotel in London. During the meal I learnt Bertie's father's family were Italian immigrants who arrived in England around the same time as Theodosia. I found Bertie an easy person to like, a gentle, caring man who worked hard and made an honest living as a jeweller.'

Ivy looked out of the window, remembering Bertie talking about his family. She had been crestfallen, thinking the last thing a gentleman like him would want was to be lumbered with someone else's child. The idea of her niece living with her once she married was impossible. She squared her shoulders. She would meet the right man. Perhaps it wasn't Herbert Joseph Primavesi.

'After the dinner we met as often as possible; Bertie stayed in London and attended my performances at weekends, then returned to Bournemouth each Sunday evening. I missed him more each time he left and he assured me he felt the same. I found him very easy to talk to and my admiration for him grew when he told me his sisters were involved with the suffrage movement. He had even accompanied them to a suffragist rally.'

'Will I meet them, Bertie's sisters?'

'Yes. Their names are Lena, Isabel and Gertrude. Lena is 27, Isabel is 26 and Gertrude is 24. Bertie also has a brother called Leo who is 22. I think you will all get along very well.'

'I'd like to learn about the suffrage movement. Will Bertie's sisters tell me?'

'I think they will be delighted to tell you everything you

want to know. The work is very important in paving the way for greater freedoms for women.'

As Ivy got to know Bertie, she knew she needed to be honest with him. He listened when she set out the circumstances leading to her sister's abandonment of her child. She said she took her responsibility to her niece seriously and if Mona was never found, she would want Ena to live with her. She waited, expecting rejection. It didn't come, and she allowed herself to fall in love with Bertie. She leant across the carriage and took Ena's hands.

'You know things are going to be all right now, don't you?' Ivy watched Ena nod slowly. She hoped her niece could put her troubles behind her.

'Right. Back to *'Madame Butterfly'*. Do you know the story or any of the songs?'

Ena shook her head.

'Your grandmother taught me and your mother about the magic and beauty to be found in music and stories. Do you remember her?'

Ena nodded. Ivy continued to tread carefully. She knew Ena was neglected during their years apart, and she hadn't pressed for details. Perhaps talking about Theodosia would help. Ivy's own memories of her mother were bittersweet. Theodosia Brown, Tee to her friends, Frannie La Fleur on stage. Ivy was proud of her mother's allure, her difference. A Frenchwoman living in Gateshead, Theodosia was unique. She instilled in her daughters a determination to fight for their rights and refuse to allow society to overlook them. She had been dead for nine years and Ivy's heart broke anew when she pictured her remarkable, beautiful mother. She felt her loss as keenly now as the day she registered her death. She squeezed Ena's hand.

'Do you want to talk about her?'

Chapter 5

Ena

Ena met her aunt's eyes and nodded. She had called Theodosia Grama, and during her years of separation from her family, she fought for scraps of memories. Memories comforted her, reminded her she had been loved, once. When her desperate situation threatened to overwhelm her, she battled to hold onto these precious memories. When she was hungry and cold and her alcoholic guardian Lizzie was nowhere to be found, she clung to glimpses of her life before everything changed. She longed for her grama's warm cuddles and lullabies and the unconditional love that filled her life before her grama went to be with the angels. She could still recall the dancing lilt of Theodosia's voice, it was stored in her memory, never to be lost. Ena listened to her aunt.

'One of the first things I remember your grandmother teaching me and your mother was her trapdoor trick, *'le truc de la trappe'* in French. When she was young and living in Paris, her mother told her about the magic of daydreams, a trick to escape in difficult times. She said Theodosia could open a trapdoor in her mind and go anywhere. Your grandmother told me and your mother to close our eyes and imagine the most wonderful place we could, then put ourselves there. Can you guess what my place looked like?'

Ena's eyes were wide. 'No, I can't.'

'My place was a meadow full of beautiful summer flowers and a lake, the water cool and refreshing in the sun's heat.'

Ena smiled. 'What did my mother's place look like?'

Ivy sighed. 'Your mother described a glittering ballroom full of people in beautiful dresses, dancing to the latest music, laughing and having fun. I think she used the trick a lot.'

Ena rolled her eyes; the description was typical of her mother. She frowned.

'What is it?'

Ena took a deep breath. Hazy memories flitted through her mind. Hunger gnawing at her empty stomach and a small, suffocating cupboard. She turned to look out of the window. The train moved rhythmically through lush green countryside and she pursed her lips. Would it help to voice the dark memories she fought so hard to hide away?

'You don't have to talk about anything unless you want to.'

A lump formed in Ena's throat and tears filled her eyes. She swallowed and faced her aunt. Her voice was a whisper. 'I think I remember you telling me about the trapdoor trick. I didn't understand it until my first day at school. I understood it when I needed to use it.'

Ena shuddered, allowing the memory to form. She remembered shivering in the schoolyard, her heart racing. One by one the other children moved away from her. A teacher appeared and called them in with a large, loud bell. Ena held back and entered the classroom last. There were two empty desks, right at the back. She stared straight ahead, trying to ignore the spiteful glances and the girl who held her nose when she walked past. An image of her aunt appeared in her mind and she smiled to herself. Her aunt gave her a gift, a trick her classmates knew nothing about. She could make herself invisible and go somewhere else in her head. She whispered to her aunt. 'I am a pretty flower growing in the stinking mud of Gateshead.' She wasn't walking the gauntlet of sly looks and whispered jibes in Miss Kinghorn's classroom any longer, she was strolling in a beautiful garden with her aunt.

Now, Ena sat back and closed her eyes. She felt her aunt squeeze her hand.

'Thank you for telling me, my dear. I am so glad your grandmother's trick helped you. Now, let's return to 'Madame Butterfly."

Ivy

'I should warn you Ena, the music is beautiful but is a tragic tale of unrequited love. The composer, an Italian man called Giacomo Puccini, wrote a sorrowful musical score to accompany the forlorn tale of a young Japanese girl called Butterfly.'

'What a lovely name.'

'Her real name was Cio Cio San. *'Chōchō'* is Japanese for butterfly. She falls in love with an American naval officer, Pinkerton, but their romance has devastating consequences.'

'What happened to her?'

Ivy frowned, her niece needed cheerful stories, not tragedies.

'It's all right, I know it's only a story.'

Ivy continued. 'Butterfly was 15 when she married Pinkerton. She didn't know he married her for convenience, intending to leave once he found an American wife.'

Ena crinkled her nose and crossed her arms. 'I don't like him.'

'No. But in real life, people can be cruel.'

Ena nodded slowly; her eyes told Ivy she knew this from bitter experience.

'Soon after they were married, Pinkerton left Butterfly, promising to return in the spring, *'when the robins nest.'*

'He didn't come back, did he?'

Ivy swallowed to hide her despair at her niece's lost innocence. 'Not for three years. Butterfly insisted he would return. When the American consul visited her with a letter from Pinkerton stating he was travelling to Japan, Butterfly became very excited. She said she had given birth to their son after Pinkerton left.'

Ena narrowed her eyes. 'It was a happy ending, then?'

Ivy shook her head. 'From their house on the hill, Butterfly watched Pinkerton's ship enter the harbour. She and her maid prepared for his arrival, then they waited. Butterfly stayed up all night. When he arrived, his new American wife was with him. When Pinkerton saw Butterfly had decorated the house for him, he realised he should not have returned. Admitting he was a coward; he left, asking the others to break the news to Butterfly. She agreed to give up her child if Pinkerton would come and see her, then she prayed to statues of her ancestral gods and said goodbye to her son. She placed a small American flag in his hands before picking up her father's knife.' Ivy stopped; this story was a mistake.

'She died, didn't she?'

Ivy looked at her niece. 'Yes, I'm afraid so. Pinkerton rushed in, but he was too late.'

Ena smiled weakly but Ivy saw tears in her eyes. Pinkerton's cowardice reminded Ivy of Ena's father Louis and his cowardly actions in London, abandoning Mona to an uncertain fate. Ivy kept those thoughts to herself. 'My favourite song from *Madame Butterfly* is *One Fine Day.* When Butterfly sings it, she believes her husband will return to her.'

'Tell me some of the words, Aunt Ivy. I want to learn about music.'

'Very well. These lines come as Butterfly spots Pinkerton.'
From out the crowded city,
There is coming a man.
A little speck in the distance,
Climbing the hillock.
Can you guess who it is?
And when he's reached the summit,
Can you guess what he'll say?
He will call, 'Butterfly' from the distance.'

Ena pursed her lips. 'Why did she wait for him? I wouldn't wait.'

'Good. You deserve better.'

'I would like to know more of these stories and songs, Aunt Ivy. And to read more books now I have spectacles and can see properly.'

Ivy's heart soared. Lizzie's neglect stretched to ignoring Ena's damaged eyesight. Soon after Ena arrived in London Ivy noticed her niece didn't read well, often screwing her eyes up or closing one to try and make out words or numbers. Ivy sprang into action and before long, Ena was being examined by an eye-doctor. Ivy watched as the contraptions were placed on Ena's face, and she was instructed to read from a page of letters the eye-doctor held out in front of her. Suddenly Ena exclaimed and Ivy knew he had found the right lenses. A few days later a package arrived and Ivy clapped her hands when Ena opened the box. Ena positioned the spectacles on her face and Ivy passed her a newspaper. Ena smiled; the biggest, broadest smile Ivy had ever seen. A whole new, marvellous world opened up for Ena. Mrs Newbold and Clara gave her books and Ivy took her to a bookshop. All Ena needed to correct her eyesight were spectacles. Her reading ability went from strength to strength. Ivy smiled, picturing the book her mother gave her for her 16th birthday, 'Dr Jekyll and Mr Hyde.' Her mother's inscription called it 'a dark tale' and Ivy agreed, reading it quickly and repeatedly. She looked at Ena. Her niece would be 13 in six weeks, was she too young for the gothic tale? Ivy thought not, resolving to buy Ena a copy for her birthday.

Ena

Aunt Ivy said it was over 100 miles from London to Bournemouth. Ena compared it to their journey from Newcastle to London when she came to Mrs Newbold's in January. She couldn't remember anything of the journey. What stayed with her was the taste and smell of a hot, sweet drink Aunt Ivy gave her when she tucked her up in bed. She remembered drinking the hot chocolate greedily and starting to cry when the long-forgotten nectar soothed her dry mouth. She remembered closing her eyes and Aunt Ivy singing her a lullaby. Then she slept as she had never slept before.

She tried to picture Butterfly waiting for Pinkerton to come back. If Butterfly had been her friend, she would have told her not to wait. Pinkerton treated her very badly and he didn't deserve her love. Ena pictured her friend Nancy and a lump grew in her throat. She waited for Nancy on the day they planned to run away from Gateshead. She waited until it grew dark, facing a brutal beating from Lizzie when she reluctantly returned to Pipewellgate. She could have continued with their plan and caught the train to London to find her mother, but she wouldn't have abandoned Nancy. She sighed; she understood Butterfly now, Butterfly loved Pinkerton the way she loved Nancy. She shook herself, determined to concentrate on the future. There was so much to look forward to.

Ena stole a glance at her aunt. Ena admired her aunt's calm grace; she never raised her voice and Ena couldn't imagine her lifting a hand in anger. Aunt Ivy brought joy, elegance and lightness into a room. Ena stroked the skirt of her smart blue wool travelling suit. Aunt Ivy took her to Selfridges to choose her outfits for their stay in Bournemouth. As they approached the huge revolving doors she remembered her first visit to the department store, when she hid behind Aunt Ivy. They went to choose her dress for the wedding and she expected to be thrown out, convinced the assistants would know about her disgraceful beginnings in life and think she didn't belong in Selfridges. To her surprise, they welcomed her. When they arrived in the bridal wear department, Ena caught her breath at the sight of the beautiful dresses. Her unease gone, she pointed at one thing then another, settling on a luxurious, layered garment of soft white silk, accentuated with sprays of hand-made, embroidered silk flowers. On their more recent visit Aunt Ivy led her towards the smart suits designed for travelling and they chose matching outfits in different colours. Aunt Ivy's, a shade of her favourite green, accentuated her piercing blue eyes. Ena hadn't known which colour to choose and Aunt Ivy suggested the navy blue, blue being Theodosia's favourite colour.

Aunt Ivy took her to the hairdresser, where her long, tatted hair was washed and trimmed. Aunt Ivy decided to keep her own hair long until after the wedding. Ena listened to her talking to the hairdresser about a style for her special day. She wanted something similar to her hairstyle when she met Bertie at the Langham. In her dressing room at the West London Theatre, Grace helped Ivy, pulling her long, wavy auburn hair up and away from her face then pinning it into pompadours and puffs. The overall effect, a cluster of soft, graceful curls and coils, framed Ivy's beautiful face. Ena watched her aunt caressing her engagement ring. She didn't know the name of the green stone set in the middle of the gold band, but it reminded her of the trees in Mrs Newbold's garden. Clara said they were English Oak trees. Ena pictured the shiny dark green leaves. Clara described the leaves as having smooth edges and rounded lobes. When Ena frowned Clara laughed and gently tugged Ena's ear lobe. 'Like this!'

Ena giggled. 'It tickles!'

Ena smiled at the memory before asking her aunt how much further Bournemouth was.

Ivy

Ivy laughed. 'There's still a way to go, my dear. Should we use the lavatory then visit the restaurant car?' Ivy saw Ena look down and shuffle her feet. Ivy had taken her to the roof terrace café at Selfridges but this would be her first visit to a restaurant. 'Don't worry, I'll be with you.' Ivy took Ena's hand. A waiter met them at the door to the restaurant car and showed them to a small table with two high-backed seats. The table was covered with a pristine white cloth. Ivy saw Ena flush as she stared at the array of cutlery. She leant across and whispered. 'Start at the outside and work your way in.' The waiter flourished their napkins and Ena sat rigid when he placed hers on her lap. She muttered her thanks. The waiter handed Ivy a menu. 'Should I read it out?'

Ena nodded.

'First, there is a choice of tomato juice or grapefruit juice. Then pea soup with small pieces of fried or toasted bread or a clear soup made with concentrated stock. Next there is grilled turbot in a tomato sauce then roast beef with horseradish sauce, mashed potatoes and vegetables or pork chops with apple sauce, mashed potatoes and vegetables. For dessert you can have apple pie or plum pudding with custard or ice cream. To finish there is cheese and biscuits and coffee.'

Ena said she would have grapefruit juice, roast beef and ice cream.

'Are you sure, my dear? You can have some soup and the fish as well, if you like.'

'No, thank you, Aunt Ivy.'

The waiter returned and Ivy ordered for them.

'Would you like a glass of wine, Madam?' Ivy chose a glass of French red wine and made a toast. 'To us, Ena. And to our new life in Bournemouth with Bertie!' Ena copied her aunt, raising her grapefruit juice. She smiled and Ivy saw her relax. When they returned to their carriage, Ivy suggested Ena might want to have a nap, given how early they left Mrs Newbold's and how much longer the journey would take. Ena agreed and placed her head on the cushion on her aunt's lap. Within minutes Ivy heard her breathing change. Ivy gently stroked Ena's hair and thought about her sister. Where did she go when she left London? When Mona failed to join her to travel to Gateshead for Ena, Ivy hurried to Peggy Willow's flat, where Mona was staying. She learnt they disappeared before it was light and left no forwarding address. Since then, nothing. Four months with no word of explanation. Ena shifted in her sleep and Ivy sighed. She couldn't waste any more time on her errant sister. She needed to concentrate on Ena. Mona had proved herself resilient. Wherever she was, she would be all right.

'Wake up, Ena! We're entering the New Forest. This is Ashurst, it's beautiful.'

Ena stretched and rubbed her eyes then gasped when she looked out of the window.

'The New Forest is one of the largest areas of pasture, heath and forest in Southern England. Bertie said when the Southampton to Dorchester railway opened, Ashurst's fortunes changed overnight. It became a popular tourist destination and I can see why. The woodlands have oak, alder and birch trees and in the wetlands there are many different wild birds, insects and flowers.'

Ena looked blank and Ivy berated herself; her niece lived a very narrow life in Gateshead. It was unlikely she would have seen woodlands or wild birds before.

'Don't worry. We can come back later this year, after the wedding. We'll bring a picnic and see as much of the forest as we can.' Ena smiled and Ivy remembered the promise she made herself at Hampson Hall. Soon after she started working there, she learnt about the family's annual picnic. It was a splendid affair, with the household staff allowed to enjoy themselves, once the family had eaten. The picnic was held by the river, beyond the bluebell woods. There was a small canopy for the family to sit under and the table holding the food groaned with the weight of Cook's labours. Everyone ate, drank and sang along to the band. Ivy remembered the musicians playing a piece she knew from the church hall dances in Gateshead, and her thoughts turned to her niece. The piece was called *'The Village Maiden'* and Ivy listened to the words as she sat in the shade of an old oak tree, appreciating the birdsong and the aroma of wild garlic on the gentle breeze blowing from the riverbank.

'The village bells are ringing,
And merrily they chime;
The village choir is singing,
For 'tis a happy time;
The chapel walls are laden with garlands rich and gay,
To greet the village maiden upon her wedding day.'

Her happiness was tempered by concern for Ena. She promised herself when they were reunited, she would prepare a magnificent picnic. She watched Ena taking in the majestic scenery around them and vowed to keep her promise. Once the train left the New Forest, Ivy told Ena it wouldn't be long before they reached Bournemouth. Picturesque woodland and charming little villages were replaced by railway mechanics and high-pitched whistles as their destination came into view. The station was decorated with beautiful multicoloured floral displays, from one end of the platform to the other. Ivy smiled; the warmth of Bournemouth's early evening wrapped itself around her like a soft blanket. She turned to Ena. 'This is Bournemouth Central! Bertie will be waiting to meet us!'

Chapter 6

Mona

Mona and Peggy approached the elegant oak doors to *Titanic's* First-Class Lounge. Mona hesitated but Peggy swept inside, nodding briefly at the steward holding the door open. Mona smiled and thanked him as she followed Peggy. She stopped and stared at the ornate carved boiseries, the dominant feature of the room. The steward leant towards her, saying if she looked closely she would see small motifs of musical instruments interspersed within the beautiful oak panelling. Mona spotted a flute and a trumpet before a waiter led them to a table in the middle of the room. Her eyes darted from one elaborate feature to another; the bronze sconces and large rounded mirrors, and the magnificent centrepiece the waiter delighted in pointing out.

'Ladies, you are sitting directly underneath the 49-light opaque glass and ormolu Electrolier with crystal embellishment! The central recess of the ceiling, where the Electrolier sits, is itself elaborately moulded with instrumental motifs!'

Mona mumbled her appreciation but Peggy, ever the actress, enthused over the chandelier's electrical lights. Encouraged, the waiter made much of other aspects of the sophisticated room. The cosy alcoves with inset mirrors and tall bay windows of leaded and stained glass adjoining the open seating areas, and the decorative grey marble fireplace (he assured them there was no danger of fire because it contained only an electric heater). He pointed towards the opposite end of the lounge where the curved wall contained a wide mahogany bookcase.

'It serves as a lending library for first-class passengers. You can choose from a collection of classics and the latest releases.

They are freshly stocked on every voyage.'

Peggy opened her mouth but before she could speak, he continued.

'This room is used for socialising, playing cards, reading and the taking of tea, coffee and light refreshments before and after dinner. The small pantry allows first-class stewards to serve you with beverages, buttered toast and sandwiches. Afternoon tea is served at 4 o'clock each day, if you choose to dine here rather than the Café Parisien on B Deck. The First-Class Lounge is available to both men and women but is largely a female domain; ladies feel very comfortable here.'

Mona smiled to herself. The waiter didn't know Peggy would feel very comfortable in a room full of men, would probably prefer it. He continued, telling them about the replica statue of Diana of Versailles standing on the mantlepiece, crowned by a large mirror. Peggy spoke suddenly. 'I'm sorry to interrupt, but could we look at the menu, please?'

'Of course. Please forgive me. I get carried away by *Titanic's* magnificence!'

As the waiter hurried away, Mona raised her eyebrows at Peggy. 'Well, he did go on a bit. And I'm ready for a cocktail, aren't you?'

Mona nodded but the significance of Peggy's interruption wasn't lost on her. The waiter had mentioned Diana of Versailles. A name so much like her sister's, Dinah, before she changed it to Ivy. Mona's change of name, from Margaret Brown to Mona Leighton, was about leaving her old life behind. Ivy explained her reasoning for changing her name when the sisters were reunited in London three months earlier. She needed a name for the stage and chose her landlady's Christian name. When Mona asked Ivy about her surname, her sister took her hand.

'In all the years we were apart, I needed to feel connected to you. Using the same surname as the one you chose helped me to feel closer to you.'

Now, in the imposing surroundings of *Titanic's* First-Class Lounge, tears filled Mona's eyes and she yearned for her sister. How would Ivy ever forgive her?

'Have you seen the menu, Mona? There are so many different liqueurs!'

Mona swallowed. 'What is there?'

'You can have berry, chocolate, coffee, cream, flower, herbal, honey or nut. Or I'm sure they would give you a combination! I think we can have whatever we want on this voyage!'

Mona lowered her eyes, the liqueurs held little appeal for her. An image of other drinks and men watching dancers in a dark club crept into her mind and she willed it away. Even here, she couldn't escape her shame. She didn't belong in *Titanic's* First-Class Lounge.

'Do you fancy a Tom Collins, Mona? It's gin, soda, fresh lemon juice and sweet syrup.'

Mona nodded.

'This is it, Mona. This is the life we deserve, not working in dull coastal towns in second-rate repertory theatres! We're on our way back to New York City!'

The waiter delivered their strained cocktails in tall, flat-bottomed tumblers, garnished with slices of orange and maraschino cherries. Mona sipped her drink. She looked around. Dining tables and chairs, sofas and armchairs upholstered in plush velvet with green and gold patterns, occupied by immaculately coiffured and elaborately behatted ladies, so far from where she started in life.

'Drink up, Mona! Then we'll go on deck and get a good position at the rail!'

Mona frowned, they had no-one to wave farewell to. But Peggy was all about appearances, how things looked to other people. Stepping on deck, Mona turned her face towards the cool breeze blowing off the sea. She took deep breaths of the tangy air. Peggy hurried to the rail and pulled Mona in beside her. She pointed to a well-dressed, middle-aged couple on the dock. 'Look, they're perfect! Wave your handkerchief as if we are their daughters setting off on an exciting voyage! Make them proud!'

Mona hesitated, but when bagpipes signalled their departure, she raised her handkerchief in imitation of Peggy. She couldn't replicate her friend's smile. Her parents were dead and her actions were nothing to be proud of. A well-dressed, well-proportioned middle-aged woman wielded her elaborate parasol and secured a comfortable position further along the rail. Bella Holliday smiled as cheers from the quayside were drowned out by the ship's deep boom of farewell. Steam gushed from the giant whistle on the funnels. Two more blasts rang out when tugs dragged *Titanic* into the coal-black sea, followed by swarms of gulls in the billowing black smoke.

A breeze blew up, threatening the stability of Mona's hat. Peggy took her elbow, guiding her away from the rail. They walked along the deck, passing occupants of steamer chairs. Mona's eyes rested on a young couple; their heads close together. Unbidden, her mind reeled back to another time, a time when it could have been her sitting there with Louis. She shook her head. Louis betrayed her, abandoned her to a life of depravity, working as an exotic dancer at the Diamond, a rundown music hall in London. He left her, without a second thought. As her anger rose, she pictured her daughter. Hadn't she done the same thing to her, and wasn't that so much worse? A mother abandoning her own child? She realised Peggy was speaking and turned to face her friend.

'What do you say, Mona? Should we discover where luncheon is being served? Then we can spend the afternoon exploring. Let's see what else this fabulous ship has to offer. We're going to have so much fun and excitement on this voyage. We'll remember it forever.'

Mona nodded and tried to smile as Peggy took her arm.

Bournemouth

When Ivy and Ena stepped from the train, Bertie moved forward to greet them. His light grey, loose-fitting wool suit matched his bowler hat. He took their suitcases from the station porter and smiled. 'My dear girls, I have missed you.'

He embraced Ivy and Ena smiled when her aunt relaxed into his arms. He released Ivy then bent down and gently placed his gloved hands on Ena's shoulders. He met her gaze. 'Welcome to Bournemouth, Ena. I hope you will be very happy living here after your aunt and I are married. There are many picturesque places to visit; The Pine Walk, the Winter Gardens and the pier, to name a few. There are also many grisly tales of smugglers to tell you!'

Bertie's pocket watch was attached to the buttonhole in his waistcoat by a slender gold chain. He removed it, positioning his small pince-nez in front of his eyes. Ena smiled, seeing him wearing his pince-nez in London helped to ease her anxiety about wearing her new spectacles. 'Your train arrived punctually. Home isn't a great distance away and we shall make good time to Lansdowne Road, where Hilda is preparing a meal. Mother has anticipated your return with joy my dear, and she is very much looking forward to meeting Ena.'

Ivy smiled. Hilda Tilley was an accomplished cook and she knew Mrs Primavesi was delighted to have secured her as an employee when Hilda left The Royal Bath Hotel. Hilda was happy working as a cook at Bournemouth's first hotel until the arrival of a self-opinionated French chef. Her departure and decision to work in a private household was the hotel's loss and Mrs Primavesi's gain. With Hilda's skill in the kitchen and their maid

41

Gladys Upward keeping the house in order, the Primavesis' home on Lansdowne Road was a very pleasant place to stay. Bertie led them towards a motor car and Ena gasped when he placed their suitcases inside. He held the doors open and made a small bow towards them. 'Ladies, your carriage awaits!'

'Why thank you, kind sir!'

Ena giggled when her aunt affected a curtsy. Bertie took her aunt's arm and she lowered herself elegantly onto the leather seat at the front of the motor car. He closed the door with a satisfying click and offered Ena his hand. 'Miss, may I help you?'

Ena giggled again. She took Bertie's hand and slipped into the back seat. The clean, earthy smell of the leather upholstery and horsehair cushions filled her nostrils and she smiled. The previous year she trudged to school in over-sized shoes stuffed with newspaper because Lizzie was too mean to spend money on her. Now she had travelled in a first-class train carriage and was about to be driven in a motor car. She ran her hand along the empty seat beside her, picturing her friend Nancy. She wished Nancy had escaped from Gateshead with her, that she was sitting beside her in Bertie's motor car. But Nancy was dead. She still talked to Nancy, using the sign language her deaf and dumb friend taught her. Their own secret form of communication set them apart from the other children at South Street Infants School. They were glad of the division; their friendship strengthened because of it. Ena survived the darkest, most dismal days of her life because of Nancy's love. She would never forget her. She jumped at the sound of a loud horn and thoughts of Nancy were pushed from her mind. Bertie's laugh filled the motor car and he blew the horn again. 'All aboard! Off we go!'

Ivy laughed and Ena grabbed the door handle when the engine started. She stared out of the window as the motor car moved steadily through Bournemouth's pretty streets. An image of Lizzie's ramshackle room in the rundown tenement building on Pipewellgate flashed through her mind. She shook her head. Pipewellgate and Lizzie were in the past, her future was here, in Bournemouth.

Mona

Luncheon was served in the First-Class Dining Saloon on D Deck. Vernon told them the room could seat 554 passengers, at 115 tables for between two and 12 people. Peggy asked for a table and the *maître d* led them through the white, wooden panelled room. Mona studied Peggy's leather boots as they clicked on the linoleum tiles. She concentrated on the elaborate red and yellow pattern of the tiles, to avoid making eye contact with other diners. In contrast, Peggy nodded and smiled at everyone they passed. The *maître d* stopped at a small table set for two. Mona gazed at the numerous pieces of cutlery and glasses of various shapes and sizes set out on the pristine white tablecloth. In the centre of the table a small vase of daffodils sat alongside a white shaded lamp which glowed with a muted yellow light. The *maître d* pulled out their chairs and flourished one bright white napkin then another, placing them gently on their laps. He said a waiter would be with them directly.

'Isn't this magnificent, Mona? Look, the portholes are hidden by leaded-glass windows, you wouldn't know our restaurant is at sea!'

Mona nodded and stole a glance around the room. Theodosia wanted this for her daughters. For them to rise above their low birthplace and escape to places like this. She lowered her eyes. Heat rose into her cheeks. How would her mother have reacted, had she known the actions that brought Mona to this seat on a grand, lavish ship? Theodosia supported Mona when she discovered she was pregnant, never wavering from fighting to keep their family together. Mona tore that same family apart. Her lip trembled but before tears could overwhelm her, a waiter appeared and handed them each a small cream card, upon which was printed the luncheon menu. He said they could choose from the buffet or order courses to be delivered to their table.

'What is your choice of aperitif, ladies?'

'Two Manhattans, please!' The waiter nodded at Peggy and left them to peruse the menu. The words blurred as Mona frowned, trying to remember the French Theodosia taught her and Ivy. Her sister was always better at learning the exotic, lilting language. Her heart ached when she thought of Ivy. She forgave her and Mona let her down again. Now she doubted Ivy would ever want to see her again.

'Mona! Look at the delicious food. I think I'll have one of everything!' Peggy's laugh tinkled around the room as the waiter arrived with their expertly strained Manhattans; sweet red vermouth, whiskey and a dash of bitters, served in an ice-cold glass. Peggy thanked him before lifting her drink. She held the elegant coupe glass out towards Mona and gestured for her to do the same. Mona obliged and Peggy clinked the broad, round glass against her friend's.

Mona turned back to the menu. When she stayed with Peggy in New York the previous year, they fell into an easy routine of rehearsals at the Paradise, shopping and eating out. They visited several good restaurants around Broadway, but Mona had never seen a menu like the one on *Titanic*. It began with *'Consommé fermier'* and Mona decided the clear vegetable broth was the perfect way to start her meal, rather than the thicker, more filling *'Cock-a-leekie'* soup. An unwanted memory forced its way into the plush surroundings of *Titanic*'s First-Class Dining Saloon and she shuddered. An image of a different broth. Skilly. The cold, foul-smelling, greasy liquid she and the other dancers at the Diamond were given. Her friend Violet described it as watered-down porridge. Sometimes it was flavoured with meat but not often. Occasionally it contained potato skin or oatmeal but usually, the disgusting brew was tasteless. Mona tried to push the image away and concentrate on the menu in front of her. For the next course the choices were *'Fillets of Brill'* or *'Eggs a l'Argenteuil'*. Mona ordered the scrambled eggs and poached asparagus served with a cream sauce while Peggy enjoyed the sweet taste and firm texture of the brill. The waiter said the *'Chicken a la Maryland,'* the fried boneless chicken dressed with gravy and bananas, was prepared with a French twist. When Peggy asked what it was he put a finger over his lips and shook his head.

'I could not possibly divulge that information; Miss. Chef Rousseau would have me deported without a second thought. Suffice to say, *'C'est magnifique!'*'

Peggy ordered the 'magnificent' chicken with the secret twist and Mona chose grilled mutton chops with mashed potatoes. The friends returned to the menu to choose between custard pudding, apple meringue or pastry for dessert. When Peggy had polished off her apple meringue, she pushed back her chair and fanned herself with the menu.

'Tomorrow we should try the buffet, Mona!'

'No, don't mention food! I couldn't eat another thing!'

Peggy ignored her and laughed. She started to list the buffet items. 'There's salmon mayonnaise, Norwegian anchovies, potted shrimps and soused herrings, plain and smoked sardines, roast and spiced beef, veal and ham pie…'

'No! Please stop!' Mona put her hands over her ears but Peggy continued, in a louder, sing-song voice. 'The meal is completed with a selection of cheeses such as Cheshire, Stilton, Gorgonzola, Edam, Camembert, Roquefort, St Ivel and Cheddar.' Peggy signalled to the waiter to bring them both another Manhattan. 'After our drinks we must explore this fabulous ship some more, before changing for dinner.'

Mona nodded and tried to relax into the luxury of her new-found situation.

Chapter 7

Bournemouth

Bertie stopped the motor car. 'Here we are, Ena. This is my parents' house.' Ena looked out of the window. A woman stood outside the front door of the house on Lansdowne Road. The woman raised a hand and waved. Ena watched Aunt Ivy wave back. Ena slowly raised her own hand and the woman smiled as she walked up the garden path towards them. Bertie jumped out of the motor car and opened the doors for his passengers. Ena hung back as Aunt Ivy and Mrs Primavesi embraced. Aunt Ivy turned to Ena and gently brought her towards Bertie's mother. 'Please let me introduce you to my niece, Ena.'

Ena looked up and Mrs Primavesi smiled. Her kind eyes crinkled when she spoke. 'It is a pleasure to meet you, Ena. I hope you will be very happy living in Bournemouth.'

Ena took in Mrs Primavesi's silk blouse, ankle-length skirt and smart shoes. A thin string of pearls around her neck matched a row running down the front of the cream blouse and her tan, low-heeled shoes contrasted with her cream skirt. Bertie held the door open and ushered them inside. Ena walked in Mrs Primavesi's wake of sweet, lemony cologne, mesmerised by the shiny coils of dark-brown hair wound at the back of her head. The door opened onto a long, bright hallway with a high ceiling. Ena's eyes followed a curved staircase to her left.

'My dear daughter-in-law to be! How marvellous to see you again.'

Ena turned towards the voice. A broad, suited man stood in a doorway to her right. His ruddy cheeks were partially hidden by the biggest moustache she had ever seen. Bushy eyebrows topped bright eyes and a precise centre parting ran through the middle of his oiled black hair. Behind him was a large, polished desk and shelves full of books. The man smiled and Ena's cheeks flamed.

'And who do we have here? Ivy, is this your niece we have heard so much about?'

Ena's discomfort grew, what had this man heard? Did he know about her disgraceful beginnings in life? She moved to stand behind Aunt Ivy. Bertie spoke. 'Yes, Father. This is Ivy's niece Ena. Ena, this is my father, Mr Giulio Cesare Primavesi.'

Ena giggled at the way Bertie pronounced his father's name. The man looked down at her and smiled. 'It sounds like Julius Caesar, doesn't it? You may call me that, if you like!'

Ena stifled another giggle and shook her head, deciding she liked Mr Julius Caesar. Mrs Primavesi led them to the dining room, where a large table was set. A young woman was reaching up to light the gas mantles and she turned. 'Cook is ready for me to serve, Mrs Primavesi.'

'Thank you, Gladys. I'm sure you remember Bertie's fiancée, Ivy Leighton? And this is Ivy's niece, Ena.'

Gladys smiled at Ena, her open face a picture of kindness. 'I'm very pleased to meet you, Miss.' Ena smiled back and said hello. Gladys reminded her of Clara and she hoped they would become friends.

'Gladys; would you call the others, please?'

'Of course, Mrs Primavesi. They are all at home.'

As Gladys left the room Aunt Ivy touched Ena's arm and gestured towards the table. 'Here, Ena. Sit in between Bertie and me.' Suddenly the room filled with people and noise. Ena's head spun as one after another, people sat at the table. Her cheeks flamed again and she looked down. She tried to concentrate on smoothing her napkin over her lap but looked up when Bertie spoke.

'Look, Ena. My sisters and brother are sitting opposite you, in order of their ages, to help you remember who they are. I have never seen them so well organised!'

Ena smiled at her aunt's fiancé. She had never met her own father but she couldn't imagine he could be any kinder than Bertie.

'From left to right we have…' Bertie gestured for his siblings to introduce themselves.

'I am Lena, Bertie's eldest sister.'

'I am Isabel, Bertie's next sister.'

'I am Gertrude, Bertie's youngest sister.'

'I am Leo. Bertie's brother and the baby of the family.'

Ena looked from one end of the table to the other. She counted nine people including herself. An image of Lizzie shoving a mouldy piece of stale bread towards her flashed through her mind. She pushed the image away as Gladys arrived carrying a tray. Julius Caesar smacked his lips and clapped his hands. 'Cook's very own vegetable broth and homemade bread, excellent!'

Gladys placed the tray on a side table before serving each of them with a bowl of the steaming sweet-smelling broth and a warm bread roll. Ena watched Aunt Ivy select a spoon then copied her, scooping a small amount of the flavoursome orange liquid from the side of the bowl furthest away from her. The broth was packed with small pieces of succulent vegetables and Ena ate quickly, pushing her memories of starvation away.

'I see your niece has a good appetite, Ivy.' Julius Caesar grinned and Ena blushed but managed to polish off the last of her broth. As Gladys cleared the dishes away Ena studied Bertie's brother and sisters. They were like peas in a pod; all with thick, jet-black hair and angular features and all with a friendly, welcoming manner. As her eyes rested on Leo, Lena spoke. 'Ena, I believe you know about our involvement with the suffrage movement?'

Ena felt her colour rising but took a deep breath and spoke slowly and clearly. 'Yes, and I would like to learn more, if you have time to tell me.'

Lena's eyes glistened. 'Oh yes, we have time, don't we, sisters?' Isabel and Gertrude agreed and their chatter rose when Gladys returned with the fish course.

Ivy sat back in her chair and watched Ena finish her dessert. The Eve's pudding with custard was the perfect dish to round off a delicious meal. With Bertie and his family, she would make sure Ena's life in Bournemouth was as good as it could be. She would make sure Ena had wings, as the magnificent Theodosia wanted for her daughters and granddaughter. Wings to take her wherever she wanted to go. Ena looked around the room, now bathed in a muted light from the gas lamps. She caught Aunt Ivy's eye and smiled. The Primavesis were kind and welcoming and she longed to feel like part of their large family.

Mona

After luncheon Mona and Peggy took the air on deck before making their way to the Café Parisien. Despite the late afternoon sunshine, a cool wind blew off the sea. A helpful steward gave them directions to places of interest including the writing room, the smoke room, the powder room and the library. He extolled the virtues of the gymnasium; the mechanical camel, row-boat machine and punch bag before whispering about seeing 'men in white vests' using the equipment. Peggy feigned shock but later she and Mona laughed about the steward's modesty. They were accustomed to much more risqué sights during their time working in the theatre.

The last rays of sunlight found the veranda where the Café Parisien was located. Beautifully adorned with trellis decorations, Vernon told them it resembled the boutique cafes of Paris and offered the best French *haute cuisine* for first-class passengers.

Taking her seat, Mona puffed out her cheeks. 'I don't think I can eat anything else, Peggy. I'm still full.'

'Let's look at the menu.' Peggy's eyes grew wide as she read. 'Smoked salmon or cucumber sandwiches, scones with clotted cream and preserves, chocolate eclairs with French vanilla cream, pastries and a choice of teas.'

'Peggy! How do you stay so slim when you eat so much?'

Peggy's laugh drifted around the room and she shook her head. 'I don't know. But I intend to make the most of the food on this voyage. We'll dance it off in New York!'

Back in their cabin, Mona and Peggy giggled like schoolgirls. Peggy put her hands on her hips and strutted around the room with her nose in the air. 'My good man, as I have already told you, I must have my darling Lulu with me! She is named after one of our dear departed Queen's beloved canine companions.' Peggy shrieked with laughter and Mona begged her to stop. 'No more, please! I can hardly breathe!'

Peggy fell onto the sofa, continuing to mimic the rude woman from the Café Parisien. Her arrogant pleading proved unsuccessful in persuading the *maître d* to allow her treasured Pomeranian to join her for afternoon tea. Despite her dog's regal name and the woman flourishing an elaborately embroidered silk cushion while declaring '*Titanic's* precious upholstery will be well-protected,' the *maître d* ejected the woman and '*her darling Lulu*' with practised aplomb.

Peggy surprised Mona with a question. 'Who should we look out for at dinner, Mona?'

Mona frowned; she didn't know anyone else on board. 'What do you mean?'

'Look at this booklet on the writing desk.'

'What is it?'

'Do you remember our names were taken when we boarded?'

Mona nodded.

'All first-class passenger names are listed, so we can see who's on board.'

Mona looked blank and Peggy tapped her on the arm with the booklet. 'It's so we can find people we want to meet, you silly goose.'

Mona turned away. Something struck her and she went cold. 'What does it say?'

'It's only our names. You don't have to worry.'

Mona frowned and Peggy laughed. 'You know me, Mona. I'm an expert at spotting a good opportunity.' Peggy winked and Mona shook her head. As they dressed for dinner, Peggy said they were sailing across the English Channel to France. They were due to arrive at Cherbourg, *Titanic's* first port of call, at 6 o'clock that evening. They would be there for two hours while some new passengers embarked, and some who boarded at Southampton left the ship. Mona didn't know how far Cherbourg was from Paris, where her mother had lived. She pictured Theodosia, her beautiful, elegant mother. She remembered Theodosia's trapdoor trick, *'le truc de la trappe,'* passed down by her own mother. The ability to open a trapdoor in her mind and go anywhere. Mona sighed; this majestic ship was the sort of place she'd always escaped to. Now she was here, what would she use the trick for? A lump formed in her throat and she turned away from Peggy. She would wish for her mother, sister and daughter to be with her, experiencing this luxury. For them to be a family again.

Mona and Peggy knew dinner would be an elegant affair. According to a document from the shipping company *'What to Pack for Your Ocean Voyage'*, ladies were advised to bring an evening gown and matching leather or satin shoes, long white gloves, an opera bag, a fan and a scarf. Hats were not to be worn at dinner. Mona and Peggy chose their outfits carefully. While adhering to the guidance, they also wanted to stand out as independent, confident women. They both wore full length evening gowns but in contrasting colours. Mona's dupion silk gown in teal had a beautiful beaded lace panel across the top of the bodice and around the empire waist. The fitting beneath the bust created a silhouette that floated away from her waist and hips. The silhouette was emphasised by a chiffon overskirt, studded with shiny black beads. A trim of black lace around the hem of the gown provided the perfect finishing touch. When Mona pulled on her long silk gloves, also in teal, Peggy exclaimed. 'You look fabulous! Go on, swish across the room!'

Mona hesitated before taking a few small steps. She saw Peggy miming a swishing motion. She smiled then put her hands on her hips, pushed her shoulders back and glided towards Peggy. The luxurious silk rustled as she moved.

'That's more like it!'

'You don't think we'll get into trouble for not wearing white gloves?'

Peggy threw her head back and laughed. 'Let them try to criticise us!'

Peggy's gown was equally beautiful. The smooth cotton sateen in gold had an over layer of black scalloped lace and a beaded trim. A beaded lace panel around the waist and the empire fitting provided Peggy with the same silhouetted effect. The gown was completed by three quarter length sleeves with stylish frills. They helped each other with their hair, adding beaded headbands to the short, parted styles; teal for Mona and black for Peggy. They slipped on their heeled satin shoes, collected their bags, fans and scarves and left their cabin. They could return to the First-Class Dining Saloon or eat in the A La Carte Restaurant. They chose the latter, despite it not being included in the cost of their tickets. Peggy said Marv sent them some money, saying he wanted them to experience everything the voyage had to offer. Vernon said the Italian chef's cuisine was reputedly as good as any in a Ritz hotel, leading passengers to nickname Luigi Gatti's floating restaurant *'The Ritz.'* Adjoining the Café Parisien, it was smaller than the First-Class Dining Saloon but had its own reception room where passengers could enjoy an aperitif.

'Should we have champagne to celebrate being on this marvellous ship, Mona?'

Mona nodded hesitantly. She wasn't entirely comfortable being there on Marv's hospitality but Peggy told her to relax and enjoy herself. When they entered the restaurant, Mona's eyes were drawn to the exquisite furnishings and decorations. She stared at the floor-to-ceiling panelling of delicate fawn mahogany. Mounted carvings and ornaments highlighted with gold leaf gave the room a regal quality. Candle-style lamps in the centre of each panel reflected a soft, muted light across the panels, casting shadows around the room. Plain silk curtains covered the large bay windows. The tables were laid with porcelain plates and silver cutlery and decorated with small vases of pink roses and white daisies. A stringed orchestra played from a raised platform and Mona smiled, recognising the piece of music from Tchaikovsky's *'Swan Lake.'* She danced to it for her audition with Marv at the Paradise. She pictured herself, gliding onto the stage, arms outstretched, toes pointed, the embodiment of Odette, the Black Swan. When she finished Marv shouted she was in the chorus of his production and should return for rehearsals the next day. The memory warmed her and she found herself looking forward to working at the Paradise again.

'What are you looking so happy about?'

Mona turned to Peggy. 'I'm enjoying the music.'

'Isn't it wonderful? Like everything else on this ship. Look at all the latest fashions and jewellery on show in here and smell the exotic perfumes. And what about the immaculately, well-groomed gentlemen in their dinner suits? This place is like nowhere I've ever been Mona, and I intend to make the most of it.'

As Mona and Peggy took their seats for dinner *Titanic* entered Cherbourg harbour via the Passe de l'Ouest. They laughed when the waiter handed them each a menu.

'I'm not sure I can eat anything, Peggy. Not after luncheon and afternoon tea!'

'Should we save the oysters for another evening and have something light? How about Cream of Barley soup then Sautéed Chicken with Veal Sauce and Chateau Potatoes?'

'Alright. Soup then chicken and what about French Ice Cream for dessert? Tomorrow I intend to skip luncheon and afternoon tea!'

Peggy nodded and signalled for the waiter. At 8 o'clock, as Mona and Peggy finished their meal, *Titanic* left Cherbourg harbour and headed across the Irish Sea to Ireland.

Chapter 8

Bournemouth - Thursday 11th of April 1912

After breakfast, Aunt Ivy told Ena she and Bertie wanted to show her something of the town. Bertie said they should start by walking to the pier. As they left Lansdowne Road, he explained Bournemouth residents wanted a pier for years before its completion in 1856. Before then, when the waves were high it was impossible to approach the shore without being drenched. The first structure, a jetty with a retractable platform, was damaged by a severe storm. It was replaced five years later by a wooden pier. Soon Bournemouth's fashionably clad residents strolled along the pier while their carriages waited for them at the entrance. Within another five years the pier's wooden piles were so badly damaged by shipworm they were replaced by cast iron.

Ena frowned. 'What's shipworm?'

Bertie stopped and made a wiggling motion towards Ena with his index finger. 'They're clams, with worm-like bodies. I'm told they're very tasty!'

Ena shrieked and giggled as she moved away from Bertie's finger.

Bertie laughed. 'In 1867 a gale destroyed more of the pier but it wasn't replaced for 13 years. It was opened in August 1880 by the Lord Mayor of London. The covered shelters and bandstand were added five years later and the pier was extended again in 1894 and 1905.'

'How do you know so much about it?'

'My father taught me everything he knows about his birthplace in Italy, but he also insisted I should learn about the history of Bournemouth.'

Ena looked around; apart from her friends there, she wanted to forget about her own birthplace. Walking down the steep hill, Bertie pointed towards the pier's grand entrance. Above it, a clock in the ornate tower chimed 11 times. Bertie waited for the chimes to end before leading Ena towards the entrance. The cool, shady building was protected from the warm spring sunshine, but the contrast when they stepped onto the pier took Ena's breath away. She gasped and her eyes followed Bertie as he pointed in one direction then the other.

'On one side you can see the Isle of Wight and on the other, the Purbeck Hills. And over there, the public baths. Would you like to go swimming one day?'

Ena's colour rose and she lowered her eyes. Aunt Ivy touched her arm. 'I think they offer swimming lessons, Ena. Should we enquire?'

Ena nodded. 'Yes, please.'

In the distance to Ena's left was the island Bertie called the Isle of Wight. He said the beautiful green landscape was home to the poet Alfred, Lord Tennyson and Queen Victoria's summer residence and final home, Osborne House, was there. Aunt Ivy asked Ena if she would like to borrow her volume of Tennyson's poetry. 'My favourite, *The Lady of Shallot* is about a young noblewoman, Elaine of Astolat. She is stranded in a tower upriver from Camelot, castle of the legendary King Arthur.'

Ena concentrated on the horizon. She was like Elaine of Astolat in Gateshead, her river the stinking, coaly Tyne. She shook her head. She was free and living with people who wanted to teach her about books and music. People who loved her. She imagined a black box wrapped in chains. She placed Lizzie and Pipewellgate inside the box, locked it and pushed the image to the back of her mind.

'Now ladies, before we visit the public gardens, would anyone like an ice cream?'

Ena laughed. 'Yes, please!'

Queenstown, South Coast of County Cork, Ireland - Thursday 11th of April 1912

Mona and Peggy were relaxing in deck chairs when *Titanic* arrived at Queenstown on the south coast of County Cork in Ireland at 11.30 that morning. More passengers were dropped off and new ones embarked for the voyage to New York. The friends walked to the rail and watched their new travelling companions chattering excitedly about the style and sophistication of the ship. Peggy took Mona's arm. 'Time for luncheon, Mona?'

Mona nodded; she had never eaten as well. When they were making their way to the First-Class Dining Saloon, a familiar figure walked towards them. Vernon Revill, the first ship's steward they met. 'Hello, ladies. How are you enjoying your voyage?'

Peggy smiled. 'Very well, thank you.'

'I am pleased to hear it. Do you have any questions about anything you have seen?'

Peggy didn't hesitate. 'Would I be correct in thinking it is customary for passengers to socialise on the open deck, while promenading or relaxing on the wooden benches?'

'Oh yes, Miss. It's an ideal way to meet people. There is also the booklet of passenger names which is compiled for first-class travellers.'

'Yes, I've noticed it in our cabin.'

Vernon leant in towards them and spoke in a low voice. 'Between us, in my experience it is not uncommon for ambitious mothers to use the list to identify wealthy bachelors among the great and the good, to introduce their marriageable daughters to during the voyage.'

Peggy's eyes widened when Vernon provided some colourful examples of this behaviour from previous voyages. Mona looked away; the stories held no interest for her.

'The voyage also provides many opportunities for young ladies such as yourselves to meet eligible gentlemen. At dinner and while dancing.'

Peggy nudged Mona. 'Thank you, we shall make the most of our time on board. Remind me, when are we due to dock in New York Harbor?'

'Our scheduled arrival date is Wednesday the 17th of April, Miss. We will travel a good distance, almost 400 miles, between today and tomorrow and over 500 miles on Saturday. I hope you both enjoy the sumptuous dinners and dancing to *Titanic*'s wonderful orchestra while you are on board.'

'Oh, we will!' Peggy giggled and pulled Mona away. 'We're going to have so much fun, Mona. Every night, but especially on Sunday.'

'Why? What's happening on Sunday?'

'It's my birthday! I'll be 29 years old!'

Mona sighed; Peggy was the same age as Ivy. After years apart she and her sister were reunited earlier that year, on Ivy's 29th birthday. Then Mona let Ivy down and now they were estranged again.

'Did you hear what I said? Sunday is my birthday.'

'I'm sorry, Peggy. Yes, of course, we must celebrate.'

Peggy linked her arm through Mona's and they made their way to luncheon. Vernon smiled as he watched them walk away, proud to be part of *Titanic*'s crew. He looked out over the sea as the massive vessel sailed through calm waters.

Bournemouth

After their ice creams Bertie said they should visit Bournemouth Gardens. As they walked, he continued regaling Ena and Ivy with his local history knowledge. 'Bournemouth's beautiful public gardens began as marshy land. The land was cleared to create an area of what were called pleasure gardens. It was part of the work to develop Bournemouth into a seaside resort. Footpaths were laid then 4,000 trees and shrubs were planted. The gardens were opened to the public in 1859 and a competition to design the Lower Pleasure Ground was held some years later.' Bertie paused and looked at Ena, a glint in his eyes. 'Can you guess what the winner's name was, Ena?'

Ena shook her head. 'I don't know.'

'He was the most aptly named Philip Henry Tree!'

Ena laughed. 'The winner of the competition was Mr Tree?'

Bertie nodded. 'Yes. Funny, don't you think? His design included new walks, plantations and flowerbeds.' They walked on and Bertie continued. 'There is a magnificent path bordered on both sides by pine trees. Pines like the salty air; it helps them grow to great heights. Squirrels love pine cones, Ena. See if you can spot any gnawed ones on the ground. Some of the town's most beautiful trees are here; cedar, oak, redwood, cypress and birch.' While Ena didn't know which trees were which, they were the most beautiful gardens she had ever seen. She hung back, allowing her aunt and Bertie to walk on ahead. She looked around and breathed deeply, wanting to take in every detail. She pictured another park; Gateshead's People's Park. Aunt Ivy told her the park was built for the benefit of everyone in Gateshead. The northeast's heavy industry polluted the air, and Ena was grateful for the oasis of green space. She remembered a precious day, sitting under a tree with her friend Jack Todd. A day when she was meant to go to Sunday School, but instead she and Jack walked to the park. Jack jumped up to kick a ball around with some other boys. Ena leant back against the tree trunk and smiled. She could count days like this on the fingers of one hand. Days when a bright light shone in her dark life. Friends were in short supply. Who would want to befriend the scruffy, dirty-looking girl? Something in her memory had told her it was important to be neat and clean and she tried, but she found it hard without help. She learnt at an early age not to ask Lizzie for anything, everything led to an argument. She existed in a small, miserable space at Lizzie's, but kept her few possessions and what little room she had, clean and tidy. It was something she could control, a sense of order amidst the chaos of life with slovenly Lizzie. Jack never mentioned her shabby clothes and second-hand shoes. Jack looked out for her. Bertie's voice interrupted her thoughts.

'Ena? Come on, you need to see the stream!'

Before hurrying to catch up, Ena closed her eyes and imagined a brightly coloured box, loosely tied with pretty ribbons. She carefully placed her memories of Jack Todd into the box, along with those of Nancy and her grama. Bertie spoke and she opened her eyes.

'There you are. Now, are you interested in birds and nature, Ena?'

Ena bit the inside of her cheek, her knowledge stretched to what she had learnt at school, which wasn't much. Bertie bent down and pointed towards the gently meandering stream. 'The stream is teeming with wildlife; you will soon learn what to look out for. And what to listen for, the views and sounds change with the seasons. 'Bertie put a finger over his lips and whispered. 'Look! There's a goldcrest. It's Britain's smallest bird. They love to make nests in the pine trees. You can't see them but their nests look like little hammocks.'

Ivy touched Ena's arm. 'Would you like a notebook to record things like this in, Ena?'

Ena nodded and smiled at her aunt. 'Yes, please.'

Bertie pointed towards the water again. 'You must write about the beautiful demoiselle damselflies, Ena. They look like dragonflies but are bigger. You can spot them all year round, in nymph form in winter and on the wing in summer. The males are metallic blue and the females have brown wings and green bodies. You'll see them flitting and fluttering overhead as the male tries to attract a female with his impressive display.' Ena stared at the water but she couldn't spot the damselflies.

'Soon the fresh spring shoots will change to full summer leaves then before we know it, the bright autumn colours will give way to stark winter branches. You'll be able to record how everything changes through the seasons in your notebook.'

Ena frowned. Other than from winter to spring, she dreaded Gateshead's changing seasons. Each spring, she dared to hope that along with the new shoots, her life would improve. Summer's heat made the stench and filth of Pipewellgate unbearable and when autumn leaves fell each year; she lost hope. Winter brought ice and snow and Lizzie's constant gripes about the cold. Bournemouth's seasons sounded worth recording.

'Ena! You must see this tree. It is known as the 'Bournemouth Pine'. It is said to be a descendant of one of the earliest trees planted in Bournemouth in the 16th century. Its needles can be up to four feet long! Now, I think we should leave the Winter Gardens for another day and head back to Lansdowne Road, don't you, ladies?'

Ivy nodded. 'Yes, and on the way, I think we should find Ena a notebook.'

Bertie grinned. 'We'll go to Bright's department store.'

Ena smiled. She had never owned a notebook. She couldn't wait to start writing. She crossed her fingers behind her back. She pictured a page headed 'New Friends.' There was a spring in her step on the way back to Lansdowne Road.

Chapter 9

Friday 12th of April 1912

Mona

Taking their seats for breakfast in the A La Carte Restaurant, Mona and Peggy looked around at their fellow passengers. They were greeted by polite smiles and nods as a dish of fresh strawberries was delivered to their table.

'Could you ever have dreamt of travelling and dining in such luxury, Peggy? Fresh strawberries in April, in the middle of the ocean!'

'Yes, it is magnificent. And I overheard someone say there are rumours of an early arrival in New York. We may be there by Tuesday night, rather than Wednesday morning.'

Mona pursed her lips. 'I am looking forward to being back in New York now, but I could stay on this splendid ship for ever!'

Peggy laughed, picking up the menu. 'Me too! Should I read the breakfast choices?'

'Go on then, although I still feel full after everything we ate yesterday!'

Peggy cleared her throat and spoke in an affected cut-glass English accent, reeling off the menu items. 'Baked apples, stewed prunes, porridge oats, haddock, smoked salmon, kidneys and bacon, grilled sausage, fried, poached or boiled eggs, mashed, sautéed or jacket potatoes, cold meats and scones with blackcurrant conserve or marmalade.'

'Enough!'

'Phew! I'm glad you stopped me; I was running out of breath.'

Mona laughed. 'I'm not sure I want much at all.'

Peggy wagged an elegant finger towards Mona's face. 'You need to have a good breakfast, because afterwards I think we should visit the gymnasium!'

Mona laughed at Peggy's suggestion.

'Why not? We're dancers and we need to take regular exercise. Imagine not being able to dance for Marv when we reach New York!'

'Yes, but what is it like, this gymnasium?'

'It's ladies only in the morning, as are the salt-water baths. The gymnasium is near the Grand Staircase and it's equipped with state-of-the-art exercise equipment.'

'I can't swim, can you?'

Peggy shook her head. 'No.'

Mona's eyes widened. 'Is there a barre for dancers to practice at?'

'I don't think so but there are two electric camels, an electric horse, a rowing machine, a punching bag, a weightlifting machine and mechanical bicycles. I think it'll be fun!'

Mona laughed. 'Whatever do the electric camel and the electric horse do?'

'The camel mimics the animal's gait and the horse simulates an equestrian ride!'

Mona smiled. 'It sounds very different to our usual dance practice, more like exercise for rich people with time on their hands. But let's try it!'

Having eaten what she could, Mona folded her napkin and placed it on the table. A waiter appeared as if by magic and pulled out her chair when she stood.

'Thank you.'

'It is my pleasure, Miss. I do hope you have a pleasant morning.'

Mona brushed the skirt of her tailored wool suit with her hand and stepped away from the table. She glanced at Peggy, a mirror-image in her tight-fitting costume with a hip-length jacket. Their smart suits were paired with crisp white blouses featuring Peter Pan collars. Their shiny, lace-up leather boots peeped out from under their skirts as they walked, and their small, felt hats sat neatly upon their perfectly styled hair.

A little later, when Mona and Peggy were being guided in the use of the gymnasium's equipment, the waiters in the A La Carte Restaurant cleared all traces of breakfast away and started preparing the restaurant for luncheon service. Out of sight and sound of the *maître d*, they talked of their plans, should the ship arrive in New York earlier than scheduled. They were also aware of other, more troubling whispers, telling of an unusually active ice season. Without any official notifications having been received, they dismissed these as rumours and concentrated on the excitement awaiting them in New York.

Giggling uncontrollably, Mona and Peggy left the gymnasium. Peggy grabbed Mona's arm and pulled her to the side of the corridor. 'Did you see the lady with the large bosom trying to use one of the electric camels?'

Mona laughed. 'You couldn't miss her! She refused to remove her hat!'

'I know! It was like a real bird's nest, covered in feathers, flowers and what looked like a stuffed blackbird! Her hat was the same size as the camel's hump!'

They laughed all the way back to their cabin, where they collapsed onto the sofa like schoolgirls. When she caught her breath, Mona turned to Peggy, her face serious.

'What is it, Mona? A moment ago you couldn't stop laughing.'

'That's the point. I've never had as much fun in my whole life. Thank you, my dear friend, for helping me to leave my awful past behind.'

Peggy took Mona's hand. 'I need to thank you too, Mona.'

'Whatever for?'

Peggy's beautiful features took on a grotesque mask as she opened up to Mona. 'Ever since my father died, I've lived in fear of having no money and being homeless. I've always imagined I'm standing on a trapdoor that could open and swallow me at any time. That's why I work so hard and keep people at a distance. I've never loved anybody fully, never had a true friend. I've always protected my heart. But I was lonely. When we met on RMS *Matilda*, I hoped that would change.'

Mona looked at her friend. Peggy hid her insecurities well; Mona hadn't known she was so scared. She squeezed Peggy's arm. 'You saved my life on RMS *Matilda*.'

'I also saved you from having to stay in ghastly steerage accommodation!'

For a moment Mona allowed herself to remember the journey. The atrocious things she did to get on the ship and her fear at being caught and sent back to London. Peggy saved her.

'No, don't.' Peggy waved a finger in Mona's face. 'You've left that life behind.'

Mona nodded and pushed the memories away. Later, with their friendship deeper and more meaningful than ever, Mona and Peggy relaxed and enjoyed another delicious dinner. While they were eating, the captain of the French ocean liner SS *La Touraine*, travelling westbound from Le Havre into New York City, addressed a message warning of dense fog and thick ice to Captain Edward J. Smith on RMS *Titanic*. One of *Titanic*'s wireless operators took the message to the bridge. Captain Smith stroked his neat white beard as he read the message. Untroubled, he turned to 4th Officer Joseph Boxhall and provided him with the position of the reported ice. 'Mark the position on the map in the chart room.'

'Yes, Sir.' Officer Boxhall touched the fingers of his right hand to his forehead in salute. He hesitated before leaving the bridge. 'Is there cause for concern, Sir?'

'Not a bit of it. Ice is common in the early spring.'

Bournemouth
Ena

In her bedroom at Lansdowne Road, Ena picked up her note-book. She stroked the soft leather of the light blue cover then carefully opened the black oblong box on her dressing table. As well as the notebook, Aunt Ivy bought her a fountain pen and pencil set. Ena removed the pen from the cushioned box. She read her neat words on the lined pages and shook her head. A few months ago she couldn't see properly, let alone write anything. Now, thanks to her spectacles and the gifts from Aunt Ivy, she could write and read her own words. On the first page she wrote the date and her statement of ownership.

Thursday 11ᵗʰ of April 1912
This notebook belongs to Ena Leighton, aged 12,
of Lansdowne Road, Bournemouth

She turned to the first page. The heading was *'Family.'* Two names were listed; Aunt Ivy and Bertie. She frowned and positioned her pen above the next available line, her hand shaking. She hesitated and put the pen down. She had other family, her mother and father and her mother's cruel cousin Lizzie, but did they deserve to be included in her new life? She turned the page and smiled at the heading. *'Friends.'* The names listed warmed her and she pictured her two friends from Gateshead. Friends who helped her to survive some of the darkest times in her life. Friends without whom she dreaded to think what might have happened to her. She traced a finger across the first line. 'Nancy Glover.' Tears pricked her eyes and she swallowed. She touched the name on the second line. 'Jack Todd.' She knew she would never see Nancy again, but hoped to cross paths with Jack in the future. But Jack lived in Gateshead and she didn't know if she would ever go back to the place that held such dismal memories for her. Mrs Newbold and her house maid Clara were included in Ena's list of friends and she pictured the friendly, welcoming guest house on Chestnut Tree Avenue in London.

Earlier, Aunt Ivy and Bertie said they should take advantage of the mild weather and show Ena more of the town. Their stroll along the pretty tree-lined avenues took them to the Winter Gardens. Bertie said the impressive glass-domed building with trees on three sides, was constructed in 1875 as an exhibition centre. Ena smiled when he described the grounds as 'delightful' and 'alluring,' resolving to add a new page to her notebook with the heading, '*Good Words.*' Bertie said the venue had been a theatre and concert hall since 1893, when Bournemouth became the first town to regularly provide music for the public. He stopped walking and puffed out his chest before proclaiming, 'the Bournemouth Symphony Orchestra was founded in the same year! Visiting conductors have included Edward Elgar, Jean Sibelius and Gustav Holst.' Ena wished she could feel the same pride for Gateshead as Bertie did for Bournemouth. Aunt Ivy told her Bertie's father's family were Italian immigrants who arrived in England around the same time as Theodosia. Ena knew nothing about Italy or France, where her grama came from, but she wanted to learn everything she could. A question occurred to her. 'How many people live in Bournemouth?'

Bertie's eyes twinkled, his delight at her question evident. 'Well, let's see, shall we? Should we knock on people's doors and ask to count them?'

Ena laughed. 'No, we can't! Don't you know?'

'Well, by 1901 the population of Bournemouth had reached 59,000.'

'That was 11 years ago. What about now?'

'I think we should visit the Central Library to see what we can learn. It is in a converted house opposite Horseshoe Common.'

Aunt Ivy nodded. 'What a wonderful idea, Bertie. As a Bournemouth resident Ena could join the library.'

Ena shrugged her shoulders. She had never set foot in a library. Her aunt explained. 'The library has a collection of books for members of the public to borrow.'

'Do you have to pay for them?'

Aunt Ivy smiled. 'No, my dear. Libraries don't charge people for borrowing books.'

Ena gave a low whistle. 'That sounds delightful and alluring!'

They laughed and continued walking.

Chapter 10

Saturday 13th April 1912

Mona

Mona and Peggy made themselves comfortable on one of the wooden slatted benches on the Promenade Deck. Mona looked out to sea. Peggy reached across and tapped her on the arm with a long, beautifully manicured fingernail. 'What did you think of him?'

Mona continued watching the ocean. 'Who?'

Peggy tutted and tapped her arm again, harder this time. 'You know who!'

Mona turned, smiling mischievously. 'Do you mean Mr Behr?'

'Yes! Wasn't he dashing?'

'He is also in pursuit of Miss Newsom, Peggy. He made that very clear.'

Peggy pursed her lips. 'He is a tennis player and a banker.'

Mona continued. 'I found Mr Andrews very engaging. He is one of *Titanic's* architects and knows a lot about the ship. He is here to ensure everything is up to the right standard.'

Peggy laughed. 'Yes, but can he dance?'

'I don't know, you could write to his wife and ask her. Anyway, the person I found most intriguing last night was Miss Elsie Bowerman.'

Peggy sighed. 'Very well. Tell me about her.'

'Weren't you listening? Her conversation was fascinating.'

The friends had discovered the most popular pastime on *Titanic;* the after-dinner concerts in the Reception Room, where juicy gossip about the wealthiest and most famous passengers buzzed around. There were also opportunities to talk to other travellers. 'What was so fascinating about her?'

'She's a suffragette and she once had Emmeline Pankhurst to stay with her.'

At the mention of the founder of the Women's Social and Political Union (WSPU), Peggy paid attention. 'She knows Emmeline Pankhurst?'

'Yes, and while campaigning for the WSPU she addressed a meeting of 1,000 people!'

Peggy stood and smoothed her white twill skirt. 'Should we walk around the deck?'

'To look for Mr Behr?'

Peggy laughed; her friend knew her well. They took in the sights and sounds of the ship as they walked. Friendly shouts from a group of passengers playing quoits reached them and they paused to watch the game. A young man aimed a wooden ring in the direction of an upright metal spike and his friends jeered and hollered to try and distract him. The man narrowed his eyes and focussed on the target. He launched the ring and his friends booed. Resolute in his task, the ring landed directly above the spike and slid down to the deck. His friends cheered and applauded and he took a bow. He looked in their direction and raised his cap. 'Good afternoon, ladies.'

Peggy gave the man a quick nod and Mona felt her colour rise. They carried on walking, passing two men playing shuffleboard. Peggy craned her neck to get a good view. One used a cue-stick to push coloured disks along an area of the deck marked with lines denoting different scoring sections. Peggy tutted. 'Perhaps he is indoors; he could be playing chess or cards.'

Mona took her friend's arm. 'Should we see if we can find him?'

Peggy shook her head. 'No. Let's style each other's hair and decide what to wear for dinner tonight. I'm sure we'll see Mr Behr and your fascinating Miss Bowerman then.'

While Mona and Peggy were walking back to their cabin, Captain Smith called Joseph Bruce Ismay, Chairman and Managing Director of the British Shipping Company's White Star Line, to the Reception Room outside the A La Carte Restaurant. Captain Smith said he wanted a definitive answer regarding the time of *Titanic's* arrival in New York.

'There is talk among some of the passengers and crew, Ismay. Will we dock on Tuesday evening or Wednesday morning?'

Ismay shifted in his seat before replying. 'We made a better run today than yesterday and will make a still better run tomorrow. Everything is going smoothly; the machinery is bearing the test and the boilers are working well. I am confident we will get into New York on Tuesday.'

Bournemouth
Ena

From the moment she learnt about the library, Ena couldn't wait to join. Aunt Ivy said it was the first thing they would do once she and Bertie returned from their honeymoon. The wedding was two days away. Afterwards, Aunt Ivy and Bertie were going to stay in a hotel along the coast in a place called Boscombe, while Ena stayed with the Primavesis for a few days. Aunt Ivy said they could visit the library on Monday the 22nd of April. Ena counted the days on her fingers then made a new heading in her notebook, *'Important Dates.'* On the first line she wrote the date and details of the wedding. On the second line, in the best handwriting she could manage, she wrote *'Monday 22nd of April 1912, first visit to Bournemouth Central Library.'*

Today she was looking forward to having tea with Aunt Ivy, Bertie, his sisters and brother. She had learnt a little about the suffrage movement and Bertie's sisters had promised to tell her more. She knew there were two groups involved in trying to gain advances for women. The suffragists were peaceful campaigners.

71

They started a national organisation which men were allowed to join. The suffragettes called for direct, militant action and some of their activities were violent. Their organisation was smaller, and men were not allowed to join. She also learnt about something called Shabbat. Aunt Ivy told Ena about the Primavesis' neighbours and good friends, The Leamans. Aunt Ivy said their daughter Rachel was the same age as Ena. Ena hoped they would hit it off and she would be able to add Rachel's name to the list of friends in her notebook. Aunt Ivy explained the Leamans wouldn't be there because their Jewish faith meant they celebrated Shabbat on Saturdays.

'What is Shabbat?' Ena had never heard of it.

Aunt Ivy explained the tradition. 'Shabbat is the seventh day of the Jewish week. It is the day of rest and abstention from work as commanded by God.'

'Like our Sunday?' Ena remembered the two occasions when Lizzie allowed her to go to Sunday School in Gateshead.

'Yes, precisely. The Shabbat ceremony involves two similar commandments; to remember and to observe. I'm sure Rachel will be happy to tell you more about it once you become friends.'

Ena smiled. She crossed her fingers behind her back, hoping Rachel would like her. She closed her notebook and brushed her hair before making her way downstairs for tea. She heard the voices as soon as she left her bedroom. Lena, Isabel, Gertrude and Leo were laughing and joking and Ena grinned as a warm feeling spread through her body. Once Aunt Ivy married Bertie, she could add Bertie's sisters and brother to her list of friends.

'There she is! Ena, come and sit down. We have so much to tell you!' Lena smiled, gesturing for Ena to sit next to her. By the time Ena returned to her bedroom, her head was spinning. She reached for her notebook, eager to record what she had learnt before she forgot anything. When Lena and her sisters talked about the suffrage movement, Ena realised women could do anything, if they were determined enough. Lena said the number of women entering professions previously closed to them, such as medicine, was increasing. She leant in closer to Ena and whispered. 'A good friend of mine has met two female doctors in London!'

Ena's eyes were wide. 'Who are they?'

'One was Louisa Garrett Anderson. She was sent to Holloway Prison for her suffragette activities which included breaking a window by throwing a brick. My friend waited outside the prison to applaud her when she was released.'

'And the other one?'

'Flora Murray. With Louisa Garrett Anderson, she founded the Women's Hospital for Children on Harrow Road in London. The hospital provides health care for working-class children in the area. It also provides female doctors with an opportunity, the only one available to women, to gain clinical experience in paediatrics in London.'

'What is paediatrics?'

Lena laughed. 'Our Ena is like a little sponge, our very own Geordie suffragist! Paediatrics is the area of medicine dealing with children and their diseases.'

Ena beamed. Lena said the hospital's motto was *Deeds Not Words* and Ena committed it to memory, determined to add it to her notebook as soon as she got back to her bedroom. Lena sipped her tea and Isabel took up Ena's history lesson.

'Have you heard of Ethel Smyth, Ena?'

'Yes!' The women laughed at the excited shout from their newest recruit.

'What do you know about her?' Isabel smiled at Ena across the table.

'She wrote *The March of the Women*.'

'She did. How do you know about the feisty composer-turned-suffragist?'

'Clara told me about her and taught me the song.'

73

Ena proceeded to tell the Primavesi siblings about Mrs Newbold's guest house on Chestnut Tree Avenue, explaining it offered accommodation to theatrical types. When she mentioned some of the colourful characters she met there, the table fell silent. They were listening. To her. Despite her accent. She smiled, warming to her subject. 'I think you will meet some of them at the wedding.' She looked at Aunt Ivy for confirmation.

'They will. And what a celebration it will be!'

Isabel returned to her anecdote. 'Did you hear about Ethel Smyth's toothbrush, Ena?'

Ena shook her head.

'Last month, Emmeline Pankhurst coordinated a suffragette march in London. Hundreds of women blocked Westminster's busiest roads, from Piccadilly to Regent Street. The march erupted into a riot when the women pulled hammers and rocks out of their handbags and began smashing the windows of shops and political offices opposing a woman's right to vote. By the end of the night, 148 women had been arrested, including Ethel Smyth. She was jailed for hurling a rock through the window of Lewis Harcourt, an avowed anti-suffragist. When Ethel's friend, the musician Thomas Beecham visited her at Holloway Prison, dozens of suffragettes were gathered in the prison yard, singing 'The March of the Women.' Inside, Ethel grabbed a toothbrush, stuck her arms out of the bars of her cell window, and conducted the chorus below.'

Ena smiled at Isabel. 'What a wonderful story.'

Not to be left out, Bertie's youngest sister Gertrude asked Ena a question. 'Do you know about last year's census boycott, Ena?'

Ena shook her head again. She looked down, she didn't know what a boycott was.

'It was an ingenious idea! Emmeline Pankhurst called on

women to boycott the census in protest at the Liberal Government's reluctance to give women the vote. She said, 'If women don't count, neither shall they be counted'. It was a rallying call for suffragettes on the night of the 1911 census. She urged women to protest passively, asking those who were at home on census night to refuse to complete the return, risking a £5 fine or a month's imprisonment, or to avoid the census by being out of the house.' Lena warmed to her subject, saying some women spoiled the census form by refusing to provide information or by scribbling comments and slogans on it. 'One woman gave the name of a male servant and added 'no other persons, but many women."

Aunt Ivy nodded, agreeing with Bertie's sisters about the power of peaceful protest. 'Some women gathered in secret *'safe houses'* and a group of suffragettes hired the Aldwych rink and skated through the night. Another group in Wimbledon took secret night-time treks but Emily Wilding Davison carried out the most audacious act. She hid in a cupboard in the crypt of the Palace of Westminster to be recorded as resident at the House of Commons on census night.' Ivy looked at Ena. 'I know your grama would have hidden us, if she had still been alive. She would have squeezed the four of us into a hiding place somewhere in Gateshead. She always told me and your mother we could do anything and go anywhere, if we were determined enough.'

Brushing her teeth later, Ena imitated Ethel Smyth conducting the women in the prison yard. When she closed her eyes, she saw the women who were dedicated to making life better for those to come. This house was full of those women, and she resolved to be one herself.

Mona

Peggy strutted around their cabin, imitating the rude woman with the Pomeranian. She puffed out her chest, raised her chin and affected a plummy, upper-class accent.

'My man, my darling Lulu must join me for dinner! She will pine for me if I leave her alone in my cabin. By the time I return she may have expired with grief!'

Peggy lowered her chin and her voice before imitating the *maître d's* reply. 'Madam, as I have already explained, 'darling Lulu' is not permitted to enter the restaurant. 'Darling Lulu' should be in the ship's kennels, rather than in your cabin.'

'Kennels? Never, not for my beloved Lulu!' Peggy put the back of her hand to her brow and pretended to swoon. Mona flourished her fan over her friend's perfect features before they collapsed laughing onto the sofa.

As they made their way to dinner, Mona shivered and pulled her fur wrap tighter around her neck. A passing steward, noticing her discomfort, offered to turn on the electric fire in their cabin while they were dining. Mona smiled and accepted his offer.

'It is my pleasure, Miss. It is much colder outside this evening.'

When Mona and Peggy arrived at the A La Carte Restaurant, they noticed Thomas Andrews sitting in the Reception Room. He raised a hand in their direction and Mona turned around to see who he was acknowledging. Peggy gave her sleeve a quick tug.

'It's us, you silly goose. Let's join him.'

Mona hesitated but Peggy took her arm and led her towards his table.

'Good evening, ladies. I am delighted to see you again. Are you dining in the A La Carte Restaurant this evening?'

'We are, Mr Andrews.' Mona could always rely on Peggy's self-confidence when her own deserted her.

'Would you like to join me for an aperitif?'

'Yes, thank you.' Peggy took the chair closest to Thomas Andrews and Mona sat opposite the debonair ship's architect.

'Now, what would you like to drink?'

'Champagne, please.'

Mona turned away, embarrassed by Peggy's boldness. Thomas Andrews appeared unoffended and signalled to the waiter.

'How are you ladies enjoying your time on this floating luxury hotel?'

Peggy gave Thomas her most dazzling smile and spoke like an actress. 'It is as if we are not on board a ship at all, rather we have entered some great mansion on shore.'

The waiter returned with their champagne and Thomas raised his glass in a toast.

'To RMS *Titanic*, the most magnificent mansion to sail the ocean!'

Mona and Peggy clinked their glasses and repeated the toast.

RMS *Titanic*

John George Phillips, Jack to his friends, took a seat in front of the transmitter in *Titanic*'s radio room at the start of his shift. He adjusted his position, his back poker-straight in the wooden chair. He looked around. Although *Titanic* was the greatest vessel afloat, boasting the latest equipment and decorated in a style more lavish than any hotel of the era, its radio room was little more than a cupboard with a Morse code transmitter and straight key. The key consisted of a metal bar fixed to a small block of wood, with a knob on top. A spring and electrical contact sat underneath. Wireless operators were trained to press the metal bar down onto the spring, creating a closed electric circuit. This enabled them to transmit a string of dots and dashes, to be decoded by the receiver.

Jack was proud to be *Titanic's* senior wireless operator, although strictly speaking he and the junior operator Harold Sydney Bride weren't part of the crew. They were employed by the British Marconi Company, whose equipment was installed on board, but they were paid by the White Star Line. Using a mutually agreed shift system, Jack and Harold took turns sleeping, keeping the radio in operation for 24 hours a day. During the day, the powerful equipment had a 400-mile transmission range. At night, the range could increase to nearly three times the distance, messages being sent and received via the large antennae slung between *Titanic's* masts. Jack and Harold listened to continental Morse code coming in from nearby ships, and tapped out replies. They were also responsible for sending passenger messages. *Titanic's* wealthy voyagers delighted in using the service and as slips of paper were delivered to the operators, they tapped away at the state-of-the-art machinery designed by Guglielmo Marconi.

About three hours after Jack's shift started, he noticed a problem with the wireless system.

The power output had dropped, making it increasingly difficult to send and receive messages. Jack cocked his head to one side and chewed the inside of his cheek. He suspected there was an issue with a particular component of the wireless transmitter. He knew according to the Marconi manual and company policy; wireless operators were not permitted to try and fix this component. They were instructed to wait until getting into port where a Marconi engineer could be called to repair the fault. Jack rubbed his chin; he could follow the rules, or he could break them. As some passengers enjoyed their last drinks and card games of the evening and others made their way to bed, Jack decided. He called Harold out of bed to help him repair the transmitter.

Harold arrived in the radio room yawning and rubbing his eyes. 'What is it?'

Jack explained the problem and started taking the wireless system apart.

Harold gasped. 'Do you know what you're doing? Have you been trained to do that?'

Jack looked up from the exposed components of the system. 'No, do you have a better suggestion?'

Harold looked towards the door of the radio room. He checked the door was firmly closed and Jack started examining the condensers. Harold checked the door again then got down on his hands and knees next to his colleague.

Jack smiled. 'We can fix this, I'm certain of it.'

By the time Mona and Peggy were walking back to their cabin after dinner, Jack and Harold were still trying to repair the transmitter. As they worked, private passenger messages piled up. When Mona and Peggy were getting ready to turn in for the night, *Titanic* passed SS *Rappahannock*, eastbound from Halifax to London. The damaged steamship used its morse lamp to blink a warning to *Titanic*. The warning told of dangerous, heavy pack ice ahead. *Titanic* flashed back an acknowledgement and sailed on into the night.

Chapter 11

Sunday 14th of April 1912

RMS *Titanic*

While *Titanic's* passengers slept and the huge liner continued across the ocean, Jack and Harold worked to repair the transmitter. In the early hours of the morning, Jack yawned and stretched to ease his aching back. Harold frowned. 'You should be off duty by now, you need to sleep.'

'I'm staying until this is fixed.' Jack brushed his hair back with his fingers then rubbed the back of his neck. At around 5 o'clock, a slow smile crept across his face and he leant in towards Harold. 'Got the little rascal!'

'What was it?' Harold peered inside the exposed transmitter and Jack pointed to the source of the problem; a short in the secondary winding of a transformer. 'What luck you were here, Jack.'

'When we get the system running again we can start working our way through this huge backlog of passenger messages.'

'No, Jack. Once it's fixed you need to get some sleep.'

Jack shook his head. 'I want to finish the job, including dealing with the messages.'

Later, Harold persuaded Jack to go and get some much needed rest. As *Titanic's* passengers enjoyed breakfast, Harold received a message from RMS *Caronia* warning of '*bergs, growlers and field ice.*' He smiled, remembering when he first heard the term *growlers* during his training. He and the other new recruits laughed, imagining a variety of growling animals in the middle of the ocean. He learnt *growlers* were pieces of ice. About the size of a grand piano, they extended less than three feet above the surface of the ocean. Shortly before midday, Harold received a further report from SS *Noordam* of *'much ice'* in the area previously identified by *Caronia*. Captain Smith appeared unalarmed and instructed Harold to reply to *Caronia* and *Noordam*, thanking them and acknowledging the messages. When *Titanic's* passengers were taking their seats for luncheon, Jack returned to the radio room and took over, allowing Harold to eat in the mess area allocated to the Marconi and postal workers on C Deck. Later, Harold and Jack overheard a warning sent by SS *Amerika* to the United States Hydrographic Office in Washington DC. The warning was a sighting of two large icebergs. Harold and Jack knew the office prepared and published maps, charts and nautical books needed for navigation, but it was a private message and they didn't report it to the bridge. When Harold received a message from RMS *Baltic* warning of *'large quantities of field ice'* at a latitude 250 miles ahead of *Titanic,* he delivered it to Captain Smith. The captain passed it to Joseph Ismay. Ismay read the message then slipped it into the pocket of his waistcoat. Over luncheon Mona and Peggy heard people discussing the change in the weather. One said the temperature outside had plummeted even further and they wouldn't be venturing on deck.

Despite the electric fire in their cabin being on all day, Mona and Peggy shivered as they dressed for dinner. They agreed to leave the fire on while they were out.

'What do you think? Will I impress our fellow passengers?'

Mona looked; Peggy took her breath away. Her evening gown shimmered as she twirled. The delicate fabric caught the light, giving the impression of an outfit comprising layer upon dazzling layer of silver. Peggy's choice of organdie; a crisp cotton fabric, allowed the gown to float despite its narrow bodice and slim skirt. A diaphanous, almost sheer underlayer of cream lace contrasted with the vibrant silver. A silver beaded ribbon was tied tightly around the raised waistline, emphasising Peggy's petite figure. Mona looked down but before she could compare herself to Peggy, her friend spoke. 'Your turn now!'

Peggy's enthusiasm triumphed over Mona's apprehension. She pointed her right toe and twirled around, allowing Peggy to see the full extent of her outfit. Their dressmaker gave both gowns an Oriental, kimono-style look and when Mona moved, the heavily beaded and embroidered black tunic of lightweight velveteen rustled. The contrasting rose-gold silk underlayer stood out against the black tunic and a thick velvet waistband completed the long, columnar line of the gown.

'Ravishing, my dear friend. Now, shall we take our pretty dancing shoes out and join our fellow passengers?'

'Before we go, I have something for you.'

Having only discovered it was Peggy's birthday after they set sail, Mona worried she had nothing to give her. She didn't know if she would find a suitable gift on board but Vernon came to her rescue. The previous morning, while Peggy was still asleep, Mona tiptoed from their cabin and followed him to *Titanic's* gift shop. On the way, Vernon asked how she was finding the voyage. She hesitated, trying to conjure up Peggy's confidence. Vernon looked at her. 'Has everything been as you expected, Miss?' His kind eyes disarmed her and she smiled sadly. 'I didn't know what to expect, Mr Revill. I never imagined being on such a voyage.' Vernon raised his eyebrows. 'I am surprised, Miss. You appear very much at home on *Titanic.*' Mona shook her head. Vernon spoke quietly. 'I meet people from all walks of life in my job, Miss. I remember my nerves on my first voyage, convinced I would drop something or say the wrong thing to someone. Before long, I learnt most people are pleasant and understanding. Although there are exceptions who break the rule!' Mona managed a tight smile.

She didn't know what it was about Vernon Revill, but his honesty allowed her to ask about something that had troubled her since they left Southampton.

'Tell me, Mr Revill, what are the conditions like in steerage on *Titanic?*'

Vernon stopped walking. He met Mona's eyes. 'I'm pleased to say *Titanic's* third-class accommodations are excellent, Miss. Some passengers say they are better than their living conditions at home.'

Mona swallowed. An image of a flea-ridden guest house opposite a rundown music hall tried to snake its way into her mind and she pushed it away.

Vernon continued. '*Titanic's* third-class accommodations resemble other steamships' second-class accommodations. The cabins have running water, washbasins and electricity and beds have mattresses, pillows and blankets. Most third-class passengers on *Titanic* bring their own sheets and pillowcases because they plan to settle permanently in America. They have the use of two dining rooms and are provided with three meals a day. The menus are simple but the food is plentiful. Have I put your mind at rest, Miss?'

Mona admired Vernon's discretion; he didn't ask why she wanted to know. 'Yes, thank you, Mr Revill.'

Vernon smiled. 'Please Miss, call me Vernon.'

'I'm Mona.'

Vernon extended his hand. 'Very glad to know you, Mona.'

Mona stopped walking and put her hand on Vernon's arm. 'Could I ask you one more question, Vernon? What sort of entertainments do third-class passengers have?'

Vernon laughed. 'Oh, they have tremendous parties! There is a room where they can pass the time reading or playing cards but when they gather in the evenings it's a sight to behold. Fiddle players appear from nowhere and there is plenty of beer, dancing and laughter.'

Mona pictured the scene; a dance in full swing, men whooping as they swept the women around in a figure of eight.

'Here we are, Mona. *Titanic's* gift shop. I hope you find something suitable.'

'Thank you, Vernon. For everything.' Mona knew she would have to continue putting on a show in first-class, she didn't belong there. She lifted her chin, determined to make the most of her unexpected good fortune. She pushed the gift shop door open and a bell tinkled.

Now, she handed Peggy a small box.

Peggy hesitated. 'For me?'

'It is your birthday, isn't it?'

'Yes, but I didn't expect anything.'

The woman in the gift shop had wrapped the gift in tissue paper before carefully placing it inside a small silver box. She wrapped the box in bright red paper and tied a red ribbon in a bow on top. There were tears in Peggy's eyes as she took the gift. 'It looks too good to open.' Peggy gasped when she removed the delicate brooch. 'Oh Mona, it is perfect. Thank you.'

'You are most welcome, my dear friend. Should I pin it on for you?'

Peggy nodded and Mona attached the pin brooch to her gown, just below her left shoulder. A tiny pair of ballet shoes, made of pale pink crystal stones, hung from a silver diamond bow. The shoes glistened and twinkled when Peggy moved. At the door to their cabin Peggy placed a gloved hand on Mona's arm. 'You are the only person who has given me a gift since my father died, Mona. I will treasure this always, I promise.'

Mona embraced her friend, thinking how good it felt to have made someone she cared about so happy. She couldn't remember feeling like that before.

Bournemouth
Ivy

Ivy re-read Ruby's letter. It arrived in response to the wedding invitation she sent. She smiled at her friend's familiar, child-like hand, picturing Ruby's cheerful smile and freckled face. Ruby Rogers was one of the first people Ivy met when she started working as a scullery maid at Hampson Hall, and they remained friends when Ivy moved to London. Ruby started work at the age of 13 and hadn't spent much time at school. Ivy appreciated the effort she took to write to her.

'To my dear friend,

Thank you for your letter and kind invitation to the wedding with Mr Bertie. I am very happy for both and smiled when I read it. I am happy Ena is with you and not in trouble now at Gateshead. I will be a bridesmaid for you! It is very exciting for me but there is one thing you need to do. You need to write to your missing sister. It is not right I will be there but she will not. I know she is trouble for you but she is your sister. I always wish I had a sister! I have to go because Mrs Jackson is shouting and I am not where I am meant to be.

Always your friend Ruby Rogers Miss.'

Ruby's simple words broke Ivy's heart, she couldn't write to Mona because she didn't know where she was. Ivy was surprised Ruby could come to her wedding. In a rare act of compassion, Mrs Jackson, the stern housekeeper at Hampson Hall and Ruby's nemesis, allowed her the time off. Ruby had arrived earlier and was joining them for dinner. Ivy folded the letter, determined to concentrate on the people around her and the happiness of the occasion, rather than the one person who was missing.

Ena

As Ena turned the page of her notebook and started to read her entries under the heading *'Nature,'* there was a knock on her bedroom door. 'Ena? Gladys is serving drinks and the Leamans will be arriving soon. Ruby is excited to meet you. Are you coming down?'

Ena opened the door. 'Yes, Aunt Ivy. I'm coming.' She picked up her hairbrush. She was looking forward to meeting Ruby and the Leamans and this meal the night before Aunt Ivy and Bertie's wedding was the perfect opportunity. Her hands shook as she brushed her hair. She studied her reflection in the mirror. What would the Leamans make of her, this abandoned girl from the dirty streets of Gateshead? Despite her conversations about the suffrage movement with Bertie's sisters and everything Aunt Ivy had done to make her feel at home, she felt her difference keenly. She looked at the book lying on her bedside table; *'Anne of Green Gables'* by L. M. Montgomery. Aunt Ivy had given it to her and Ena was entranced by Anne Shirley's story. After a bleak childhood, orphaned Anne longs for a real home. She goes to live on a farm called Green Gables in the fictional town of Avonlea, and thrives in the close-knit village. Ena studied the picture of Anne on the cover; her red hair and freckles and her pale, thin face. She moved somewhere new and managed to fit in, why couldn't Ena do the same? She closed her eyes and pictured her version of Green Gables. It wasn't a farm; it was a pretty little house in a welcoming village like Avonlea, where everyone knew her and sounded like her. Ena opened her eyes and sighed.

She adjusted the collar of her blue checked gingham dress and opened her bedroom door. She heard voices in the hallway and tiptoed to the top of the stairs. Looking down, she watched Julius Caesar shake hands with a tall, thin man then embrace the woman next to him. 'Edwin, my good fellow. And Meta, my dear. How are you?'

Edwin removed his black bowler hat and placed it on the polished wooden stand behind the front door before answering. 'We are very well thank you, Giulio. And you?'

'Everyone is well, thank you. And we have much to celebrate in the coming days.'

'Oh yes, where is the bride to be?' Ena leant over the staircase to see Rachel's mother more clearly. Meta looked up and smiled. When their eyes met, a warmth spread through Ena. It sent her back in time. Back to a time of being surrounded by a love so strong she could hardly breathe. To a time of safety. To her grama. She smiled and Julius Caesar looked up.

'Ah, Ena. Do come down and meet our good friends the Leamans.'

Ena hurried downstairs; her fears swept away by Meta Leaman's smile.

'Ena, let me introduce you to Mr Edwin Leaman and Mrs Meta Leaman. Friends, this is Ivy's niece, Miss Ena Leighton.'

Ena beamed at Julius Caesar's use of her new name. No one in Bournemouth would associate her with downtrodden, dishevelled Evie Brown from Gateshead. Her hand shook as she raised it. She said she was very pleased to meet them. She spoke quietly, acutely aware of her accent and pronunciation.

'Lurking behind their parents are Cyril, Donovan and Rachel.' Julius Caesar pointed towards Edwin and Meta's children and Ena's eyes moved from one brother to the other before settling on Rachel. Their eyes locked and Ena would later discover Rachel's first impression of her was the same as her own. It was as if they were staring into a looking glass. Rachel was a little taller than Ena but they shared the same dark-brown eyes and shoulder length auburn hair. They exchanged wide smiles and Ena knew Rachel's name would be added to her notebook.

'Come on everyone, Hilda has prepared a sumptuous meal for us!' Julius Caesar led them towards the dining room and Ena fell into an easy step next to Rachel. When they walked into the room, a young woman jumped up from the table, arms outstretched. She looked from Ena to Rachel and back again before speaking. 'Ena?'

Ena nodded and Ruby enveloped her in a warm, sweet-smelling hug. 'I'm Ruby Rogers, your aunt's friend and bridesmaid!'

Ena smiled. 'Pleased to meet you, Ruby.'

Ruby took her place at the table as Aunt Ivy and Bertie's mother led Ena and Rachel to seats next to each other. Once they were all seated, Julius Caesar formally introduced Ena to Rachel's brothers, 16-year-old Cyril and 14-year-old Donovan. Cyril and Donovan smiled and said hello to Ena from across the table. She felt her cheeks starting to heat up and was grateful when Gladys arrived with the first course. As Gladys moved around the table, Ena stole a glance at Donovan. Their eyes met and his friendly smile reminded Ena of another boy. Jack Todd. She smiled back and Donovan's eyes sparkled mischievously.

Chapter 12

Mona and Peggy

Mona and Peggy were delighted to have received an invitation to dine with Thomas Andrews. The bugle sounded for the start of dinner service and they made their way into the elegant restaurant. The tables were lit by small lamps and decorated with cream vases full of white lilies. The aromatic scent followed them as they were led to Thomas's table. Thomas made introductions.

'Miss Mona Leighton, Miss Peggy Willow, please meet Colonel John Jacob Astor, Mrs Madeleine Talmage Astor, Sir Cosmo Edmund Duff-Gordon and Lucy, Lady Duff-Gordon.'

Mona and Peggy exchanged a quick glance before saying how delighted they were to meet Thomas's guests. Mona swallowed, she wished her sister and mother could see her dining in such illustrious company. While they waited for their champagne, a man in uniform approached their table. He apologised for interrupting them but said he needed to speak to Mr Andrews. The men stepped away from the table but remained within Mona's earshot. The uniformed man spoke first.

'Captain Smith has ordered a slight alteration to our course from southwest to due west, Mr Andrews.'

Mona saw Thomas Andrews frown before quickly regaining his composure.

'Why is that, Second Officer Lightoller?'

'Merely a precaution to avoid the reported ice, Mr Andrews.'

'Very well, thank you for informing me.'

As Thomas started walking back to the table, the uniformed man stepped in front of him, with his back to Mona. He leant close to Thomas and said something she couldn't hear. When

Thomas took his seat, Mona asked him if the change of course and the ice were cause for concern.

'Not at all, Miss. RMS *Titanic* is as nearly perfect as human brains can make her.'

Mona smiled and nodded, reassured by Thomas's calm manner. As Thomas sipped his champagne, his mind wandered. He knew the change of course should have directed *Titanic* into an area of the gulf stream free from icebergs; in any normal year this would have been the case. He also knew 1912 was not a normal year for ice; cold water pushed the warm gulf stream further south and the change in direction put the ship on a collision course with the reported ice. While the outside temperature was dropping, Thomas knew the lack of wind and calm waters would make spotting an iceberg more difficult. Without wind they would be unable to see water breaking upon it. The lack of moonlight would also limit the chance of reflected light from an iceberg. Lightoller also told him about the message warning of *'large quantities of field ice'* from RMS *Baltic*. The message had now been returned to Captain Smith, but not before Joseph Ismay shared it with several passengers. When Lightoller moved closer to Thomas he whispered, 'rumours are circulating, Mr Andrews'. Thomas looked around. The great and the good sitting in *Titanic's* First-Class Restaurant appeared unaffected by rumours or anything else, as they drank and ate their way across the ocean. His thoughts were interrupted by the arrival of another of his dinner guests. Bella Holliday had swapped her parasol for a gigantic orange hat with a blue rim, across which lay a large stuffed bird. The hat needed its own seat, such was its size and flamboyance. The wealthy American's commanding presence was evident as she swept through the restaurant towards them. Thomas stood to greet Bella and a waiter hurried to pull out her chair. She extended a gloved hand towards Thomas before collapsing onto the chair in an explosion of apricot tulle.

She fanned herself with the menu as Thomas made introductions. She looked around the table, nodding at Thomas's other guests. She stopped suddenly, narrowing her eyes.

'As I live and breathe! Miss Mona Leighton! It is you, isn't it?'

Mona's cheeks burned. 'Mrs Holliday. What a pleasure to see you again.'

'The pleasure is all mine, my dear. I am delighted to see you voyaging in style on this luxurious ship.' Bella's words dripped with curiosity and Mona crossed her fingers under the table. With a few words Bella could ruin her reputation in front of Thomas Andrews and his well-heeled guests. Peggy touched Mona's hand under the table and nodded reassuringly.

'Mona and I have been working tremendously hard, performing night and day in repertory theatre all over England, and saving every penny in order to embark upon this voyage of a lifetime.'

Mona was grateful for Peggy's attempt to convince Bella of their right to be there, without mentioning Marv's handout, but she saw questions in Bella's eyes. Bella was her companion on her return voyage to England the previous year. She helped Mona when anxiety overwhelmed her in front of the stern *maître d.* Mona told Bella something of her reasons for leaving New York. She talked about the man who followed her and about Marv's Folies Bergère production. She lowered her eyes when she remembered telling Bella how uncomfortable she was, having to dance almost naked. Bella surprised Mona by saying she thought they had a lot in common. Mona hadn't seen the similarities, Bella was rich, she dressed like a film star and knew a thing or two about life. Mona, for all her experiences in New York, remained a naive young woman from the North East of England. When she met Bella, she was returning to England a nervous wreck, devoid of self-confidence. Bella explained about her humble beginnings in Colorado, saying her father hadn't always been successful. A lucky investment led to an unexpected expansion in his business and their fortunes changed overnight. It was Bella who told Mona about the women known as *'The Charlottes'*, Bella who planted the seed in her mind. But she was the one, the only one to blame, for attempting the disgraceful deception. Mona started to shake as Bella's words rang in her mind, *'remember, you need to make your own luck'*. She breathed a huge sigh of relief when Thomas stood and extended his hand to greet the last of his dinner guests. All eyes turned to look at the man.

'Edward, my dear fellow. How splendid to see you again.'

Edward Pomeroy Colley shook Thomas's hand. They remained standing as Thomas introduced his friend. 'I am delighted to introduce Mr Edward Pomeroy Colley of Celbridge, County Kildare, Ireland. Edward is a civil engineer of some note. During the Klondike Gold Rush he opened a brokerage firm in Vancouver and made some very successful investments in mining stocks. Most importantly he is a dear friend of mine who laughs a lot and is tremendous company!'

Before Edward could sit down, Bella waved a gloved hand in his direction. 'Mrs Isabella Holliday, of Denver Colorado. Delighted to make your acquaintance, Mr Colley.'

Edward took Bella's hand. 'The pleasure is all mine, Mrs Holliday.'

When Thomas introduced Mona and Peggy, Edward's eyes moved away from Bella. He smiled at Mona, saying how pleased he was to meet her. Then his eyes settled on Peggy. Mona raised her eyebrows as she watched her friend. Peggy was never stuck for words. An image formed in her mind. Louis, her daughter's father. She remembered her first sight of him at the church hall dance in Gateshead. When the handsome, rebellious Louis Levy with his jet-black hair and dark-brown eyes showed an interest in her, she didn't hesitate. She knew she was treading a thin line between respectability and scandal, but her desire for a different life overwhelmed her. All she saw was Louis and the promise of a better life. She fell head over heels in love and when she discovered she was pregnant, he declared they would be married. His promises came to nothing and led to one of the worst times in her life. But she would never forget how she felt the first time she saw him. She looked at Peggy, had the lightning bolt struck her friend? The inescapable attraction her mother called *'l'étincelle,'* the spark?

'What is it you do, Miss Willow?'

Peggy smiled but Mona saw her hesitate. Mona helped her friend, as Peggy had helped her so many times before. 'Peggy is a wonderful, all-round theatrical performer, Mr Colley. She acts, dances and sings. She has the most lyrical voice.' Mona was astonished to see Peggy blush.

'Well, I don't know about that, Mona.'

'We have our very own singer at the table, how splendid! You must entertain us with a performance after dinner, Miss Willow.' Thomas Andrews's guests joined him in encouraging Peggy to sing and eventually she agreed.

RMS *Titanic*

When Mona picked up the menu, she nudged Peggy and mouthed, 'ten courses?' Peggy gave a slight shrug and took a sip of champagne. To begin, Thomas's guests could avail themselves of hors d'oeuvres then oysters, followed by *'Consommé Olga'* or Cream of Barley soup. The next course was poached salmon with a mousseline sauce and slices of cucumber. Mona looked around the table as a waiter discreetly removed her untouched plate. Bella and the men ate with gusto, demolishing everything the waiter put in front of them. Lady Duff-Gordon, Madeleine Astor and Peggy also cleared their plates but more slowly than

Bella and the men. Mona swallowed to try and dislodge the lump in her throat. Ten courses of the most delicious food, but she had no appetite. She pictured her mother sitting next to her at the table. Her remarkable mother. The woman who insisted Mona and Ivy could do anything and go anywhere, if they were determined enough. And here she was, eating a first-class dinner on the most sophisticated ocean liner in history. Why then, couldn't she relax and enjoy it?

'Mona? Lady Duff-Gordon asked us a question!'

Peggy nudged Mona with her elbow and Mona turned to look at the exquisite woman sitting opposite. 'Please forgive me, Lady Duff-Gordon. What was your question?'

'I asked you and Miss Willow about your dress designer. Your outfits are impeccable!'

'I told Lady Duff-Gordon they were tailor-made for us by an exclusive London dressmaker.'

Mona nodded. 'Yes, we are very happy with our travelling wardrobe.'

'You must come to me next time. I will ensure your designs are unique. I have fashion houses in London, Chicago, New York and Paris.'

Peggy smiled. 'Thank you, Lady Duff-Gordon, that is extremely kind of you.'

'Please, call me Lucy. Or, when you visit one of my fashion houses, ask for me by my professional name, Lucile.'

Mona and Peggy exchanged a smile. One of Britain's leading fashion designers had offered to dress them! Peggy raised her champagne glass towards her friend and Mona reciprocated. Waiters swerved expertly between tables, balancing huge serving dishes on the palm of one hand over their heads. By the time the cheerful party around Thomas's table were deciding between Lobster a la Newburg (an American dish of lobster, butter, cream, cognac, sherry, eggs and Cayenne pepper,) lamb with mint sauce or haunch of mutton with currant jelly, warnings of three large icebergs had been sent to the *Antillian,* a British Leyland Line steamship, by the SS *Californian.* Harold intercepted the *Antillian's* messages and delivered them to the bridge, but Captain Smith had left to attend a dinner party. In the Captain's absence, Harold passed the telegram to another officer. No mention of this warning was posted in the chart room and *Titanic* continued on her altered course. Captain Smith, dining in the A La Carte Restaurant and oblivious to the messages, decided on the sirloin of beef with horseradish sauce. When Harold left the bridge, he heard Second Officer Charles Lightoller issue an order to *Titanic's* crew to look after the ship's fresh water supply, as the temperature of the surrounding sea water was close to freezing.

Mona breathed a sigh of relief when the sixth course arrived. The palate cleanser, Punch à la Romaine, came in a large coupe glass and Mona sipped at the shaved-ice concoction of rum and champagne, savouring the refreshing, citrusy flavours. When the final course arrived, Peggy leant across and whispered in Mona's ear.

'I think we should try and eat dessert, don't you? We wouldn't want to appear rude.'

Mona nodded. Bella tucked into her Waldorf Pudding, shovelling each spoonful into her mouth as if it was the last meal she would ever eat. Lady Duff-Gordon, much more elegantly, took small delicate forkfuls of her chocolate and vanilla eclairs. When Mona and Peggy were finishing their desserts, an intermittent and minute flickering of the electric lights began. Mona looked at Thomas Andrews but he appeared not to have noticed. He caught Mona's eye and smiled.

'Miss Leighton, have you visited the Waldorf Hotel in New York?'

Mona shook her head, grateful for the distraction from the flickering lights. 'No, Mr Andrews, I have not.'

'Well, our dinner companion Colonel Astor built the Astoria Hotel in New York, which adjoins the Waldorf Hotel. I don't believe there is a connection between the hotel and the pudding Mrs Holliday so enthusiastically enjoyed, but perhaps Colonel Astor can enlighten us?'

Bella laughed and belched before having the good grace to blush. Colonel Astor continued the story. 'You are correct, Thomas. There is no connection with the pudding but the Waldorf Salad was created by the hotel's *maître d,* Oscar Tschirky. He devised the recipe for a charity ball given in honour of the St. Mary's Hospital for Children in 1896.'

Bella regained her composure. 'How wonderful, Colonel Astor. We should all do more for charitable causes. Don't you agree?'

'I do, Mrs Holliday.'

Mona felt Peggy touch her arm. 'Should we take a stroll before the dancing starts?'

Mona nodded and they excused themselves from the dinner table. The men stood and Thomas spoke. 'Remember, Miss Willow, you have promised to sing for us.'

Peggy nodded and Mona saw her look towards Edward Colley. 'I have, and sing for you I shall.' Peggy linked her arm through Mona's and they started walking towards the Promenade Deck. Suddenly Peggy stopped. 'Let's send Marv a telegram!'

'What? How?'

'I've heard people mention it. There's a radio on the ship that allows you to send telegrams. Everyone is doing it!'

Mona frowned. 'And what do you want to say to Marv?'

'Oh, you know. 'Look out. Stop. Glamorous dancers on way. Stop.' Something like that. You could send one to your sister, too.'

Mona looked down and shuffled her feet. Even if she had known what to say, she didn't know where Ivy was. When they met in the Lyons Cafe on Shaftesbury Avenue three months earlier, Mona told Ivy what happened to her in London, but she didn't learn much about her sister's life in the time they were apart. Mona sighed; why hadn't she asked Ivy about her life? Ivy said the most important thing was for them to go to Gateshead and bring Mona's daughter to London, where she would be safe. A wave of nausea hit Mona as she accepted the consequences of her actions. She abandoned her daughter to a life of poverty, and when the opportunity came to be reunited with her, she ran away again. Mona pressed a gloved hand against her lips to stifle a sob; she knew Ivy would take care of her daughter; she had always been more of a mother to her. She had missed her chance. She pushed away the images of her daughter and sister, determined to be her old, confident self. She lifted her chin and looked at Peggy.

'No. Let's send one to Marv. From both of us.'

'Very well. I'm sure he'll be thrilled to hear from us.'

When Harold returned to the radio room, he was surprised to see Jack. 'What are you doing here? Your shift doesn't start for a few hours and you must be exhausted after staying up all night to fix the transmitter.'

Jack moved closer and whispered. 'Is it right we've had warnings of ice ahead?'

Harold whispered back. 'Yes, I've just delivered another telegram to the bridge.'

'Are you worried?'

Harold pursed his lips before answering. 'Well, the officers don't seem concerned.'

Jack shrugged. 'Alright. I'll grab another couple of hours sleep before my shift.'

As Jack tried to get back to sleep, Captain Smith left the A La Carte Restaurant and returned to the bridge. Before retiring for the night, he discussed the visibility of icebergs and the weather conditions with Lightoller, noting the moonless night and the calm ocean. Captain Smith steepled his fingers across his mouth then nodded decisively. 'If it becomes at all doubtful let me know at once; I will be inside.'

Lightoller saluted. 'Yes, Sir!'

Chapter 13

Mona and Peggy

As Mona and Peggy walked to the First-Class Lounge for an after-dinner drink, they heard the ship's orchestra tuning up. Vernon told them after dinner, space was made in *Titanic*'s A La Carte Restaurant to allow first-class passengers to dance, accompanied by the orchestra.

They entered the First-Class Lounge and sank into large leather armchairs. Peggy glanced at the cocktail list before suggesting they order Tom Collins's. Mona nodded, a long drink with ice would be perfect. Peggy gave a low whistle and Mona turned to her friend; eyebrows raised. 'We ate dinner with Lucy, Lady Duff-Gordon! With Lucile!'

Mona joined in. 'And she offered to dress us! She is proof you can be married *and* have an occupation of your own. We don't need men to act for us, we can take control of our own destinies!'

When their cocktails arrived Peggy raised her tall glass and declared, 'to Lucile and all the women who take control!'

Mona raised her glass and repeated Peggy's toast. As she sipped the refreshing drink, she spotted Edward Colley at the entrance to the Lounge. She watched him looking around the room. He caught her eye and waved self-consciously before walking towards their table. Mona nudged Peggy and gestured in Edward's direction. Peggy turned, smiling broadly. When he reached them, Edward smoothed his neatly parted brown hair and smiled awkwardly.

'Ladies, please excuse my intrusion but may I please seek your advice?'

In an accomplished move worthy of a professional dancer, Peggy gestured for a waiter to bring another chair and indicated that Edward should sit. Then she moved her own chair closer and leant in towards him, her eyes wide. 'How can we help, Mr Colley?'

'I hope you don't think me too bold, but I wanted to ask how you became dancers.'

Mona went cold. It was the last thing she wanted to talk about. Peggy sat up straight in her chair and fixed her bright eyes on Edward. 'May I ask why?'

'Oh yes, of course you may. I do apologise, Miss Willow. The reason for my curiosity is I have a 14-year-old niece who has always dreamt of becoming a dancer. I have accompanied her to the ballet and I know she has attended some classes close to my brother's home in Chelsea but I wonder whether, that is, my question is…' Edward stopped speaking and cleared his throat.

Peggy tilted her head and sighed heavily. 'You want to know whether it is safe to be a dancer. Whether it is a suitable job for a young woman from a good family.' These were statements rather than questions. Edward nodded. Peggy gave a small shrug. 'In some theatres and music halls, no, it is not safe.' Mona moved her trembling hands out of Edward's sight. 'However, there are many reputable theatres and production companies where your niece could audition and possibly be successful, if she is talented enough.'

'Thank you, Miss Willow. I am most grateful for your candid answer.'

Peggy then gave Edward what Mona knew was a shortened, slightly embellished account of her rise to fame on the international stage. She didn't say her mother died in childbirth and her father brought her up on his own. She didn't tell Edward she and her father lived above one theatre or another, and instead of going to school, she went with him to his jobs as a stage manager in London's West End. She said being brought up around the music, personalities and excitement of the theatre, there was never any doubt she would become a dancer or an actress. Edward smiled and Peggy continued, saying she worked in London and on the south coast in repertory theatre before learning about the opportunities in New York. She ended by saying she was her own woman, not answerable to anyone other than her current employer. Mona leant back in her chair and smiled at her friend. Edward Colley could be in no doubt as to the character of the woman he appeared to have set his cap at.

'Your niece should start by writing to some reputable theatres in London. I can suggest some, if that is helpful. You should also advise her it is a very tough business, Mr Colley. It is not for the faint-hearted.'

'Thank you very much, Miss Willow. I shall write to my brother later this evening. May I also ask, whereabouts in New York will you and Miss Leighton be performing? I should very much like to attend one of your shows.'

Peggy lifted her chin. 'You can find us at the Paradise Theatre on Broadway.'

As they walked back to the A La Carte Restaurant, Peggy asked Edward about his business interests in New York. 'What will you be doing in Manhattan, Mr Colley?'

'I have several meetings arranged, to investigate possible investment opportunities for my business. After which I shall return to Vancouver where I work as a consultant to the prominent British Columbia industrialist James Dunsmuir. I have business interests on both sides of the Atlantic and I regularly travel between Dublin and my home on Vancouver Island in Victoria's English Bay neighbourhood. Have you ever visited Vancouver, Miss Willow?'

'No, Mr Colley. Is it a pleasant place?'

Edward touched his hair before answering. 'It is delightful,

Miss Willow. Perhaps we can exchange addresses and correspond once you arrive in New York? At an acceptable time, I would be very glad if you wished to visit Vancouver and you permitted me to show you around. Miss Leighton, you would also be very welcome, if you wish to accompany Miss Willow.'

Peggy smiled. 'Thank you, Mr Colley. I shall consider your kind invitation.'

When they entered the A La Carte Restaurant, Edward excused himself and went to join a group of friends. He explained they had become acquainted with the American socialite Mrs Helen Candee during the voyage, but assured Peggy all eyes would be on her during her performance. Mona looked towards the raised palm-decked dais, where the ship's orchestra introduced itself with a whine of strings and the tinkle of a piano. A large, three-pronged candle stand had been placed at one side of the dais. Mona's shoes sank into the plush Rose du Barry Axminster carpet, the pink perfectly matching the rose-patterned Aubusson tapestry of the luxurious French walnut chairs. Thomas Andrews waved, directing them to a table decorated with pink roses and white daisies. Mona raised a hand to Thomas but Peggy hung back.

'What is it? I've never seen you hesitate before a performance.'

Peggy looked around before answering. 'It's him, Mr Colley.'

'You like him, don't you?'

Peggy nodded. 'Yes, I've never felt that pull of attraction before.'

Mona took Peggy's arm. 'Well, he said he was travelling to New York to investigate business opportunities there. Perhaps he will stay long enough for the two of you to meet up.'

Peggy's eyes glistened. 'I hope so.'

As Thomas pulled out a chair for Mona the *maître d* approached Peggy and led her towards the side of the raised dais.

Peggy disappeared and Thomas ordered champagne. Mona looked around at the large crowd; Peggy's reputation preceded her and word must have spread. They waited eagerly for the star of Broadway and London's West End. Mona knew how good Peggy was, and she couldn't wait to see people's reactions when her friend sang. Suddenly the room went dark, then it was illuminated by three huge pillar candles positioned in the stand at the side of the dais. The orchestra began quietly; the sweet strains of a violin and pianissimo piano notes, then a second violin and a cello joined the ensemble. The crowd gasped when Peggy's slim silhouette appeared in the candlelight, her silver gown shining, apparition-like. Mona didn't know what Peggy would sing, but her friend had a wide repertoire to choose from. When Peggy started singing, Mona smiled. She expected something upbeat, perhaps slightly *risqué*. But this was a different Peggy. She had chosen to sing a love song. *'All that I ask of you is love.'*

'I care not what the world may say, or if it mock and jeer,
I care not for its smiles or frowns, if you were always near.
You are my very all in all; beneath the heaven's blue,
And all else is as naught to me, the breath of life is you.
All that I ask is love, all that I want is you,
And I swear by all the stars, I'll be forever true.
All that I seek to know, all that I want above,
All that I crave in this wide, wide world,
All that I ask of you is love.'

The applause rang out and Mona watched Peggy. Her friend's eyes found Edward Colley. Edward stood and his companions joined him in applauding Peggy's performance. Peggy stepped down from the dais and joined Mona and Thomas. Thomas handed her a glass of champagne and made a toast. 'To Miss Peggy Willow, our very own songbird.'

Mona repeated the toast and held her glass towards her friend. 'That was beautiful, Peggy. I've never heard you sing that song before.'

Peggy's eyes sparkled. 'I think it's this voyage, Mona. I feel as though anything is possible.'

Edward Colley approached them, clapping his hands. 'Bravo, Miss Willow. Bravo!'

'Thank you, Mr Colley.'

'I wonder, once you have your breath back, could I introduce you and Miss Leighton to Mrs Helen Candee? She is looking forward to meeting you both.'

'Yes, that would be marvellous, Mr Colley.'

They crossed the restaurant with Edward carrying Mona and Peggy's drinks. He marvelled at the graceful movement of the huge ship. 'Look, the glasses don't tilt at all!' He led them to a table where Helen Candee, the American author, journalist and feminist sat. 'Miss Willow! Miss Leighton! What a pleasure it is to meet you. Please, do sit.'

Mona stared at the self-assured, elegant woman holding court at a table of men. Helen's long white gloves contrasted with her short-sleeved emerald crepe de chine gown. The V neck gown was decorated with a rich silk brocade, the raised gold patterns criss-crossing from just below the sheer white lace bodice. Mona surprised herself by asking Mrs Candee something. When Edward told her and Peggy their hostess was a feminist, evidenced by her best-selling book '*How Women May Earn a Living*', Mona's mind reeled back to her friend Violet, a dancer at the Diamond. Not long before the ever-hopeful Violet disappeared, she tried to convince Mona things were changing for women in Great Britain. Mona questioned how the changes could reach women like them, working for a pittance in a rundown music hall. She took a deep breath and asked Mrs Candee if she truly believed things had changed for women.

Helen Candee smiled. 'Thank you, Miss Leighton. How refreshing to be challenged by an intelligent young woman!' Her eyes swept around the table, taking in her well-meaning, but privileged group of male admirers. Mona lifted her chin and pushed her shoulders back as she and Helen Candee talked. Edward sat next to Peggy and the snatches of conversation Mona heard made her smile. Suddenly Helen stood up. Mona raised her eyebrows when the full length of Helen's gown was revealed. The high waistline and gold silk brocade, shimmering down to Helen's white satin shoes, showed off her slim figure.

'I adore this piece! Who will partner me?' Helen's admirers vied for her attention and Edward held out his hand to Peggy. Mona looked down but was surprised by a voice behind her. 'Miss Leighton, could I have the pleasure of this dance?' She looked up to see Thomas Andrews holding out his hand. She nodded. The music that tempted Helen was 'The Mosquitoes' Parade.' Mona and Peggy took position opposite their partners, following the other couples in an anti-clockwise circle around the room. Thomas, with Mona to his right-hand side, gently placed his right arm around her waist. Mona put her left hand on Thomas's right shoulder. With everyone in position, the orchestra began again. The couples moved flawlessly, hopping then touching their heels and toes on the ground before walking forward, then turning to face the opposite direction. Any shyness Mona felt about dancing with Thomas disappeared the moment they were in position. She faced him, smiling playfully, her eyes bright. She held out her hands to take his as the music continued. The couples jumped and kicked to the left then jumped and kicked to the right. Mona turned expertly under Thomas's left arm before taking his hands and stepping around the room with the other couples in the final move. When the music finished, the couples applauded each other and Thomas smiled. 'What a pleasure to dance with someone so accomplished. Thank you, Miss Leighton.' Mona gave Thomas a short nod. Her heart thudded against her chest. She knew she could dance but she wanted to believe she deserved to be on *Titanic*, performing the Military Twostep with the debonair Thomas Andrews. She pushed her shoulders back and held her head high as they returned to their seats.

Peggy caught up with them at the table. 'Mr Colley has asked if I would like to go to a concert in the Reception Room; do you want to join us?'

Mona glanced towards Helen's table. Elsie Bowerman had joined her. Helen waved in Mona's direction and pointed at the empty chair next to Elsie.

'Thank you, Peggy, but I think I'll join Mrs Candee and Miss Bowerman.'

'Very well, Mona. Should I see you back at our cabin later?'

Mona nodded. She heard some of Peggy and Edward's conversation as they walked away.

'It is my birthday tomorrow; I will be 37 years old. We must celebrate!'

'What a coincidence, Mr Colley. Today it is my birthday!'

'Oh. I would have given you a gift, if I had known. Instead, you must allow me to take you out for dinner in Manhattan.'

'That would be delightful, thank you.'

Mona stared at Peggy's back. She had never heard her friend agree to have dinner with an admirer before.

Chapter 14

RMS *Titanic*

While Peggy and Edward enjoyed the quintet in the Reception Room at the foot of the Grand Staircase, Lightoller advised the lookouts in the crow's nest to watch carefully for icebergs until the following morning. A little later, a warning of heavy pack ice and a sighting of an iceberg was received from SS Mesaba. The message was overlooked in the radio room as Jack and Harold continued struggling with the backlog of passenger traffic.

After the concert, Peggy and Edward had supper in the Café Parisien. Lightoller was relieved on the bridge by First Officer William Murdoch. The lookouts were also relieved and the new crew advised to watch for icebergs. As Edward walked Peggy back to her cabin, they overheard a steward telling passengers the temperature of the sea had dropped to almost freezing. Peggy said she was glad they left the electric fire on in their cabin before they went to dinner.

Edward sighed. 'Sadly, I did not have your foresight. I fear my cabin will be chilly.'

Peggy smiled up at him. 'I hope it is not too uncomfortable for you. I shall look forward to seeing you tomorrow, on your birthday.'

'I had a wonderful evening, thank you.' Edward placed a light kiss on Peggy's gloved hand before saying goodnight. Earlier, he had arranged to meet friends in the First-Class Smoking Room to play poker, but now he decided to return to his cabin and write to his brother. There would be other opportunities to play poker before they docked in New York. Back in his cabin, he turned on the electric fire then wrapped a blanket around his shoulders. He made himself comfortable at the writing desk. He lit a cigar and started to write.

'My dear brother,

When we set sail, this huge ship appeared only half full but lots of people embarked at Cherbourg and Queenstown. The dining room is full of tables for two, three and more in secluded corners. I thought it unlikely to meet anyone I liked on board, but I was wrong! I have become entranced by an English theatrical performer by the name of Miss Peggy Willow. Now brother, before you enquire as to her social standing, know this. She and her companion Miss Mona Leighton have been welcomed into the distinguished company of Co-lonel John Jacob Astor and Mrs Madeleine Talmage Astor, as well as Sir Cosmo Edmund Duff-Gordon and Lucy, Lady Duff-Gordon. I intend to correspond with Miss Willow once we arrive in New York and invite her to visit me in Victoria Bay. Largely, the passage has been without incident although we nearly had a collision coming out of Southampton. We passed close to a ship tied up alongside the Oceanic and the suction of our ship drew her out into the stream, snapping the ropes holding her. She swung around and across our bows! She had no steam up so was pulled back by tugs and we had to reverse. She was called the New York in case you see it in the papers.'

Edward stopped writing and rubbed his hands together. He held them in front of the electric fire before deciding he would be warmer in bed. As he prepared to retire for the night, a steam-ship travelling about ten to 15 miles north of *Titanic's* position became trapped in field ice. SS *Californian's* radio operators sent out warnings to all shipping in the area, including *Titanic*. As Edward climbed into bed, Jack Phillips received the message *'we are stopped and surrounded by ice'* from the *Californian*. The strong signal interrupted *Titanic's* regular communications and Jack replied, asking the *Californian* to keep the channel clear, before continuing to work his way through the backlog of passenger messages. In *Titanic's* crow's nest, the lookouts noticed a slight haze in front of them. Sleep eluded Edward. Lying awake, he frowned, suddenly aware of the increased vibration of the ship.

Mona and Peggy

Sipping their hot chocolate in front of the electric fire, Mona and Peggy shared stories of their evenings. Mona beamed as she entertained Peggy with snippets from her conversations with Helen Candee and Elsie Bowerman. 'They are women doing things for themselves, without mention of a man!' Peggy smiled. When Mona stopped to have a drink, Peggy took the opportunity to talk about Edward. 'He wants to take me out for dinner in Manhattan and buy me a gift when we visit him in Vancouver. You will come with me, won't you?'

'Of course, as long as you don't think I would be in the way.'

'Not at all! Edward explained he will have to work during the day but said he would arrange for a guide to show us around. In the evenings he will take us to the theatre and the many first-class restaurants Victoria Bay has to offer.'

'That sounds wonderful.'

'We're going to see the big wide world, Mona! We'll see out our contracts with Marv then head to Victoria Bay, the rest of Vancouver and how about Australia?'

'Australia?'

'Yes! I've heard about a theatre in Sydney. The Tivoli, which is so well regarded, we'll become international stars!'

'You already are, Peggy!' Mona stretched and yawned. 'All this talk of travelling has worn me out, I need to go to bed.' As she stood, she staggered and almost fell.

Peggy laughed, 'too much champagne, darling?'

Mona stared; her eyes wide. 'No, there was a bump.'

Peggy's brow furrowed, 'what do you mean, a bump?'

'I don't know, a bit like a train pulling into a station.' It was 11.40 pm.

RMS *Titanic*

No more than a minute after the lookouts in *Titanic*'s crow's nest noticed the slight haze in front of them, they saw an iceberg directly ahead. Speechless, they stared at each other, their eyes like saucers. Then they sounded the warning bell with three rings and telephoned the bridge. 'Iceberg right ahead!'

Murdoch remained calm when he received the message. He took immediate action, barking orders to try and prevent *Titanic* from colliding with the iceberg.

'Hard to starboard, helmsman!'

Titanic's helmsman steered the ship's rudder hard to the right to turn her away from the iceberg. At the same time Murdoch ordered *Titanic*'s engines to be stopped. He continued shouting orders at the helmsman. 'Full astern!' As the helmsman moved the ship backwards, Murdoch activated the watertight doors below. He allowed himself to breathe when *Titanic* began to veer to port, away from the iceberg. Murdoch swore, realising it wasn't enough; manoeuvres to prevent *Titanic* from colliding with the iceberg had failed. He turned towards the sound of heavy footsteps marching through the wheelhouse. Captain Smith's question was low and grave.

'What have we struck?'

Murdoch lifted his chin and pushed back his shoulders. 'An iceberg, Sir.'

'Where?'

'Starboard quarter, Sir. We've moved her away now.'

'Keep the engines stopped until I order otherwise.'

'Yes, Sir.'

Thomas Andrews returned to his cabin when the dancing ended. He was at his desk, planning changes he wanted to make to *Titanic,* when he realised the ship's engines had stopped. He opened his cabin door to find a steward who said Captain Smith had summoned him to the bridge. He narrowed his eyes and spoke to the steward, his voice level. 'What happened?'

The steward looked around before quickly replying. 'I believe she has hit an iceberg, Sir. Apparently, there were warning messages.'

Thomas hurried to the bridge and stood alongside Captain Smith. 'These messages. Tell me what they said.'

'Walk with me, Andrews. We need to examine the extent of the damage.'

Edward's friends, playing poker in the First-Class Smoking Room and oblivious to the conversation on the bridge, discussed how long it would take Edward to propose to Peggy. One tutted and reminded them of Bella Holliday's comment earlier. 'It won't happen. Men don't propose to actressy women!' Edward's friends weren't convinced; they had never seen him so smitten. As they agreed to play a final hand, the room shook, the lights flickered and their brandy glasses slid from the table, shattering on the tiled floor. They looked at one another and two of them half-stood. They were waved back into their seats and various theories were shared. Had *Titanic* hit another ship, lost a propeller, or highly unlikely, but, knocked against an iceberg? They convinced one another it was nothing to worry about and the engines would start again at any moment. They dealt another hand.

Captain Smith walked quickly, reassuring passengers there was no cause for concern. Thomas kept his eyes lowered, not wanting to draw attention to the ominous creaks and groans he heard as they walked.

'Radio room first, Andrews. I'll instruct them to get ready to send the distress call, but to wait for my order. First, I need to know how bad the damage is.'

Harold and Jack were discussing the rumours of *Titanic* hitting an iceberg when Captain Smith and Thomas Andrews arrived in the radio room. The wireless operators dismissed the rumours as idle gossip. They barely felt any impact and didn't think it could be serious. They believed, if necessary, the watertight compartments could close off portions of the ship and keep it afloat. After all, *Titanic* was supposed to be unsinkable. They stood and faced Captain Smith, leaning towards him to hear his quiet, serious words. 'This is notice you may need to send an SOS signal, but do not send it until I instruct you to do so. Do you understand?' They nodded. Captain Smith turned on his heel and marched out of the room. Thomas Andrews followed. Harold and Jack looked at each other, SOS was a distress call. *Titanic* was in trouble. As Captain Smith and Thomas Andrews toured the ship, they received reports of damage to the vessel. After ten minutes Thomas stopped and leant against the wall outside the engine room.

'What is it, man? Spit it out!'

Thomas raised his eyes. 'It's bad, Sir. I estimate the first five of the ship's watertight compartments are flooding rapidly.'

Captain Smith moved closer to Thomas and spat his words. 'Isn't your blasted *unsinkable ship* supposed to withstand such flooding?'

'She can withstand four flooded compartments, but no more.'

'What are you telling me?'

Thomas sighed. 'I am afraid it is a mathematical certainty she will sink.'

'How long do we have?'

'In my opinion Sir, she has an hour, perhaps two, before foundering.'

Captain Smith clenched his hands into fists and raised his eyes. 'Good God, how could this happen?' He took a deep breath. 'Still, we have time. Enough time to send distress signals, enough time to uncover the lifeboats and muster crew and passengers.'

Thomas shook his head and Captain Smith moved closer again, taking hold of his lapels. 'What? You disagree?'

'It's the lifeboats, Sir. Or rather, the lack of them.'

Captain Smith pushed his red face into Thomas's. 'Explain yourself. Now!'

'I'm sorry Sir, but there is a severe shortage of lifeboats on board.'

Captain Smith pursed his lips. 'There is no time now but we will return to this matter. Do I make myself clear?' Thomas's reply was lost as Captain Smith charged away.

Jack's head whipped around when the door to the radio room banged open. Captain Smith stood in the doorway and gave instructions to send the distress call. 'Tell whoever responds we're going down by the head and need immediate assistance.'

Face impassive and hands steady, Jack turned back to the transmitter and tapped out the distress call then the ship's coordinates. 'SOS. SOS. *Titanic* to all ships.'

The international Morse code of three dots, three dashes, and another three dots told anyone listening *Titanic* was in a perilous situation. Other ships quickly replied. 'What's wrong?'

Jack didn't hesitate. 'Come at once. We have struck a berg.' He sat back and stared at the transmitter. Harold whispered in his ear. 'What a miracle you fixed it, Jack. If you hadn't, we wouldn't be able to send and receive messages.' Jack nodded when Harold clapped him on the back. Eyes fixed on the transmitter, they waited for replies. When Captain Smith returned to the bridge, he received reports that *Titanic's* squash court was awash and the ship's mail room, located 24 feet above the keel, was flooded with enough water to float the mailbags. He swallowed to dislodge the lump in his throat when he received the

113

next message; some of the boiler rooms were filling with water. He knew the weight would start to pull the ship down. In the crow's nest, the lookouts heard the boatswain's call 'all hands standby, you may be wanted at any moment'. Captain Smith gripped the edge of the ornate desk in the wheelhouse then gave the order. 'Swing out the boats ready for lowering and have passengers be called up with lifejackets on!'

Chapter 15

Mona and Peggy

Peggy wagged her finger in front of Mona's face. 'I didn't feel anything. Honestly Mona, are you sure you haven't drunk too much champagne?'

Mona shook her head. 'No, I felt a bump. And what's that noise in the corridor?'

Peggy moved towards the door. She turned back to Mona, frowning. 'It sounds like footsteps, like someone running.' She reached for the door handle.

'No! Don't open the door!'

Peggy turned to face Mona. Her friend's face was ashen. 'What do you suggest we do? We need to know what's going on.'

'But what if…'

'What? It's probably nothing, but if we don't open the door, we'll never know.' Peggy opened the door and Mona watched her look one way then the other. Mona heard a man's voice then Peggy closed the door and walked quickly towards the bedroom, carrying something bulky.

'What's that, Peggy? What's happening? I heard voices in the corridor.'

Peggy didn't answer. She collected their coats and hats. 'Put these on.'

'Why? Where are we going? We're warm in here.'

'Listen. Do you trust me?' Mona nodded; Peggy was the only person she had trusted in a long time. Peggy held Mona's elbows. She spoke slowly and calmly. 'The stewards in the corridor are giving people lifejackets and directing them onto the deck. They said to wear as many clothes as possible under our lifejackets and take nothing other than what we can put in our coat pockets.'

Mona's knees buckled but Peggy held her steady.

'Why would we need lifejackets?'

Peggy didn't answer. They put their coats on over their evening gowns then tied the strings of each other's cork-filled lifejackets. Peggy led Mona to the door. Mona shivered when a blast of cold air blew along the corridor. Outside was chaos and she started to shake as Peggy elbowed her way through people in varying states of undress. They fought their way to the packed foyer where an incongruous sight greeted them. Dressing gowns and bath robes worn with gloves, scarves, fur tippets and stoles. Women with their hair loose, men tie-less. Peggy pointed. 'Look, there's Vernon. Let's ask him what's going on.'

Mona had never seen the helpful steward without a ready smile, but this was a different Vernon. When Peggy tapped him on the shoulder he turned, his face a grotesque mask of fear. He met Peggy's eyes and immediately tried to produce his usual greeting. But the smile didn't reach his eyes. He said something to Peggy that Mona couldn't hear then hurried away. Peggy turned back to Mona; her eyes steely. 'Vernon said we need to make our way outside. Quickly.'

'Why?' Mona's lip trembled as people barged past her.

Peggy looked around then whispered in Mona's ear. 'We've hit an iceberg. Vernon said people are panicking but we should stay calm and get to a lifeboat as quickly as we can. Once we're in a lifeboat another ship will come to pick us up.'

Mona stuttered her question. 'Is the ship going to sink?'

'RMS *Titanic*? Good gracious, no! Don't you know she's unsinkable?'

Peggy threw back her pretty head and laughed, but not before Mona spotted her eyes. She had never seen fear in Peggy's eyes before. They walked quickly, heeding a steward's instructions to take the elevator to the Boat Deck. Nodding repeatedly, he tried to reassure the steady flow of passengers. 'You'll be back on board for breakfast.' People squeezed into the elevator. Those left outside tutted at the room taken up by thick coats and impossibly large hats. The same hats, viewed as the height of fashion and sophistication earlier in the day, were now invidious and ridiculous. The elevator rose slowly; the silence from those within magnified by the thunderous mechanism taking them to an unknown fate.

RMS *Titanic*

Thomas Andrews raced up the staircase towards the bridge, taking three steps at a time. Captain Smith stood with his back to Thomas. He spoke slowly, in a low, deep voice. 'I demand to know why there is a severe shortage of lifeboats on board. You will explain later, once we have completed the shipwreck process. Now, we must make every endeavour to fill all available lifeboats to capacity. Give me a figure. How many passengers can we take?'

Thomas started speaking but was silenced by an earth-shattering crash. Captain Smith whirled around and roared. 'How many, man?' Thomas hesitated. In his mind, he replayed his conversation with Bruce Ismay as final preparations were made in the weeks before *Titanic* left Southampton. He argued for more lifeboats but was rebuffed on the grounds they would ruin the view. Ismay insisted they had more than the legally required number and any extra would clutter up the beautiful open expanse of the upper deck, where first-class passengers would want to stroll. Thomas listened despondently as Ismay recorded *Titanic* would set sail with 16 wooden lifeboats and four collapsible cork rafts. Thomas met Captain Smith's eyes. 'We can take 1,178 passengers, Sir. If every lifeboat is filled to capacity.'

'But we have more than 2,200 on board! What do you suggest will happen to those we can't accommodate in a lifeboat? Should they swim for it?'

Thomas looked down. 'I am deeply sorry, Sir. I did try to argue…' His words were lost in the wake of another crash from below and Captain Smith pushed past him, his face a dangerous shade of puce. He took in the scene on the Boat Deck. Passengers milled around, hats askew or missing, clutching the now cold hands of children plucked from warm beds, bewildered by their sudden change in circumstance. Captain Smith gave the order to load the lifeboats with women and children. Women came willingly before realising their husbands were being prevented from joining them. Madeleine Astor gripped her husband's arm as they hurried along the Boat Deck. Colonel Astor appeared unperturbed. 'I find it ridiculous we should trade these solid decks of RMS *Titanic* for a small lifeboat.' He pointed a gloved finger towards their intended rescue vehicle. 'We are safer here than in that little boat.' Madeleine Astor held fast to her husband's arm when a quartermaster directed her towards a lifeboat. Her foot shook as she lifted it to step over the side of *Titanic*. The black velvet heel which just hours earlier graced the dance floor, now hung in mid-air. The quartermaster spoke. 'The boat must leave, Madam.' She turned back, her eyes dark with fear. 'John?' Her husband stepped forward but the quartermaster barred his way. 'Women and children only, Sir.' Colonel Astor, unused to refusal, glared at the officer. He leant closer and spoke quietly. 'May I join her? She is in a delicate condition.' The quartermaster looked at Madeleine Astor as if deliberating. He turned back to Colonel Astor and raised his chin. 'I am afraid not, Sir. No men may enter the lifeboats until all the women and children have been loaded.' Madeleine Astor cried out when her husband stood back. 'No! John!' Colonel Astor looked over the side and called down as the lifeboat was lowered. 'I will be in the next one, my dear. We will be picked up by another ship. I will see you very soon, I promise.'

From his position back on the bridge, Captain Smith

watched passengers surrounding his officers and the stewards, desperate for help. He turned at the sound of quick footsteps behind him. 'Sir.' Boxhall saluted then brandished a scrap of paper. 'What's this?'

'SOS coordinates, Sir. I believe these to be more accurate than those you had.'

Captain Smith shook his head then shouted. 'Take them to the radio room. Now!'

Jack listened intently to the corrected position and Boxhall's instruction to send another distress call. He immediately began tapping out the coded message. 'We have collision with iceberg. Sinking. Can hear nothing for noise of steam.' On deck, as if confirming the message, deafening blasts of steam escaped from the ship's funnels, shaking the black night like thunder. Jack leant close to the transmitter and whispered. 'Someone respond, please.'

Mona and Peggy

Mona and Peggy took in the scene on the Boat Deck. Mothers clung to children, fathers argued to be allowed into lifeboats, dogs released from kennels ran up and down the deck. A woman stumbled past them screaming there were no lifeboats and all hope was lost. Mona rubbed her gloved hands together and pulled her coat tighter against the cold night.

'Where do we go, Peggy?'

'I don't know. We need to find someone to ask.'

'This lifeboat is full. One is loading on the other side.' The officer's shout gave them the information they needed and they pushed through the throng to reach the waiting lifeboat.

'Miss Leighton! Miss Willow! Where are you going?'

Bella's customary hat sat crookedly atop her unusually ashen face. Her teeth chattered when she spoke. 'I heard the orchestra was playing in the First-Class Lounge. People have gathered there to avoid the biting cold until we receive further instructions. Will you come?'

Mona looked at Peggy and something shifted. She didn't know where the courage came from. 'No. We're heading towards a lifeboat on the other side of the deck. Come with us.' Mona's words were quiet but stern, her determination overwhelming everything else. She had faced danger before and did what she needed to, to survive. She surprised herself then and would do whatever it took now. She reached for Bella's hand and the older woman grabbed it, as if grabbing a chance for life. Mona nodded. 'Good. We need to hurry; the lifeboats are filling up quickly.'

'Mrs Holliday. Have you seen Edward? Mr Colley?' Peggy hadn't moved.

'No. I saw some of his acquaintances but he wasn't with them.'

'I need to find him, Mona.'

'No. Come with us now and find him once we're all safe.' Mona's eyes beseeched her friend and she grabbed Peggy's hand.

Peggy shook her head. 'I need to know he is all right. I'll find him then I'll find you again.' Her hand slipped out of Mona's.

'No! Peggy! Come back, please!'

Peggy gave them a cheery wave and started moving away. 'Save room in the lifeboat for us, darling! We'll see you soon!'

Mona stared at the back of Peggy's honey-coloured fur coat as she was swallowed up by the agitated crowds. She put her hand to her mouth to stifle a scream and pulled Bella towards the waiting lifeboat. An officer shouted at them to hurry. Mona went first and with shaking legs she stepped over the side. Icy hands helped her into the small wooden vessel, held at the side of the mighty *Titanic* by thick ropes. She reached up to help Bella. They sat on cold wet slats of wood, pressing together for warmth. Suddenly they were plunged into darkness when *Titanic's* lights went out. The bitter night air was filled with screams and Mona felt for Bella's hand. They sat, suspended in mid-air, shaking with cold and fear. Mona looked up into the inky sky. A bright white light came into view and she blinked. The light shot up into the black, arrow-straight. It emitted a high-pitched screech as it travelled then burst with a tremendous bang, illuminating the sky and showering the horizon with tiny lights. A shout went out from above. 'Rockets! Now we will be saved!' Then the darkness closed in again.

Chapter 16

Bournemouth - Monday 15th April 1912

Ena lay awake in the dark hours of early morning. In her mind she replayed conversations from the night before. When they finished eating, the adults started discussing arrangements for the wedding. Rachel tapped Ena on the hand and asked which school she would be going to in Bournemouth. Sometime later, Aunt Ivy said it was time for Rachel to go home. The girls parted reluctantly with a promise to continue their conversation at the wedding. Ena stretched and smiled; she never imagined she would have another friend like Nancy. She sat up then placed her feet on the floor. An unwanted image filled her mind, the black memory box. Sometimes the bad memories escaped and she struggled to lock them away again. This was different; someone she hadn't put in the black box but couldn't bring herself to put in the brightly coloured box either. The image persisted. She padded barefoot to her bedroom door and turned the handle without making a sound. She tiptoed towards the bathroom; her feet swallowed by Mrs Primavesi's plush carpet. The gentle lilt of singing stopped her and she paused outside Aunt Ivy's bedroom door.

'I care not what the world may say, or if it mock and jeer,
I care not for its smiles or frowns, if you were always near.'

Ena tapped on her aunt's bedroom door. The singing stopped and the door opened, revealing Aunt Ivy in a long, white nightgown embroidered with small green flowers. She smiled and pulled her niece inside. 'Can't you sleep either?' Ena shook her head. 'Are you excited about today?' Ena looked up at her aunt, the consistent source of love throughout her life. 'Yes'…, Ena hesitated. Aunt Ivy sat on the bed and patted the space beside her. 'What is it?' Ena hesitated again and Aunt Ivy waited. 'It's just…, I've been thinking about the Primavesis and the Leamans and Ruby and your friends from London, but…' Aunt Ivy took her hand. 'There's someone missing, isn't there?' Ena nodded and tears she didn't expect filled her eyes. 'How can I miss someone I've never known?' Ivy's heart ached. She hugged Ena. 'Perhaps you can miss the idea of someone. I wish she was here too.' 'Where is she?' Ena whispered the anguished words. Aunt Ivy squeezed her hand. 'I don't know.' Ena leant into her aunt. She hated admitting to missing the woman who abandoned her, but the tightness in her chest was real. Ivy lifted Ena's chin and looked into her eyes. 'One thing I know about your mother, is she has an astonishing ability to land upright in any given situation. I am sure she's safe and well, dancing in a grand theatre somewhere.' Ena sniffed and nodded. 'Try not to hate her, Ena. She loved you but in chasing her dreams she lost sight of what mattered. I'm trying to forgive her; I hope you can too.'

'But why isn't she here? She should be with you, her only sister, on your wedding day.' Ivy sighed, she wanted that more than anything. 'Listen, Ena. I'm sure wherever she is, she will be thinking about us. And we have Ruby, who has become like another sister to me. Now, I think you should try and get some sleep, we have a very busy day ahead of us.' She placed a light kiss on Ena's head and Ena nodded. After Ena went back to her own room, Ivy sat on the edge of the bed with her head in her hands. The trapdoor trick returned her to life before everything changed, when her mother was still alive and Ena was a baby. She and Mona worked at the Gateshead Ropery and while the heavy dirty jobs didn't pay much, their mother ensured they had decent clothes and enough to eat. She longed for her mother's advice. What would she have said about Mona's behaviour? She encouraged her daughters to be ambitious, to strive for a better life and recognise their own value. Ivy walked to the window and placed her palms on the glass. She looked up at the moon. Wherever Mona was in the world, Ivy imagined her looking at the same moon. As Ivy pictured her sister, the horizon blazed orange with the first light of day.

Peggy

When Peggy left Mona and Bella, she made her way to the First-Class Lounge. Bella had said the orchestra was playing and some passengers were waiting there until there was more information. Peggy thought Edward might be among them. She pushed through the frantic crowds, trying to ignore the anguished faces and cries of people who, less than an hour ago, believed they were taking the voyage of a lifetime on an unsinkable ship. Peggy shook her head; *Titanic* was made of iron, of course she could sink. She slowed her pace when she reached the door to the Grand Staircase. People shoved their way through the wood-panelled door, now hanging dejectedly from its hinges. A gloved hand gripped her arm when she tried to pass.

'Not that way, Miss! This is the way to the lifeboats and safety!'

Peggy looked up into the sea-worn face of a member of *Titanic's* crew. His eyes pleaded with her but one by one, she peeled his fingers from her arm. 'Please Miss, I beg you. Don't go down there. Come with me.' She turned from the smell of whiskey on the man's breath and forced her way to the balustrade. Her foot slipped on the linoleum floor and she collided with the rail. She looked down at the cream tiles, interspersed with black medallions. Her shoes were soaked and she held the rail to shake first one then the other. She heard the orchestra and looked down. The doors to the First-Class Lounge stood open and the sound of music drifted into the chaos above. The strains of Archibald Joyce's *'Vision of Salome'* reached her and for a moment she imagined waltzing with Edward. The lights went out and she took deep breaths, trying to stay calm amid the screams around her. She looked up at the large wrought iron and glass dome but everything was black. She heard a shout from outside. 'Women and children first!' She turned back in the direction of the door but was knocked over when someone barged past her. On her hands and knees, she felt for the balustrade. Suddenly a bright white light appeared outside the glass dome. The light shot up into the sky, emitting a high-pitched screech. Peggy's eyes followed it until it burst with a tremendous bang. Light flooded in through the stained-glass skylight, illuminating the statues of Honour and Glory and the clock in the great carved panel. She heard a shout. 'Rockets! Thank God!' Her breathing steadied and she took advantage of the light to look down again.

'Peggy!' Edward stood at the foot of the staircase, next to the small bronze cherub angel. He started running up the stairs then darkness descended once more. 'Peggy? Where are you?'

'Go left at the top of the stairs, I'm standing at the balustrade.'

'I'm making my way to you. Don't move.'

Peggy felt Edward's hand on hers. The lights came back on. They burned less brightly than before, but the dim light allowed her to see his face. His customary neatly parted hair was dishevelled and his eyes darted from side to side. 'Are you all right?'

Peggy nodded. 'I am, now I have found you.'

'Where is Miss Leighton?'

'She and Mrs Holliday are in a lifeboat. They wanted me to go but I wanted to find you.'

'You should go, now!' Edward squeezed Peggy's hand.

'What about you?'

'Thomas said they're only taking women and children at

first; I'm going back down to help him persuade others to leave. You must go now, my darling.'

'I don't want to leave you.'

Edward enveloped her and placed a light kiss on her forehead. 'I want you to be safe. Go now and I'll follow once they allow men into the lifeboats.'

'But…' Peggy looked into the eyes of the man who had unexpectedly stolen her heart.

'But nothing. Go now.' Edward released her and turned her towards the door. He watched her walk away. From the top of the Grand Staircase, he saw Thomas shepherding a group of passengers from the First-Class Lounge. The water was up to their ankles.

RMS *Titanic*

Bella screamed when the lifeboat dropped suddenly. It lurched unsteadily towards the black water. Mona looked up. People hung over *Titanic*'s rail, shouting at them to wait.

'That lifeboat isn't full! Come back!'

Titanic's crew continued lowering the lifeboat, the passengers' pleas lost to the night.

'Mona! Tell them to wait!' Mona narrowed her eyes. Peggy's hair, beautifully coiffured and styled in anticipation of the evening's entertainment, was now sodden.

'I found Edward! He and Thomas Andrews are bringing more people! Tell them to wait!'

Mona called to the officer in charge of the lifeboat. 'We must wait! We can take more people!' Before the officer could reply, a piercing scream echoed around them and a man's head hit the side of the lifeboat with a sickening crunch before continuing the terrible drop into the ocean. A woman wailed above them and the lifeboat rocked perilously from side to side.

'He thought he could make it.' Bella's words dripped with sorrow.

The officer signalled to the crew above to continue lowering the lifeboat. Mona looked up. Bella rubbed Mona's arm. 'She will be in another lifeboat; mark my words. She has an iron will, that one.'

Mona looked at Bella and tried to smile. 'Yes, you're right.' Mona's eyes searched the ship's rail but there was no sign of her beloved friend.

Jack was staring at the transmitter when the beeps started. He pulled his chair closer and recorded the message from SS *Frankfurt*. Immediately he replied with *Titanic's* position and a request to tell *Frankfurt's* captain to 'come to our help, we are on ice.' Jack held his breath until *Frankfurt* acknowledged his request. He turned to see Harold waiting at the door. 'Run and tell Captain Smith *Frankfurt* has responded to our distress call.'

Harold hurried to find Captain Smith but was hampered by crowds of passengers, shouting and jostling for position at the rails, desperate to be accommodated in the dwindling number of lifeboats. He navigated his way around huge chunks of ice sliding on the deck and tried to ignore the grim faces, silent now they realised their floating palace had been brought to a standstill. He found Captain Smith on the Boat Deck, overseeing the loading and lowering of lifeboats. He relayed the message from *Frankfurt* and returned to the radio room with Captain Smith's instruction to learn *Frankfurt's* position. On gaining this information, Jack tapped out another message. 'Are you coming to our assistance?'

Frankfurt replied. 'What is the matter with you?'

Jack tutted and turned to Harold. 'I've already told them; they're wasting time.'

'Tell them again. Insist they come.'

Jack tapped. 'We have struck iceberg and are sinking; please tell captain to come.'

Frankfurt replied. 'Ok; will tell the bridge right away.'

Jack breathed a sigh of relief and tapped again. 'Ok; yes; quick.'

Minutes that felt like hours passed as Jack and Harold stared at the silent transmitter. 'Why don't they respond, Jack? Is anyone coming to save us?'

Jack shrugged, remembering telling the *Californian* to keep the channel clear. She was closer, he was sure of it. The transmitter started beeping and Jack recorded the message from RMS *Carpathia*. 'Quick, Harold! Go and tell Captain Smith *Carpathia* is coming!'

Harold found Captain Smith in the wheelhouse. Breathlessly, he relayed the message. '*Carpathia* is making full steam to us, Sir!'

'Is she the only one who has responded?'

'A few have made contact but she's the only one close, Sir. They say she can be here in four hours.'

'Four hours?' Captain Smith blanched, thinking at least half an hour of Thomas Andrews's estimated two hours had already passed. The radio room held its collective breath as Jack tapped and the message to *Carpathia* travelled across the icy ocean.

The lifeboat hit the freezing water with a huge splash and Mona covered her ears to try and drown out the screams around her. Bella's hand shook and she gripped Mona's knee. Mona turned to the older woman, Bella had protected Mona once and she hadn't forgotten it.

'It's going to be all right. Another ship will come and pick us up.'

Bella held Mona's gaze. 'Do you believe that?'

Mona nodded. 'Yes. We must believe it.'

Bella nudged closer and Mona caught the remnants of her scent. A mixture of spice, lemon, lavender and vanilla; the same as her mother's perfume. What would Theodosia have done in this situation? She had an idea. 'Bella. Can you help me with something, please?'

Bella nodded. Mona pointed towards *Titanic's* rail and Bella slowly raised her eyes.

'I'll start looking from one end and could you start looking from the other end? We must find Peggy.' Bella nodded again and turned her head up and to the right. Mona, looking in the other direction, focussed her eyes on *Titanic's* bow. She blinked into the darkness, longing for a flash of Peggy's blond hair or her coat, but all she could make out were black figures, like large ants, running along the rail and hanging over the side of the stricken ship. Another distress rocket exploded in the night sky, casting light on the scene. Bella gasped and Mona stared, unable to drag her eyes from the scene above them. Some of the human ants took their chances and jumped from the rail, others grabbed hold of one of the ropes lowering the lifeboats and tried to climb down to safety. There was no sign of Peggy. Mona saw the water had reached the second row of portholes under *Titanic's* name on the bow and the ship now tilted slightly to the left. Anyone still on the lower decks would drown. Mona tore her eyes away from *Titanic* and looked forward. The officer in charge of their lifeboat gave the order to row and Bella started sobbing. Mona bit her lip in an attempt not to scream. Pieces of ice shone like starlight against the black water as the oars sliced through the ocean.

Chapter 17

Church of the Sacred Heart, Richmond Hill, Bournemouth

Ivy slept fitfully after Ena returned to her own bedroom. She dreamt about Mona. Her sister was dancing in a rundown music hall with drunken men leering at her. When she woke, Ivy sat on the edge of her bed and breathed deeply. Mona had escaped from her life of debauchery in London. Ivy didn't know where her sister was, but she knew her capacity for survival. Mona would be all right, whatever happened. Ivy smiled. Her wedding day had dawned to a warm sun rising majestically into a clear blue sky. The day brought the promise of happiness for her and Bertie and for Ena, who now knew how it felt to be loved and cared for. She stretched and made her way to the bathroom.

Ivy and Ena were having breakfast when they heard a knock on the front door. Voices in the hallway told them Ruby had arrived. Gladys opened the dining room door and the bundle of energy burst in. 'I'm so excited!'

Ruby plonked herself down at the table. Gladys brought another cup and saucer and poured Ruby's tea. Ruby thanked Gladys.

'You're very welcome, Miss.'

'Call me Ruby, Gladys. We're all friends here.'

Gladys smiled and thanked Ruby.

'Where are the dresses and the flowers? Where is Bertie? Who's coming from London? What are we having to eat after the wedding? Where will you live once you're married?' Ruby's questions came thick and fast.

Ivy smiled, grateful for Ruby's infectious high spirits. 'After breakfast you can come upstairs and help me dress. While we're getting ready, I'll tell you who's coming, what we'll be having to eat and all about our lovely new home on Heron Court Road. The flowers are keeping cool in the pantry and Bertie is at the Leamans. He stayed there last night because it's unlucky for him to see me before we meet at the church.'

Ruby finished her tea and stood up. 'Let's get you ready then, Mrs Primavesi to-be!'

Ena smiled and followed her aunt and Ruby upstairs. The beautiful gowns from Selfridges hung on the outside of Ivy's wardrobe. Ruby helped Ena to dress. She and Ivy laughed as Ena twirled around, swishing her skirt and humming a tune. Ivy took Ena's hand and looked into her eyes. 'Do you like it, my dear?'

Ena embraced her aunt. 'Very much, Aunt Ivy. Thank you.'

Ruby turned her attention to Ivy and Ena sat on the bed, watching and writing in her notebook. Ruby fastened the small pearl buttons running down the back of Ivy's wedding dress and around the lace cuffs of her tight-fitting silk sleeves. She moved to stand behind her friend. Ivy's mother's necklace, once the cause of much despair, was back where it belonged. When Ivy confronted Ena's father for abandoning Mona, Louis at least had the decency to return the necklace. Ruby secured the clasp and Ivy caressed the delicate silver stones that once sparkled against her mother's skin. Ruby positioned Ivy's headpiece and veil. The front of the head-piece was adorned with a row of tiny pink roses and the scent reached Ivy's nostrils as her friend carefully pinned it in place. The veil of delicate white lace hung down her back and pooled around her on the floor. The women turned and examined their reflections in the mirror. Ivy's slim figure was shown off by the tight-fitting, full-length dress. The underskirt of white lace sitting beneath luxurious layers of soft white silk hugged her skin. Pretty flowers were embroidered onto the bodice and the long sleek skirt. When Ivy moved, the dress shimmered. Ivy looked at Ruby and Ena's dresses and nodded. When Ruby agreed to be her bridesmaid, Ivy returned to Selfridges and ordered a similar dress as the one she had bought for Ena, but with a fitted, rather than a frilly skirt. Ivy laughed. 'Do you remember the first time we met, in the attic bedroom at Hampson Hall?'

Ruby shrieked. 'Of course I do!'

'And what we were wearing then?' The women laughed, recalling their scullery maid uniforms. Ruby's cheerful disposition rubbed off on Ivy. 'We made beautiful scullery maids, but we make an even more beautiful bride and bridesmaid, don't you agree, Ruby?'

'I do!'

'You asked who was coming from London.'

'Did you invite your friends from Mrs Newbold's guest house?'

'Yes, and I think they're all coming! Walter and Grace will also be there.' Ivy pictured her friend Grace Opal and her husband Walter Hampson. Walter was the son of Ivy's employer at Hampson Hall, and he had become a dear friend. Ruby reeled off the characters she met when she visited Ivy in London. 'Mrs Newbold, guest house proprietor, her housemaid Clara, famous stage actress Bessie Bentley, Harold Barnes whose act included catching plates in his mouth and juggling joints of meat, Lawrence and Celia Stratton, husband and wife trick cyclists.'

Ivy clapped her hands. 'What a good memory you have, Ruby. They've all replied to say they are coming. Even Monsieur le Grand, my director from the West London Theatre, will be there. He still hasn't been able to return to his beloved Paris to retire because *'Toujours Belle'* has turned into one of the longest-running shows in London!'

Ruby gave a low whistle. She stayed at Mrs Newbold's when

she attended a performance of '*Toujours Belle*' with Walter and Grace. Ivy explained the production, based on writings of a Parisian friend of Monsieur's, concentrated on a period during '*La Belle Époque*' in Paris. It brought to life the optimism, love and beauty of the era through elaborate dance routines and colourful, uplifting songs. The cheerful story celebrated love and beauty in all its forms. Ivy told her she knew a little about '*La Belle Époque*' from her mother, and the idea of being part of a stage production celebrating everything Theodosia adored about Paris was perfect.

'I had a lot of fun when I stayed at Mrs Newbold's. Is your new house the same?'

Ivy smiled, delighted to talk about the large, detached house she, Bertie and Ena would move into a few days after the wedding. The square, three-storied house was set back from the road and hidden from view by mature trees and shrubs. There were two large bay windows at the front and a solid black wooden door, varnished until it shone. On the ground floor were two large reception rooms, a study with a welcoming inglenook fireplace and Ivy's pride and joy, the parlour. When she was forced to leave Gateshead and go to Hampson Hall to work as a scullery maid, Ivy promised, when she had her own house, to recreate her mother's favourite room. A piano stood in one corner of the parlour and elegant curtains draped the windows. Two pairs of plush French needlepoint armchairs were positioned on either side of a pretty, circular rug. She insisted on the chairs being easy to move to create space for dancing, because the pièce de resistance of the room was a gramophone. She smiled, remembering taking one of her mother's records to Hampson Hall. On her first Sunday evening there, to her great surprise, the butler carried bottles of beer into the kitchen and the usually stern housekeeper poured each of the women a small sherry. Her jaw dropped when the butler called for help with the gramophone. Ivy started looking forward to Sunday evenings but her mother's record stayed in the suitcase under her bed. She knew grief would accompany the record into the kitchen. Now, in her own parlour, the record waited on the turntable. She intended to make happy memories in this room. The kitchen was equipped with modern appliances and the bathroom on the first floor had hot-running water and a large claw-foot bath. There were four bedrooms with the sumptuous master bedroom boasting a large four-poster bed. Ena's room was smaller but equally luxurious. The garden at the back of the house was everything Ivy dreamt of, and she looked forward to teaching Ena about different flowers and herbs.

She gave Ruby a short description of the house and her friend's eyes grew wide as she spoke. 'It sounds wonderful. What about the food? I'm starving!'

Ivy laughed, thinking Ruby would enjoy the story attached to her choice of menu. 'Have you heard of the ocean liner RMS *Titanic?*'

Ruby tutted. 'Of course, it's been the talk of the kitchen. *'The unsinkable ship!'*'

'When I read about it in the newspaper, I decided to have some of the items from their lavish first-class dinner menu for my wedding breakfast. If it's good enough for *Titanic's* passengers, it's good enough for my guests.'

Ruby gasped. 'What did you choose?'

Ivy smiled. 'The wedding breakfast begins with a clear vegetable soup, a *'Consommé Jardinière.'* Ivy told the caterers the menu must remain recognisable so no one was intimidated by any of the dishes. She knew Ena had existed on next to nothing in Gateshead.

Ruby nodded. 'Carry on. What next?'

'The consommé is followed by poached salmon with a delicate lemon sauce and slices of cucumber. My mother used to make it, substituting salmon for a less-expensive fish. Her sauce was always delicious.'

'You're making my mouth water!'

'After the salmon we'll have a palette-cleansing sorbet, then there is a choice of main-course dishes. '*Filet Mignon Lili*' on a bed of crispy potatoes with a rich Cognac, Madeira and red wine sauce. The steak is topped with seared foie gras and sliced truffles. Or you can have succulent duck fillets with Parmentier potatoes coated in herbs and spices.'

'Stop! I won't be able to move after eating all that!'

'Well, I wanted to treat my guests on my wedding day! There's dessert too!'

'No, no more!'

The friends laughed and Ruby crouched down to spread out Ivy's veil. 'Can you imagine travelling all the way to America on *Titanic* and eating food like that every day?' Ruby paused and looked up at Ivy. 'Didn't you go to America to look for your sister?'

Ivy saw Ena's head shoot up at the mention of her mother. Ivy studied her reflection in the mirror. She searched for Mona in London and New York City, without success. Following their eventual reunion in London, Mona disappeared again and Ivy decided her sister was on her own. But America? On *Titanic*? Was it possible? Ivy shook her head. She thought it precisely the kind of voyage her sister, who harboured grand ambitions, would have wanted to be part of. The majestic new ship and the publicity surrounding the wealthy people due to embark from Southampton on the 10th of April, Mona's birthday, would have added to the attraction. But how would she have afforded it? Ivy read a newspaper article putting the price of a third-class ticket at £7, second-class at £12, a first-class berth at £30 and a first-class suite at £870. Ivy didn't think Mona would have settled for third-class. She looked at Ena and Ruby and smiled.

'Never mind that now; are we ready?'

Ruby and Ena nodded and they left Ivy's bedroom. Bertie's

father was waiting in the bright hallway. He looked up when Ivy came to the top of the stairs. When they reached the hallway, Gladys handed Ivy her bouquet of roses and freesia and gave Ruby and Ena smaller posies. Bertie's father placed a brown envelope in his inside jacket pocket before holding out his hand. 'Dear Ivy, may I accompany you to church and walk you down the aisle?'

Ivy smiled and nodded. 'You may, Mr Primavesi.'

Chapter 18

RMS *Titanic*

Mona tried to block out the screams above her. She counted 28 people in the lifeboat including herself and Bella. She hung her head; they could have taken a lot more, including Peggy. She forced herself to look up. Another distress rocket bathed *Titanic* in light and shadow figures danced on the deck and at the rail. Lifeboats hung perilously in mid-air, occupants screaming and shouting to loved ones left behind.

Peggy searched for an officer, hoping to persuade someone to allow a lifeboat to wait for the passengers Edward and Thomas were bringing. She was brushed off. 'Save yourself, Miss. It's all you can do.' She forced her way through the crowds and hooked an arm through the frozen rail. Through chattering teeth, she took deep breaths to try and steady her nerves.

By the time Edward reached the foot of the Grand Staircase, the water was almost to his knees. He called for Thomas but his words were lost in the chaos and confusion. He tried to direct people up the stairs and out onto the Boat Deck, but panic had set in and no one listened. People pushed past him, shouting for missing family and friends. Someone grabbed his arm and he looked into the face of a middle-aged woman. Her make-up ran down her face but she made no effort to remove the black marks on her cheeks. 'My man, have you seen my darling Lulu?' Edward stared; not long ago the woman would have been in her luxurious first-class cabin, preparing to retire for the night and wake up well on the way to America. Now, a lifejacket belted tightly around a sodden fur coat hampered her steps towards safety. 'My little Pomeranian, have you seen her? There is a dog

137

show in the morning and she must be groomed.' Edward shook his head and the woman's tears flowed anew. 'I'm afraid not Madam. You must make your way on deck and into a lifeboat.' She wailed. 'Never! Not without my beloved Lulu!' He watched her turn away, attempting to lift her heavy coat out of the water, calling repeatedly and he suspected, in vain, for her treasured Lulu.

In the radio room, Jack and Harold continued staring at the transmitter. When the beeps began Jack grabbed his headphones. 'Harold, it's RMS *Baltic*!' Harold waited.

'They're making for us! They say to keep in touch! They're coming, Harold!'

Harold clapped Jack on the back. 'We're saved!'

When Edward reached the First-Class Lounge, the musicians were leaving. 'Have you seen Mr Andrews? I last saw him here, directing a group of passengers out to the Boat Deck.' The bandmaster, holding his violin in the air, gestured in the direction of the first-class staterooms. 'I think he wanted to persuade more passengers to put on lifejackets and go on deck.' Edward nodded. 'Are you going that way yourselves now?' The man nodded and wished him luck. Edward started wading through the icy water towards the first-class staterooms. A blond-haired woman crashed into him in her hurry to reach the stairs and he stopped. What was he doing? Why hadn't he gone with Peggy? He turned back. He would make sure Peggy was safe then return to help Thomas.

Peggy heard lifeboats being lowered and men shouting. One voice rang out over the others and she turned to see Edward making his way to her through the crowds. She unhooked her arm from the rail and held her shaking hands out to him. He grabbed her hands and held tight. 'Let's get you to a lifeboat.' Her reply was lost when a loud rumbling began. It was like nothing she had ever heard before, as if a giant hand was playing bowls. A sudden rush of water bore her aloft, tearing her from the safety of Edward's hands. Her piercing screams echoed across the deck as water swept her over the side. Edward ran to the rail and watched helplessly as Peggy fell, as if she was dancing on a vast, black stage, her grand jeté propelling her relentlessly downwards. When she hit the unforgiving ocean, he glimpsed a flash of silver. Peggy's sparkling pin brooch was torn from her gown before her blond head disappeared beneath the water. Edward yelled into the black night.

Ena

Ena watched the guests gathering at the church. She was determined to make her aunt's wedding day as happy as possible, despite the dark cloud caused by their absent guest. She shook her head; she refused to think about her mother now. Once the guests were seated, she and Ruby waited in the vestibule, standing behind Aunt Ivy and Bertie's father. When the music began, Julius Caesar turned around and smiled. 'Are you ready?' Ena nodded and started walking slowly into church.

Ena breathed deeply, wanting to capture the smell of her posy and Aunt Ivy's perfume as she followed her. She swished her skirt; Ruby called it a *frou-frou* and Ena mouthed the word to herself. The stirring music started slowly then the organist played faster fanfares, building to an ostentatious flourish as the bride walked down the aisle. Aunt Ivy told her *'The Trumpet Voluntary'* was written more than 200 years ago, by an English composer called Jeremiah Clarke. Ena thought it was the perfect music to announce her aunt's arrival in church. She stole glances at the people who were there to share her aunt's day. Bertie's family had welcomed her with open arms and she was overwhelmed by the kind people around her. At the altar, Julius Caesar gave way to his son. Ena watched, thinking if she ever got married, she would want her husband to look at her the way Bertie looked at her aunt.

Ivy

Mendelssohn's Wedding March began and Ivy and Bertie made their way back down the aisle amidst cheers and congratulations. Mrs Ivy Dinah Jane Primavesi smiled broadly. She and Bertie had made solemn, binding vows and she would love him until the day she died. Passing the happy faces of the congregation she searched in vain for Mona. Today of all days and despite everything, she wanted her sister by her side. She turned and spotted Ena. Ena smiled and Ivy's heart soared. Today wasn't a day for sadness, it was a day for happiness. As the consommé was served Ivy glanced along the table, where Ena sat next to Ruby. Ivy's cheery friend whispered something to her niece and Ena stole a glance at a rotund aunt of Bertie's. Ena giggled and Ivy beamed. She and Bertie would make sure Ena never wanted for anything ever again. Ivy imagined Theodosia at the table. Everything would have delighted her; her kind, handsome son-in-law, the beautiful dresses and flowers and her happy granddaughter. Ivy sipped her champagne and Bertie indicated the serving staff could bring the meat and poultry dishes.

After the dishes were cleared away the waiters replenished glasses and Ena sat back, grateful for a rest before dessert. It was her first Peach Melba, and as the soft peaches in raspberry sauce melted deliciously on her tongue, she followed the sensation with vanilla ice cream. She licked her lips, savouring the sweet flavour. Bertie's mother sipped her champagne, her manicured little finger raised. Ena copied her and Ruby laughed.

For the final course, Ivy chose the same selection of cheeses she had at her first dinner with Bertie. The champagne flowed and for a while Ivy managed to push away thoughts of her missing sister. Once they finished eating Bertie's father stood. He cleared his throat, preparing to deliver his speech in place of Ivy's father. He kept the speech short, congratulating the happy couple and instructing his son to look after his new wife throughout what he was certain would be their long and happy marriage. Before toasting the newly-weds he reached inside his jacket.

'Ladies and gentlemen, please indulge me for a moment before we toast the happy couple with this excellent champagne.' All eyes turned as he held aloft a thin brown envelope.

'A telegram arrived this morning, addressed to Miss Ivy Dinah Jane Leighton, care of the Primavesi family of Lansdowne Road, Bournemouth. Now, we do not have a Miss Ivy Dinah Jane Leighton here, do we?' The room erupted into pleasant laughter. 'Forgive me, my dear. Of course, this is for you.' He handed Ivy the envelope. She frowned. Who would have sent her a telegram? The thin envelope shook in her unsteady hand. Was it possible? It would be typical of Mona to contact her out of the blue. But how did Mona know where she was? She held her breath and the room fell silent as she slipped the thin sheet of paper from the envelope. She read the short message then bowed her head. Bertie took the telegram. He imagined what Ivy had allowed herself to believe and he caught himself before speaking. He pressed his lips together. His sister-in-law, a woman he had never met, had caused such distress to her daughter and sister. He glanced along the table; Mona didn't even know her daughter was safe. For all she knew Ena was still in Pipewellgate, suffering at the hands of abusive, neglectful Lizzie. His wife wasn't responsible for her sister's poor choices and while Ivy might be able to forgive Mona, Bertie couldn't. He squeezed Ivy's hand and she lifted her head. He read the telegram out to their guests.

'SENDING YOU ALL OUR VERY BEST WISHES ON
YOUR WEDDING DAY STOP
SORRY WE WERE UNABLE TO JOIN YOU STOP
LORD AND LADY HAMPSON STOP'

Bertie waved the telegram and their guests applauded. His father raised his glass and proposed a toast. 'Please join me in drinking to the good health and happiness of this splendid couple!' The room erupted and Ivy smiled at her guests, her heart aching.

Ena

When Julius Caesar produced the telegram, Ena imagined what her aunt might have allowed herself to believe. She looked around the room, most people were blissfully unaware of her mother's behaviour. Wherever she was, Ena's mother cast a long shadow. Ena twisted her napkin, rooted in her seat next to Ruby. Hot tears pricked her lids and she rubbed her eyes, determined not to cry. Ruby passed her a handkerchief and Ena blew her nose. The musicians struck up and Ruby pointed to the dance floor. 'Ena, it's your aunt and Bertie's first dance as Mr and Mrs Primavesi!' Ena looked up. The newly-weds faced each other in the middle of the room. Bertie placed his right hand on Ivy's back and she took his left hand. Ena knew their wedding song by heart because her aunt played the record all the time. She reached for Ruby's hand and sang along.

'I care not what the world may say, or if it mock and jeer,
I care not for its smiles or frowns, if you were always near,
You are my very all in all, beneath the heaven's blue,
And all else is as naught to me, the breath of life is you.
All that I ask is love, all that I want is you,
And I swear by all the stars, I'll be forever true.
All that I seek to know, all that I want above,
All that I crave in this wide, wide world,
All that I ask of you is love.'

As they danced, Bertie whispered to Ivy. 'I never met her but I know your independent, determined mother would be very proud of her independent, determined daughter.' Ivy smiled up at him. Bertie's love for her and Ena were the best wedding presents she could wish for. When they took their seats after the first dance, Ivy leant across to Ena and whispered. 'Now we are married, Bertie would like you to call him Uncle. What do you think?' Ena smiled and nodded.

Chapter 19

RMS *Titanic*

Mona didn't know how long they'd been in the lifeboat. The officer had given the order to stop rowing and now they and several other lifeboats drifted, with no sign of rescue in sight. Mona concentrated on Bella, trying to distract herself from the screams in the water around them. Chunks of ice shone in the moonlit ocean and Bella shivered uncontrollably. Mona's hands shook when she reached out to her. She rubbed Bella's arms. 'Stay awake, Bella. It's important.'

Bella mumbled something Mona couldn't make out. She moved closer and put her ear to Bella's mouth. Her teeth chattered. 'What did you say, Bella?'

'Are we nearly there?'

Mona's lip trembled and she squeezed her eyes shut. She wished she was back on *Titanic* with Peggy, in their luxurious cabin, sharing stories and hot chocolate. Not drifting in a lifeboat listening to Bella's slurred speech and shallow breathing, soaked to the skin and freezing cold. What could she say? 'Yes.' With Mona's reassurance, Bella leant into her and closed her eyes.

The musicians found chaos on deck. Crowds of people pushing and shoving their way towards the rail. Women screaming and children shouting for their mothers. The men looked at each other as the reality of their situation became clear. Calls of 'all hands on deck!' were drowned out by passengers' screams. 'There is no information! Where are the lifeboats? Won't someone help us?' The bandmaster positioned his violin under his chin. 'Men, will you join me in playing something cheerful? How about *'Put Your Arms Around Me Honey?'* The musicians, grateful for the distraction, took up their instruments and started to play. Passengers stamped their frozen feet in time to the music as they waited to be rescued.

'Put your arms around me honey,
Hold me tight,
Huddle up and cuddle up with all your might,
Oh babe! Won't you roll them eyes?
Eyes that I just idolize.'

Second Officer Lightoller watched the next lifeboat being lowered. He nodded at the two seamen in charge, this one at least was fully loaded. He'd shouted at the previous one to come back, having counted only 12 people in a lifeboat with capacity to take 40. It hadn't come back. Lightoller shook his head; there would be questions to answer when they arrived in New York. The lifeboat got stuck part-way down and the seamen shouted up to the crew holding the ropes. 'There's at least 50 feet to go yet; what are you doing?' The crew above swore and grunted as they pulled on the heavy, dirty ropes. They roared and Lightoller saw they had lost their grip. The occupants screamed when the lifeboat shot towards the icy water. It smashed into the side of the ship before colliding with the edge of another lifeboat that had made it down safely. People were tipped into the ocean from both lifeboats. Their screams were lost as the frigid water claimed them.

Thomas fought his way through the ever-rising water to reach the first-class staterooms. He repeated a mantra in his head; *'I tried to argue for more lifeboats, I tried.'* Still, he felt responsible and needed to do whatever he could to get as many people to safety as possible. He clutched the lifejackets he'd been able to lay his hands on, thrusting them at anyone he met. He knocked on cabin doors and shouted at people to get out, to save themselves. Time ticked away and he knew the further he went, the more likely it was he wouldn't be able to get back. He kept going.

Rooted to the spot, Edward stared over the rail into the black water. His tears for Peggy froze on his cheeks. He yelled again and raised his shaking fists to the sky. Another distress rocket bathed the ship and the ocean in light. Nausea rose into his throat at the sight below. The powerful wave that swept Peggy overboard had taken numerous lives. Bodies bobbed on the ocean's surface, their hastily fitted lifejackets keeping them afloat. He turned at angry shouts behind him. People surged towards the rail, desperate for a space in one of the few remaining lifeboats. Two men jumped into a lifeboat as it was being lowered. Edward ducked and screams rang out when an officer drew his gun and fired two shots. The officer shouted up as his lifeboat continued downwards. 'Keep back! This boat won't stand a sudden jerk!'

Thomas took a deep breath at the entrance to another corridor of first-class staterooms. He had two lifejackets left. He decided to give them to the first two passengers he found then make his way onto the Boat Deck. A dishevelled couple stumbled along the corridor and he opened his mouth to call to them. His words were swallowed by a roaring wave of water rushing towards them from the end of the corridor. 'Run!' He shouted then turned back. His muscles screamed as he ploughed through the water to the foot of the grand staircase. When he reached the bronze cherub, water crashed through the dome over the top of the staircase. Water cascaded down through the lights of the magnificent chandelier and rushed down the stairs towards him. A man beside him gasped for breath and Thomas watched him grab hold of the bronze cherub. The man spoke through chattering teeth. 'I'm staying here, I'm not moving!' Thomas grasped the man by the shoulders. 'It's not safe here! You need to get on deck and into a lifeboat!' The man stared and the water swept him away when the foot of the bronze cherub came loose from the base.

Harold moved closer to Jack and spoke quietly. 'Anything

more from *Carpathia* or *Baltic*?' Jack shook his head. 'I last heard from *Olympic*. I've told her we are putting women and children off in small boats. All we can do now is wait.'

Lightoller shepherded women and children towards one of the remaining lifeboats. He counted 64 heads as the vessel was lowered. Seconds later and before he could order them to wait, another equally full lifeboat was lowered. He shouted when the second lifeboat was swept towards the first by a rush of steam from one of *Titanic*'s condenser pumps. His heart raced as the collision was narrowly avoided. He turned to see men from the boiler room arriving on deck. 'We were told to get out, Sir. We did everything we could.' Lightoller stared at the life-jacketed firemen, trimmers and greasers who worked tirelessly in *Titanic*'s hot, hidden bowels. Startled eyes stared out from sooty faces and he nodded. As the men searched the deck for their best chance of escape, *Titanic* listed suddenly. The men, knowing most of the forward lifeboats would have gone, hurried towards *Titanic*'s stern. Crowds of desperate passengers followed in their wake.

Harold was alone in the radio room when *Baltic* called. He didn't hesitate and tapped out the latest information from the bridge. 'Engine room getting flooded.' When Jack returned, he said much of the deck and the crew's quarters in the bow of the ship were now awash. Harold raised his hands. 'What should we do?' Jack shrugged his shoulders. 'We're doing all we can.'

The musicians continued playing as people ran the length of the deck, searching for a lifeboat with space and calling without success to missing loved ones. Water moved relentlessly towards them as they produced the final strains of Archibald Joyce's *'Songe d'Automne'*. The musicians packed their instruments away and nodded at each other before separating. As they walked away the bandmaster spoke. 'It has been a privilege playing with you tonight.' They watched him position his violin under his chin and begin to caress the strings with his bow. They didn't hesitate and joined him to play the final piece of their lives. *'Nearer My God to Thee'* rang out across *Titanic's* flooded decks as people took their chances.

Edward stood, surrounded by the deck's chaos. He heard snippets of conversation, *'...no lifeboats..., the ship is torn to pieces below!'* He saw the men from the boiler room pushing through the crowds to reach the back of the ship. He followed. He grasped a metal rail to steady himself on the icy deck and looked down towards the bow. *Titanic's* majestic face curtsied into the water, taking people down with it. As it sank, the propellers at the back of the ship became visible above the ocean. The advancing water smashed against the sides of the ship, now just a few feet below the Promenade Deck. Edward watched people clinging to anything that was tied down.

Jack and Harold stood when Captain Smith entered the radio room. The captain gestured at them to sit. 'Thank you for your perseverance. You can do nothing more and are freed from your duties. Now it's every man for himself.' Captain Smith left and Harold moved to follow him. Jack stayed where he was. Harold turned to his colleague and friend. 'Come on, we need to leave.'

'I'm not going.'

'Are you mad? You'll die in here.'

'I need to continue sending distress calls advising on our latest position. I must convince other vessels to assist in the rescue of people taking to the boats.'

'But…' Harold stared.

'Go and save yourself. Please.'

Harold hesitated for a moment then wrapped a lifejacket around Jack and handed him a heavy coat. He moved to the door and ran. When he arrived breathless on the Boat Deck, a white distress rocket exploded above him. A cascade of stars illuminated the dark night sky and the ship. He took in the devastation all around him then ran towards the officers' quarters.

After Harold had gone, Jack hung his head. If he hadn't been so determined to clear the backlog of passenger messages, he would have responded differently to the *Californian*. She hadn't replied to subsequent messages and now it was too late. Even so, he turned back to the transmitter and started tapping out another distress call. '*Titanic* to all ships. Cannot last much longer.'

On his way back to the bridge, Captain Smith passed the now abandoned First-Class Smoking Room. A figure stood in darkness and he shouted to get the man's attention. 'You need to get out. Now!' The man turned and he recognised Thomas Andrews, although the ship's architect was a shadow of himself. His gaunt face told a story of guilt and regret. He turned back, his expressionless eyes staring at the painting above the fireplace. A lifejacket lay on the table behind him. Captain Smith shook his head and left the room. He made his way to the wheelhouse and closed the door behind him.

In between supervising the lowering of lifeboats, Lightoller watched the bow of the ship getting steadily lower. He ran forward and looked at the staircase leading down from the Boat Deck. Three or four decks down, step by terrifying step, green water crept up the staircase. He ran in the same direction as Harold. One of the rafts with collapsible canvas sides was stored upside down on the roof of the officer's quarters, above the Boat Deck beside *Titanic's* first funnel. He helped Harold and other crew members to remove the raft, but before they could launch it *Titanic* listed sharply and the raft was washed off the deck, upside down. Harold shouted as the water took him with it. He flailed around beneath the overturned raft before holding his breath and managing to swim out from underneath. He climbed onto the overturned raft and lay there, gasping for breath.

Lightoller didn't hesitate when Harold was swept into the

ocean. He dived into the freezing water and came up alongside the raft. He managed to grab one of the raft's ropes and clung on as the water threw him from side to side. Breathing deeply, he reached his hands up onto the bottom of the raft. He clambered for purchase on the slippery canvas, his stinging red hands like blocks of ice. When he pulled himself up the overturned raft began to float away from *Titanic*. Crewmen in the water scrambled to climb onto the raft before it drifted out of reach. Lightoller counted heads, determined he and the men would stay on the raft until rescue arrived. He looked back to the once majestic ship. It listed sadly amid passengers' shouts and screams. He watched people jumping into the bitter sea below, now acknowledging this as their best chance of survival. As he turned to focus on the raft, a loud grating sound came from the ship. The wires holding the first funnel in place snapped off one by one and the huge steel structure fell towards the ocean. It smashed down in an explosion of soot, crushing people in the water. The massive wave created by the fallen funnel picked up the raft and threw it clear of *Titanic*.

As *Titanic's* bow dipped deeper into the water, Edward clung to the metal rail at the back of the ship. It rose higher and he watched people sliding down the deck, yelling and screaming and grabbing hold of anything to slow their descent. Thinking like an engineer, Edward decided his best way off the ship was to climb over the side. He prised one hand from the frozen metal and reached up for the next rail. He tried to ignore the screams behind him as he climbed. The freezing night air stole his breath and his teeth chattered uncontrollably as he tried to steady his numb feet on the slippery rails. At the top of *Titanic's* stern, he paused. He turned to look over his shoulder and immediately wished he hadn't. He gasped for breath at the sight below. Bodies collided as deck chairs and wooden benches flew along the deck, smashing into anything and anyone in their way. He turned back and looked into the churning, unforgiving water below. His shaking legs took him over the side and he held fast to the outer rail.

Jack stared at the silent transmitter. There were no replies to his last distress call. He stood and pushed his chair under the desk. He fastened the coat Harold had given him and secured his lifejacket. He walked to the door and left the radio room.

The raft stood shakily on the unpredictable water and Lightoller took control, organising the men into two halves. He ordered them, mostly crew, to stand and keep the raft balanced. They floated further away from *Titanic*. From his position on the raft, he watched the bow sinking and the stern rising out of the water. He heard a sullen, rumbling roar as *Titanic's* massive boilers came free from their beds and crashed down through the bulkheads and everything in their way. People clung on like bees to a hive, before losing their grip and falling. When the boilers broke away, the lights blinked then went out permanently, plunging the ship into darkness. Until then she stood out clearly with her rows of electric lights burning. Lightoller stared; *Titanic's* huge black outline was distinct up against the stars and sky. He watched in disbelief when *Titanic* split in two between the third and fourth funnels and the bow disappeared below the waves. The ship's broken stern remained afloat and briefly settled back into the water. The stern continued to fill with water, rising towards the stars until it was vertical. There was a sound like heavy thunder and Lightoller steadied his feet on the raft. *Titanic* began her final plunge, faster and faster until she slid beneath the surface of the ocean. Lightoller spoke quietly. '*Titanic* is gone, submerged into the North Atlantic Ocean.'

Edward clung to the rail, his arms and legs shaking. All around him people jumped into the water and he watched in horror as heads and limbs smashed into *Titanic's* exposed propellers. He pictured Peggy in Victoria Bay, dancing and singing.

He yelled into the night. He shuddered and one of his hands slipped from the rail. From his position he couldn't see what was happening on deck, but the sound of metal splitting apart and explosions from deep within the ship told him *Titanic* couldn't be saved. Suddenly the stern dropped sharply and his other hand came loose from the rail. Edward fell straight into the path of the propellers.

Bella's weight was heavy against Mona's shoulder. Mona shifted her position and Bella moaned. 'Bella, can you open your eyes?' Bella's eyelids flickered then closed again. Mona held her tight as the lifeboat made its unsteady way between obstacles in the water. She stared into the black night. She had watched the mighty *Titanic* split in two then disappear into the ocean, but she still didn't believe it. How could such a magnificent piece of engineering meet such a tragic end? Her neck was stiff with the cold but she looked over her shoulder to the officer in charge. Through chattering teeth, she managed to ask him where they were. 'Somewhere off the coast of Newfoundland, Miss.' She opened her mouth to ask Peggy where Newfoundland was then stopped. She hung her head. Why hadn't she insisted Peggy come with them? Why hadn't she made the lifeboat wait? Her steadfast friend who helped her on so many occasions. Peggy was resourceful, she would have found her way to safety; Mona was sure of it. She had to have hope. The lifeboat lurched when it smashed into something in the water. Mona saw the flash of a lifejacket and looked the other way. She whispered to her daughter and sister, imagining her words collected by the icy breeze and carried across the freezing ocean. The lifeboat rocked from side to side and she wept.

ACT TWO

Chapter 20

Bournemouth - two years later
Ivy

Ivy buttered her toast. Bertie smiled at her from across the table then opened his newspaper. Their usual breakfast routine was suddenly shattered. 'Good God!' Ivy's head shot up. 'What is it, my dear?' Bertie put the newspaper down and pinched the top of his nose. 'We're at war with Germany.' Ivy put her hand to her mouth and gestured towards Ena. Her niece wrinkled her nose. 'What does it mean, Uncle Bertie?' Ivy looked at Bertie and gave a quick shake of her head. Ena tutted. 'I'm 15, you don't have to treat me like a child.' Ivy sighed; Ena had matured considerably in the last two years but she still felt an overwhelming urge to protect her.

Bertie cleared his throat. 'It means the Prime Minister and his Government have decided Britain must protect Belgium and France from Germany.'

'Why do they need protection?'

Ivy raised her eyebrows at Bertie, knowing Ena's questions would continue.

'Well, it's complicated but Germany has been threatening some smaller countries and now they have invaded Belgium.'

Ena opened her mouth but Ivy interrupted. 'Aren't you meeting Rachel this morning?'

Ena pursed her lips. 'Yes, we're going to the library.'

'Then you need to brush your teeth and get on your way. You don't want to be late.'

'All right. But can we talk about this later? I'm interested.'

Ivy nodded. 'Very well.' After Ena left the table and closed the door behind her, Ivy turned to Bertie. 'What does it mean?'

Bertie sighed. 'Some say it will be over before the autumn leaves fall, but others…'

'What do others say?'

Bertie shook his head. 'In all honesty my dear, I don't know. I'll ask around at work and see if I can learn anymore.'

Ivy raised her lips for Bertie's farewell kiss. After he'd gone, she picked up the newspaper and started to read. '*Owing to the rejection by the German Government of the request made by his Majesty's Government for assurances that the neutrality of Belgium will be respected, …. his Majesty's Government declared to the German Government that a state of war exists between Great Britain and Germany as from 11 p.m. on August the 4th, 1914.*' Ivy swallowed a lump of fear before continuing '*…there is a call for medical practitioners, tradesmen and motorcyclists to join the army.*' The paper shook in her hands; she expected Bertie would be classed as a tradesman.

The news took her back to the morning after their wedding two years earlier. They were staying in a charming hotel in Boscombe. When they entered the dining room for breakfast, they stopped suddenly. The room was silent, save for muffled sniffs and sobs. Bertie picked up a newspaper from the table at the door. The stark headline explained the room's atmosphere. '*Disaster for RMS Titanic. World's largest ship collides with an iceberg in the Atlantic during her maiden voyage.*' A woman ran past them, clutching a sodden handkerchief. Bertie took Ivy's arm and led her to a table. A waitress brought tea and toast but they had no appetite. Gradually people left the room until the newly-weds were alone. Ivy reached for Bertie's hand across the table.

'Did you know anyone on board?'

'I don't think so but a colleague said his brother was considering taking the voyage.'

'I'm so sorry. Wouldn't there have been appropriate rescue procedures and equipment?'

'I expect so.'

Ivy stared at the headline. She went cold, remembering Ruby's question about her going to America to look for Mona and their conversation about *Titanic*. Bertie squeezed her hand.

'My dear, what is it? You've gone as white as a sheet.'

Bertie moved to sit beside her. She opened her mouth to speak but words wouldn't come.

'It's all right my dear, take your time.'

She swallowed before pointing at the newspaper. 'The article about *Titanic*.'

Bertie frowned. 'You asked me if I knew anyone on board. Do you?'

'I don't know, but…' Bertie waited. Ivy whispered. 'Mona.'

Bertie looked away and ran his fingers through his hair. His troublesome sister-in-law. Again. He turned back. 'Are you sure she was on board?'

Ivy shrugged. 'No, but it sounds like something Mona would want to be part of.'

Gently, Bertie placed his hands on Ivy's shoulders. He held her gaze. 'We'll find out, one way or the other. I promise.'

Ivy nodded. 'I need to know, Bertie.'

He embraced her. 'Of course you do, my darling.'

Ivy remembered little about the rest of their honeymoon. She would have gone back to Bournemouth that first morning, but Bertie persuaded her to stay. He reasoned news of survivors would take a few days to arrive from America and there was no point upsetting Ena until they knew the facts. Ivy agreed but spent the rest of her time in Boscombe scouring the newspapers for information. Everything she read about the grandeur and magnificence of *Titanic* strengthened her belief Mona would have wanted to be on board. When they arrived back at Heron

Court Road, Bertie held the door open with his foot, ready to carry his new wife over the threshold. Ivy hesitated. How could she carry on as if everything was normal? Bertie waited. Ivy saw the kindness in his eyes and scolded herself. She didn't know anything for certain yet and Mona's shadow had cast gloom over their lives for long enough. She lifted her chin and opened her arms.

'Are you going to carry your new wife over the threshold, Mr Primavesi?'

Bertie laughed and scooped her up. 'I am, Mrs Primavesi!'

Ivy nestled into Bertie's shoulder and tried not to think about her sister. They hadn't been back long when Bertie's mother brought Ena home. Ivy offered tea but Catherine Primavesi declined, saying she was expected back at Lansdowne Road. Ivy watched Bertie bid his mother farewell, noting their exchanged whisper at the door. *Titanic* was on everyone's lips. Ivy led Ena into the parlour and her niece gasped. 'I've never seen such a beautiful room!' Ivy embraced her. 'I'm so glad you like it. Do you want to see the rest of your new home?' Ena nodded. Ivy was grateful for the distraction. As they made their way around the house, Ena's questions came thick and fast. 'What was your hotel like? Did you go to the beach? Is there a garden here? When can Rachel come and visit?' Despite her dread, Ivy smiled when she opened Ena's bedroom door. She knew her niece had slept in appalling conditions in Pipewellgate and she was delighted to give her a beautiful room of her own. She bought a pretty lace counterpane for the bed and she watched Ena wrap herself in the soft, luxurious material. Ivy hoped all thoughts of Pipewellgate and Lizzie would disappear from Ena's mind as her eyes took in the room that was hers and hers alone.

The next day, Ivy walked from room to room, waiting for Bertie to come home with news of *Titanic*. She picked up a book. Before the wedding she started reading '*The Scarlet Pimpernel*'.

She was immediately drawn into the adventure and intrigue of the story and entranced by the eponymous hero's defiance in the face of authority. The Paris setting of Baroness Orczy's tale only served to captivate her further, as she imagined her mother's ancestors as characters. But thoughts of historical adventure and romantic escape did nothing to calm her restless mind and she put the book down. She flicked through one of her theatrical newspapers. 'The Era' was widely regarded as invaluable for reviews, news, general theatrical information and gossip. Usually Ivy devoured every word, particularly the advertisements by and for actors and companies. She always searched for word of Mona and had started looking for opportunities for herself. Bertie made a good living as a jeweller, but Ivy missed the buzz of the theatre, the thrill when the curtain lifted and the camaraderie between the players. She wanted to be home when Ena returned from school and hoped to be considered for matinee performances only, if possible. She and Bertie had also talked about starting a family. Despite her anxiety she managed a small smile at the thought of their son or daughter. A cousin for Ena.

She returned the newspaper to the coffee table and walked slowly into the parlour. She sat on the piano stool and stared at the keys. The small black and white rectangles blurred before her eyes and she stifled a sob. She glanced at the gramophone. Her hands shook as she wound the handle then lifted the arm and placed the needle on the edge of the record. She waited for the familiar crackle. Her spine tingled when Hamilton Hill's melodious tones filled the room. 'A Bird in a Gilded Cage' was one of her mother's favourite songs.

A ballroom was filled with fashions grand,
And shone with a thousand lights,
There was a woman who passed along,
The fairest of all the sights.
A girl to her lover then softly said,

She has riches at her command,
She's married for wealth,
Not for love, he cried,
And she lives in a mansion grand.'

Ivy removed the needle from the record, returning the room to silence. Thoughts of her sister filled her mind. Her flighty, dreamy sister who caused so much worry and whose actions led to disastrous circumstances for Ena. Ivy sighed, Mona would always be her sister and Ena's mother and she couldn't stop loving her. She stared out of the window. If Mona was on *Titanic,* she would have had her 28th birthday on board. Ivy remembered earlier birthdays, when they were all together, before their mother died. Theodosia always managed to conjure up a delicious spread and presents for her daughters and granddaughter, despite their lack of money. They never wanted for anything and Ivy silently thanked her mother. If Mona had taken the voyage, Ivy imagined she wouldn't have gone alone. Ivy shivered, for all her sister's bravado, she was vulnerable.

Ivy checked her wristwatch. The solid gold timepiece, a wedding present from Bertie's father, was inscribed. *'Ivy from Father 15th April 1912.'* She stared at the delicate hands on the watch. She only had vague memories of her own father, he died in a terrible railway accident when she was ten and Mona nine. Minutes then hours ticked by as she waited. She tried to keep herself busy; she prepared their evening meal and set out ingredients to bake a cake. She was sifting flour into a bowl when she heard Bertie's key in the lock. She froze, the sieve shaking in mid-air.

'Hello?'

Ivy ran into the hallway and embraced her husband. Her eyes searched his for answers but he shook his head. 'I'm so sorry my dear, the news is all very confused.'

'News about what?' Ena followed Bertie in through the open door.

Ivy led Ena into the front room. 'Sit down, Ena. There is something we need to tell you.' Ivy watched the colour drain from Ena's face and she shivered. Her niece had received more than her fair share of bad news in her 12 years. Ena looked from her aunt to her uncle. 'What is it?' Bertie stood with his back to the fireplace and calmly told Ena about *Titanic*. Ena put her hands in her lap and raised her head. Her voice was steady. 'What awful news.' Bertie looked at Ivy and she nodded briefly. 'We think it's possible, but it hasn't been confirmed yet, that your mother was on board *Titanic*, Ena.' Ena blinked then looked at her aunt. 'As Uncle Bertie says, we don't know definitely.' Ena stood up. 'Is it all right if I go to my room?'

Later that month Bertie came home with news. He learnt survivors of the disaster were due to arrive at Southampton docks on Monday the 29th of April. His father knew someone at the White Star Line who had seen a list of survivors. Mona and Peggy weren't among them. Sometime later Bertie showed Ivy a newspaper article laying out the stark facts of the fateful voyage. *'Of 2,224 persons on board RMS Titanic, only 735 were saved.'* The pain in Ivy's temples made it difficult to focus. A line jumped out from the article. *'The ship's band continued to play as the giant of the seas disappeared into the black water of the night.'* Ivy pictured Mona straining to hear the music as she took her final breath. Bertie tried to offer some consolation. 'Father did say reportedly some names have been misspelled or even omitted. New reports continue to come in and there is a lot of ambiguity surrounding the facts of the disaster.' Ivy searched for hope in his kind face. 'So she may not have been on board or even if she was, she could have survived?' Bertie shrugged his shoulders. 'I'm sorry my darling, we simply don't know.'

Two years later, there was no word from Mona. They still

didn't know if she was on *Titanic* and if she was, whether she survived. Ivy had kept the newspaper article and she slid it out from an old copy of '*The Era*'. It shook in her hands and a wave of nausea hit her. She put the article down; she knew the words by heart. She also knew in all likelihood; her sister was dead.

Chapter 21

Ena

During the short walk to Rachel's house on Capstone Road, Ena considered how much her life had changed since she came to live in Bournemouth. She knew how fortunate she was to be there. She had made a best friend in Rachel and she liked most things about her school. She should have felt like a different person, like a happy teenager with a bright future. But despite everything, she didn't. Whenever she spoke, she was conscious of her accent and imagined people could see inside her, could see where she came from. Aunt Ivy and Uncle Bertie had taken her to some of the best restaurants in Bournemouth and to the theatre. She shuddered, remembering telling her English teacher about the Christmas Pantomime they attended at Bournemouth's Theatre Royal.

'Ena, please remember to pronounce your 't' sounds properly.'

She started a page in her notebook with the heading 'New Accent' when the teacher said she had a problem with glottalisation. A thick silence filled the classroom and Ena stared at the floor. After some trouble, she managed to find it in Uncle Bertie's dictionary. She noted the definition, 'the complete or partial closure of the glottis during the articulation of another sound'. Then she looked up glottis and noted, 'opening between the vocal folds.' The definitions didn't help and she relied on her English teacher telling her when she went wrong. Some words continued to trip her up; theatre, thank you and people. She tried saying bathroom as if there was an 'r' before the 't' but the word got stuck on her tongue.

When she started attending Moorfield, Aunt Ivy asked her what the other pupils were like. Ena lied, saying they were all very nice. In truth, some of them made fun of her Geordie accent. With the Primavesis and the Leamans, Ena spoke without thinking. It was different at school. Aunt Ivy asked if she would like elocution lessons; the skill of clear and expressive speech.

Ena frowned. 'Will I lose my accent?'

Aunt Ivy nodded. 'Yes, you might. Or it might not be as noticeable after the lessons.'

Ena promised to think about it but the conversation made her realise her accent was part of her identity, part of where she came from. It was one of the things tugging at her, pulling her back to Gateshead, despite her miserable life there. She didn't want to lose it.

As she walked, she remembered her first visit to the library two years earlier. A week after the wedding Aunt Ivy kept her promise, despite her distress about *Titanic*. The day after they told Ena what they suspected had befallen her mother, her aunt and uncle were unusually quiet at breakfast. Her aunt's eyes were red-rimmed and Ena noticed she didn't eat anything. Ena's anger towards her mother grew when she watched her aunt's grief take hold. Seeing her aunt's lip tremble, she moved to sit beside her. From the little she knew about her mother, Ena thought she might have deliberately gone missing after *Titanic* sank. If she and her friend were on board and survived the disaster, Ena suspected they were alive and well, that this was another of her mother's tricks.

When Ena arrived at Horseshoe Common for the first time, she fell in love with the quiet beauty of Old Library House. Uncle Bertie said it was a Victorian villa built with George Jennings's brick from South-Western Pottery. Ena listened politely but her interest lay inside the building. Stepping over the threshold, she wrinkled her nose then breathed deeply. Dust shimmered in the light from the high windows and she inhaled the woody, earthy fragrance. She looked around, her eyes wide. The polished wooden shelves held books of all shapes and sizes. Her heels tapped on the ceramic black and white geometric floor tiles and she walked on tip toe, aware of the noise in the otherwise silent room. Aunt Ivy led her towards a gleaming dark wood desk, where an auburn-haired woman sat. A shiny nameplate on the desk introduced her as Miss Maud Quick – Librarian.

'Good-day, Miss Quick.'

The woman raised her head from a sheet of figures. She smiled and dimples appeared in her soft cheeks. She pushed an unruly curl out of her eyes and removed her spectacles. Attached to a delicate silver chain, they sat snugly against her smart dark green jacket.

'Mrs Primavesi, how nice to see you. Is this your niece Ena you told me about?'

Aunt Ivy nodded. 'It is. Could I take out a membership card for her, please?'

'Yes, of course.'

Miss Quick reached into a drawer and Ena watched her remove a small brown card. She positioned her pen above the card and looked up. 'Miss…? What is your surname Ena?'

Ena pulled herself up to her full height and spoke clearly. 'I am Miss Ena Leighton of Heron Court Road, Bournemouth.' Ena tingled when Miss Quick wrote her name and address on the card. She explained the card allowed Ena to borrow two books at a time, for up to two weeks. She mentioned the fine should a book be returned late and Ena smiled. She intended to start reading her first two books straightaway. She was confident she would be back at the library before the books were due to be returned. She asked Miss Quick where she would find a particular book then hurried in the direction indicated, clutching her precious card. She stared at the shelf; books, gleaming with promise. Her eyes moved along the alphabetically arranged volumes until she reached '*Little Women*' by Louisa May Alcott. Rachel had told her some of the story and Ena couldn't wait to read it. She carefully removed the book from the shelf, holding it to her nose to take in the leathery, smoky smell of the dust jacket. She turned towards the desk then stopped. Miss Quick said the card allowed her to borrow two books. She pursed her lips, what else should she choose? An image popped into her mind; the train journey and the story of '*Madame Butterfly*'. When Aunt Ivy told her Butterfly's tragic tale, Ena decided she would like to learn more about opera. She looked at the high stacks and countless books and sighed. Where would a book about opera be?

'What have you chosen, my dear?'

Ena turned to her aunt and held up '*Little Women*'.

'A good choice.'

Ena explained her dilemma and Aunt Ivy directed her towards the appropriate section. Ena reached for a book called '*Opera Through the Ages*'. They returned to Miss Quick's desk where she asked for Ena's library card. Ena watched her remove a small white card from a pocket glued to the inside front cover of the books. She showed Ena the card, upon which was written the author and title of the book. She slotted the white cards from both books into Ena's library card before filing it in a wooden box on her desk. 'They are filed in order of the date they are due back. When you return them I'll put the cards inside the books again and put them back on the shelves, ready for someone else to borrow.'

Ena frowned. 'What will happen if I forget when they are due back?'

Miss Quick pointed to the right hand side of the open book. Opposite the pocket was a glued white sheet with the library's details. Miss Quick picked up a metal stamp and pressed it firmly into the next space on the sheet. The stamp clicked. *'Et voilà!'* Miss Quick held the book up, showing Ena the 'due back by' date stamp. She repeated the process with Ena's second book then handed them over. Ena clutched the books to her chest, making a mental note to ask Aunt Ivy what Miss Quick said. When they walked down the steps outside the building Ena pushed her shoulders back. The first thing she did when they got home was to turn to a blank page in her notebook. Under a new heading she called *'French Words'*, she wrote *'Et voilà, there you go'*, and *'Le truc de la trappe, the trapdoor trick.'* She devoured *'Little Women'* in a few days and couldn't wait to talk to Rachel about it. 'Which March sister are you?'

Ena put her head on one side before answering. She saw something of herself in each of the sisters. She agreed with Meg's traditional values but didn't think she had her beauty. She liked boys but wouldn't describe herself as a tomboy like Jo. What she shared with Jo was her love of reading and writing. Throughout the story Jo had her nose in a book and Ena learnt a new word, bookworm. She looked it up in the dictionary and wrote it in her notebook under the heading, *'New Words'*, along with its meaning; *'a person who enjoys reading'*. Beth played the piano and Ena hoped to have that in common with her soon, because Aunt Ivy asked if she would like to learn to play. Amy, the youngest sister, was the one Ena thought she was least like. Amy's longing for elegance and fine society reminded Ena of her mother. Ena asked Rachel which of the sisters she had the most in common with.

'I agreed with Meg's values and like you and Jo, I love reading. And I can play the piano like Beth.' Rachel looked up; her eyes wide. 'Did you say your aunt was arranging for you to have lessons?' Ena nodded, looking down at her hands. Aunt Ivy said her fingers were long and tapering; a pianist's fingers. 'We will be able to play duets and Cyril can accompany us on his violin!' She studied her friend; unsurprised Rachel didn't mention Meg's appearance. When she and Rachel met, Ena thought they looked very similar, but now her friend was growing into a beautiful young woman. They both had auburn hair but Rachel's grew quickly and curled in soft loops. Rachel's mother usually set it in a tight bun at the back of her daughter's head, but when it hung loose the curls bounced when she moved. Their eyes were dark-brown but without spectacles to obscure them, Rachel's eyes sparkled. Ena thought her friend's long straight nose gave her a Grecian look, like Aphrodite, the Greek goddess of love and beauty. Rachel's modesty only added to her allure.

The March sisters and their mother lived in Massachusetts in America. All Ena knew about America was Aunt Ivy went there to look for Ena's mother and sang in a theatre called the Paradise. 'Little Women' was set during the American Civil War and Ena soaked up every word, feeling the sisters' pain when their father, having lost all his money, went to serve as a chaplain for the Union Army, far from home. Ena knew how it felt to live without a father. She shuddered when she read about the family facing Christmas without him. Christmases came and went when she lived with Lizzie. There were no presents and no delicious food. Christmas Day was like any other day; cold, miserable and long. She smiled wryly at the idea of the March sisters giving their Christmas breakfast away to a poor family. The memory of sitting in front of an empty plate returned with a sickening thud. She longed for someone to help her, someone like the March family's wealthy neighbour Mr Laurence. Her friends Nancy and Jack shared what food they could with her, never mentioning her shabby clothes and second-hand shoes.

167

Reading 'Little Women' helped Ena to gain a deeper understanding of the desperate circumstances she had endured, and her sense of pride grew. She had survived. She refused to think about what might have happened if Aunt Ivy hadn't come back for her. Throughout the story the March sisters strived to help their family and to improve their characters. Meg tried to be less vain and Jo to control her temper. Beth stayed at home and helped with housework and Amy tried to be less materialistic. The sisters kept busy as war continued, until they received word their father was very ill with pneumonia. Their mother travelled to America to nurse him but while she was away Beth contracted scarlet fever.

Ena's mind reeled back to memories she tried to keep hidden. The locked black box shook and the chains around it rattled. The images of Beth with scarlet fever pushed images of other children out of the box and they swarmed in front of her. She screwed her eyes shut, willing them back inside. The memories persisted. Aunt Ivy said when her mother abandoned her, before she went to live with Lizzie in Pipewellgate, she was sent to the workhouse in Gateshead. Ena remembered the workhouse as a dark prison. On her first day a boy was lifted out of the bed next to the one she shared with two other girls. The boy was straight like a statue and covered in spots. The other children stepped back and whispered. Ena hadn't known the word. Smallpox. Lots of children became ill there and when Ena read about Beth she realised many of them must have had scarlet fever. Children died days after getting a sore throat and a rash of tiny red bumps. The children in her mind shivered, their flushed faces danced in front of her eyes. They lay on their beds, sitting up only to vomit onto the filthy floor. She forced her eyes open. She couldn't allow the memories to take root in her new life. When she continued reading she learnt Jo helped Beth to recover by keeping her temperature constant and feeding her rennet-whey and broth.

Later in the story Meg was invited to spend two weeks with rich friends. There were parties and formal balls where the girls could dance with boys and improve their social skills. Ena remembered Aunt Ivy saying her mother met her father at a dance at their local church hall. Ena knew very little about her father other than his name, Louis Levy, that he was Jewish and a musician. Like Cyril, he played the violin. Jack's uncle said it caused a scandal because Louis and Ena's mother ran away to London together, unmarried and without a chaperone. The man Meg was interested in, John Brooke, was also considered unsuitable by Meg's parents. When he confessed his love for Meg her parents were pleased but thought Meg too young to marry. John agreed to wait until Meg came of age and he joined the military. When he was wounded, he returned to find work in order to buy a house in readiness for his wedding to Meg. Jo became a published novelist and her story made Ena think about what she wanted to do with her life. She thought about Uncle Bertie's sisters and the activities of the suffrage movement. Why should men dictate what women did?

She and Rachel quickly became regulars at the library. About a year after Ena's first visit, the library moved. Miss Quick told them about the council's plans to relocate Bournemouth's Municipal College to The Lansdowne, an area in the centre of town. Her beloved library would be housed within the college building. Miss Quick said the development included a lending library, a newsroom, a reference library and a magazine room. The lending library would contain 23,000 volumes and the newsroom 34 newspapers and magazines plus railway guides and directories. Miss Quick pushed her shoulders back and said the Music Reference Library would be the first of its kind in the country. The 1,855 volumes were presented to the town by Reverend Camm, a local music lover. A magnificent clock tower costing £1,200 made the building an architectural showpiece. The mayor presided over the opening ceremony in May 1913 with Ena and Rachel among the proud spectators.

Miss Quick was always ready with new reading suggestions and Ena discovered she and her library were gold mines of information. Her library card was one of her most treasured possessions. She tucked it inside her notebook and it nestled there, promising introductions to other worlds.

Rachel was waiting at the front door and rushed out to greet her. She took Ena's arm and whispered. 'Are they talking about it in your house as well?' Ena nodded; she didn't need to ask Rachel what she meant. 'The War. Yes.' For the last two years, Ena had avoided looking at the newspapers, reasoning any news about her mother would come from her aunt and uncle. Today was different. Today she wanted to read everything she could about the war. The library was busier than usual and when they walked inside they heard it. Talk of war was everywhere. Ena saw Miss Quick walking quickly towards the newsroom. She turned as they approached. She gestured towards an empty table, her usual smile missing. She set newspapers down in front of them. Ena stared at the stark headline. *'War declared on Germany. England expects that every man will do his duty.'* She started to read. How would this news change their lives?

Chapter 22

Ivy

Ivy re-read the newspaper article. She laid her hands on her stomach. Why today, of all days? The day she was looking forward to giving Bertie the news they were longing for. News she was hoping to have confirmed by the doctor that morning. She took a deep breath. She refused to allow even the declaration of war to spoil this.

She knew Ena well enough to know she and Rachel would have gone straight to the library newsroom. Her niece would come home bursting with questions. Ivy sighed. She and Bertie would answer her as honestly as they could, but Ivy didn't know how much bad news Ena could withstand. She never asked about her mother, but Ivy never stopped hoping for news of Mona. The not knowing and the realisation, over and over again, that her only sister was missing presumed dead, haunted Ivy. She could be in the garden or listening to music, or out in Bournemouth; she could be anywhere when it happened. Her vision would blur and ice would creep up her spine. Bertie tried to discover what happened to Mona but the information was patchy. Conflicting stories about the disaster circulated like flies around dirt. Ivy tried to consult reliable sources but more than two years later they still had no knowledge of Mona's whereabouts.

Ivy recalled the sequence of events after they learnt about *Titanic*. After weeks of waiting and receiving scant information, an official inquiry was conducted by the British Wreck Commissioner on behalf of the British Board of Trade. During 42 days of investigation involving legal counsels, assessors and experts in marine law and shipping architecture, questions were levelled at White Star Line and government officials, surviving passengers and crew and people involved in the rescue efforts. Nearly 100 witnesses testified, with the questioning resulting in a report containing a detailed description of the ship, an account of the journey, the damage caused by the iceberg and an account of the evacuation and rescue. The report brought Ivy no comfort. It found *Titanic's* sinking was the result of colliding with an iceberg, by travelling at a dangerously fast speed in icy waters. There were no inherent flaws with the ship. The report's recommendations led to changes in safety practices but it was of no help to Ivy. She threw the report on the floor, saying her questions remained unanswered. Was her sister alive? And if not, where was her body? She needed to bring Mona home, dead or alive. Ivy knew, having read more than she should about the disaster, that hundreds of souls lost their lives to hypothermia in the freezing water. She knew about people jumping from the ship as it plummeted into the ocean and others being crushed by a huge funnel when it collapsed. Many people had never been found and others were impossible to identify after being in the water.

By August of 1912, Ivy needed to try and restore some sense of normality in their lives. She remembered her promise to have a picnic for Ena. She decided to do it before Ena went back to school in September and she threw herself into making the arrangements. She had another reason to celebrate; she was pregnant. She and Bertie hadn't told Ena or their families yet because they wanted the picnic to be about Ena. She remembered the Hampson family's annual picnic when she worked in Northumberland. The picnic was held on the last Sunday in July and the staff were invited to attend along with the family. On the day of Ena's picnic Ivy watched the friendship between her niece and Rachel Leaman growing stronger. Ivy hoped new, happy memories would help to banish the sinister ghosts from Ena's past.

In the last two years Ena had settled well at school. Since her first day at Moorfield Council School, she and Rachel walked the 20 minutes to East Way together, sometimes with one or both of Rachel's brothers for company. Ena didn't say much about her past but Ivy suspected the school was a distinct improvement on Gateshead's South Street. Ena's favourite subjects were reading, writing, music and surprisingly, arithmetic. Ivy smiled, remembering the day Ena arrived home with this news. As usual, she ran in and placed her satchel on the kitchen table before taking the proffered glass of milk. Then she regaled her aunt with chronological details of her day. The walk to school. *'Nothing eventful happened today.'* Her morning lessons. Physical Exercise accompanied by an expression of disgust. '*Why does it have to be the first lesson on Monday morning?'* Music. '*I played 'Clair de Lune' and Mr Love commented I must have been practising."* Seymour Love was a good friend of Edwin Leaman's and in addition to teaching music at Moorfield he offered private tuition. His son William was an accomplished flautist and for some years he had given Cyril violin lessons. Rachel's natural talent as a pianist improved significantly when she became his pupil. He was happy to add Ena to his list of tutees. He reminded Ivy of Monsieur le Grand, her director at the West London Theatre. His mannerisms and voice, minus the French accent, were so similar if Ivy closed her eyes, she was back on Shaftesbury Avenue, listening to the diminutive Frenchman's instructions. There was one notable difference between the men; Mr Love's height. He was very tall and Ivy noticed Ena stifle a giggle when he curled his long legs under the piano.

Ena grimaced when she mentioned her afternoon lessons, starting with homemaking and social etiquette. *'Do we have to be taught how to make delicate conversation, Aunt Ivy?'* Ivy agreed with her niece but unfortunately part of Ena and Rachel's education was tailored towards girls' roles as wives and mothers.

In addition to the delicate conversation irking Ena, learning to sew and manage servants was compulsory. Ena told her she and Rachel thought little of the *'improvement'* classes. Ivy was pleased to learn Ena preferred the more intellectually challenging aspects of her education. She and Rachel had different ideas about their futures. Rachel's ambition stretched to performing with the Philharmonic Society like Arabella Goddard, a famous English pianist. Rachel knew all about Madame Goddard's career and proudly told Ivy she performed all over the world. When Ena delivered the news about her unexpected proficiency in arithmetic, she provided Ivy with a rare glimpse into her life in Gateshead.

'When my teacher at South Street wrote numbers on the blackboard and told us to add or subtract them, I couldn't do it.' Ena paused. 'But my friend Nancy helped me.' Ivy held her breath, she could count on one hand the number of times Ena had mentioned her past. 'I couldn't make out the numbers, they were all jumbled up like the letters when we had a spelling test. Then Nancy tilted her slate towards me and I could see them more clearly. Once I copied them, I found them easy to add or subtract. Now, with my spectacles to help, I like arithmetic and I might have a job working with numbers when I finish school. Or something to do with reading or writing.'

Ivy checked her watch. Dr Porter should arrive soon but even without his confirmation, she knew. Whatever happened with the war, she and Bertie were going to be parents. She tried not to think about what happened in 1912, but she was terrified history might repeat itself. Before she and Bertie were able to tell Ena and their families the good news, Ivy had a miscarriage. Privately, she and Bertie grieved; their tragic loss bringing them even closer together.

The bell chimed and she hurried to the door. Dr Porter was pleasant enough and confirmed what Ivy suspected. In around seven months' time, in March 1915, she would become a mother. When she asked Dr Porter what would happen next, he stared out of the window and cleared his throat before advising her to secure the services of a midwife. He bade her good day and turned to leave. When Ivy asked how she would find a midwife he mumbled over his shoulder, saying most women sought recommendations from female friends or family members. After he'd gone Ivy sat in the back garden, her faced turned to the warm summer sun. She hadn't felt able to tell Dr Porter about her previous miscarriage; she would prefer to talk to another woman about something so personal. She remembered a recent newspaper article. The previous year the Salvation Army opened their Mothers' Hospital in London. It offered facilities for unmarried pregnant girls and women whom most other maternity hospitals would not deal with. The article also provided information about two women who despite many obstacles, accomplished something remarkable. They broke into a male dominated career; medicine.

Ivy was mesmerised by the article. In 1890, at the age of 21, Flora Murray attended the London Hospital in Whitechapel as a probationer nurse, for a six-month course. The course convinced her she wanted a career in medicine and in 1897 she started studying at the London School of Medicine for Women. Then she worked as a medical assistant for 18 months at an asylum at the Crichton Royal Institution in Dumfriesshire. She completed her medical education at Durham University, receiving her Bachelor of Medicine and Bachelor of Surgery in 1903, and her Doctor of Medicine in 1905. Ivy smiled, picturing Flora among all the men at Durham University. Following her studies, Flora worked as a medical officer at London's Belgrave Hospital for Children and then as an anaesthetist at the Chelsea Hospital for Women.

Ivy discovered Flora took a prominent role in women's suffrage, starting when she became an activist in Millicent Fawcett's National Union of Women's Suffrage Societies. Ivy first learnt of Millicent Fawcett and the NUWSS from the cook at Hampson Hall. In 1910 Lady Hampson attended an NUWSS rally in London and was lucky enough to meet Millicent Fawcett who was speaking at the Suffragist International Congress. Unusually, Lord Hampson accompanied his wife to the speech. Ivy felt fortunate to have men in her life who agreed women should have greater freedoms. Flora also supported Emmeline Pankhurst's Women's Social and Political Union, working at the Pembroke Gardens Nursing Home where she cared for suffragettes recovering from force-feeding. Flora took a leadership role, demonstrating her value by speaking at public gatherings. She joined the 1911 census boycott and used her medical knowledge and skill to treat fellow suffragettes who were injured during their work as activists. She looked after Emmeline Pankhurst and other hunger-strikers after their release from prison and campaigned against the forcible feeding of prisoners.

The other woman in the article was Louisa Garrett Anderson, the daughter of Elizabeth Garrett Anderson and the niece of Millicent Fawcett. Louisa's mother set a remarkable example for her daughter. She was a suffragist and the first woman to qualify as a physician and surgeon in Britain. She was the co-founder of the first hospital staffed by women, the first dean of a British Medical School, the first woman in Britain to be elected to a school board and Britain's first female mayor. Like Flora, Louisa studied at the London School of Medicine for Women, receiving her Bachelor of Medicine and Bachelor of Surgery in 1898. She received her Doctor of Medicine in 1900 before enrolling in further postgraduate study and travelling to observe operations in Paris and Chicago. She was a medical pioneer, a member of the WSPU, a suffragette and a social reformer.

In 1912, when Louisa was 39 and Flora 43, they founded the Women's Hospital for Children. It provided health care for the area's working-class children and gave women doctors their only opportunity to gain clinical experience in paediatrics in London. Ivy smiled when she read the hospital's motto; *'Deeds not Words'*, the motto of the WSPU. Ivy had little experience of pregnancy but knew these were the sort of women she wanted around her when she gave birth. Women like her mother. Mona was only 15 when Ena was born but Ivy remembered their mother keeping her calm and telling her how to breathe, soothing her through the worst of the pain. She remembered what Ruby said about Winnie, the other scullery maid at Hampson Hall. She felt nauseous throughout her pregnancy, but when her baby arrived she told Ruby it was worth every second of pain to hold little Rose in her arms. Ruby said Winnie had a midwife to help her and Ivy decided to ask Bertie's mother if she knew anyone suitable. Her peace was disturbed when she heard Ena coming home.

'Aunt Ivy? What can I do to help us win the war? Will Uncle Bertie get a uniform?'

Chapter 23

September 1914
Ivy

Ivy clutched Bertie's hand as they walked along Undercliff Drive. The path sloped gently downwards before reaching the beach. Ivy walked slowly, wanting to delay his departure as long as possible. A week after war was declared, the newly formed Dorsetshire Regiment started recruiting and Bertie signed up. It was voluntary but he met the recruitment criteria, being taller than 5 feet 3 inches and aged between 18 and 38. His peers were signing up and having a baby on the way didn't justify not joining the army. Bertie threw his boater into the air when Ivy told him her news. He embraced her and they allowed themselves a few moments of joy before facing reality. In all likelihood, Bertie would not be at home when their son or daughter arrived the following year. Ena was delighted to hear she would become a cousin and for a short while questions about the baby took precedence over questions about the war.

Ivy asked Bertie's mother if she knew a midwife who lived locally. Catherine recommended Madeleine Proctor, saying most women gave birth at home with midwives they knew. Catherine had known Madeleine for a few years after she and her daughter Isabel became friends. The women met at Bournemouth train station and discovered they were both travelling to London to attend a meeting to discuss the 1911 census boycott. When Isabel got home, she couldn't wait to tell her sisters and mother about her new friend. During their journey Madeleine told Isabel how she became a midwife. She said thanks to the Midwives Act of 1902, which introduced training and supervision for midwives in England and Wales, her chosen profession was now regarded respectfully in most quarters of society. Uncertified and untrained midwives were outlawed and certified but untrained ones phased out. This meant women could now choose to have a qualified midwife, someone required to be registered with the Central Midwives' Board, as their birth attendant. When Ivy met Madeleine, the midwife's professional yet compassionate manner enabled Ivy to talk about her first miscarriage and her fear for this pregnancy. Madeleine explained everything in a straightforward, reassuring manner and Ivy didn't hesitate in asking her to look after her.

Ivy glanced at her husband. Bertie's woven grey tweed over-coat had six tortoiseshell buttons down the front and two on each cuff. He tipped the rounded crown of his black bowler hat when another couple walked past. The woman clutched the man's arm. She met Ivy's eyes with a pained expression. Another final walk before an enforced separation. Ivy looked out to sea and along the beachfront, taking deep breaths of the tangy air. She looked at Bertie again. She wanted to commit every detail of him to memory. She remembered the stories Bertie told Ena about Bournemouth's smuggling history. Long before the town existed, the desolate area of heathland and gorse created a perfect landing and hiding place for smugglers. Teams of packhorses and wagons waited on the barren cliff tops for cargoes of illicit goods then carried them away into the night. Bertie lowered his voice to a whisper when he told Ena about Isaac Gulliver, one of the most famous smugglers to land his cargo of contraband by the mouth of the River Bourne.

'History has it the line of wagons was two miles long.'

Ivy spotted a cove a little further along the beach. There were hidden caves in the sheltered area and for a moment her mind wandered to a ridiculous notion. Could Bertie hide there? She felt tears starting and lowered her eyes. There was no alternative, he had to go.

Back home, Ivy stared at the pristine uniform lying on the bed. She tried to picture Bertie wearing the stiff peak cap and leather chin strap. Her eyes moved down, despising every inch of the khaki serge tunic with chest patch pockets, shoulder reinforcements and epaulettes. Equally hateful were the high-waisted trousers with side slash pockets fashioned in the same harsh woollen fabric. She picked at the general service buttons on the waistband, intended for brace attachments. She longed to grab her sewing kit and replace them with the tortoiseshell buttons from Bertie's overcoat. Even the shiny brass buckle on the webbed belt couldn't lift the dull, sack-like costume. She pinched the puttees between her fingers and wrinkled her nose. Bertie explained the purpose of the long cloth strips. They were wound spirally from ankle to knee to protect and support soldiers' legs. She let the puttees fall back onto the bed and sighed. She poked her foot at one of the metal toe caps on the drab leather boots. She knocked them over before thumping down onto the bed. Her shoulders heaved and she sobbed. She didn't want Bertie to become the man in this uniform. It was a world away from his usual wardrobe. From the moment she saw him waiting in the Langham Hotel's elaborate marble entrance hall, immaculately dressed for dinner in white tie and tails, she had never seen him anything less than perfectly dressed for the given occasion. It was something, along with his kindness, that set him apart from other men and made him her beloved husband.

Bertie's regiment moved to billets in Dorchester in October. Ivy tried to explain the practice of billeting to Ena but her niece remained exasperated. 'Dorchester is only 30 miles away. I know because I looked it up at the library. Why couldn't Uncle Bertie have stayed here with us?'

Ivy paused before repeating her explanation, her usual patience starting to wear thin. In addition to missing Bertie, she was suffering from painful stomach cramps. 'The army separates soldiers from the civilian population and houses them somewhere temporarily.'

'But why couldn't he have stayed here until he has to go to war?'

'The idea is, being together for training reinforces discipline and encourages *'esprit de corps'*'. Ena raised her eyebrows. 'It's a feeling of pride and loyalty shared by members of a group.' Ena tutted. Ivy rubbed the back of her neck. 'I miss him too but it's out of our hands. We have to make the best of things until the war is over.' Ena opened her mouth then closed it again. Ivy guessed her next question would have been when that would be, but something stopped her. Instead, Ena moved towards her aunt and hugged her. 'We'll be all right, won't we?' Ivy looked down at Ena and nodded. As Ena left the room Ivy bent double when an agonising pain shot through her stomach. She stifled a scream and collapsed onto the sofa. She called for Ena to come back. 'Go to Lansdowne Road and ask Mrs Primavesi or one of Bertie's sisters to get Madeleine Proctor to come. Quickly!' Ena ran and Ivy heard the front door slam shut before she passed out.

In the days following her second miscarriage, Ivy lost count of the number of times she picked up her pen to write to Bertie. How could she tell him this in a letter? In the end she didn't need to. One evening, after Ena went to Rachel's and Ivy was trying to muster the enthusiasm to cook something, she heard the front door click quietly shut. She didn't see Bertie's hateful uniform as she fell into his arms. He anchored her and she gave into her grief. When her sobs subsided, they sat on the sofa, heads together. Bertie said his mother wrote to explain what happened. He requested leave and in the circumstances, it was approved. He took Ivy's chin and looked into her eyes. 'My love, I am so sorry but I must return to Dorchester on the first train tomorrow.' Ivy nodded slowly, desperate not to be parted from him but understanding she would be. They clung to each other throughout the silent night, united in their sorrow. In the morning, Bertie left.

Ena

After Ena's thirteenth birthday, Aunt Ivy spoke to her about puberty. She insisted society's view of keeping such matters hidden was outdated and said Ena shouldn't feel embarrassed. Ena remembered nodding but longing to retreat to her bedroom with her red face. Now she was grateful for her aunt's candour in helping her understand what happened to the baby. Aunt Ivy explained why Uncle Bertie was allowed to come home, albeit briefly, and why she was no longer pregnant. Before he left, Uncle Bertie knocked gently on Ena's bedroom door. She rubbed her eyes and stretched. He came into the room and hugged her tightly. Her lip trembled at the pain in his eyes.

'Promise me you'll look after your aunt while I'm away, Ena.'

Ena sniffed. 'I will.'

'You understand why I have to leave?'

Ena sniffed again and nodded. 'Yes. I wish you didn't but I understand.'

'Good. I'll write soon, I promise.'

He hugged her again then left. Ena allowed her tears to fall, missing him before he left the house. She heard the front door close and squared her shoulders. Aunt Ivy needed her. Within days of war being declared, Ena noticed changes. Restrictions on shining lights at night were introduced, meaning she and Rachel needed to be back in their own homes before dark. After a few weeks Aunt Ivy asked her if she could donate anything to the war effort, saying committees were trying to raise money and collect useful goods. Without hesitating, Ena asked her aunt what she needed, glad to help someone else for the first time in her life. They bagged up blankets, towels, gloves, galoshes and slightly reluctantly on Ena's part, books. She was comforted to learn from Miss Quick that the issue of books was not included in the new restrictions. If she felt the loss of any of her old books, Miss Quick would no doubt have them in stock.

As Ena approached Rachel's house the next day, she heard raised voices. She frowned; she had never seen any of the Leamans lose their temper. She lifted her hand to knock but Rachel opened the door and ushered her inside, finger on her lips. Ena mouthed 'what's going on?' Rachel led her upstairs and didn't say anything until the bedroom door was closed.

'Donovan wants to sign up but my parents are refusing to let him.'

Ena put her head on one side. 'He can't, can he?'

'No. I was there when my father explained Cyril can, because he is 18, but Donovan is too young. Cyril's horror was clear, you know all he wants to do is play the violin.'

Ena nodded. After school one day Cyril walked home with her and Rachel. Ena remembered stealing a glance at him and her cheeks growing hot when he turned his handsome face towards her. When they reached Heron Court Road he smiled down at her and said when she was older he would ask her aunt for permission to take her to the local dance. She mumbled, saying she needed to get indoors, and hurried away. Now, she looked at her friend. 'What happened next?'

'Donovan reacted differently. All he could hear was the excitement of the call to arms and he said as much to father.'

'What did your father say?'

'He said Donovan shouldn't be taken in by the authorities. He said they would be only too keen to turn a blind eye to a fit, strong boy of 16 pretending to be old enough to sign up.'

Ena gasped. 'Do you think they would?'

'I don't know. And I don't know how the conversation ended because I saw you arrive and came to meet you.' The voices continued downstairs and Ena whispered to Rachel. 'Your father won't allow Donovan to go, will he?' Ena thought of everything she had read about joining the army. Recruits must be aged between 18 and 38, although they could not be sent overseas until they were 19. Cyril was old enough, having just had his 18th birthday. But Donovan was only 16.

Rachel laughed sadly. 'No, he won't. But have you noticed what happens when anyone tells Donovan he can't do something?' Ena nodded, remembering the argument about the cello. At dinner one evening Mrs Leaman said she and her husband were keen for Donovan to learn to play. She said they could picture their children as a musical trio; Cyril with his violin, Rachel on the piano and Donovan making up the ensemble on the cello. Donovan was adamant. 'I don't want to learn to play the cello! I want to play football!' He pleaded his case, saying his sports teacher was providing coaching outside school hours and in the end, his parents agreed. Ena pictured Donovan with his endless energy and enthusiasm. She knew he wasn't interested in music but she had seen where his strength lay, on the school playing fields. She had watched his muscles pumping as he pounded the running track, around and around until she thought his lungs would burst. She started walking past the track on her way home from school, hoping for a glimpse of him. Once, when he was catching his breath at the end of a race, he looked up and their eyes met. She returned his playful smile before he set off for another lap of the track. Ena turned away from Rachel and smiled to herself. Donovan couldn't leave, he wasn't old enough.

Rachel's mother knocked on the door and asked if Ena would like to stay and eat with them. Ena was tempted to say yes then remembered her promise to Uncle Bertie. 'Thank you Mrs Leaman, but I should be going home soon, to be with my aunt.' Meta Leaman nodded, saying she was sure Ena was a great support to Ivy. 'Yes, and you should leave before it starts to get dark. Remember the restrictions.' Rachel walked Ena to the door. Passing her father's study, they stopped at the sound of Edwin Leaman's deep, rumbling voice.

'No. Think of someone other than yourself for once. Think of your mother.'

'But Cyril doesn't want to go, I could go instead!'

'For the very last time, Donovan. The answer is no.'

The girls heard a shout and jumped away from the door when Donovan ran out, his fists balled. He pushed past them and yanked the front door open. He ran up the path and jumped over the gate. Ena watched until he was out of sight, he looked as though he was running the race of his life. Back at home, Ena asked Aunt Ivy if what Rachel's father said was true; if the authorities would ignore Donovan's age and allow him to sign up. Aunt Ivy hesitated and Ena reminded her she promised to be honest, no matter how bad things were. Her aunt sighed and looked at her. Ena noticed the dark shadows beneath her eyes and regretted pushing for an answer.

'Sadly yes, I have heard it happens.'

Ena hesitated. 'Do you think Donovan would pretend to be old enough?'

Aunt Ivy gave a small nod. 'I won't lie to you, Ena. Yes, I think he might.'

In her bedroom, Ena picked up her notebook. The heading she wrote earlier blurred as tears welled in her eyes. She rubbed her sleeve across her face and sniffed. She picked up her pen and focussed on the heading. '*The War.*' She pressed her pen down hard and wrote one line under the heading. '*I hate the war.*' She curled up on her bed and wept.

Cyril

Cyril walked to violin practice, mulling over his father's words. He had no intention of going to war. Their religion forbade it. In his head he repeated the Torah's Ten Commandments, including the moral imperative 'Thou Shalt Not Kill'. He heard a group of men discussing the rights and wrongs of it at the Synagogue. He knew many others of their congregation were prepared to fight and he admired these men, but for him, the idea of taking another life was abhorrent. He would help the war effort, but from home. He would be a conscientious objector. He wasn't like his brother, who thrived on physical exertion. Cyril's satisfaction came from lyrical music and the ripple of applause for a well-played piece. Music took him away from thoughts of war; the last thing he wanted was to be in the middle of it, killing other men. He wasn't afraid but had no desire to leave home to risk life and limb overseas. He hummed *'Spring'* from Vivaldi's Four Seasons as he walked. He barely felt the woman's touch as she pushed something towards him. She sneered and carried on walking. He stopped and retrieved the white feather from his top pocket.

Chapter 24

Ivy

After Bertie returned to Dorchester Ivy tried to keep busy. Some schools were requisitioned for use as hospitals and pupils advised the future of their studies was uncertain. Ena's school remained open but staff were depleted as teachers signed up. She and Ena visited Bertie's family regularly and his sisters kept them informed of new suffrage activities. When war was declared the militant suffragette campaign came to a sudden halt with Mrs Pankhurst asking, 'what is the use of fighting for a vote if we have not got a country to vote in?' Instead, the WSPU threw their weight behind the war effort and in return, an amnesty was granted to suffragette prisoners. Ivy remembered reading about the treatment of suffragette prisoners who had gone on hunger strike, refusing to eat for days. The government's response was to force-feed the women. Ivy sighed; how many women would suffer or even die before the government listened to their demands? Key figures had been imprisoned and the previous year the movement mourned deeply at the loss of Emily Wilding Davison. She ran out in front of the King's horse at the Epsom Derby. She was trampled and died four days later, never regaining consciousness. Her death made headlines around the world.

Pressure from women for their own uniformed service to assist the war effort had already begun. Organisations sprang up, including the Women's Volunteer Reserve and Lady Londonderry's Women's Legion, which provided cooks for Army camps. Ivy was considering whether to join such an organisation when Bertie's father asked if she would help him in his jeweller's shop, while Bertie was away. She agreed, grateful for the support of her husband's family. She enjoyed the work and felt closer to Bertie, standing behind the counter where he normally stood and chatting to customers who knew him. He wrote whenever he could and his letters felt like a warm coat on a winter's day. She always replied straightaway, keeping her news light and amusing. At night, alone in their bed, she allowed herself to grieve. For her absent husband and their lost children.

At the beginning of November Ivy received a letter from Bertie with the news she was dreading. His battalion was being shipped overseas. He provided scant details, which she knew was in line with security protocols. It wasn't long before his father, through channels unknown, told her Bertie's battalion travelled to India on the troopship *Grantully Castle*. It departed from Southampton at the end of October and was due to arrive in Bombay in December. She asked Giulio if he knew why Bertie's battalion had gone there. He explained the war was being waged in Asia as well as on the Western Front. After five weeks on board a ship, Bertie would be spending Christmas and Hanukkah without his family, 4,000 miles away. Ivy thought of another ship, bound for New York City. A ship which may have claimed the life of her sister. She prayed the troopship with her beloved husband on board would arrive safely at its destination.

Like Ena, Ivy watched as things around them changed. Even the King contributed to the war effort. Ivy read he sent Boscombe Military Hospital 25 shot pheasants and 40 partridges, reportedly received with much joy. Ena told her about a dog called Queenie who sat patiently outside the tobacconist's shop on Westbourne Arcade. Supervised by the Ladies' Field Dog Collecting Brigade, Queenie collected the grand total of £1 and five shillings for the Red Cross. Some schools organised their pupils to carry out voluntary war work, but Ena was still attending Moorfield for some lessons. To Ena's displeasure, her strict arithmetic teacher Miss Rix, offered to provide Ena and

Rachel with private tuition in algebra and trigonometry. While she continued to enjoy the subject, Ena said she found Miss Rix's manner unpleasant. 'She barks instructions at us and I've never seen her smile.' Ivy urged caution, saying they didn't know what sadness the war might have brought into the teacher's life. Ena shrugged her shoulders and said Miss Rix was miserable long before war broke out. She also said she could tolerate Miss Rix's miserable countenance because her most despised subject, homemaking and social etiquette, was cancelled with immediate effect. Despite her grief, Ivy joked with Ena, saying Moorfield's Headmaster instructed parents and guardians to provide this tuition themselves, at home. Ivy stood up straight and placed a book on her head. She pushed her shoulders back and lifted her chin. A copy of '*The Mayor of Casterbridge*' by Thomas Hardy sat neatly in between her auburn curls and she saw Ena's eyes widen as she stepped precisely across the room. At the fireplace Ivy turned and, using both hands, removed the book from her head. 'Your turn.' She handed the book to Ena. Her niece took it, pressing her lips together and narrowing her eyes. She lifted it above her head then paused. She stared at her aunt and Ivy couldn't stop the laugh bursting out of her mouth. 'I'm sorry, my dear.' Ena giggled and they hugged. Ivy dropped a light kiss on the top of Ena's head. Relief flooded through her that they, unlike poor Miss Rix, could still find something to laugh at.

Later that month, Ivy read a newspaper article asking people to 'donate gramophone records they can spare'. The records were to entertain soldiers while they waited to be shipped to the front. She called for Ena to join her in the parlour and explained what she wanted to do. Ena smiled and they started looking through their record collection for cheerful songs to send the soldiers on their way. They placed the records on the turntable and listened to each song. Ivy said she would sing a few lines from each one to help them decide. The first record was *'Home Sweet Home'* by

John Howard Payne. Ivy's dulcet tones filled the parlour and for a moment, the war was forgotten.

'Mid pleasures and palaces though we may roam,
Be it ever so humble, there's no place like home.
A charm from the skies seems to hallow us there,
Which, seek thro' the world, is ne'er met with elsewhere.
Home, home, sweet, sweet home,
There's no place like home,
There's no place like home.'

Ivy put the record back underneath the gramophone. 'No, it's too sad. We need something more uplifting.' 'This one?' Ena handed a record over and Ivy studied the cover. She nodded. 'Yes, this is perfect.' Ena's choice was *'In the Good Old Summertime'* and she joined in when Ivy started singing.

'There's a time in each year that we always hold dear,
Good old summertime.
With the birds and the trees and sweet-scented breezes,
Good old summertime.
When your day's work is over then you are in clover,
And life is one beautiful rhyme.
No trouble annoying, each one is enjoying,
The good old summertime.'

Ena stopped suddenly and Ivy raised her eyebrows. Ena looked down and mumbled. 'My teacher said I sound like a frog when I sing.' Ivy shook her head. 'Not at all, you sing beautifully. Now, what's next?' Ena smiled and picked up another record. In the end they agreed on five songs they thought would cheer the soldiers. Ivy looked at her niece. Ena had already shown she could overcome extreme adversity. Ivy hoped together they could withstand whatever was to come.

Ena

After hearing about the request for knitted garments to protect soldiers serving on the Western Front, Aunt Ivy asked Ena if she would like to learn to knit. They hoped hand-made knits would comfort soldiers' souls and their bodies, as they battled harsh winters and an even harsher enemy. When Aunt Ivy was showing her how to use four needles to knit socks, Ena asked what the Western Front was. Her aunt continued knitting. 'When the Germans failed to capture Paris or force the French to surrender, they stopped and started digging trenches for their soldiers to use as shelter from enemy fire. Our army and the French also dug trenches to use as defence from German machine guns. Our soldiers are stuck in terrible conditions in those trenches so anything we can do to help is greatly appreciated. I've heard some people are putting a message for the soldier in with the socks. I think it's a nice touch, don't you?' Ena nodded, already thinking about her message.

When they were ready to take their knitting to the community hall, Ena pulled her overcoat on and followed Aunt Ivy to the front door. Outside, Rachel was coming through the gate. Her shoulders heaved and Aunt Ivy took Ena's parcel, saying she would deliver the knitting. When Rachel stopped crying Ena asked her what was wrong. Rachel stuttered.

'Th-th-they've gone!'

'Who's gone?' Ena stared at her friend. A cold shiver crept up her spine.

'My brothers. They've gone to war.'

Ena couldn't speak. As far as she knew, Cyril hadn't wanted to go and Donovan wasn't allowed to. 'What happened?'

'Cyril came home in uniform saying he'd signed up. When my mother asked him why, he refused to answer.'

'But he didn't want to go, did he?'

'No, but he changed his mind.' Ena waited for Rachel to continue. 'I heard him speaking to Father about it; the white feather.' Ena shrugged her shoulders. Rachel looked down and picked at her skirt. 'Women are handing them to men they think are old enough to fight. They try to shame them into joining the army. I heard my mother crying, saying they are being fooled by the 'Your Country Needs You' posters. She said they are designed to guilt-trip underage boys into signing themselves up for bloody slaughter."' Ena pictured Uncle Bertie in his uniform. She refused to let her mind wander to the terrifying scenarios Rachel's mother portrayed.

'What does it mean, the white feather?'

Rachel met Ena's eyes. 'It's a symbol of cowardice.'

Ena gasped. 'I'm so sorry, Rachel.' She longed to ask her next question but didn't want to hear the answer. 'And Donovan?'

Rachel sighed. 'He's disappeared.'

Ena waited for Rachel to continue. 'You know how stubborn he can be. Once he knew Cyril was going, that was it. My father tried to stop him but he refused to listen. He's gone.'

After walking Rachel home, Ena made her way to the running track. She stared at the empty lanes, picturing Donovan. She hadn't imagined he would leave. She dug her foot into the dirt at the side of the track and kicked soil into the air. She hadn't acknowledged the strength of her feelings for Donovan until Rachel said he had gone. She was in love with him. Whenever she stayed at the Leamans overnight, she and Rachel drank cocoa and talked for hours, sharing their teenage secrets and dreams. With Rachel, Ena could be herself. She never feared judgement about her accent or her lack of social niceties. But she didn't mention her feelings for Donovan. Rachel kept a picture of her brothers on the table next to her bed. If Ena was alone in the room, she traced Donovan's face with her finger. She was looking forward to celebrating Christmas with the Primavesis and

Hanukkah with the Leamans. The war changed all that. A cold wind whipped up and she pulled her overcoat tighter before heading home.

Back in her bedroom, she flicked through her notebook. She looked at the page headed *'Nature'* and remembered her last walk with Uncle Bertie before he left. He had shown her the beauty of Bournemouth. She wrote about the sandy beaches and the lush, green countryside. She included his description of the purple-spotted stem, fernlike leaves, small white flowers and unpleasant smell of the highly poisonous hemlock, with a note. *'Warning, it is very similar in appearance to harmless parsley.'* On one walk he pointed out yellow iris flowers saying they represented friendship and happiness, on another the pretty purple marsh thistle and meadowsweet, a plant with fluffy white flowers containing a natural aspirin. He told her how much butterflies love elms but said they stay in the very top of the trees for safety, occasionally coming down to drink nectar from privet and bramble. And she would never forget his stories of smugglers. In addition to Isaac Gulliver, another who regularly smuggled goods at the steep coastal gorges was Edward Beake. Uncle Bertie said he was one of 19 smugglers involved in a violent affray at Bourne Heath. He told her the men were angry with customs officers from Christchurch who seized a wagon containing 60 tubs of spirits. One officer, Jasper Bursey, was thrown over the wagon but managed to chase the smugglers. Later, the other officers found Jasper on the beach with 25 casks. Ena closed her eyes and pictured Uncle Bertie, the man who told her stories and taught her so much. The only father she had ever known.

She opened her eyes and turned back to the first page of her notebook. Under the heading *'Family'* she had written *'Aunt Ivy'* and *'Uncle Bertie'*. There was now a longer list on the next page under *'Friends.'* In addition to Nancy and Jack from Gateshead,

Rachel was there with her brothers. Uncle Bertie's three sisters and brother were also listed. Ena considered her mother but still couldn't bring herself to add her name. She knew it was possible her mother had died on *Titanic* but she abandoned her long before that, and as the years passed Ena felt further away from her than ever, dead or alive. An image of her mother's cruel cousin Lizzie played at the corners of her mind but she pushed it away. She turned to the page headed *'War'* and wrote *'War changes everything.'*

Chapter 25

1915
Ivy

Ivy turned away from the window. Snow covered the garden, hiding any trace of green. She sighed and tapped her fingernails on the table. The first bomb fell on British soil on Christmas Eve, in a man's vegetable garden in Dover. For her and Ena, Christmas and Hanukkah passed in a strange, muted way. The Leamans joined the Primavesis for tea one day but no one was in celebratory mood. The empty seats at the table spoke louder than anyone sitting around it. Bertie and his brother Leo, Cyril and Donovan Leaman; all absent. News from their loved ones was scarce. Ivy felt lucky to have received a postcard from Bertie. 'Writing letter later, no envelopes or note paper procurable.' It told her he was alive, at least at the time of writing. Of Cyril and Leo, there was no word. A letter arrived from Donovan and Meta Leaman carried it with her wherever she went. It brought a measure of comfort, Meta and Edwin knew their younger son was alive. Repeatedly, Meta removed the letter from her apron pocket and tried to smooth the creases away. She handled the flimsy paper, stained and ripped when it arrived, like crystal. 'Shall I read it?' Ivy nodded patiently, to refuse a mother's request in these circumstances was unthinkable.

'Dear Mother, Father and Rachel,

We are in the trenches and our little dugout has just been flooded by a heavy thunderstorm. We cleared it out and are under cover now. Before coming here we had rigorous training and I was commended for my fitness. My commanding officer was impressed by my steady eye and ability to shoot straight and hit a target. I have a military haircut and am very smart, if I say so myself! Father, I think you would be proud of your son. Mother, do not worry; we will triumph over the enemy and be home before long. Rachel, I hope you and Ena are not getting up to mischief.'

The letter ended abruptly. Meta looked up; her eyes full of pain. 'There's no more.' Ivy nodded. Reports from the war worsened after their men left, but some word was better than nothing. In a matter of months, the country began to endure Zeppelin bombing raids. Dorset avoided any direct hits, but the carnage wreaked in London and on the East Coast made for solemn reading. That month, the rigid cigar-shaped airships dropped bombs on the seaside towns of Great Yarmouth and King's Lynn. When Ena asked how far away the towns were, Ivy was honest, knowing Ena would look it up at the library. 'Around 200 miles away.' She saw Ena frown. 'That's not close, is it?' Ivy said it wasn't but they couldn't be complacent. They needed to be watchful.

Before long Ivy heard about pieces of crashed Zeppelin being fashioned into brooches to be sold to the highest bidders to help the war effort. Bertie's father admitted to having mixed feelings about it but said he needed to stay in business. He shook his head and apologised when he told Ivy he no longer needed her help in the jeweller's shop. Business had virtually dried up. She and Ena continued to knit for soldiers but wool supplies were dwindling. When the Queen's Needlework Guild requested garments for soldiers and refugees, Ivy went straight to her wardrobe. She stared at Bertie's side; the row of pristine shirts and suits screamed his absence into the room. On her side, an-ever decreasing number of dresses and coats. She didn't hesitate in donating whatever she could. She beamed when Ena brought her contribution downstairs. So much generosity from a young girl who once had little to call her own. They took their donations to a collection point in town. When Ivy opened the door to the community hall, they were met by a loud, rhythmic noise.

196

A tall woman walked quickly towards them; her spectacles balanced precariously in a mound of curly, coppery hair. She opened her arms. 'Thank you, we need everything we can get.'

Ivy felt Ena's hand on her arm. 'What is that noise?' Ivy's gaze followed her niece's, turning towards double doors on their right. 'Would you like to see?' As the woman led them to the doors the noise increased. She reached for the handle then paused. 'It's something special.' She opened the doors and gestured for them to follow her inside. Ena put her hands over her ears and stared. Rows of women, knitting and singing. The needles clicked out the rhythm of the knitting army. Hundreds of them, recruited, according to the tall woman, who shouted to be heard, to produce cotton slings for wounded troops. The woman led them out of the room. 'I'm sorry, I didn't introduce myself. I'm Olga Curwen.' Ivy shook Olga's hand then introduced herself and Ena. 'That's a London accent, isn't it?' Olga nodded. 'Born and bred and proud of it!'

'What brought you to Bournemouth?' Ivy noticed since war broke out people were more inclined to make conversation. Faced with a stranger, people wanted to know who they were.

'I was working at St. James's Palace when war was declared. It became the Guild's headquarters and they asked me to set up centres here and in Christchurch, Poole and Weymouth.'

Ivy smiled. Olga's independent nature struck a chord with her. 'Why Dorset?'

It was Olga's turn to smile. 'The Guild was established in 1882 when the matron of a Dorset orphanage asked Edith Amelia Ward, otherwise known as Lady Wolverton, for 24 pairs of knitted socks and 12 jerseys for the children in her care. Lady Wolverton and a group of friends provided two garments for each child and clothing for other charitable institutions. By 1894 The London Needlework Guild was making and distributing over 52,000 garments a year.'

Ena gave a low whistle. 'How did you get to all those places in Dorset?'

'I drove.' Olga said it as if it was the most ordinary thing. Ivy appraised the woman standing next to her. She was the future, the type of woman her mother encouraged her daughters to be. Women who fought to do things previously reserved for men, women who wouldn't be told no.

'What war work are you doing?' Olga's question caught Ivy off-guard. She hesitated before saying she was working in her father-in-law's jewellery shop in addition to knitting and collecting donations. She knew how trivial it sounded. 'What more could I do?' Olga threw her head back and laughed, a glorious sound amidst the horror of war. She told Ivy about the thousands of women who answered the government's cry for help by joining the war effort. She said they signed up in droves to fill the gaps left by men, working in transport, engineering, mills and factories. Olga stirred something in Ivy. She realised following her second miscarriage she shut herself off and stayed close to home in her efforts to help. She wanted to do more.

Ena

Rachel's mouth fell open when Ena described Olga.

'She smoked, drove a motor car and was wearing trousers!'

'And what did she say about the war? About what women are doing?'

Ena repeated what Olga said about the jobs women were doing now so many men had gone to war. Rachel listened intently. When Ena stopped talking, her friend moved closer and spoke in a low voice. 'Could we do something, do you think? Leave school and work? What could we do?' Ena sighed. She longed to help the war effort but didn't think her aunt and Rachel's parents would agree to them leaving school early. She said as much to Rachel before something occurred to her. 'There might be a way to find out what we could do.' Rachel sat up straight. Ena's eyes sparkled. 'Let's visit the library tomorrow and speak to Miss Quick.' Rachel clapped her hands. There was a knock on Rachel's bedroom door and Meta Leaman's voice interrupted them. 'It's time you were going home, Ena. Father will walk you to your aunt's.' Ena walked backwards to the door with her finger on her lips. 'We'll talk about our war work tomorrow.' Rachel nodded.

When they arrived at the library the next day, Miss Quick was flicking through the wooden boxes on her desk to find index cards for a pile of returned books. She looked up as they approached. 'Hello, girls. I hoped you would be here today. I have something to show you.' Ena and Rachel followed the librarian into the newsroom. Miss Quick pointed to a newspaper spread open on the table. 'Look at this.' Ena and Rachel stood on either side of Miss Quick. Their eyes followed her pointed finger to the headline. *'Free a man for the front!'* Ena smiled slowly, her eyes twinkling. 'We came today to ask if you knew of anything we could do!' Miss Quick gestured towards the article. 'Read on, girls.'

When Ena and Rachel left the library, Rachel sighed and tutted. Ena touched her friend's arm. 'What is it? Don't you think we could do it?'

'I think we could, but do you think your aunt and my parents will agree?' Ena grabbed Rachel's hands and laughed. 'Let's find out, shall we?' Rachel nodded and they hurried home.

Ivy

Ivy smiled at Ena and Rachel's reactions. Her niece looked at her friend and frowned then she shrugged her shoulders. Ivy suppressed a laugh. 'What?' Ena turned to face her. 'We didn't think you would agree so easily. We thought you would insist we continued going to school.'

'Rachel's parents and I have already discussed it because we expected you might both be keen to help. We agreed because your classes have dwindled, you should make yourselves useful to the war effort. Do you have anything in mind you would like to do?'

Ena and Rachel exchanged a smile and Ivy laughed. Of course they did; these two young women knew their own minds. Ena's words came out in a rush when she described the newspaper article Miss Quick showed them. Under the headline *'Free a man for the front!'* various possibilities for war work were listed. Some were occupations vacated by men while others were designed to offer comfort and a semblance of connectivity to home. Ena and Rachel's choices fell into the second category. They read about voluntary organisations asking people to write songs and compose music for travelling entertainment groups to perform for soldiers. Rachel knew their music teacher Mr Love was too old to have signed up, and said she would like to talk to him about composing something on the piano. In addition to wanting to join the knitting army, Ena spotted the request for people to write short stories to be sent to soldiers in the trenches. She immediately pictured her notebook and her descriptions of the walks and nature trails she took with Uncle Bertie. Ivy agreed these were perfect ways for them to help.

Writing to Bertie later, Ivy remembered her conversation with Meta and Edwin. Ivy knew their decision to allow Ena and Rachel to take up war work bothered Edwin. When they began to discuss the situation, Edwin was adamant. He would not permit their only daughter to leave school and get involved in 'who knows what'. Ivy watched Meta quietly and cleverly manoeuvre her husband around to her way of thinking. Didn't he want Rachel to feel proud that along with her brothers, she made a valuable contribution to the war effort? Would her education suffer so greatly, given her one ambition was to be the next Arabella Goddard and play piano with the Philharmonic Society? The decision also troubled Ivy. Ena only had two years of structured education before war broke out. She gazed at the framed photograph of Ena and Bertie taken in their garden before he left for India. She traced her finger across their faces. Bertie resplendent in the uniform she despised and Ena smiling in her dark blue shift dress. She set out her concerns in her letter. *'I promised myself she would receive the best of everything I could provide, including a decent education. She has shown aptitude in arithmetic and her love of literature and writing is clear, but what opportunities will there be for her in the future?'* Ivy felt Bertie's absence keenly. The Leamans wanted more for their daughter, as Ivy did for Ena.

She rubbed her forehead and sighed. What would she do now Bertie's father no longer needed her at the jeweller's shop? She positioned her pen above a new sheet of paper and imagined she was talking to Bertie. *'I met a remarkable young woman called Olga Curwen at the community hall when Ena and I delivered some donations. She told me of plans for the establishment of a military hospital on Endell Street in London. And my dear, the marvellous thing about this hospital is it will be run and staffed entirely by women! It is being set up by two female doctors, Flora Murray and Louisa Garrett Anderson. What do you think of that?'* Ivy smiled to herself; she knew Bertie would have recognised the significance of the hospital. For the first time, female doctors and nurses were being permitted to use their qualifications and provide much needed care for wounded soldiers. *'Olga does some work for the doctors and she suggested I could apply for a job at Endell Street.'* Ivy read her words back and heard Bertie's voice, loud and clear.

'Of course you must apply to work there, my dear. It will be ideal.'

Ivy shook her head. How could she go? She had promised to look after Ena. She heard footsteps and looked up when her niece came into the room. She opened her mouth to speak.

Ena laughed. 'Yes!'

'What do you mean?'

'You should go to Endell Street.'

'How…?'

'I saw how excited you were when Olga mentioned it at the community hall.'

'I didn't know it was so obvious.'

'It was, and it would be perfect for you. I'll be all right here.'

Ivy beamed. The next day, she called at the community hall to ask Olga how she could apply to work at Endell Street. Olga smiled broadly. 'That's the ticket, we need women like you!'

'The thing is, I don't have any medical training, Olga. Didn't you say the doctors were drawing on their clinical connections to recruit staff?'

'Yes, but they're also interested in women who are sympathetic to the suffrage movement. I think you could be put to good use as an orderly.' Olga explained orderlies assisted clinical staff with routine nursing and medical interventions, where there was no risk for the patient. 'You will need to go up to London for an interview but I think Endell Street will be lucky to have you. Write a letter of application and I'll pass it on for you.' While Ivy was waiting for news from Endell Street, she took Ena to join the knitting army. While they were there, Olga told Ivy all she could about the hospital. She said it was originally designed to accommodate 520 beds, but soon after opening orders came to put up as many extra beds as possible. Beds and staff were in place to tend to the first patients, who arrived two weeks earlier than the War Office promised.

Olga told her how annoyed Flora Murray was to find the patients were convalescent cases transferred from other military hospitals. *'No doubt sent here to clear beds for more casualties expected from the front.'* Flora, or Flo to her friends, described by Olga as *'our dear, dour Scot'*, took this as a sign the male-dominated establishment still viewed Endell Street as a second-class hospital. When Ivy asked what the doctors were like, Olga laughed. 'Two more independent, determined women you couldn't hope to meet! They have particularly exacting standards and Flora revels in chastisement. Watch out, her words can bite!' Ivy smiled, picturing her aunt in Gateshead. When their mother died leaving them in debt to Aunt Agatha, the woman held a sword over Ivy and Mona's heads for years. Ivy lifted her chin; she triumphed over Agatha Brown. She didn't think Flora Murray would be a problem. 'And Louisa Garrett Anderson?'

'She is equally exacting but more demonstrative and gregarious than Flo.'

'How did they come to establish Endell Street?'

Olga explained not long after war was declared, Flora and Louisa visited the French Embassy in London. As suffragettes with records of political protest and criminal defiance, they knew it was pointless approaching the British government or the army. They knew a female surgeon who volunteered her skills to army medical chiefs in Scotland only to be told to *'go home and sit still'*. At the French Embassy Flora and Louisa offered to organise a surgical unit for France. The official, Flora later admitted, probably expected them to finance and equip a unit rather than treat wounded soldiers themselves. Nonetheless, they were referred to the London headquarters of the French Red Cross who accepted their offer. By mid-September 1914, Flora and Louisa, accompanied by fourteen younger women, were at Victoria Station ready to board a train to France.

'Why did the British government change their mind?' Ivy was keen to know what convinced the anti-suffrage administration to shift their position. Olga's eyes sparkled. 'As both sides dug in for the first winter of the war, the weather, rather than the enemy, proved harder to contend with. Artillery bombardment rapidly destroyed quickly-built, flimsy trenches and the destruction of pre-war drainage ditches led to widespread flooding. By February this year, news of Flora and Louisa's success in France reached London and they were invited to the War Office for a meeting with Sir Alfred Keogh, Director General of the Army Medical Services. He acknowledged that with a new offensive about to begin on the Western Front and more battle zones opening up further afield, he urgently needed more hospital beds and more doctors in Britain. He invited Flora and Louisa to set up and run a military hospital in the heart of London. They readily accepted and Endell Street opened three days after the Allies launched their joint Spring Offensives against the German Army on the Western Front.'

Chapter 26

Donovan

Donovan crouched in the filthy trench. He pulled his knees into his chest and lowered his head, trying to make himself invisible to the enemy's brutal attack. This wasn't how he'd imagined army life when he signed up. After the argument with his father, he ran straight to the recruiting station in Bournemouth. Tall and well-built for his age, he had no trouble persuading the sergeant to approve him for a medical examination. He lied, saying he was 18, but later discovered the medical examiners had discretion to decide a recruit's 'apparent age' based on appearance and physical stature, when they didn't have satisfactory proof-of-age documentation. A recruit behind him in the queue said he'd heard one sergeant tell a boy to *'go outside, have a birthday, then come back'*. Another soldier told anyone who'd listen his mother followed him to the recruiting station and argued with the commanding officer, saying he was too young. The officer asked him if he wanted to go home with her and he said no. He was 16.

The training Donovan referred to in his letter home was much tougher than he expected, but his physical strength and fitness equipped him well. He watched other new recruits collapse under the strain and heard officers scream at them to get up and carry on. He learnt about military discipline, drills and how to fight with a rifle and bayonet. After months of living in tents to undergo the gruelling training, the recruits were instructed to prepare for mobilisation. A pale scrawny boy in the bunk next to Donovan asked him what it meant.

'All I know is we have to prepare for active service somewhere in France or Belgium.' Donovan watched the boy cross himself

205

and mouth 'God help us.' He took hold of the boy's shoulders and looked him straight in the eyes. 'You're a soldier now. We all have to look out for each other. Do you understand?' The boy nodded and Donovan pointed to the pay book on his bunk. 'Don't forget that, it's your identity document, it proves who you are. You need to put it in your top right-hand breast pocket and produce it if an officer or non-commissioned officer demands to see it. Are you wearing your identity discs?' The boy nodded and Donovan turned away, pushing aside thoughts of other circumstances in which someone might need to identify them. He couldn't allow himself to think like that, he was going to fight and help his country to win the war. He picked up his own pay book and re-read the message from Lord Kitchener.

'Be courteous, considerate and kind to local people and allied soldiers and avoid the temptations both in wine and women.'

At the ferry port, a brass band was playing. As the soldiers marched through the throng of well-wishers, people threw halfpennies to them and girls ran out to glue pieces of paper onto their arms. Their addresses and a request to write to them, Donovan would later learn. Loaded to the gunnels, the ferry travelled across the English Channel. The soldiers, their feet not yet on the first rung of the ladder of manhood, heard the band playing and the crowd cheering them away. Donovan pulled the girl's address from his arm and stuck it onto the soldier next to him. There was only one girl he wanted to write to. When they arrived in France, they were ordered into lines and instructed to march. Donovan thought back to their training. The first time they were given their Field Service Marching Order he watched some trainees struggle with the weight of the items they had to carry. He took a deep breath and pictured the running track in Bournemouth, before hoisting the packs onto his back. The heaviest items were his rifle, sling and ammunition but he knew everything they carried and wore was essential for their survival, all 61 pounds of it. Eyes front, he marched on. Night had fallen by the time they arrived at their destination; a train station. They boarded silently and slept where they sat or fell. Outside was black as the train moved through the French countryside. Donovan was woken by the train thumping to a halt. Dawn was breaking when they filed onto the station platform. Orange lines streaked the sky as the soldiers blinked themselves awake. Their commanding officer called them to order and shouted.

Donovan shivered in the fetid mud of his trench, trying to block out the whistling shells overhead. He pictured his brother. Was Cyril in an equally horrific trench somewhere along this line? He pictured Ena, a girl who could make him laugh. A girl he was in love with.

Ivy

Preparing to travel to London for her interview, Ivy considered the journey ahead. She was surprised to learn people could still travel, despite the railways being under military control, if their purpose was war-related or otherwise reasonable. Olga reassured her while trains from Bournemouth to London were full of troops and supplies for the front, she would be able to board. As the train steamed towards London, Ivy looked around. She had read about journeys just after war broke out, where trains were packed with soldiers desperate to fight for their country. Bands filled the station with cheery songs and the mood was optimistic. Friends and relatives waved handkerchiefs and sang to send loved ones on their way.

'Come on and hear, come on and hear Alexander's Ragtime Band,
Come on and hear, come on and hear 'bout the best band in the land....'

Ivy's train was subdued. There was no band on the platform and the small number of well-wishers struggled to hide their despair. Maimed fathers, sons and brothers and many who failed to return, brought the truth of war home. Ivy made small talk with those prepared to do so but for most of the journey she read. Earlier in the year, precious letters from Bertie started to arrive. She understood he needed to be vague about certain aspects of his military service but whatever his letters contained; they told her he was alive. She knew he had arrived safely in India and while it was hot, he described their conditions as *'bearable in the circumstances'*. He reassured her of his love and said how proud he was of her intention to work at Endell Street. After re-reading his latest letter, she took a book from her bag. It was one she had read before but Emily Brontë's *'Wuthering Heights'* provided her with the perfect escape from thoughts of war.

She paused outside the iron gates to Endell Street Military Hospital. Olga told her about the bomb damage in some parts of London, but nothing could have prepared her for Shaftesbury Avenue. She wanted to see the West London Theatre, where she worked when she first came to London in 1910. She walked along the opposite side of the street, to get a full view of the theatre's grand entrance. She stared; the building bore no resemblance to the one she worked in. The grand portico, huge temple-style pillars and ornate stonework were gone, obliterated into mounds of rubble spread across the street. The formidable entrance theatregoers marvelled over was no more. A man raised his fist to the sky as he walked past. 'Bloody Zeppelins!' Tears stung her eyes and she nodded, too heartbroken to reply. She stumbled to the end of the street and turned right. Red Cross motor ambulances lined the street leading to the hospital. Olga explained the building was the former St Giles Union Workhouse. An image of the workhouse in Gateshead appeared in Ivy's mind and she pushed it away. She would never forgive those responsible for her niece's incarceration in the horrific place.

Pushing open the heavy black gates, Ivy felt a mixture of

apprehension and excitement. A business-like woman wearing a nurse's uniform walked briskly towards her. Ivy took in the woman's starched white apron with a red cross on the bib. The apron was fastened firmly over a blue-grey dress and a white handkerchief-style cap was tied at the nape of her neck. She introduced herself as Victoria Burdon, a Voluntary Aid Detachment volunteer. Known as VADs, Ivy quickly learnt these women were worth their weight in gold. They worked tirelessly; organising medical squads for the arrival of patients, unloading trains and moving the wounded into ambulances, and attending to luggage and stretchers. Ivy explained she was there to be interviewed for a position as an orderly and Victoria ushered her inside. 'Follow me.' Victoria walked away, her dress rustling. Ivy hurried to keep up as Victoria regaled her with an endless list of facts about the hospital. 'We have an operating theatre and an X-ray room and the once-grim exercise yard has been transformed into a tranquil green space. Our 17 wards have the names of female saints rather than military-style numbers, apart from the 'Johnnie Walker ward' in the basement, where drunks are put to sober up!' Her jocular manner calmed Ivy's nerves and she smiled when Victoria pointed out wards decorated with colourful quilts and fresh flowers. 'It is part of the psychological techniques promoted by Dr Anderson to heal men 'often more wounded in their minds than their bodies.' Ivy learnt the hospital library had over 5,000 books and there was a rolling programme of outings and entertainments, with the chance of a pantomime at Christmas. When she asked how it had all been possible, Victoria smiled. 'With the help of some remarkable women. Women such as Elizabeth Robins and Beatrice Harraden.' Suddenly, Victoria stopped. 'Here we are. Knock and wait.' She started walking away then turned back. 'I'll tell you about Elizabeth and Beatrice the next time we meet, which I'm sure we will. Good luck!'

Ivy stared at the brown door. She lifted her hand and knocked. 'Come.' She knew from Olga the crisp voice belonged to Flora Murray. She opened the door and walked in. Flora and Louisa stood to greet her; hands outstretched. Flora was slightly taller than Louisa and they wore their hair in the same style, brushed back into a tight bun with a precise centre parting. Their uniform was a dull khaki with red piping, jackets belted at the waist. Ivy smiled, it was the first time she had seen women wearing ties and white shirts, other than as part of a theatrical performance. She gave them both a firm handshake and Flora gestured at her to sit.

'Mrs Primavesi, I understand you are here on the recommendation of Olga Curwen?'

'Yes, I met Olga at the community hall in Bournemouth.'

'Olga is an asset to us, is she not, Dr Anderson?'

Louisa Garret Anderson nodded. 'She is, Dr Murray. Anything we need collecting or delivering, she is at the wheel of her large motor car in an instant.' Louisa's cut-glass English accent was in direct contrast with Flora's Scottish burr. Flora straightened her papers and looked up.

'I don't know how much Olga has told you about our operation here, Mrs Primavesi.'

'Please, call me Ivy.'

'Very well. We look for certain qualities in our orderlies, Ivy. Medical or nursing experience is preferable but overall we want intelligent, determined, good humoured women. I see from your letter of application you are 32 years of age. What can you tell us about your life to demonstrate you have the aspects of character essential to the distinctive Endell Street spirit?'

Ivy looked from Flora to Louisa, wondering where to begin. From the moment her mother died, she was required to be resilient. She started there, saying after her mother died she worked as a scullery maid at a country house in

Northumberland. 'I think the constant scrubbing and cleaning will have prepared me well for the rigorous cleaning required to fight the spread of infection here.' She saw Flora nod and both women wrote something down.

'Are you from Northumberland?'

Ivy shook her head. 'No, I was born and brought up in Gateshead in the North East of England.'

Louisa laughed. 'My mother knows Gateshead!'

Ivy smiled. 'She does?'

'Yes, when my mother was 13 and her sister Louie 15 they attended the Boarding School for Ladies in Blackheath, London. They met sisters Jane and Annie Crow there. In 1848 the Crow family moved to Gateshead and in 1854, my mother and aunt went to visit Jane and Annie. The Crow sisters were friends with Emily Davies; my mother met her in Gateshead and they became lifelong friends.'

Ivy smiled again, delighted to learn this remarkable woman had a connection with her home town. 'I know about Emily Davies; didn't she establish the first women's college in Cambridge?'

'Yes, with Barbara Bodichon. Emily was a dear confidante of my mother's, always ready to give sound advice regarding the important decisions of her career. In Gateshead, Annie helped Emily to found a weekly reading class for servants and young women.'

Ivy imagined her mother listening to this conversation. To be in the company of these remarkable women, discussing others who had achieved so much, was something Theodosia dreamt of for her daughters.

'I'm sorry for the digression. After you worked in Northumberland, you came to London?'

Ivy nodded. 'Yes, I was very fortunate to be offered an audition at the West London theatre on Shaftesbury Avenue.'

She pushed away an image of the brutal bomb damage around the corner from Endell Street and continued. 'I worked there for almost two years and I can assure you, theatrical employment demands good humour!'

'Why did you stop performing?'

Ivy hesitated. Olga warned her the doctors would ask some questions about her personal life, in addition to any work she'd done. 'I had family responsibilities.' Flora raised her eyebrows. 'I needed to take care of my niece.' The room was suddenly warm and the air heavy as the doctors waited. 'Her mother…' Ivy pictured her missing sister. 'Her mother?' Louisa prompted her to continue. 'She couldn't look after her daughter.' Ivy's lip trembled when she remembered the sequence of events that took her to London then New York City to try and track Mona down. Ena's mother had never taken responsibility for her daughter and now here she was, being interviewed for a job that would take her away too.

Flora took control. 'Your niece, where is she now?'

'My husband's family live in Bournemouth. She is with them.'

'And your husband? Do you know where he is?'

'He is stationed somewhere in India.'

'What does your niece think about you coming for this interview?'

Ivy pictured Ena's smiling face. 'She encouraged me to come.'

'Good. We need orderlies to focus on the task at hand without distraction. Can you do that?'

Ivy nodded. 'Yes.'

Flora maintained eye contact while she wrote something on her notepad. 'Olga mentioned you were helping your father-in-law in his jewellery shop?'

Ivy felt her cheeks redden, the work with Giulio seemed

unimportant now. She looked up and met Flora's steady gaze. 'I'm not needed there. I think my father-in-law offered me work to keep me from thinking about my husband and...' Ivy stopped, this wasn't the place to divulge such personal information. 'I'm sorry.'

Flora stared. 'No, continue. And...?'

Ivy took a deep breath; Flora and Louisa were doctors after all.

'Three years ago...I suffered a miscarriage and then last year...another.' After she said it, Ivy realised it was the first time she had spoken to anyone outside the Primavesi or Leaman families about her failed pregnancies. Flora and Louisa stopped writing. 'I am very sorry to hear that, my dear. Are you well in yourself now?'

Ivy nodded, not trusting herself to speak. Flora turned to Louisa and they exchanged a glance. Then Flora nodded. 'Very well, we are prepared to give you a one month trial. You will start with cooking, cleaning, laundry and running errands. Then you will be shown basic nursing duties under the watchful eye of our formidable ward sisters. Orderlies work six days a week and you will be required to live in. We do grant occasional weekends off, so some visits home may be possible.'

Chapter 27

Bertie

Wafting flies away from his face, Bertie tried to read Ivy's letter. Correspondence from home was sporadic and took a long time to arrive. No one minded, they were just glad to receive news from friends and family. He remembered his first sight of Ivy, at the Langham Hotel in London. He was in town to attend a show that Grace Opal, his friend Walter's fiancée, was performing in. Walter and Grace invited him to dinner, saying Grace's friend and fellow performer Ivy Leighton would also be joining them. When the women stepped into the Langham's elaborate marble entrance hall, Bertie caught his breath at the sight of Ivy in her gold evening gown. Her wavy auburn hair was pinned up and a cluster of soft, graceful curls and coils framed her beautiful face. He lifted her gloved hand to his lips, held her gaze and brushed a kiss against her fingertips. He would never forget her piercing blue eyes. During dinner, he learnt about Ivy's missing sister. He and Walter offered to hire a private detective to try and find Mona. He admired Ivy for her loyalty towards her sister, but he didn't share her feelings. From his perspective, this woman, whom he'd never met, brought nothing but despair to his wife. After abandoning her child, she left Ivy to pick up the pieces and take responsibility for Ena. Then she led Ivy a merry dance to London and New York City, in trying to find her. When they were reunited, she reneged on her promise to return to Gateshead with Ivy and bring Ena to safety. Her latest adventure or perhaps tragic downfall, might be to have embarked on the disastrous RMS *Titanic*. Bertie sighed; he knew Ivy would never give up on her sister.

When war broke out he knew he needed to sign up. The

billets in Dorchester weren't too far away and still the talk was the war would be over in a matter of months. When his mother wrote to tell him about Ivy's miscarriage, his commanding officer permitted him to take some home leave. He comforted Ivy as best he could but his own heart was breaking; this had happened twice now and he longed for them to become parents. It took all his willpower to leave again.

When his battalion set sail for India, they didn't know what to expect from the five-week journey. As their passage progressed the main problem was the heat, not helped by the number of them crammed on board. Hundreds of men slept on deck to escape the heat in their cabins. Those overcome by sea-sickness spent their days hanging over the side and their nights sweating and moaning. Listening to men in his battalion discussing journeys others had endured, Bertie knew how fortunate he was. They arrived in India in December and continued their journey by train to the army camp at Poona, four hours south of Bombay. Poona was built on a plain and Bertie wrote to Ivy during the journey, describing the countryside and native villages. He asked her to convey his descriptions to Ena; the flat land and sparsity of trees, the herdsmen driving skinny cows along the side of the road and the low houses, more like huts, built of mud baked hard by the ferocious sun. He smiled, picturing Ena writing everything down in her notebook.

Their barracks loomed into view as the sun dropped below the horizon. Bertie saw the outline of low white huts. He squared his shoulders and marched through the gates. The poor ventilation inside their hut offered little protection from the unrelenting heat. After an almost sleepless night, he was woken at sunrise by the reveille. The loud bugle call from the barrack square signalled the start of their first day of duty in India. Hurrying outside, Bertie looked up. He imagined standing on the beach at Boscombe with Ivy, watching the sun peek over the colourful horizon, a gentle promise of a warm, English day. Here, the harsh golden ball against an azure sky brought no such comfort, even at this coolest part of the morning.

'Fall in!'

Bertie stood to attention with the rest of his battalion in one of the silent, neat rows.

'You will eat at set meal-times in the mess hall. Be late, you do not eat! You will practice marching and loading your weapons, until I am satisfied you can protect yourself and your comrades! You will do physical training until your muscles ache! You will carry out regular chores and a period of guard duty each day! Do I make myself clear?'

'Yes, Sir!' Bertie joined the shout ringing out across the hot barrack square.

'Fall out! Dismissed!'

Over the coming weeks Bertie watched more men choosing to sleep on the barrack square. He chose the stifling heat over turning himself into easy prey for the ever-present mosquitoes. Before long, his battalion combined with others to form a division. One battalion was a cavalry and Bertie watched with admiration as soldiers mounted the large, strong horses. He learnt they were used to break enemy formations and give commanders mobile firepower on the battlefield. Their division was ordered to join and strengthen others already in the Mesopotamia region. They were there to protect the oil pipeline supplying the Royal Navy, threatened by the Ottoman Empire's Turkish army after the Turks declared themselves allied to Germany. The assault force, there since November 1914, had achieved some early success and the British Government wanted it to continue. Along with the rest of his division, Bertie steeled himself for the arduous march ahead.

Ivy

Back in Bournemouth, Ivy gathered Ena and the others together. She watched them take their seats around her dining table. Ena sat next to her with Rachel on the other side, then came Bertie's mother and sisters with Meta Leaman completing the group. Ivy smiled. She knew how keenly the women felt the absence of their sons and brothers, yet they appeared undaunted. They were all contributing to the war effort through work or voluntary activities. Ivy raised her chin and pushed her shoulders back. 'What an impressive group you are.' She took in their smiles before telling them everything she had learnt about Endell Street. Later, when she went to Ena's room to say goodnight, she found her niece writing a short story for soldiers in the trenches. Ivy had barely seen Ena without a pen in her hand since she learnt about this work. 'What is this one about?' Ena's eyes sparkled. 'I'm writing a story about smugglers in the coves around Bournemouth. I hope it distracts the soldiers for a while.' Ivy kissed her niece. Ena was intelligent enough to know what she was trying to distract the soldiers from. Ivy closed her bedroom door and sat down heavily on the bed. She picked up Bertie's photograph and sobbed; silent sobs that shook her whole body.

She waited until after Ena's 16th birthday to leave. Both Catherine Primavesi and Meta Leaman offered to have Ena to stay. Unsurprisingly, Ena chose the Leamans. Knowing Ena was safe, Ivy made her way to London. Victoria met her at the hospital gates. Inside, she handed her a uniform and directed her towards a changing area. While Ivy dressed, Victoria said the work at Endell Street was unrelenting but rewarding. 'We also have fun! Do you remember I mentioned Elizabeth Robins and Beatrice Harraden? The doctors rallied family, friends and suffrage comrades to support their enterprise, asking for money, talents and gifts. Elizabeth and Beatrice were among the first to respond. Elizabeth made her name as an actress on the London stage, turning to writing novels after she retired. She also threw herself into the suffrage movement. She responded to her friend Beatrice's appeal to help set up a library here.' Ivy listened, donning the pale brown buttoned-up jacket and skirt. The outfit reminded her of Hampson Hall and her friend Ruby. She pictured them in their scullery maid uniforms. She tutted; she hadn't written to Ruby for some time. She resolved to put pen to paper as soon as possible. Fixing her bonnet cap and long gauze veil in place, she pulled the curtain to one side, ready for her first shift.

She threw herself into the work. When Victoria showed her to the cold cramped dormitory, she reminded herself of people, including her husband, who were sleeping in far worse conditions as the war raged on. Orderlies rose at dawn, ready to start work at 7 o'clock. Ivy's initial duties included collecting large bins of soiled dressings from the wards and taking them to the incinerator in the yard. She emptied ash bins from the fires then filled coal scuttles before hauling them back to the wards. After a quick breakfast, she swept floors and stoked fires. Ivy told herself it wasn't dissimilar to her work as a scullery maid. Although at Hampson Hall she never faced the smell of death and decay that permeated Endell Street. She didn't consider herself squeamish, but nausea threatened to overwhelm her at the sight of soldiers tied to their beds. Often ravaged by fever and delirious after huge doses of morphine, without restraints the men could be a danger to themselves. She tried to ignore their moans and screams as she worked.

The days passed in an endless round of scrubbing floors, emptying bedpans and pushing trolleys. Victoria impressed upon her the need for their patients to have hygienic conditions. Before long Ivy was asked to help with the wounded. The first time she watched casualties arriving, Victoria reassured her. 'You do get used to it.' The powerful artillery and high-explosive shells used by Germany caused deep ragged wounds and complex multiple fractures. Bursting shrapnel shells left dozens of splinters embedded in bone and muscle. Soldiers screamed in pain, faces unrecognisable, as they were wheeled into Endell Street on metal gurneys. Shouts of 'kill me, please!' would echo in Ivy's head for weeks, until she learnt to block them out. She also learnt to force pictures of Bertie from her mind, unable to bear the thought of him suffering like the soldiers there. How did Catherine and Meta cope with thoughts of their absent sons? Ivy knew nothing of what Bertie was enduring in India. She could only pray if he was injured, there was a hospital like Endell Street and a nurse with Victoria's compassion looking after him.

Donovan

Donovan pushed himself back into the unsteady walls of his trench. Putrid mud oozed over his shoulders and down the front of his jacket. He watched a shell drop into the trench, some distance away but close enough for him to see arms, legs and other fragments of men tossed into the air in a swirl of yellow, brown and red. When the shell dust settled he heard the wails and screams. He tried to distract himself by thinking of something else. His diary. It was different to his letters home. He could never tell his family the truth about the Western Front, it was too horrific. Instead, he glossed over the brutal facts of war and tried to be cheerful. He expected they were hearing reports in the news that didn't match his version of events but he couldn't bring himself to tell them the truth. He often wrote about food in his diary. *I long for a piece of chocolate or a tinned apple pudding. It's strange how the idea of food obsesses you when you can't get any.'* His stomach rumbled as if in response. He closed his eyes and pictured a plate of roast beef with all the trimmings.

When another shell dropped, he looked to his left where his comrade in arms and friend, Private Johnny Johnson, crouched low. When they first met, Donovan and Johnny realised they lived not far from each other in Bournemouth. They shared stories of local schools, dances and people, and Johnny was sure he knew Donovan's sister Rachel. Donovan told Johnny about a girl back home. He started calling her his girl, but he hadn't asked her yet. He pictured Ena when she came to live with her aunt and uncle in Bournemouth. He remembered thinking she was different, and not because of her accent. There was something about her that appealed to his sense of fun and adventure. She would be 16 now and he wondered how the war had changed things for her. He didn't know much about her but what he knew, he liked. He saw her fall off her bicycle once and rather than complaining she got back on and cycled away, laughing. After seeing her at the running track on her way home from school, he started watching out for her. He could run faster when she was watching and the smiles they exchanged made his heart skip a beat. He knew she came from Gateshead in the North East of England and from snatches of overheard conversations, knew her start in life was rough. But he never saw her downhearted and admired her strength in overcoming whatever had happened in her past. She was clever and sparky and thinking about her made him smile. He nodded to himself. He would write and tell her how he felt. He would tell her about the Christmas truce in December 1914. He thought she would enjoy that. But first he would try and sleep for a while. He lowered his head and dirty rain water dripped from his cap and ran down his face.

Chapter 28

Bertie

Bertie watched in disbelief as the horrific conditions affected his division. Despite the best efforts of medical staff, soldiers struggled with the extreme heat, lack of clean water, flies, mosquitoes and vermin. Many collapsed from heat exhaustion and dehydration as they marched. Bertie kept going. Weeks turned into months and they kept advancing. When they were ordered to halt, he sank to the ground. He didn't know how far they had marched but his legs and back screamed in agony. Some soldiers started to construct their bivouacs and he sighed. They used whatever they could lay their hands on to make the temporary structures; branches, leaves, ferns, anything to offer some protection from the harsh elements and even harsher enemy. Bertie got up slowly, his head swam and his vision blurred as he steeled himself to make his shelter. Later, after eating a plate of indifferent rations, he took out his diary. He started it when they left Poona. It was a distraction and helped him to keep track of the days.

'Friday 4th of June 1915. After marching over 100 miles along the River Tigris, often through mud up above our boots, we captured the town of Amara. As we marched, our aeroplanes worked hard, dropping sacks of grain, parcels of chocolate, anything to help us carry on for a few more days. I watched men fall. We had no choice but to leave them. I cannot allow myself to consider their fate. We march and fight, march and fight. Our division is severely weakened by sickness and a lack of artillery, general supplies and ammunition. Tomorrow we push on, to the town of Kut, and then the city of Baghdad, some 250 miles away. I have no words for how weary I am. But we have no alternative than to continue.'

It had grown dark. Bertie stopped writing and slumped against his flimsy shelter. He closed his eyes and pictured Ivy on their wedding day. He opened his cracked, dry mouth and sang quietly.

'I care not what the world may say, or if it mock and jeer,
I care not for its smiles or frowns, if you were always near,
You are my very all in all, beneath the heaven's blue,
And all else is as naught to me, the breath of life is you.'

A deep bass voice joined him, drifting across the black desert night.

'All that I ask is love, all that I want is you,
And I swear by all the stars, I'll be forever true.'

Ivy

Ivy was woken by the now-familiar clanging of the courtyard bell. Two loud strikes signalled the arrival of a convoy of wounded soldiers. She pulled her uniform on over her nightdress and pushed her hair into her cap, before hurrying to the yard for stretcher-bearing duty. She rubbed her eyes and tried not to yawn as she and the other orderlies waited for the ambulances. They delivered each patient to their allocated ward then returned to the yard, over and over, until the final ambulance was empty. Victoria called her to help with a stretcher she was pulling from an ambulance. 'Quick, Ivy. Get the other end!' Ivy jumped into the ambulance and her head swam when she saw what remained of the soldier. His wounded leg lay at an impossible angle on the blood-stained stretcher and she bit her bottom lip hard to distract herself from the stench. As she lifted one end of the stretcher Victoria shouted at her to hurry. She looked up and her eyes were drawn to the mess that was once the soldier's right leg. The wound started below his knee and travelled down to his ankle. Slimy green and red gore oozed from the foul dressings, hastily applied at the front. The bone was clear to see and Ivy pictured Bertie's puttees, pristine on the bed in Bournemouth. Did they look like this now? 'Ivy!' Startled by Victoria's shout, she apologised. She lifted her end of the stretcher and they carried the wounded soldier inside.

Once the last ambulance was empty, the orderlies were instructed to try and get some sleep. Ivy collapsed onto her bed and tried to ignore the cries and groans of patients from the wards below. Her bone-weary body longed for rest but the sun was rising and sleep wouldn't come. She reached for her copy of William Makepeace Thackeray's *'Vanity Fair.'* The story of Becky Sharp, the strong-willed, cunning but moneyless daughter of an art teacher and a French dancer, determined to make her way in society, removed Ivy from the horrors of Endell Street for a while. Over the following months the convoys became more frequent and soldiers' injuries more horrific. Stories about the latest scientific weaponry being employed by the Germans buzzed around the hospital long before they saw first-hand the terrible effects of poisonous gas on their men. The Germans used chlorine gas for the first time when they attempted to capture the Ypres Salient, a bulge in the Allied line occupied by British, French, Canadian and Belgian troops. The noxious substance opened a hole in the line four miles wide. The devastating effect sent the stunned Allied troops fleeing in panic towards the Belgian city of Ypres. Ivy was changing a dressing on a soldier's arm when she overheard Victoria and another nurse discussing the attack.

'Over 10,000 men were gassed and around half of them died.'

'And the injured?'

'We can expect to see many of them here and they'll be in a bad way.'

Victoria hadn't underestimated the damage. When the arrivals began, the orderlies hurried into the courtyard.

Ambulance doors were opened and silence filled the yard. Ivy watched an orderly reel backwards before vomiting. She held her breath and stepped forward. A motionless shape lay under a grey blanket on a stretcher. Nothing told her it was a soldier. A charred claw, once a hand, slipped out from beneath the blanket and a sob caught in Ivy's throat. She checked herself, the man needed care. She nodded towards another orderly. They lifted the stretcher and carried the soldier inside. A doctor directed them to the operating theatre. They pushed the stretcher through the double doors and another doctor instructed a nurse to carry out routine observations. The nurse wasted no time, calling out as she worked. 'He's bradycardic with signs of cyanosis.' Ivy had learnt bradycardia was a slow heart rate and cyanosis, associated with cold temperatures, heart failure, lung disease and smothering, could be caused by a lack of oxygen in the blood. The doctor took over. 'Check him for signs of bronchial irritation, he won't last long if he can't breathe.' Ivy dragged her eyes away; she would be needed in the yard; this poor man was one of many who would arrive in a similar condition. She met another orderly hurrying down the stone steps. 'Have you seen the state of our soldiers?' Ivy nodded. The young woman spat her words. 'Do you know how those wretched Germans can poison our men without poisoning themselves?' Ivy wasn't sure she wanted to know, but the woman continued. 'They wear India rubber suits and respirators. They release the gas from cylinders and blow it towards our trenches. Bloody cowards!' Ivy kept walking, the less she thought about it, the better she could do her work.

Ivy was always delighted to receive Ena's letters. Her niece mentioned the Shell Scandal and the newly established Ministry of Munitions. Ivy was impressed by Ena's knowledge; she knew the failure of British forces to break the deadlock of the Western Front had been blamed on insufficient and poor quality artillery shells. The scandal became a political crisis and led to the collapse of the Liberal government. The new coalition appointed David Lloyd-George as Minister for Munitions, recognising the economy needed to be prepared for total war if the Allies were to triumph on the Western Front. It became clear the war effort required the recruitment of more women. Women were directly encouraged to enrol for work in munitions factories.

Ivy knew Bertie's sisters had committed themselves to some of the more dangerous occupations. They took jobs in transport and engineering to keep the country moving. Lena wrote to tell her the WSPU had called for compulsory national service for war work by women. Ivy wasn't surprised to read Bertie's daredevil sister, with her zest for adventure, wanted to volunteer. Lena said the WSPU organised a procession of 30,000 women and they marched under the slogan 'we demand the right to serve'. As a result, more factories and businesses began to hire women. Not long after, Ivy learnt Lena, Isabel and Gertrude were working as munitionettes, manufacturing highly explosive TNT. Initially, Catherine and Giulio tried to dissuade their daughters from the dangerous work. But they quickly realised how important it was to their young women to contribute in the way they chose. Munitionettes worked with hazardous chemicals without adequate protection. For those working with TNT, prolonged exposure to the nitric acid used in the process could turn their skin and hair yellow. Lena explained this in a letter to Ivy, saying it prompted the nickname 'Canary Girls'. 'Thankfully, we are all still our normal colour!' Exposure to other chemicals was also a serious health risk for munitionettes, potentially harming the immune system with liver failure, anaemia and spleen enlargement being significant risks. Munitionettes also faced the daily risk of explosions due to the nature of the materials they handled. Their factories were prime targets for enemy fire, with sites routinely flattened by bombs. Ivy's admiration for Bertie's sisters being prepared to risk life and limb to supply ammunition to the frontline matched her fear for them; the war put them all in great danger, one way or another.

In the little free time she had, Ivy wrote to Bertie. She never knew if he received her letters, she had only received one from him since his postcard the previous year. She also wrote to Ena, the Primavesis and the Leamans. Olga collected and delivered her letters when her duties brought her to Endell Street. Ivy knew she was fortunate to have a link with home; many orderlies felt cut off from their families. Olga also brought Ivy a much-needed connection with Ena. Despite Ena encouraging her to go to Endell Street, Ivy felt guilty for leaving her. Olga's joyous laugh filled the room when Ivy mentioned this. 'My dear, you have no need to worry! Young Ena has come into her own this year!' Olga explained Ena had started doing the book-keeping at the community hall in Bournemouth. 'She no doubt explains it all in her latest letter, but let me tell you, she is an extremely efficient worker. We're very lucky to have her!' Ivy couldn't wait to read Ena's letter. Her niece always made her smile and today was no exception.

'Dear Aunt Ivy,

I hope you are well and not too upset by our poor soldiers' injuries (I read about the poisonous gas attacks in the newspapers at the library). You are doing a very good job there; I am very proud of you. Much is the same here, Rachel is still writing songs and composing music with Mr Love and he is still very tall! Sadly there is little word from our brave men although Rachel's mother has received another cheery letter from Donovan. It sits alongside the first one in her apron pocket. What of me? Well, I was knitting at the community hall recently when there was an almighty commotion! An argument between two women who previously shared the book-keeping duties. One accused the other of not being able to add up properly and making mistakes. She made as if to attack her with a knitting needle and Olga had to step in! She told them both to leave and not return which left a vacancy for a book-keeper. I asked Olga to show me the records and I spotted the errors. Both women made mistakes in their calculations and when I pointed them out to Olga she asked if I would take over. I accepted, so now knit less and add up more. I still write my stories and I hope they bring some comfort to soldiers far from home.'

Ivy grinned. Her niece asking Olga to show her the records demonstrated how much Ena's confidence had grown since her arrival in Bournemouth. Despite Ivy not being there, Ena was surrounded by positive role models and women who encouraged others to fulfil their potential. She returned to Ena's words and her mention of Donovan's 'cheery' letters. Ivy had seen the reality of the front line, it lay in Endell Street's wards and mortuary. It was personified by men on stretchers, grey ghosts of their former selves. Ivy suspected Donovan's letters were a smokescreen to protect his family from the brutality of his situation.

By November, Ivy was feeling the effects of the long hours, gruelling work and tight discipline. On a rare day off, she sat on her bed, trying to decide what to do. She longed to talk to Bertie or at least hear from him, to know he was safe. She remembered their walks in Hyde Park when she lived in London and their walks with Ena in Bournemouth. She sighed; she needed some fresh air to lift her melancholy mood. Leaving the hospital, she bumped into a young woman. 'I'm sorry, I was miles away.' The woman stopped and stared. 'It's all right Ivy, I was coming to see you anyway.' Ivy's lip trembled and she embraced the woman. 'Clara! What are you doing here?' Clara laughed. 'A little bird told me you were working here and I was in the area so decided to call in.' Ivy joined in with Clara's laughter. 'A little bird called Ena, by any chance?' Clara nodded. 'Yes! Now, should we take a walk and catch up with all the news?' Ivy smiled and linked her arm through Clara's. The young woman who had been Mrs

Newbold's housemaid was a welcome surprise amidst the gloom. Clara explained she was meant to be attending a WSPU meeting at the Royal Albert Hall but it was cancelled, because the Hall's management saw a leaflet criticising the Government. She tutted. 'As you see, not much has changed.' Ivy turned to look at Clara. Her support for the suffrage movement was ever-present, in the form of a small purple, white and green pin on her coat.

Their eyes met and Clara smiled. 'I have news.' Clara's expression sent a shiver up Ivy's spine and she steeled herself. 'You know I got married earlier this year?' Ivy nodded, rooted to the spot. 'I'm pregnant!' A lump appeared in Ivy's throat and she swallowed. The relentless work at Endell Street helped to distract her from thinking about her miscarriages but here it was, the all-too-familiar, stabbing pain. She took a deep breath. 'I'm very happy for you.' Clara put her head on one side. 'What's wrong, Ivy? You've gone as white as a sheet.' Ivy knew she needed to be honest. 'I lost a baby last year, just after Bertie was billeted.' Ivy didn't say it was her second miscarriage. Clara put her hand to her mouth. 'Oh no, I'm so sorry! Here I am going on and poor you…' Clara stopped and stared at Ivy. 'It's all right. The doctors here say it happens sometimes and I can get pregnant again…' Ivy's words hung in the cold air. She wondered if Clara was finishing the sentence in her head, as she was, '…if Bertie comes home.' Clara shook her head. 'I'm very sorry, Ivy.' Gently, Ivy put her hands on the younger woman's cheeks and looked into her eyes. 'It's wonderful news. Losing my own baby doesn't mean I can't be happy for you.' Clara sniffed and thanked her and they walked on, arm in arm. Ivy stared straight ahead. The truth lay somewhere in between what she told Clara. She could be happy for other women but the heartbreak of losing her babies was as raw as ever.

Christmas delivered the best present Ivy could have wished for. Endell Street remained busy and home leave was cancelled, but Olga brought Ena, Rachel and Bertie's sisters to visit her. They walked and talked, laughed, drank tea and ate cake and Ivy wanted them to stay forever. When it was time for them to leave, Ivy looked at them, assembled beside Olga's large motor car. She hugged them one by one, ending with Ena. Her niece had grown in the months they'd been apart, in height and character. 'I am very proud of you, Ena.' 'As I am of you, Aunt Ivy.' As Olga drove away, her passengers waved from the motor car. Ivy waved back at the remarkable women. Women who could do anything they wanted. Women who would say 'who's going to stop me?'

Chapter 29

1916
Ena

Ena opened her new notebook, a Christmas present from Aunt Ivy. Her final entry in her previous one was an account of her visit to London. When Olga asked if she wanted to visit her aunt at Endell Street, Ena burst into tears. Olga, unaccustomed to displays of emotion, patted her on the head. Ena apologised, saying she didn't know what came over her. To herself, she knew her reaction reflected how much she had missed her aunt since she went to London. Staying at the Leamans was the next best thing to being at Heron Court Road with her aunt and uncle, but it wasn't home. She discovered Rachel's mother had a nickname. She was known locally as Ma Leaman because of her unfailing ability to look after anyone who crossed her path. Ena remembered the warmth she felt the first time she saw Meta. She was happy to call her 'Ma', after all, her own mother was nowhere to be seen. Carefully, she folded the cover back and smoothed her hand over the first page in her new notebook. She started to write.

'I have no idea what this year will bring. War has changed our lives but I feel very fortunate compared to many other people. We have enough to eat and are warm despite coal now being rationed. What of everyone here? Rachel's father, being too old to sign up, has wound up his decorating business. He and Uncle Bertie's father, whose jewellery shop has closed, have more than enough to do. They are kept busy repairing damage done to people's houses by the relentless Zeppelin raids. Ma Leaman and Mrs Primavesi, along with Gladys and Hilda, look after the houses. They also provide what food they can for the community hall. Rachel and I help to take

meals to refugees and people who have been made homeless. We try to help in whatever way we can. Uncle Bertie's sisters continue to work in the munitions factories. The work is exhausting and dangerous but they are determined to carry on. Rachel has written a lot of songs with Mr Love and I like to imagine our soldiers finding some comfort in their music. I still knit and write stories when I can, but I have been concentrating on the book-keeping at the community hall. Air raids are something new we have to contend with. Loud, shrill whistles sound the alarm and we run for cover. Aunt Ivy said a lot of people there use the London Underground stations. We make for the basement here at Capstone Road while Bertie's parents have a surface shelter at their house. It is not so bad; there is often singing and we all try to keep each other's spirits up. We stay hidden until the all clear sounds; sometimes we sleep there. Sadly, we have no recent news from our men. Ma Leaman carries Donovan's letters with her but of the others, there is little word. I know Aunt Ivy longs to hear from Uncle Bertie, as do I.'

Ena put her pen down and closed her notebook. It was time to go to work. Before leaving the house, she knocked on Rachel's bedroom door. She knew her friend had gone to meet Mr Love but she knocked anyway. This was her secret. She tiptoed into the room and picked up the picture on the bedside table. She looked into Donovan's eyes, wondering where he was and what the conditions were like. She tried to imagine him, handsome in his soldier's uniform. She traced her finger across his face then replaced the picture. She sat on Rachel's bed and closed her eyes. She imagined life after the war. A life where they didn't constantly listen for sirens or Zeppelins, a life where they were all back around the table, eating and laughing together. And when she was older, a life with a man she loved, in a house in the pretty little village she dreamt of. A house with a garden and good neighbours. A quiet, happy life. She opened her eyes and smoothed out the creases on Rachel's bedspread. She left the house and walked along the snowy streets, trying not to look too closely at the damaged buildings. She sighed, she knew people were more important than bricks and mortar but Bournemouth had been such an elegant town. She shook herself. They would win the war and the town would be rebuilt. It would be elegant again and Uncle Bertie and Donovan would be astounded to see it when they came home.

Bertie

The thick mist over their trench began to lift and Bertie winced as he pulled himself up. He reached for his diary and blew a layer of desert dust from the cover. He turned the yellowing pages. He couldn't remember when he last wrote anything, or sent a letter home, but the events of the previous six months were etched into his mind. He positioned a pen in between his injured fingers then hesitated. He wasn't sure he wanted to commit the horrific details to paper. He steadied his hand, perhaps writing it down would help.

'Wednesday 8th of December 1915. I wish I could say the second half of 1915 was an improvement on the first, but I cannot. Our first tactical advance on the city of Baghdad, including the capture of Kut, started on Sunday 12th of September. Our commanding officer said the seizure of Mesopotamia's capital was a vital strategic step in the defence of our oil pipeline. The small town of Kut stands on a peninsula two miles long by one mile wide at the southern end of a loop in the River Tigris. The banks of the river are low, flat and muddy, and palm trees grow along the sides. Desert lies beyond the palms. We advanced upriver through thick mud and intense heat, over ground which afforded neither cover nor surprise. Still we continued, marching through the night. By the time we entered Kut, exhausted and with a thirst we could not quench, we had inflicted heavy losses on the Turks. By mid-November, we were only 25 miles from Baghdad.'

Bertie's pen flew from his hand when a deafening explosion rang out, followed by a heavy thunder shower. He hunkered down and covered his head with his hands. A tortured scream travelled along the trench and he opened his mouth to offer some words of comfort to the wounded man. His blistered lips sent hot, agonising bolts of pain through his face. He tried to raise a hand in the man's direction but fell back against the filth of the trench, drained by the action. The deep roar of a cannon reverberated in response to the enemy's attack and the rattle of rifle fire intensified as the action developed. Bertie stayed low in his trench. He tried to assess their success, based on enemy fire being punctuated by the regular, heavy boom of their cannon. He looked into the distance where his division's shrapnel shells were bursting in the air, forming snow white clouds. Then he heard a long drawn out rushing, finishing with a hollow sound like the clop of a horse's hoof on a country road. He retreated further into the trench but knew above, the ground was being churned up by the enemy's shrapnel shells. Following the sun's position, he estimated the shelling continued for at least three hours. He tried but failed to block out the sounds and smells as men were torn apart and left in pieces all around him. When the attack ended and the dust settled, he steeled himself to glance along the trench. Surrounded by blood and body parts, a dirty, smiling soldier stared at him.

'It's there! Can you see it? The cool water?'

The man mumbled incoherently and pointed a filthy finger towards the top of the trench. The arid desert terrain, where the only water was found in river beds or an occasional oasis, played cruel tricks. Men were fooled into thinking they could see an inviting stretch of water. Wherever the men went, the mirage went on ahead of them and their desperate thirst grew. Bertie shook his head and with a shaking hand, returned to his diary.

'From Kut we advanced further towards Ctesiphon, 20 miles south of Baghdad. Despite it being the site of a palace built by the Persian Emperor Chosroes, our orders were to capture it and advance to Baghdad. When we reached the ancient site towards the end of November, we discovered the Turks had already dug elaborate trenches and built fortified structures to strengthen their divisions against us. We battled with everything we had to hold our position, but after three days and nights of heavy fighting and even heavier losses, we knew we were blocked. We knew, even if our division had been strong enough to capture Baghdad, we did not have the necessary reserves or logistical support to retain it. There was no alternative for our commanders than to order our retreat back to Kut.'

Bertie's stomach rumbled and he reached for his water bottle. The salty river water did little to quench his thirst and his stomach remained empty as shells continued to explode.

'The march back was a miserable affair. We were orderly at first but as the Turks advanced quickly, we fell into disarray. Some soldiers were remnants of men not fit to march a few miles, fit for nothing more than camp and guard duties. Weak from starvation, they were full of disease; dysentery, beri-beri and malaria. Many fell and were left. At Kut, where we arrived yesterday, we had to start digging in before the Turks started shelling. Not just shell fire but artillery, rifle and machine-gun fire. It made us work because the more you dug down the more sheltered and the safer you were. I dug furiously but I wasn't fast enough. The whistle of shell fire still rings in my ears but yesterday, one was much closer than the others. I remember its screech when it exploded and my scream as it ripped into my right leg. I remember bits of the soldier next to me flying up into the air and landing in a mess of blood, bone and tissue.'

Bertie leant back in the trench and closed his eyes. He dreamt he was with Ivy and Ena, in the back garden at Heron Court Road. They were sitting at a bronze aluminium table, drinking tea and eating scones. In his mind's eye picture, Ivy reached out and gently rocked a cradle positioned next to her at the table. The baby cooed and Bertie wept for his lost children.

Ivy

The war continued with one disastrous defeat after another. The convoys of casualties were relentless. Shadows of men, often ravaged by rapidly spreading infections, were delivered to wards and operating theatres on a daily basis. The solution was often the amputation of one or more limbs. Ivy held her breath when an odour, described by an orderly as the dead mouse smell, filled her nostrils. Dr Anderson explained the foul, sweet-smelling discharge from the lesions on the man's skin was gas gangrene. She said left untreated it could lead to the death of muscle tissue and sepsis, proving fatal. She pointed to the distinctive black, bubble-like lesions on the man's discoloured skin then pressed down on his leg, causing a loud grating sound. She looked up. 'Yes, crepitus. Produced by friction between bone and cartilage or the fractured parts of a bone.' Ivy held a damp cloth to the man's brow to try and calm his fever. She knew Dr Anderson's only hope was to amputate his leg.

They knew their soldiers were marching, sleeping and fighting in damp, unhygienic conditions. Filthy trenches spread diseases carried by rats, lice and mosquitoes. Dysentery, measles, meningitis and diphtheria thrived. Men arrived with black feet, caused by prolonged immersion in cold water and mud. Sometimes trench foot triumphed and feet couldn't be saved. Some soldiers appeared beyond help, their heads almost obliterated by sniper fire and artillery bombardment. Doctors tried to repair their devastating wounds, despite dwindling supplies of ether and chloroform. Ivy moved to the next stretcher, pushing away an image of a patient waking up mid-operation. In addition to appalling physical injuries, increasing numbers of men started to arrive with unusual symptoms. At first, their tremors, night terrors, mutism and deafness mystified the doctors. One young soldier, apparently unperturbed by his lice infestation and the severe lacerations to his face and arms, muttered under his breath as Ivy tended to his wounds. Once he was bandaged up, she tried talking to him. His eyes moved rapidly from side to side when she spoke.

'Can you tell me your name and where you come from?'

He jerked his head, looking in every direction around the room, anywhere other than at her. Gently, she held his shoulders and followed his eyes. 'What is it? What do you see?' He laughed maniacally, then started shrieking. He threw his hands on top of his head and crouched down on the floor, shouting. 'Take cover, men! Take cover!' Ivy shook her head; what horrors lay in this poor man's mind? The doctors knew some soldiers presenting with these symptoms were accused of shirking and risked being treated as cowards. Flora and Louisa held a different view; the soldiers were in shock, devastated by what they had seen and done, haunted by the horrific deaths of friends and enemies alike. At Endell Street they were treated with compassion and understanding.

Since meeting the previous year, Ivy and Clara started exchanging letters. Clara gave birth to a baby girl and Ivy had every confidence Christabel would be brought up as a suffragist. Clara wrote, 'she is named after Emmeline Pankhurst's daughter Christabel, nicknamed 'Queen of the Mob.'' Clara updated Ivy with news of the cause. While the militant suffragette campaign had halted, other activities continued. Earlier that year a Committee of Women's Suffrage Societies was formed in response to the Government's proposed changes to the electoral register. By the summer, the Prime Minister had converted to the suffrage cause. Clara wrote her next sentence in block capitals. *'He announced he was persuaded by the argument, 'if a new class of electors on whatever ground of State Service is formed, women who have rendered as effective service in the prosecution of the War as any class of the community', also had a claim.'* Clara went on to say, in simple language, it was a declaration of allegiance to giving women the right to vote, but she would wait to see if it happened. Ivy noticed women being recruited into jobs previously reserved for men; railway guards and ticket collectors, bus and tram conductors, postal workers, police, firefighters and bank tellers. Annoyingly, they were paid a lower wage than their male counterparts. She also saw younger women enjoying greater freedoms. Working and earning their own money, they behaved more independently. They went to pubs unescorted and on the orderlies' rare days off, Ivy watched some meet male friends on leave from the front. They went to Harrods for afternoon tea and shopped on the Strand. Ivy preferred to walk alone in Hyde Park, lost in memories of happier times.

Chapter 30

Ena

Ena checked the column of numbers one last time. She smiled, donations to the charities continued to come in, despite the hardship suffered by so many people. She knew from personal experience there was always someone worse off than yourself. As she closed the ledger, the door to the office opened and Olga appeared, her coppery curls escaping from under her cap. 'You should be getting home, Ena. It's almost dusk.' Ena nodded and pulled her coat on. 'I can give you a lift, if you like.' Ena thanked her but said she enjoyed the walk. 'Well make sure you get back before it's dark.' Ena promised she would and Olga left.

Ena took her usual route home, past the running track. She stood at the side of the overgrown lanes and pictured Donovan. His mother had received a number of letters from him. Meta read them aloud so many times, Ena knew the words by heart. She sighed, from everything she knew about the war, she didn't think Donovan was being truthful. She had an idea of the conditions on the Western Front and it wasn't at all how he described it. She admired him for trying to protect his mother. She shivered, it was starting to get dark and she should be at home. Hurrying along Capstone Road, she decided to ask Olga how people sent letters to soldiers at the front. The stories she wrote were sent in a bundle, but she wanted to know how to address a letter to an individual soldier. To Bombardier Donovan Ernest Leaman of the Royal Field Artillery.

She closed the front door behind her and removed her coat. As she hung it up, Ma Leaman came out of the kitchen. 'I'm pleased you're back Ena, it's dark outside now.'

Ena reached for Meta's warm hand. 'Thank you. But I can look after myself, you know.'

Meta nodded. 'I know, but I still worry about you. It's my job! Now come on into the kitchen, there's hot vegetable broth.' Meta started to walk away then stopped. 'Gladys collected post from your aunt's house today. She said there was a letter for you.'

'For me?' Ena felt a mixture of dread and excitement. Who could it be from? Most probably Aunt Ivy but Ena had only recently received a letter from Endell Street. Would another one come so quickly? Meta's voice trailed off when she opened the kitchen door. 'I don't know who it's from.'

Ena turned. She hadn't noticed the envelope on the hall table when she came in. She approached the table and reached out a shaking hand. She picked up the envelope and wheeled around. She was alone. If Meta had looked at the envelope, she would have known who the letter was from. She would have recognised her younger son's handwriting. Ena peered at the envelope; it was addressed to her.

'Miss Ena Leighton,
c/o The Leaman Family at 173, Capstone Road,
Bournemouth,
England,
Great Britain.'

In the top left-hand corner, for the avoidance of any doubt, was written, *'From Bombardier Donovan Ernest Leaman of the Royal Field Artillery'.* She glanced longingly up the stairs but pushed the envelope into her pocket. She hurried into the kitchen to join the others. As soon as she could, she excused herself and pushed her chair back. Grateful to Rachel for offering to help Meta with the dishes, Ena left the kitchen, slipped off her shoes and ran upstairs. She pushed her bedroom door shut and fell onto the bed. Carefully, she removed the envelope from her pocket and read the address again. She opened the envelope and pulled out the single sheet of thin paper. Smiling, she read Donovan's words.

'Dear Ena,

I imagine you did not expect to receive this letter. I hope you do not think it too forward of me, but every fellow here needs a word or two from home. I received word from my father; he mentioned you are staying with them at Capstone Road. I suspect you know about my letters to Ma. With your interest in reading, I am sure you know the picture here is different. With your permission, I would like to paint a more accurate version of events for you. I would be delighted to receive a reply from you, but until then I will tell you a story which I think you might enjoy.

It is about Christmas 1914, the first year we found ourselves in this unimaginable outpost. We were huddled together in our filthy trench, fighting a brutal enemy and an equally brutal winter. Late on Christmas Eve, some of our number heard voices drifting across the black night air. They listened carefully and realised the Germans were singing Christmas carols. Raising themselves slightly to peer over the parapet of our trenches, they saw lights in the darkness. German soldiers placed candles on tiny Christmas trees and displayed signs proposing a temporary ceasefire the following morning. We didn't think we could trust this unexpected action from our enemy, but as the sun rose on Christmas Day, something extraordinary happened. We saw small groups of unarmed (yes, unarmed!) Germans climbing slowly from their trenches. Some of our men laid down their guns and stepped forward to meet them. Of course, their officers tried to stop them but before long, they joined them. We heard afterwards our commanders shook hands, exchanged gifts and agreed the terms of a truce. It was the most remarkable thing. For a short time we soldiers were not at war with each other. We were in a place called no-man's land, a strip of land between our opposing trenches. We chatted and swapped gifts of tobacco and food. Even buttons that we tore from our uniforms! I played football with German soldiers and one German, who was a barber before the war, offered our men free haircuts. We were also able to collect our dead from the battlefield without being fired upon, as they were able to collect theirs. At dusk, the truce ended. We returned to our posts and guns were soon firing again. Sadly, it did not happen in 1915. Our leaders were furious and gave orders to shell no-man's land throughout the Christmas season.'

Ena picked up her pen and replied immediately.

Bertie

Their commanding officer issued a statement when they arrived at Kut. He said the Turks had surrounded them but he intended to defend the town and not retire further. He was optimistic about the siege, saying supplies were stockpiled in preparation for an advance on Baghdad, and reinforcements were expected within the month. He said because supplies were plentiful and reinforcements imminent, most of Kut's native population, around 7,000 people, were allowed to stay in the town. He called it a humanitarian decision because the harsh winter would soon arrive.

Bertie tried to concentrate on his words but his wounded leg throbbed and his head pounded. They had marched 44 miles in the last 36 hours. Those who could still stand needed to rest. When they were dismissed, Bertie turned to follow what remained of his division. The next thing he remembered was waking up in the hospital inside their garrison with a medical officer peering at his leg. He winced and the doctor looked up. The wound no longer throbbed and a clean dressing had been applied, but red hot pain shot through his body when the doctor touched his leg.

'You are back with us, Private Primavesi. Good. It is a miracle you made it back with this leg. It is badly damaged, but to walk with a limp is preferable to not walking at all, do you agree?'

Bertie managed a croaked, 'yes, Sir.'

'Very good. Now try and get some rest.'

The doctor moved to examine another soldier. Bertie focused on the rhythmic drips of rain falling from the hospital ceiling. He closed his eyes. He was jolted awake by a cacophony of noise outside.

'Turks have surrounded the garrison! We are under attack!'

The town was subjected to shelling, sniper fire and aircraft attack. The Turks proved to be a deadly and difficult foe. Over the coming weeks, they continued to launch attacks on the Kut defences. As the steady toll on the garrison worsened with their losses numbering between 150 and 200 each day, the reality of their situation became clear. Their food would last for around two and a half months. The garrison was starving to death. Bertie picked up his pen and a sheet of paper, intending to write to Ivy. He sighed and reached for his diary instead. The events of recent months were too gruesome to put in a letter. He knew from Ivy's correspondence she was routinely seeing horrifically wounded soldiers at Endell Street. His wife was unflinching in her duty and never complained, but he suspected the relentless arrival of casualties would be taking a toll on her. He didn't want to add to her burden. Perhaps he would tell her some of the detail when he was back home. For now, his diary was the best place to record his living nightmare.

'Saturday 15th of January 1916. Our command was right in trying to protect the local population from the winter weather, although our food supplies are now seriously depleted. Fresh meat ran out towards the end of December, and half rations have been introduced. I heard a soldier say the decision has been taken to slaughter the oxen and horses and add them to the larder. It is no surprise the bowels and stomachs of some of our number are disintegrating. Previously lean men are changed into leathery skeletons. What I wouldn't give for a bowl of hot spaghetti covered in a rich tomato

sauce. My stomach rumbles at the thought of it. The nights are bitterly cold and for the last few weeks the monsoon has brought torrential rain. The constant, heavy rain soaks us to the skin and leaves men feeling cold and miserable. Our trenches are filled with water and the hospital roof is more leaks than not. Now the intense heat of the sun is draining the moisture from the earth, the moist conditions and humidity are only serving to worsen fever among many men, to say nothing of diseases such as malaria and cholera.'

Bertie stopped writing and rubbed his leg. He knew he was fortunate to have been seen by a medical officer before the wound became infected, or worse, gangrenous. Almost 21,000 people were trapped there, many of them sick or wounded and medical supplies were proving inadequate. His wound was clean, which was something to be grateful for. Dressings and medicine were in short supply and many men were not so lucky. Their original field dressings weren't removed and replaced in time and the stench of open, infected wounds was indescribable. When the medical officer cleared him to return to duty, he limped away from the hospital, relieved to be of use once more.

'Wednesday 29ᵗʰ of March 1916. I have neither the strength nor the desire to recount my experience of this siege. However, I will try to describe how badly we are faring, but I expect to fail. Some things defy description. By mid-February our food supplies were worryingly low. The bread allocation was 12 ounces a day and meat eight ounces. We heard this was to be cut once more. The hospitals are overflowing with men suffering from all manner of infectious diseases; scurvy, malaria, gastroenteritis, diarrhoea, dysentery and pneumonia. Hunger has made us irritable. Add to this the ever-present, typhus-carrying lice, and you have the picture. We de-louse ourselves regularly, stripping to the waist and laying out our army-issue collarless shirts on the parapets of the trenches. We bake the revolting pests in the scorching sun. Sand-flies provide an equally disturbing problem. These evil creatures burrow inside you and lay

their eggs. The biting, blood-sucking scourges are sometimes blown away by a much-prayed-for wind; then the problem is the choking dust-storm it brings. Add snakes, centipedes, scorpions and in their myriads, common flies. Their numbers and persistence are exhausting. We exist within an inch of death. The medical staff do what they can, but their working conditions are appalling. Minor illnesses and wounds, treatable in a fit man, are a problem here because so many are seriously malnourished. Septic sores will kill a man here. My wounded leg has recently started to smell bad and I worry it has become infected. I must not think of it; I have endured floods, rats, enemy fire and worse to get this far. We are told reinforcements are coming soon. I must continue.'

Bertie stopped writing when a soldier sat down next to him. He looked at Bertie's words and scoffed. 'It's not true, you know.'

'What?'

'That reinforcements are coming. They've been beaten back.'

Bertie stared and the man walked away. Four weeks later Bertie knew the man was right. There were no reinforcements and they were going to surrender. There were rumours of a final assault but he thought it unlikely. They had nothing left; no strength, little in the way of ammunition and no desire to fight.

'Friday 28th of April 1916. Over the last three months, attempts by the relief force to attack the enemy and rescue our besieged troops have all failed, with losses of around 23,000 men. We have been here for 147 days and thankfully our horrific ordeal is over. Our commanding officer has surrendered our position. We don't know what comes next other than we are ordered to march to imprisonment at a place called Aleppo, where there is talk of an exchange of prisoners. Surely it can be no worse than our present situation. In addition to constant Turkish shellfire, we are starving and sickness is rife. We are plagued by dysentery and typhus, besieged by lice and sand-flies and harassed by hostile locals. I drag my useless right leg around with me but it serves no real purpose now, other than being

an inconvenience. I will drag it to Aleppo and continue my diary there.'

Suddenly a shout echoed around the courtyard. 'Take up arms!'

Bertie threw down his pen and limped outside as fast as he could.

'We're not beaten yet! Attack!'

Bertie hurried to his defensive position. He heard a warning shout and turned to see a cavalry horse charging towards him. He froze and took a vicious kick to his right leg as it hurtled past. He hit the ground and everything went black.

Chapter 31

Ena

When Ena finished writing her first letter to Donovan, she read it back to herself repeatedly, trying to make sure it was friendly and not soppy. She wanted her words to make him smile and think of home, without upsetting him. She knew from the newspapers that conditions in the trenches were appalling and letters from home were greeted with joy. She hoped her words would help him to endure whatever the war threw at him.

'Dear Donovan,

I was very surprised (but pleasantly so) to receive your letter. Thankfully Ma didn't see it or I think there would have been questions. Gladys collected post from my aunt's house today and she brought your letter to Capstone Road. I read the newspapers and am aware of your efforts to protect Ma. I applaud you for it. I enjoyed your story about the Christmas truce. How wonderful you men put your differences aside and stopped fighting, albeit for such a short space of time. I can picture you playing football in no-man's land, I hope you scored a goal against the Germans! I continue to write short stories for soldiers in the trenches (perhaps you have seen one?) and I am working as a book-keeper at the community hall. We – that is, me, your family and the Primavesis, along with Gladys and Hilda, look after the houses between us. We all try to keep busy and help the war effort as much as possible. We long for your safe return. Please write to me again soon.'

Ena agonised over how to sign the letter. She wanted to be his girl but he hadn't asked her yet so that wasn't appropriate. But *'yours sincerely'* was too formal. In the end she settled for, *'Your friend, Ena'.*

Ivy

Ivy was checking stores in the linen room when she heard the door open behind her. She turned around, losing count of the sheets and pillowcases. Olga. Ivy started to smile then stopped. Olga was never without a ready smile. Olga held something and Ivy started backing away.

'No. I don't want it. Don't give it to me. Please don't.'

'I'm sorry, Ivy. It's addressed to you.'

Olga held out her hand and Ivy let the telegram fall to the floor. Olga picked it up and together, they opened it. The floor gave way under Ivy's feet and Olga caught her. Ivy allowed herself to be held then Olga led her to the door. 'We need to see Dr Murray.'

Olga knocked on Flora Murray's office door. Ivy stood mute beside her. 'Come!' Inside, without speaking, Olga handed Ivy's telegram to Flora. The doctor gave a quick shake of her head before looking up at Ivy.

'Your husband?'

Ivy said nothing but Olga confirmed the telegram related to Bertie.

'Please accept my condolences and those of Dr Anderson. You may take some leave and return home to be with your family.'

In the dormitory, Olga packed some things into Ivy's suitcase. Neither of them spoke on the drive to Bournemouth. When Olga pulled up outside the house on Lansdowne Road, she handed Ivy her suitcase and offered to come inside to help break the news to Bertie's family. Ivy shook her head then stepped out of the motor car. She opened the garden gate and walked up the path to the Primavesis' front door. She didn't look back.

Donovan

Donovan struggled to hear Johnny over the enemy's machine gun fire. He cupped a hand to his ear and moved closer.

'I said, is it another letter from your girl?'

Donovan smiled. 'From Ena, yes. But I don't know if she's my girl yet.'

Johnny's reply was lost as the barrage continued overhead. Donovan quickly scanned Ena's letter to see if there was an answer to his question. There it was, sitting snugly among the lines of news from home. *In answer to your question, no, I'm not already someone's girl and yes, I would like to be yours. There was a boy, back in Gateshead. A boy called Jack. He was a true friend to me, years ago. I don't know where he is now; he might even be where you are.* Donovan's heart leapt. Here, in the middle of his nightmare, was a glimmer of hope, a light for him to move towards. He would survive and go home to his family. And to Ena.

He and his comrades had heard talk of a new offensive and they waited with a mixture of excitement and dread. After his commanding officer noted his ability to shoot straight and hit a target during their training, Donovan was proud to learn how to fix his bayonet onto his rifle in readiness for battle. Now, after seeing first-hand the damage wreaked by their weapons, he longed to lay down his gun. He lost count of the number of traumatised soldiers he'd seen trying to inflict their own 'Blighty wounds'. Men who would shoot themselves in the hand or foot in an attempt to be sent home or at least to a field hospital. A man desperate enough to place a rifle against his foot and drive a bullet through his own bones and flesh. Desperate enough to risk being found guilty of this capital offence, punishable by execution by firing-squad or being sent to prison. Before Donovan could read the rest of Ena's letter, they received word they would be leaving their trenches. He knew only too well what came next. They would drink a glass of coffee with rum. It was vital to lift their spirits, because they knew just above the trench was the possibility of death. Death from bullets, death from bombs, death from one or another of the horrific things awaiting them. Once they were out of their trenches, they crouched low and ran or crawled, weapons ready to fire at all times, throwing themselves forward until they arrived at the front line. Once there they fired guns and shells all day and all night. They were there for four days then relieved for four days.

This assault was different. They were given notice of the order to leave, but told to wait. For the next week they crouched low in their trenches, while a devastating artillery barrage of shells hurtled across no-man's land. Donovan and Johnny were reassured by the thunderous attack, designed, according to their officers, to kill any enemy soldiers hiding in the vicinity. When the barrage stopped they were ordered out and told to advance slowly in long lines, across no-man's land towards the German trenches. Those who survived would later learn of their commanding officers' fatal mistake. Their barrage failed because thousands of German troops remained protected by sitting deep in their trenches, safe from even the largest shells. As Donovan, Johnny and their comrades in arms calmly crossed no-man's land, enemy troops spilled out from their underground bunkers, dragging machine guns, grenades and boxes of ammunition with them. Donovan flattened himself in the mud, his gun in position, as the air around him hissed with the sound of bullets ripping through their lines. He crawled forward, only to find a thick barrier of barbed wire blocking his path. He watched men try and fail to hack their way through. He dropped into a shell hole and tried to catch his breath while all around him shells whistled and men screamed. He readied himself and inched towards the top of the hole. Keeping his body hidden, with his rifle in position, he started firing and kept firing until his arms burned. He slid back down into the hole and waited for the enemy fire to end.

Ena

After she received Donovan's first letter, Ena offered to collect the post from Heron Court Road each day. She told Gladys it made sense because she could walk past the house on her way home from work. Gladys readily agreed and Ena smiled, she wanted her correspondence with Donovan to be their secret. They exchanged a few letters before the news about Uncle Bertie arrived. She tried to keep her letters light and amusing, but knew she needed to tell him.

'Dear Donovan,

It causes me such sadness to write this, but you should know we have received the worst news about Uncle Bertie. We are all grieving and cannot believe he will not be coming home. I am doing my best to help Aunt Ivy but she is out of reach, lost in her sorrow. She speaks little but I will keep trying. We are staying with the Primavesis but Aunt Ivy wants to go back to Heron Court Road. Mrs Primavesi is trying to dissuade her; I think she is worried Aunt Ivy's grief will worsen if she returns to the house she shared with Uncle Bertie. I will write separately about other, less terrible matters. I am sorry to be the bearer of such awful tidings.

Yours, Ena.'

The following day, she hurried to Heron Court Road after work, longing for news from Donovan. She opened the door and looked down. On the mat, a single envelope, filled with promise. She grabbed it and sat down on the stairs.

'Dear Ena,

You do not know how much light your words bring into an otherwise black place. I was amused to hear about the bickering between women in the knitting army. I could not have imagined such aggressive behaviour over misplaced wool. I was very interested to hear about the book you are reading. 'The Thirty-Nine Steps' sounds like a story we men would like to read. The man you describe as 'the very ordinary Richard Hannay, who manages to do extraordinary things', appears to be a man who puts his country's interests before his own safety. He would fit in very well here. I think the story would be greatly appreciated in the midst of mud, rain and shells, and everything else that makes trench life depressing. Perhaps you could send a copy, if you are able? We go on in much the same way here, fighting and trying to sleep, not sleeping then fighting again. It is relentless but necessary.

You asked for a description of our trenches and conditions here. It is not a pretty scene but I think I know you well enough now to realise you want the truth. The line of fortified trenches stretches from the North Sea to the Swiss frontier with France. The long, narrow ditches are deep and there is dirty, sticky mud on all sides. When it rains (which it does, a lot), we are often up to our stomachs in freezing, muddy water, and our rifles get all plugged up with it. In addition to mud we have rats and often no food for days at a time. We are under constant enemy fire from shells, machine and rifle-gun fire and don't forget the gas. When we first went in, we could walk in the deep trench without our heads showing (if they show they will be shot at!). When we want to shoot out, we use what is called a fire-step. It runs along the entire trench and is a bit that hasn't been dug as deep. We step up a couple of feet or so and use it to peer over the side, through the parapet into no-man's land, looking towards the enemy's trench line. When the frosts came we could walk on the hard ground and it was a decent surface to sleep on. But our boots froze while we slept, which was very painful. Our greatcoats (overcoats to you!) also froze to be as stiff as boards, and we used our bayonets to hack the bottoms off and walk around in short coats, swinging our arms to keep warm.'

Ena looked up. It was dark outside. She needed to get back to Lansdowne Road before Mrs Primavesi started to worry.

Locking the door behind her, she saw Uncle Bertie fastening his coat and adjusting his hat as he prepared to take her on one of their many walks. Her chest tightened and the hollow feeling in the pit of her stomach returned her to reality. Her lip trembled and she shook herself. Uncle Bertie had asked her to look after Aunt Ivy while he was away. She turned back to look at the house that was such a happy home for the three of them. 'I promise, Uncle Bertie. I'll look after her, as the two of you looked after me.' She pulled her gloves on and walked away.

Ivy

Ivy lay on the bed, her face to the wall. She heard the front door open and close again then light footsteps on the stairs. A soft knock on the bedroom door and then Ena's voice. 'Aunt Ivy? Can I come in?' Ivy took a deep breath. Perhaps it was time. 'Yes, my dear. Come in.'

Ivy turned to face Ena. She closed her eyes and tried to hold back her tears. Ena took her hand. The tears came and Ivy sobbed like a child. Ena held her aunt as her grief filled the room. When Ivy's sobs subsided, Ena helped her into bed. 'I'll bring you some broth. You need to eat something.' Ivy started to argue but Ena held up a finger. Despite her grief, Ivy couldn't stop the smile from forming. 'Very well, you're in charge.' 'Yes I am, and don't you forget it!' Ivy watched Ena walk to the door, proud of the woman her niece had become. Ena returned with two bowls of broth on a tray. As they ate, Ivy listened to Ena's tales from the community hall. Later, for the first time in months, she slept.

The following morning, she sat on the edge of her bed, holding the telegram. She knew the cruel words by heart but today her eyes were dry.

'Deeply regret to inform you Service No: 4430 Private Herbert Joseph Primavesi 2ⁿᵈ/4ᵗʰ Bn. Dorsetshire Regiment officially reported died of his wounds 30ᵗʰ April 1916.'

She folded the telegram and placed it in her bedside drawer. Then she went downstairs to join the others for breakfast. She was greeted by smiles, a cup of hot tea and a bowl of porridge. As she started telling them about her decision to return to Heron Court Road, there was a knock on the front door. Gladys went to answer it and Ivy heard a familiar voice. Olga joined them and a cup was placed in front of her. She took one sip before asking Ivy if she was ready to return to work. Ivy swallowed; she hadn't even considered it. She opened her mouth to say no but Olga spoke first. 'Should we have a walk on the beach?' Ivy nodded, stunned into silence by Olga's intervention.

The salty air stung Ivy's eyes as she looked out to sea. She shivered and pulled her coat tighter. 'I came here the day I found out.'

Olga nodded, putting her arm through Ivy's.

'It was a dull day, a thin strip of weak light divided grey sky from grey sea. I came in the evening and the day was dying. The horizon was full of dark clouds shot through with silver light. Suddenly the crimson sun burst through and sank towards the sea. Gone, just like that. Like him.'

Olga was silent and they carried on walking.

'I had to tell his parents.' Olga nodded. 'I think they knew as soon as they saw me. Giulio tried to embrace Catherine but she kept her hands by her sides, shaking her head.'

'No. No. Please don't tell me. If I don't hear it, it can't be true.'

'Giulio took Catherine's hands, grief etched across his face.'

'I am so sorry my love, but he's gone. Our boy and Ivy's beloved husband. We've lost him.'

'Catherine's knees gave way and he caught her before she hit the floor. I helped him put her to bed. Then I went to bed myself. When I woke, Ena was holding my hand. Giulio went to Capstone Road to tell her, then he brought her to me. I prayed

I had imagined the telegram, you driving me back here, everything. The telegram said he '*died of his wounds*'. I can't stop thinking about it; what were his wounds, how much pain was he in? I can't bear to think of him suffering like the men we've seen. It tortures me, Olga.'

Olga stopped walking and took Ivy's hands. 'Come back to work. You need a distraction and the patients need you. You know the orderlies bring laughter into the wards.' Ivy looked at her friend, this tower of strength and purpose who soldiered on, no matter what. She did so much good and helped so many people. Ivy kicked the sand and looked out to sea. What use was she to anyone hiding here feeling sorry for herself? She turned to Olga. 'Alright. I'll try.'

Olga grabbed Ivy's arm and turned her around. 'Excellent! Let's go!'

'What? Now?'

'Yes! No time like the present!'

Chapter 32

Ivy

Ivy found Endell Street unchanged. Convoys of horrifically wounded soldiers continued to arrive at all hours of the day and night. Olga was right. Despite the injuries and deaths the orderlies dealt with on a daily basis, they managed to remain cheerful. People were sympathetic to her loss but they carried on because so many others needed their care and attention. Gradually, the work started to distract Ivy from her grief and feeling useful helped her regain some sense of perspective.

A few weeks after her return to work, Ivy walked past Victoria and a group of orderlies chatting animatedly in the corridor. Victoria called to her. 'I say, Ivy?' Ivy turned to face the women. 'Yes? How can I help?' Victoria smiled and gestured for her to join them. 'I think it's the other way around, don't you, girls?' The women nodded in agreement and Victoria explained. 'You know something that keeps everyone going around here is the entertainment programme, don't you?' Ivy nodded but said she hadn't found the time to be involved with anything so far. 'Well that might change, because this year we're having a Christmas pantomime!' Ivy conjured up a brief and she hoped convincing smile, but inside she was horrified. Grief crept over her shoulders and fixed her with its sharp, spiteful claws. It was never far away. The last thing she wanted to do was celebrate. She excused herself, saying one of the doctors needed her in the operating theatre. As she hurried away, Victoria called after her. 'Anyway, watch out for the entertainers. Some of them are coming in soon to start rehearsing!' Ivy raised a hand in acknowledgement, knowing she would try to stay as far away as possible.

As soon as she could, Ivy requested permission to take some time off to spend Christmas in Bournemouth with Ena and Bertie's family. When it was granted, she found she couldn't wait to leave. The prospect of having to appear cheerful and celebrate was something she couldn't imagine. On the day her leave began, she was saying goodbye to Victoria when she heard a woman's voice in the distance. She turned to see two women heading towards the library. All she saw of the one in front was the flash of a red dress, before the door closed behind them.

Victoria touched her arm. 'Ivy? What is it? You look as if you've seen a ghost.'

'It's nothing…it's just…'

'What?'

'Those women. Who are they?'

'Oh, they're two of the performers Elizabeth Robins has brought in for the pantomime. What is it? Have you changed your mind about coming?'

Ivy shook her head. 'No, but I thought one of them looked familiar.'

'Who was it?'

'I don't know, I expect it was my mind playing tricks on me.'

Victoria hugged her. 'Go home and be with your family.'

Ivy nodded and left.

1917
Ena

Donovan's letters kept coming and Ena replied straightaway. She was at Heron Court Road reading his latest letter when there was a knock on the front door. She opened it slowly, smiling when she saw Rachel.

'Hello, may I come in?'

Ena laughed and held the door open for her friend. She closed the door and turned to face Rachel. 'Is everything all right?'

Rachel looked around then turned back to Ena. 'I know you, you're up to something!'

Ena hesitated. Since becoming friends she and Rachel had told each other everything, but Donovan was Rachel's brother. She couldn't lie. 'I've been writing to Donovan. He's asked me to be his girl. I like him.' She held the letter up and Rachel laughed. 'I know, you silly goose! Your face changes every time someone mentions him.'

Ena felt her cheeks grow hot. 'Do you think anyone else knows?'

'No, I don't think so. Everyone is so caught up with worry and grief. Your secret is safe with me. Who knows, you might be my sister-in-law one day!'

Ena slipped Donovan's letter into her coat pocket. She smiled at her friend. 'Never mind Donovan, what about you and William Love?' Ena noticed Rachel wore her best dress and smartest shoes when she visited Seymour Love's house to compose music for the travelling entertainment groups. When war was declared, Mr Love's son William was one of the first to sign up and one of the first soldiers to see direct action on the Western Front. He was also one of the first to have a leg amputated following a brutal shell attack at the battle of Mons. William was invalided out of the army and after spending some time at the Colliton House VAD Hospital in Dorchester, he returned home to live with his father. Rachel turned her back on Ena and mumbled. 'What about him?' Ena laughed and moved to stand in front of Rachel. Her friend's eyes glistened. 'I knew it!'

On the walk back to Capstone Road, they talked about Donovan and William. Rachel confided in Ena that William suffered from episodes of panic and bouts of anxiety. 'Yet when he plays his flute, it's as if nothing has changed.' Ena told Rachel how much she missed her uncle. 'I haven't told Aunt Ivy because she is so sad, but I can't believe we'll never see him again.'

Rachel matched her step to Ena's and spoke slowly. 'Every day brings more bad news. I read some communities have lost whole streets of men who signed up together. Men who sang in a local choir or played for their town's football team. I've seen some soldiers come home on leave; why not my brothers and Leo Primavesi, do you think?'

Ena shrugged. 'Uncle Bertie was too far away but I don't know why some are granted leave and others aren't. Leo is in the Air Force; I don't know if it makes any difference.'

Rachel sighed. 'Their letters tell us so little, other than Donovan's attempts to make it all sound better than it is.' She looked at Ena. 'Is he more honest with you?'

Ena nodded. 'Yes, he paints a terrible picture of things on the Western Front. His most recent letter did say they now have rubber face masks and breathing equipment to shield them from the poisonous gas attacks. You know how tough he is, I'm sure he's trying to protect you and your mother. Perhaps that's the case with Cyril and Leo too. At least we know they're still alive.'

Ena just caught Rachel's whisper. 'For now.'

She tried to reassure Rachel by saying Donovan sounded cheerful in his letters, despite the graphic descriptions of conditions in the trenches. Ma Leaman was waiting with hot cocoa when they got back. Ena wrapped her hands around the warm cup. She encouraged Rachel to get a good night's sleep, knowing it was difficult for all of them these days. She picked up her pen to write to Donovan. Rachel was right, there was doom and gloom everywhere. She wanted to tell him something positive, to lift his spirits. She smiled, she would briefly mention Christmas and Hanukkah then concentrate on more positive news.

'Dear Donovan,

I would wish you a Happy Hanukkah but I do not suppose you are in celebratory mood where you are. When Aunt Ivy went back to work I returned to stay with your parents and Rachel. Aunt Ivy came home from London at Christmas but we were not a happy crowd. We feel the empty seats around the table keenly, but we hope and pray you will all be safely home soon.

Now, let me tell you something more positive! You may know Britain has become very low on food. The Government has created a Ministry to regulate its supply and consumption and encourage greater production. Here's the exciting part! The Board of Agriculture has set up a Women's Land Army! Did you ever imagine such a thing? They have called for women to work on farms, picking crops and tilling the land. Rachel and I have signed up to be 'Land Girls'. I'm not sure your poor sister is cut out for driving a plough! Still, we are trying to do our bit.

You will remember how passionate the women here are about the suffrage movement. I think you will be interested to know how activities are progressing. We value everything you are doing and we relish the opportunity to work hard in areas previously closed to us. I know the men in both yours and Uncle Bertie's family are sympathetic to our cause. The news is, women's suffrage has been approved in the House of Commons! The Speaker's Conference on Electoral Reform recommended granting the vote to women who are local government electors, or wives of local government electors, and to university graduates; in both cases the women must be over thirty. I don't think I know many women in these categories, other than possibly the doctors at Endell Street where Aunt Ivy is working. It is a start but irritatingly there was no mention of qualifying factors for men, who could all vote from the age of 21. I can also tell you the grille in the Ladies Gallery at the Houses of Parliament has been removed. The next time I visit Aunt Ivy I intend to go there and take the view, because I can!'

Ena read her words back. She bit her bottom lip. Donovan had been honest with her about his situation. Perhaps it was time to tell her story. If they were to fall properly in love when he came home, she needed to tell him how her life began. She picked up her pen.

'*Dear Donovan,*

Me again. I know you sometimes share my letters with fellows in the trenches but this one is for your eyes only. I think it is time for me to tell you about my start in life, which was not a happy one. Not right from the beginning; I have vague memories of my grandmother and I am told she was very proud to show me off in my pram around Gateshead, when I was a baby. My recollections are blurred; her sweet voice, warm cuddles and the comforting smell of cocoa. Sadly, everything changed when my grandmother died. I believe Aunt Ivy did her best, but she and my mother were left in debt to their vicious Aunt Agatha. They had to go away to work and earn money to repay her. Well, that was the plan until my mother ran away to London. For years I carried shame for her actions but now I know, the shame is all hers. I did nothing wrong.'

Ena paused. The pen trembled in her hand. She grabbed the paper and crumpled it up. She stopped and took a deep breath. If Donovan wanted to be with her, he needed to know everything. She smoothed the creases from the paper and continued.

'*For years I didn't know what happened, but Aunt Ivy told me the truth when she brought me to London. If she had not come when she did, I don't think I would have survived. When my mother abandoned me, I was sent to the workhouse in Gateshead. Life was cruel and miserable there and those are memories I want to forget. By a strange piece of good fortune, I was able to leave the workhouse and go to live with my mother's cousin Lizzie. I was treated very poorly by Lizzie, but Aunt Ivy has taught me forgiveness and now I find myself feeling sorry for her. Her life was also unhappy. Living with her in the poverty of Gateshead's Pipewellgate, I can draw some parallels between your experience and what I endured. Not the bombs and mud, but the cold, the rats and the starvation. I had two friends there; without them my world would have been even darker. I planned to run away with my friend Nancy but tragically she died before we could escape. Jack helped me in many ways; he shared his food with me and helped me to get away from Lizzie. In the end, because of him, his uncle and Aunt Ivy, I was saved.'*

Ena wiped a tear from her cheek. She had hidden these memories away for a long time, and they were no less painful all these years later. She blew her nose and continued.

'What of my mother? Well, you are so lucky to have Ma. My mother has always been a disappointment. Aunt Ivy thinks she may have been on Titanic; I don't even know if she is still alive. I have never understood how she could have abandoned me. I think she was more interested in her theatrical career than being a mother. All she ever gave me was a handkerchief and a picture. She didn't even sign the picture as being from my mother. It was signed on the back 'To my little girlie, with fond thoughts, yours lovingly, Mona.' I didn't know who she was. Can you imagine? I hope you still want me to be your girl after hearing all this. If you do, we will have fun when you return, I know it. With the misery we are all living through, I think it is more important than ever to look to the future. Shall I tell you what I dream of? To live in a pretty little village, in a house with a beautiful garden. And to be loved. If you will, tell me what you dream of, Donovan.

Yours fondly, Ena.'

Ivy

Before Ivy left Bournemouth to return to London, she received a letter from Bertie's solicitor, explaining he needed to meet her to discuss Bertie's will. Ivy stared at the letter; this was something they hadn't discussed. Why would they, at their age? She shook her head, perhaps because of the nature of Bertie's departure, they should have. But it would have been to acknowledge he might not come home, and she hadn't allowed herself to consider that. She started to worry. She had some money of her own, but didn't know if it was enough to maintain the house and support her and Ena. She told herself to stop worrying, she could get a job after the war and by then, Ena would be old enough to earn her own money.

She sat in a sturdy leather chair in Bertie's solicitor's office, her gloved hands folded neatly in her lap. The solicitor cleared his throat. He informed her the house on Heron Court Road was paid for and Bertie bequeathed it to her, in addition to his effects. His estate totalled £1419 and 14 shillings. Ivy gasped. 'When did my husband arrange this?' The solicitor adjusted his spectacles and consulted the document on his desk. He looked up. 'Tuesday the 11th of August 1914.' Ivy managed a smile. 'The same day he signed up.' She left the solicitor's office a woman of independent means. She shook her head; her loyal, steadfast husband had thought of everything.

Back at work, she was relieved to find all talk of Christmas and pantomimes over. The war's devastating impact on the economy meant their focus was on continuing to care for patients, amidst steeply rising prices and shortages of food and coal. Deadly battles continued to be waged in France and Belgium, resulting in convoy after convoy bringing the desperately wounded to Endell Street. Air raids sounded repeatedly over London as the women calmly and efficiently went about their work. By May, Ivy was firmly back into the routine although grief followed her around like an unwelcome guest. Writing to Clara, she said she felt as though part of her soul had left her, to go and search for him. She put one foot in front of the other and did all the things she needed to at work, but she drifted, like a ghost. Her happy-ever-after was snatched away in cruel fashion and while she knew she was one of many women widowed by the war, it didn't lessen her pain.

Chapter 33

Donovan

D onovan peered along the trench, squinting. They had been told their next assault would be 'the big one'. After years of being told one thing then another, now they simply followed orders and waited to see what unfolded. Spirits were high because they had received some very good news; the Americans had agreed to join the war. They were all exhausted; this much-needed boost might make all the difference. Something caught his eye and he smiled at the small mouse scurrying along the trench, searching for crumbs.

'You'll be lucky, mate! We're so hungry you could be dinner!' The mouse fixed him with its beady eyes then scampered away, as if it understood. Donovan laughed and picked up his pen.

'My dear Ena,

I have just been visited in my rotten trench by a small field mouse. I scared him off by saying he might be my next meal! We are seriously hungry, please send chocolate if you can get any, or biscuits. Anything would help. I am honoured you felt able to share your story with me. You have endured so much and yet are willing to forgive those who have wronged you. I have tremendous admiration for you. You asked what I dream of? Getting out of here alive of course and being back home. Walking along the beach with you and making plans for the future. Like you, the idea of living somewhere pretty and peaceful. The opposite of this godforsaken place.

I was cheered to hear you and Rachel have become Land Girls (although I agree with you about my sister!) and of the developments in the suffrage movement. I have long believed women are a match to men in many situations. You will no doubt know the Americans have joined the war? What a boost to our morale this is! We tied pamphlets to balloons announcing the news and released them over enemy lines! They will be no match for the fighting power of our new ally and this deadly stalemate may at last be broken.'

The order came to leave their trenches once more and Donovan stopped writing.

Ena

Ena threw herself into land work, but longed to be in her bedroom writing to Donovan. She decided to tell him about the poetry she had been reading. Soon after war was declared, she read a newspaper article about 'the first war poem'. She discovered Henry Newbolt's poem *'Vitaï Lampada'* was written years earlier, but published in August 1914 because of its theme. *'Vitaï Lampada translates as 'The Torch of Life'. The schoolboy in the poem, a future soldier, learns about selfless commitment to duty through playing cricket. That's what you and your comrades have, Donovan. Day after day you selflessly put yourselves in grave danger to keep the rest of us safe. Here are a few lines; write and tell me what you think, please.*

> *There's a breathless hush in the Close to-night,*
> *Ten to make and the match to win,*
> *A bumping pitch and a blinding light,*
> *An hour to play and the last man in.*
> *And it's not for the sake of a ribboned coat,*
> *Or the selfish hope of a season's fame,*
> *But his Captain's hand on his shoulder smote,*
> *'Play up! play up! and play the game!*
>
> *The sand of the desert is sodden red,*
> *Red with the wreck of a square that broke;*
> *The Gatling's jammed and the Colonel dead,*
> *And the regiment blind with dust and smoke.*

The river of death has brimmed his banks,
And England's far, and Honour a name,
But the voice of a schoolboy rallies the ranks:
'Play up! play up! and play the game!"

Donovan

Whenever Donovan received a letter from Ena, he was grateful
for her imagination. Her words provided a welcome distraction
from the devastation around him. Today it was the poem by
Henry Newbolt. She had asked him what he thought of it. He
read the poem repeatedly to try and make sense of it in relation
to what was happening to him and his comrades. As a sportsman, he knew all about adhering to sporting values and 'playing
the game'. He had always believed in fairness, courage and duty,
but the battlefield proved to be something different. Here the
rules of the game didn't apply. It wasn't a game, it was murder.
Kill or be killed. He understood the ideology of dying for something higher than himself; if he perished there, he would be seen
as having lived and died in the right way. If he was honest, he
would tell Ena he was weary of the deafening machine gun fire,
exploding artillery shells and the smell and discomfort of their
tight rubber masks, worn to avoid being suffocated by toxic gas
from an unseen enemy. But he would keep his dignity until the
last, he wouldn't cower in a muddy ditch waiting for the end.
No, he would reply to his dear girl and set down his dreams for
their future. That was what he intended to write, until the rain
came and he passed one of his worst nights since arriving at the
Western Front.

'Dearest Ena,

I need to set this down, but I hardly know where to start. Yes-
terday it poured with rain all day and night. Water rose steadily
until it was knee-deep and we had the order to retire to our trenches.
Foolishly, I dropped my blanket and fur coat in the water. Then I

slipped getting onto the parapet and was soaked and covered in dirty stinking mud up to my waist. I joined other boys to fill sand-bags then I was on sewer guard duty. Snipers were everywhere and some boys were hit. One lay in the open all day, we couldn't go to him for sniping. We brought him in once it was dark, he was unconscious but still alive. He passed away soon after and lies beside me still.'

He carried on writing for a little while then signed off '*Yours always, Donovan*'. He put his pen down and rain mingled with his tears as he wept. He was woken by the sharp rattle of machine-gun fire and whistles. He grabbed his rifle and scrambled through the mud to the parapet. He watched Johnny go out and then a barrage of bullets ripped through the air above him. He heard a scream and one of Johnny's arms flew past him, falling into the mud at the bottom of the trench. In the last four years he and Johnny had been through battles too numerous to mention. Donovan tried to think of this as another terrifying ordeal they would both survive, but he sensed a difference. Their numbers and ammunition were badly depleted and his hope lay somewhere in the rancid mud. He inched towards the parapet, he needed to get to Johnny. His friend lay a few feet away, separated from his helmet which Donovan saw was shot through with holes. Trembling, Donovan crept out, low and slow. A man to his right screamed, from injury or madness Donovan didn't know. A voice called out and he turned.

'Donovan? Brother?'

Donovan peered through the smoke. Cyril, his brother the musician who hadn't wanted to be here in the first place. Donovan smiled and started to move towards Cyril. A shell screeched through the air and the brothers hit the ground. Donovan drifted in and out of consciousness as the cacophony of battle faded away. He heard a voice, familiar yet distant. 'Brother? Can you hear me?' Donovan smiled weakly and reached out a hand to Cyril. He watched his brother move towards him and then Cyril flew through the air backwards, the force of the blast propelling him over the parapet and into the trench. Donovan slithered to the top of the trench on his stomach. He looked down and saw Cyril, stunned but alive. 'Brother!' Cyril looked up, and the last thing Donovan saw was the love in his brother's eyes.

THE VILLAGE ON THE HILL

ACT THREE

Chapter 34

Ivy

Ivy re-read Clara's letter. She drummed her fingernails on the table in the library.

'You look thoughtful.'

'It's my friend Clara. She wants me to go to the Patriotic Meeting at the Royal Albert Hall but I'm not sure.'

Victoria frowned. 'Why not? We're all going.'

'You are?'

'Yes, of course. It's a celebration of our suffrage efforts. Hopefully, we will have the vote by the end of the year. Both Emmeline and Christabel Pankhurst are speaking. Come with us.'

Ivy smiled. Clara had mentioned her daughter's namesake would be speaking. She wasn't sure why she hadn't wanted to go. 'Alright, I'll come.'

'Excellent!' Victoria patted her on the back and returned to work.

Later, Ivy picked up Bertie's photograph. The meeting would be her first social event since he died. When she returned to London, she threw herself into work and did little else. Perhaps it was time to move forward. She replaced Bertie's photograph on her bedside table. 'I will never forget you, my darling, whatever else happens in my life. You were my first, most precious love.'

Approaching the Royal Albert Hall, they heard women quietly singing Ethel Smyth's '*The March of the Women*'. They were subdued; still being in the midst of war and this not yet being a vote for all women. Ivy walked proudly with the women of Endell Street. It was what she needed. To do something meaningful, something important. In her speech, Emmeline Pankhurst called on the Government and businesses to retain women in factories after the war, on the basis of the equal right to work. She said they would continue to fight for the right to vote for all women, this being only permission for women over 30, university graduates or property owners. It excluded many young women who toiled in factories and on land during the war. They would also continue to fight for equal pay for equal work. After the meeting, the women from Endell Street visited the hall's cocktail lounge. Unchaperoned, they strode in with their heads high and took their seats. Olga sat opposite Ivy and asked her what she would like to drink. Ivy hesitated; she couldn't remember the last time she was in such a situation.

'I'm having a gin fizz; would you like one?'

Ivy smiled, grateful to her friend. The mixture of lemon, fizzy water and gin sounded perfect. 'Yes please, that would be nice.' Once everyone had drinks, Flora and Louisa raised their glasses and proposed a toast. 'To women everywhere!' The women repeated the words as one. As Ivy sipped her drink, Olga started discussing the speeches. Ivy didn't hear what Olga was saying. She was remembering another performance, a long time ago, at the West London Theatre on Shaftesbury Avenue, and the dinner afterwards where she first met Bertie.

'Excuse me, I couldn't help but notice your glass is empty. Would you allow me to buy you another drink?' Ivy dragged herself back to the present. She looked at the man who had approached their table. He frowned. 'You look familiar. Where might I have seen you before?' Ivy looked at Olga and her friend raised her eyebrows. She looked at the man again, trying to ignore his handsome face and impeccable manners.

'No, thank you. I am here with friends.'

'Very well. But please allow me to introduce myself and give you my business card. I would welcome the opportunity to make your acquaintance properly. I am Squadron Leader George Scott-Smith, currently on leave from the Air Force. Perhaps I could arrange to call on you sometime, Miss…?'

Ivy looked down at her left hand where her wedding ring nestled comfortably. 'It is Mrs; Mrs Ivy Primavesi. I am married.'

'Please forgive me. I meant no offence.'

Watching the man walking away, Olga whistled under her breath. Ivy waved her unspoken suggestion away.

'What? Don't you think you could be happy again?'

Ena

Ena hurried to Heron Court Road. Perhaps today there would be a letter from Donovan. They were arriving regularly until a few weeks ago when one day, they stopped. She pushed her key into the lock and opened the door. The mat was bare. She sighed and trudged back to Capstone Road. She re-read all his letters and replayed her own in her mind. Had she said something to upset him? Had she scared him off? She would rather believe that, than consider the dreadful alternative. When the telegram came, it wasn't addressed to her. As she approached the house, she heard Meta Leaman's screams and she knew. She ran to the running track. A few weeks later, she went back to Heron Court Road. She wasn't expecting to find anything, but an envelope lay on the mat. Donovan's final letter.

'Dearest Ena,

I need to set this down, but I hardly know where to start. Yesterday it poured with rain all day and night. Water rose steadily until it was knee-deep and we had the order to retire to our trenches. Foolishly, I dropped my blanket and fur coat in the water. Then I slipped getting onto the parapet and was soaked and covered in dirty stinking mud up to my waist. I joined other boys to fill sand-bags then I was on sewer guard duty. Snipers were everywhere and some boys were hit. One lay in the open all day, we couldn't go to him for sniping. We brought him in once it was dark, he was unconscious but still alive. He passed away soon after and lies beside me still. No sleep could be had. No matter how cold or wet we are, we stay here, doubled up in this muddy half-grave, this disgusting underbelly of the war. So many men have died and I may not make it home, I realise it now. For this bloodshed to have had a point, you must live. Find Jack, or another who makes you happy. Find your pretty village and your house with a garden. Live well and live free, make sure this madness meant something. Please, do it for me and all the others here. Do it for those who will not return.

Yours always, Donovan.'

Ena folded the letter and returned it to the envelope.

Ivy

When Ivy heard the news about Donovan, she asked Olga if she would drive her back to Bournemouth on her next day off. When she arrived at Capstone Road, she took a deep breath before going into the house. Meta sat in the living room, holding a photograph of her younger son. Ivy sat beside her and reached for her hand. Meta turned empty eyes towards her and nodded slowly. 'You know.' Ivy nodded back and continued to hold Meta's hand. The telegram lay on the table in front of them.

'Deeply regret to inform you Service No: 208511 Bombardier Donovan Ernest Leaman Royal Field Artillery officially reported killed in action 5th June 1918.'

'Their 'deep regret' doesn't help, does it?' Meta's voice dripped with sadness and Ivy agreed it didn't. A cup of cold tea sat on the table and Ivy took it into the kitchen. Returning with a fresh one, she placed it in front of Meta. She heard the front door open and footsteps she recognised as Ena's. Ivy frowned when her niece didn't come into the living room. She walked to the door and saw Ena moving slowly up the stairs. 'Ena?' Her niece whirled around and Ivy gasped. Ena's usual rosy cheeks were sunken and dark lines sat beneath her red eyes. 'Come to me.' Ena almost fell in her desperation to reach her aunt's arms. Ivy held her and she sobbed. Later, Ena confided in Ivy about her feelings for Donovan, saying they had been writing to each other for some time. Ivy listened, as Ena had listened to her after Bertie died. United in grief, they mourned their loved ones.

At work the next day, Ivy was as busy as ever. Even as more positive news of victories on the Western Front started to arrive, the convoys kept coming. In addition to the usual horrific injuries, a doctor at Endell Street started to record increasing numbers of *'a most peculiar new disease'* spreading through patients and staff.

Vernon

Vernon wheeled his brother into the courtyard at Endell Street. A warm breeze blew across the yard and he turned Albert towards the sun. Albert stared straight ahead. Vernon considered himself one of the lucky ones. He was one of *Titanic*'s few survivors. When war broke out he signed up and his regiment was quickly dispatched to France. Four years later he had witnessed more horror than he wanted to remember, but he came home, alive and relatively unscathed. His mother said he was saved for some greater purpose and when they received word of Albert, Vernon knew what it was. His brother lost his legs, his sight and his soul during the war. Vernon turned towards a voice to his right. A nurse, helping yet another of the walking wounded out into the fresh air. She caught Vernon's eye and smiled. As they walked past she spoke. 'Isn't it a beautiful day?' Vernon nodded but his reply stuck in his throat. The woman's accent sounded familiar but he hadn't met her before. And her eyes. Where had he seen those piercing blue eyes before?

Chapter 35

Monday 11th November 1918
Ivy

The streets surrounding Endell Street thronged with war-weary people. They held their collective breath, not yet believing the news. When the Armistice was announced at 10.30 am, joy replaced grief. Strangers embraced, lovers kissed and the streets erupted. The war was over. Those not on duty were permitted to join the celebrations and Ivy hurried outside with Victoria. As hundreds of people cheered and danced in the streets, they could not have known their celebrations were helping a new, invisible enemy to spread among them. While they danced, the authorities blamed the deadly flu virus for the rows of funeral cortèges quietly making their way through the streets.

The following day, Ivy received a visitor at work. Squadron Leader George Scott-Smith, the man from the cocktail lounge at the Royal Albert Hall. He had sought her out, he said, now the war was over, hoping she would agree to have dinner with him. Ivy hesitated, but only briefly. Perhaps it was time for a new beginning.

*

Not long after the war ended, Ivy bought a flat in London. Endell Street was still open and she wanted to continue working there but live more comfortably. Ena said she was happy to stay in Bournemouth and started looking for a job there. Meta told Ivy she was delighted Ena would continue living with them. Ivy bought a small flat situated in a block on Garrick Street, not far from the hospital. The number of wounded soldiers started decreasing, but Endell Street faced a new problem. Instances of the '*most peculiar new disease*' spotted by one of the doctors towards the end of the war, increased rapidly. The doctors were mystified; the disease wasn't like anything they dealt with during the war. It wasn't typhoid, influenza or meningitis; patients had symptoms of all three diseases. Before long the illness started to affect Endell Street's staff.

At Ivy's first dinner with George, their conversation flowed and his endless stream of anecdotes reminded her how it felt to laugh. He was always punctual and immaculately dressed when he arrived to pick her up for evenings out, and he was a gentleman. Their whirlwind romance was followed by a proposal, which she accepted. People whose opinion she valued expressed concern. Olga, 'isn't it rather quick?' Victoria, 'what do you know about him?' And Ena, 'are you sure, Aunt Ivy?' She waved the questions away. they were in love, and yes, she wanted to marry Squadron Leader George Scott-Smith. She had never been impressed by someone's social standing or how well off they were. She was attracted to George because he was kind and caring. He told her he worked as a barrister before the war, and expected to be offered a position with one of the leading chambers in London. When she asked where he lived, he said his town house in Mayfair was closed up for much of the war and was now being redecorated. She asked where he was staying and he said his club had offered him some rooms for as long as he needed.

Their wedding was a quiet affair. George said his parents died when he was young and he was brought up by his grandfather who died soon after war was declared. Ivy reasoned she had a grand wedding when she married Bertie and if George had no-one to invite, a private ceremony would be preferable. They honeymooned in a luxurious hotel in Eastbourne. It was the first time George asked her to pay for something, explaining he had a temporary cashflow problem. In the first flush of new love, she agreed. He promised to repay her once he returned to work.

After the wedding, George said they should live in her Garrick Street flat until his house was habitable. Ivy agreed, finding nothing odd in his suggestion.

Their first argument came when Ivy said she wanted to continue working at Endell Street. George argued it was war work and now the war was over, she didn't need to carry on. Ivy stood her ground. She explained how important the work was and how much satisfaction she gained from helping wounded soldiers. 'I am an independent woman, George. I want to work and I'm earning money to support our household.' George glared at her and she jumped when he slammed out of the flat. His heavy footsteps thumped down the stairs. She watched from the window. He marched along the street, barging into people on the way. She watched until he turned the corner and disappeared. It was three days before he returned. During his absence, Ivy started to wonder if she had married in haste. She realised there were warning signs, things she should have heeded. Wherever they went, she never saw George pay for anything. In restaurants and theatres she watched him approach the *maître d* or the theatre manager. He knew them, he said. She asked herself if she should have been more curious.

Their arguments became more frequent and Ivy learnt her best form of defence was silence. George would sulk, sometimes for days, eventually agreeing to a 'truce'. Ivy was baffled, unable to question him for fear of another argument. In his rare moments of calm she saw the man she had believed George to be. During one of those moments, she told him they had received an invitation. It should have been a wonderful evening. Grace Opal, the friend Ivy first met when she worked as a scullery maid at Hampson Hall, wrote to say she and her husband Walter were going to be in town. She invited Ivy and George to join them at the theatre and for dinner afterwards. Ivy was delighted. She knew from Grace that Walter's father had sadly died the previous year. Walter, now Lord Hampson, inherited the estate, but Ivy didn't expect the title to have changed him. She wrote back by return of post, thanking Grace and accepting her kind invitation.

'Who are these people? How do you know them?'

Ivy was taken aback by George's reaction; she hadn't imagined he would object to her accepting Grace's invitation. Her husband's expression didn't change as she explained how she knew the couple. 'And what? They want us to join them at some ridiculous show?'

Ivy kept her voice level. 'Yes. They are dear friends of mine and I think it is very generous of them to have invited us.'

'Is he paying, seeing as he's a 'Lord?'

George's voice dripped with cynicism but Ivy refused to rise to the bait. She was learning how to deal with her husband's sudden mood swings.

'Let's just go and have a nice time.'

The evening was a disaster. From the moment she introduced George to Walter and Grace, her husband embarrassed himself. He embarrassed her too, as she tried to make excuses for him. When they were directed to Walter's box, in a prime position with excellent views of the stage, George sneered, saying he preferred to be in the stalls. 'You can soak up more of the atmosphere down there.' Like Ivy, Walter and Grace chose not to retort. In the absence of an argument, Ivy watched George fume quietly throughout the show. When Ivy tried to get his attention he looked away, like a petulant child. During the interval, George disappeared. Ivy and Grace went to the powder room and Ivy talked about anything other than her husband. As they re-applied their lipstick, Grace met Ivy's eyes in the mirror. 'Are you all right?' Ivy shook her head.

'I don't think he's good for you.'

Ivy bit her lip in an effort not to cry. 'People said it was too quick, that I didn't know him well enough. I think they were right.'

Grace took Ivy's hands. 'Why not come home with us tonight? Allow George to cool off?'

Ivy sniffed. The idea of being away from her jealous, controlling husband was tempting, but she knew it would make matters worse. 'Thank you Grace, but I think I should go home.'

Grace shook her head. 'I think you would be better staying away from him for a while, but all right. Remember the invitation is there, call me anytime and we'll send a car for you.' Ivy nodded and they returned to their seats. There was no sign of George. When Walter and Grace dropped Ivy off on Garrick Street, she saw a light on in her flat. During the journey Grace had repeated her invitation for Ivy to come home with them. Ivy refused. 'I'm very grateful Grace, but I'm not feeling too well. I think I may be coming down with a cold.' She had been suffering from a headache all evening but now it was accompanied by the shivers.

She smelt the whiskey as soon as she opened the door. George snarled and moved towards her. Spittle hit her face as he raged. She backed away and he moved closer again, hands clenched into fists. She didn't fight back, thinking he would calm down if she didn't argue with him. She was wrong. He reached for her but the whiskey made his aim poor. She managed to get away and ran to the bathroom. Shaking uncontrollably, she locked the door and slid down onto the floor. Her breath came in ragged gasps as he pounded on the door. She curled into a ball and lay on the floor, wondering what her husband was capable of. Wondering if she knew him at all. Eventually, she heard his footsteps receding, a cacophony of crashing and banging then her front door being yanked open. She stayed on the floor. When she was as confident as she could be that he had gone, she tried to stand up. She swayed on unsteady legs and leant against the wall before reaching for the lock. As quietly as she could, with trembling hands, she unlocked the door. She turned her back to the door and leant against it. When nothing happened, she opened the door a crack. She placed her foot on the threshold and peeked out. She looked all around before stepping slowly out of the bathroom. She ran to the telephone and called Grace. Her front door swung from its hinges, a fist-shaped hole in the middle. The last thing Ivy saw before she passed out was Walter and Grace running towards her.

Vernon

Vernon was delighted to learn he could take his brother home. The doctor at Endell Street apologised, saying they had done everything they could but it was unlikely Albert's condition would improve. She said no medical benefit could be gained by keeping him in hospital and the likelihood of infection from the new disease was far greater there. Vernon was advised to take him home and keep him as far away from other people as he could. He couldn't wait to tell his mother the good news. He had hoped to see the woman with the piercing blue eyes again but learnt she was away on her honeymoon. He didn't know her but found himself smiling at this news. Everyone deserved some happiness now the war was over. While he was at the hospital, Vernon sought out other soldiers who were suffering in the same way as his brother. He knew many of them were greeted with silence on their return from the front. There was little understanding of illnesses of the mind, and he watched brave warriors who were unable to continue fighting hang their heads in inexplicable shame. He talked to them as he would any other wounded soldier. When he wheeled Albert away, Victoria called after him. 'Don't be a stranger, there are men here who need you.' Vernon promised he would come back.

Ena

Ena watched her aunt, the woman who had saved her and loved her like a mother, struggling to breathe. She closed her eyes and prayed. She had lost Uncle Bertie and Donovan; she couldn't lose Aunt Ivy. She opened her eyes and looked around. The doctors, nurses and orderlies at Endell Street were facing this new enemy with their usual suffrage-minded efficiency. Just as they should have been able to rest and recover, they were working harder than ever. She lowered her head; she knew they were losing the fight against the waves of what was being called *'Spanish flu'*. It had already killed many of their younger staff. An image of a newspaper headline was etched into her mind. *'Nurses fall like ninepins.'* She pushed it away and turned to her aunt.

When she arrived at the hospital she was denied entry. A stern orderly at the gates informed her patients and staff were being kept isolated, to lessen the risk of spreading the deadly new disease. Ena said she understood, then pushed her shoulders back and asked to see Dr Murray. At first, the orderly refused, but once Ena explained who she was, and said she didn't intend to leave, the young woman relented. Ena hadn't met Flora Murray before, but when the doctor strode across the courtyard Ena recognised her from her aunt's description. Flora explained they needed to be meticulous about hygiene, but instructed the orderly to open the gates for Ena. Inside, Flora directed Ena towards a disinfecting hut in the courtyard. 'Staff are sent there to breathe in steamy vapor twice a day. You should do it now.' Ena followed Flora's instructions to the letter; she would have done anything to see her aunt. Inside the hospital, Flora told her patients with the flu were segregated on special wards, with screens placed around their beds. 'Doctors, nurses and orderlies wear face masks and gloves at all times.' Ena fastened the mask around her nose and mouth and pulled the gloves on. She thought of Donovan.

He had told her they were given rubber face masks and breathing equipment to protect them from the poisonous gas attacks. She shook herself; she couldn't think about Donovan now.

As they walked, Flora told Ena something of the Spanish flu. So called, she said, not because it originated in Spain but because, being neutral during the war, Spain hadn't censored its news. While people all over the world became ill and died from this new flu, countries involved in the war didn't report it. Spanish newspapers did write about the devastating disease killing people, hence the term 'Spanish flu'.

'What is flu, exactly?'

Flora talked as she walked. 'The symptoms are caused by a tiny virus, too small to see under an optical microscope. It is very difficult to detect this virus and therefore very difficult to diagnose flu as the disease.'

'I know my aunt had a fever, what are the other symptoms of flu?'

'As you have identified correctly, a sudden, very high fever is a key symptom. Patients often have one or more of a range of additional symptoms including a dry cough, head and body aches, sore throat, chills, runny nose, loss of appetite and fatigue.'

'How do you treat patients who have this flu?'

Flora stopped walking and looked at Ena. 'I'm sorry to tell you there is no real treatment. We give patients aspirin, morphine and quinine to suppress the symptoms, fluids and nourishment to keep their strength up and prevent dehydration, alongside bedrest and careful nursing in the hope they will beat it themselves. We have to hope and pray your aunt's fever breaks and she survives.'

Ena stared at Flora. 'Some people are surviving it?'

The doctor nodded her head. 'Yes, but many more are not. Some of those coming through the fever are older people who would have been exposed to flu strains more closely related to this one, offering them some immunity.'

'What about prevention methods?'

'You used the disinfecting hut in the courtyard and you know about face masks and gloves. We are also trying to isolate people wherever possible and ensure our staff stay away from crowds. You will see instructions all around the hospital for washing your hands, thoroughly and often. Please make sure you do.'

Ena nodded her head and said of course, she would. She looked at Flora. The doctor was calm and professional in the face of adversity, whilst displaying compassion for her patients. Ena understood why her aunt held the doctor in such high regard. Suddenly Flora stopped. 'Your aunt is in here. I must warn you Ena, she is very unwell.' Ena took a deep breath when Flora used her elbow to push open the door to the isolation ward. Flora led her towards her aunt and behind her face mask, Ena gasped. She held back momentarily then walked towards the bed. Her aunt, always tall and elegant, looked frail under the starched hospital bedding.

Flora positioned a small, metal chair a distance away from the bed and gestured for Ena to sit. 'I know you will want to, but you must not touch your aunt. The risk of infection is too great, for both of you. Do you understand?' Ena nodded. 'If I talk to her, will she hear me?' Flora looked at Ivy then turned back to Ena. 'There is no solid scientific evidence to prove or disprove the theory.' Ena met Flora's eyes. 'What would you do, if this was someone you loved?' Flora didn't hesitate. 'I would talk to her, about anything and everything.'

Once Flora left, Ena sat down. She looked at her aunt and talked. She started at the beginning, her life in Gateshead with her grandmother, her aunt and her mother. As she talked, she imagined her words permeating her aunt's mind and pulling her back to consciousness.

Ivy

When Ivy opened her eyes, the first person she saw was Ena. Her niece was sitting next to her hospital bed, wearing a protective face mask and gloves. Ivy didn't know what day it was or how long she had been in hospital. She opened her mouth to speak but her lips were dry. Ena looked up, her eyes shining with tears above the face mask. Ivy remembered those eyes. When she found Ena in Gateshead, emaciated and bruised from her brutal life with Lizzie, her eyes still shone with love. She marvelled at her niece's capacity for survival.

'I'm not allowed to hug you or hold your hand in case you're still infectious, but I can't tell you how happy I am to be able to talk to you! Would you like some water?'

Ivy nodded.

When Flora examined Ivy, she said the fever had broken but she wanted to keep her under observation for a few more days, until she was strong enough to stand unaided. 'Ena, you need to go home now and prepare for your aunt's return. She will need bed rest and care. Do you understand?'

Ena nodded and was about to ask Flora something when Ivy spoke.

'Home where?'

Ena looked at her aunt, the woman who gave her a safe, loving home. Both the Primavesis and the Leamans had said they could stay with them. 'Home in Bournemouth.' It wasn't a question. Ivy nodded before falling asleep again. On the day Flora declared Ivy could leave, Grace was waiting outside the gates of the hospital. She had spoken to Ena and arranged for Walter's driver to take them back to Bournemouth. Ivy, clear of infection, embraced her friend. 'Thank you for rescuing me. Without you and Walter, I wouldn't be here.'

Grace waved Ivy's thanks away. 'I'm just pleased you're going to be all right. So many people are succumbing to this awful illness. Oh, Walter had a new front door and lock fitted on your flat. Here's the key.'

Ivy's hand shook as she took the key. 'Did he see George?'

Grace shook her head. 'He's probably hiding at his club with his tail between his legs. If you tell me which one it is, Walter will visit him and tell him to stay away.'

Ivy went cold; she had never asked George the name of his club. Was it because she trusted him or because she suspected the club didn't exist? There was another explanation, one she hadn't wanted to face. A man who went missing for days and returned reeking of cheap perfume. George had a mistress. She mumbled. 'I don't know.' She bowed her head and turned away; she had allowed herself to be taken for a fool. 'Oh Grace, I've made a terrible mistake.'

'Well, I don't imagine he'll come back. But you know you must leave him, don't you?'

Ivy didn't reply. As Walter's driver held the car door open for her, Victoria called out from the courtyard. 'Ivy! I forgot to tell you; a man came here looking for you. He left his address in case you wanted to look him up.'

Ivy hesitated, alert now to the possibility of people not being who they said they were. 'What was his name, this man?'

Victoria unfolded the piece of paper, saying Ivy would probably remember him. 'It was the man who came to visit his brother. He looked after him and was compassionate and understanding towards lots of our injured soldiers, particularly those other visitors don't choose to talk to. Here you are. Vernon Revill of 5, North Road, Highgate.'

Ivy shook her head. 'I don't know him. Why did he want to see me?'

Victoria shrugged and handed Ivy the piece of paper. 'I don't know.'

Reluctantly, Ivy took Vernon's details. She folded the paper and dropped it into her handbag. Ena helped her into the car. 'Come on, let's go home.' Ivy closed her eyes as she was driven away from Endell Street, all thoughts of the war, the Spanish flu, George Scott-Smith and the stranger Vernon Revill, forgotten.

Chapter 36

Ena

Once her aunt was settled at Lansdowne Road with Bertie's mother and sisters looking after her, Ena went to see Rachel. Her friend was in the living room making notes on pages of music and she looked up when Ena came in. 'I am so pleased to see you. How is your aunt?'

Ena smiled. 'Thankfully, she is getting better. She hasn't made a full recovery yet but things are heading in the right direction.'

Rachel moved to sit next to her friend. 'I've read about the Spanish flu. Your aunt was lucky to survive, it's killing people in droves. Some say more people than the war.'

Ena nodded. 'I know. I don't know what I would have done if she hadn't survived.'

'And what about this husband of hers?'

Ena made a face. 'I never liked him and I didn't trust him. I couldn't bear to be in the same room as him.'

'Why not?'

'I'm convinced he only married Aunt Ivy for her money. When they got married it was nothing like Aunt Ivy's wedding to Uncle Bertie. George arranged it and didn't invite anyone.'

'Why do you think your aunt went along with it?'

Ena shrugged. 'I don't know. I saw him once when I visited her. He was in the entrance hall of the building, flirting with one of the lift attendants. She pushed him away but his hands were all over her.'

Rachel gasped. 'Did you tell your aunt?'

Ena shook her head. 'No, and now I wish I had. Things might have turned out differently.'

'It's not your fault. It sounds as though he was a complete cad.'

Ena nodded. 'He was, and Aunt Ivy deserves better.'

'Well, he's gone now and your aunt is better off without him.'

'Yes. She can recover here without anything to worry about.'

'What will you do Ena, now the war is over?'

'I've enjoyed doing the book-keeping at the community hall and I would like to find a similar job, something with numbers.'

'Numbers rather than words?'

'I'll keep writing stories but I want to start earning my own money.'

'Will you stay here?'

'Yes. I'm going to ask Walter if he knows any local solicitors who need someone with book-keeping experience. How about you?' Ena saw a gentle blush form across her friend's face. 'What?'

Rachel looked down and when she raised her eyes, Ena saw tears.

Ena took Rachel's hands. 'What is it?'

'I'm sorry, it's just…'

'What? You know you can tell me anything, don't you?'

Rachel nodded. 'It's William.'

Ena held her breath, how much more bad news could they take? 'William?'

Rachel nodded again. 'I didn't know how to tell you, but he's asked me to marry him.'

Ena jumped up, pulling Rachel with her. 'That's the best news I've heard in years! Why are you upset?'

Rachel squeezed Ena's hands. 'You've lost so many people, Ena. It didn't seem right I should find happiness with William.'

Ena shook her head. 'No. We've all lost people, we've all suffered. You have to grab this happiness and live. Do you hear me?'

Rachel nodded.

Ivy

It took all the strength Ivy could muster to get out of bed in the morning and get washed and dressed. Her appetite had disappeared and she spent her days reclining in a chair, staring at Catherine Primavesi's back garden. Every bone in her body ached and fatigue rendered her incapable of anything constructive. She picked up a newspaper but one glance at the headlines, *'New plague devastates hospitals'* and *'Disease crept in like a thief in the night'* set her recovery back by weeks. Grief found every corner of her existence. She grieved for Bertie, for her sham of a marriage to George and for her children who would never be. She survived the deadly wave of Spanish flu, only to be told by Dr Anderson she lost another baby in the process. She hadn't even known she was pregnant. Louisa spoke to her in confidence. With her experience in gynaecological surgery, she said Ivy's miscarriages could be due to the neck of her womb being weak.

'In this scenario, at three or four months, the baby gets too heavy for you to carry. There is a technique called a cervical cerclage which might help. I would make a large stitch at the neck of the womb, when you are about 12 weeks pregnant. Perhaps consider it when you feel better.'

Now, alone with her sorrow, Ivy wept. Over the coming months she cried less, and with the loving care of Ena and Bertie's mother and sisters, she started to recover. One day, as summer was tentatively making an appearance in the garden, Ena suggested they should have a picnic. 'We could invite the Leamans and your friends from London, what do you say?'

Ivy smiled. This young woman was part of the reason she survived; she was sure of it. 'Why not? It sounds as though you already have it all worked out.'

Ena beamed. She immediately sent out invitations for 'Aunt Ivy's Summer Picnic' to the people on her list. Between her and

Rachel, Ma Leaman, Mrs Primavesi and her daughters, they set out the best table they could, although many food items were still rationed. On the day of the picnic the sun shone gently as the friends gathered, minus some who would never be forgotten. Meta, angry now, talked about her sons. She said she wouldn't allow Donovan's photograph to become faded, she would care for it and keep his memory alive. She would make sure people knew who he was. She pointed towards Cyril. 'Look at him. He's home but he's not here. He screams in the night about gas, barbed wire and fighting. He is a shadow of himself. Do you know what my boys were? Cannon fodder. And look at their father.' The women turned towards Edwin Leaman. His grey moustache, grey hair and grey eyes. He wore his sadness like a coat. Rachel touched her mother's arm and Meta tucked her grief back inside her heart. Walter and Grace were there, along with Olga and Victoria from Endell Street. Uncle Bertie's brother Leo, recently home after his service in the Air Force, and their father, Giulio. The men gravitated towards each other, with Walter, Leo and Cyril joining Edwin and Giulio. Ivy watched Ena stop as she walked past the men's table. She stood there for a while then pulled Leo up and marched him across to her.

'Leo, you must tell Aunt Ivy what you said about her husband.'

Bertie's brother shuffled his feet and looked down. Ena prodded him. 'It's important.'

Leo looked up and Ivy sighed. He was the image of Bertie and her loss stabbed at her heart.

'Well, this fellow George.'

'Yes?' Ivy didn't know what was coming but thought it couldn't be worse than anything she had imagined about her missing husband.

'He's not who he says he is.'

Ivy raised her eyebrows. 'Who is he exactly? And how do you know?'

Leo sighed. 'I'm so sorry to tell you this, but the man you know as Squadron Leader George Scott-Smith is the lowest ranked Warrant Officer in the RAF. I met him, well, we were warned to stay away from him.'

Ivy stared, not understanding what Leo was telling her. 'Why?'

'Because he's a con man, a gambler and a fraud. He tried to borrow money from anyone he could start a conversation with. I'm so sorry you had the misfortune to cross his path.'

Ivy absorbed Leo's words. She hadn't crossed George's path; he had walked into hers.

Leo sat down beside her. 'Did you ever meet his family?'

Ivy shook her head. 'He said his parents died when he was young and he was brought up by his grandfather who died soon after war was declared.'

'Very convenient. What else did he say?'

'He said his grandfather was a magistrate. And after the war he would return to work as a barrister.'

Grace spoke from across the table and Ivy looked at her friend. 'I'm sorry my dear, when George disappeared, Walter hired a private detective to look into his life. There is no record of him practising law in England. Walter asked his colleagues in the legal profession to check and no trace of him was found, anywhere.'

Ivy's voice shook. 'How could I have been so foolish?'

'The war. The war made fools of us all.' All eyes turned towards Cyril, who spoke little these days. Rachel asked her brother to continue. 'We've all seen so much death and destruction. I can understand anyone grasping at anything looking remotely like happiness. But you are not responsible for that man's despicable behaviour Ivy, it is not your fault.' Ivy looked around. Everyone nodded, agreeing with Cyril, and Ivy started to believe they were right. Later, when they were alone, Ivy spoke to Walter and Grace. 'I want to divorce him, Walter. Can you help me?'

Walter swirled the whiskey in his glass. 'You have very good grounds, adultery and abandonment. However, it is very difficult for women to divorce their husbands.'

'Why shouldn't a woman be able to rid herself of a cruel man?'

Walter nodded. 'I agree you should be able to, but at the moment it wouldn't be straightforward. Particularly because George is nowhere to be found. I also think you need to concentrate on your recovery.' Before Ivy could speak, he continued. 'You know better than many of us how quickly things are changing with the suffrage movement, so why not wait? Who knows, in a few years, it might be possible. Once it is, I'll make sure you have the best legal team money can buy!'

Ivy smiled at her friends. 'You're right.' She surprised herself by laughing. 'It's not as though I'm in any hurry to get married again, is it?' When she went to bed, she removed the wedding ring George gave her and placed it in her bedside drawer. She picked up Bertie's photograph and kissed it. 'Goodnight, my love. I miss you.'

Ena

At the picnic, Ena asked Walter if he knew any local solicitors who needed someone with book-keeping experience. He suggested a few firms for her to write to. One of them, Reeves Solicitors on Richmond Hill, replied by return of post and invited her for an interview. She found them very welcoming and thought they must have liked her, because they offered her a job, to start immediately. The family firm was run by two of the Reeves brothers before the war; it was now run by one of their sisters, Alice. She told Ena she decided to take the business on following the tragic events that took her brothers' lives, and the passing of the 1919 Sex Disqualification (Removal) Act. Ena asked about the legislation and Alice explained.

'I had already received my LLB (Bachelor of Laws) from the University of London, but I couldn't qualify as a solicitor until the law was changed. The law ensures women's entry into the legal professions, and stipulates women will receive their degrees from universities on completion of study. It also allows women to act on juries and as magistrates.'

'About time!' Ena put her hand to her mouth. She was thinking the words but hadn't intended to say them out loud. She started to apologise but Alice laughed. 'I think you will fit in very well around here, Ena!'

On her way back to Capstone Road, Ena took a detour. Now Aunt Ivy was almost fully recovered, she expected her to return to London before long. Meta was happy having Ena to stay but she wanted a place of her own. She had learnt there were vacancies at a block of flats on Littledown Road and hoped to find the manager and introduce herself. Having secured a job and a flat, Ena fell into a satisfying routine. On her days off she and Rachel met up. Sometimes they walked to the beach and sat in their favourite spot on the sand, looking out to sea. Sometimes they packed a picnic lunch and went cycling in the New Forest. They shared news of their days; Ena's job and life on Littledown Road and Rachel's continuing musical journey and plans for her wedding to William. Rachel hadn't given up hope of being the next Arabella Goddard but more importantly, she had persuaded Cyril to start playing his violin again.

Chapter 37

Ena

Ena continued to visit the library. One Saturday, she stepped over the threshold and took her usual deep breath. Before she could breathe out Miss Quick was in front of her, propelling her to the newsroom.

'You must read this article, Ena.'

Ena laughed. 'All right. What is it about?'

Miss Quick pushed her down into a chair and pointed at the newspaper spread out on the table. 'It's about where you are from. Gateshead. Isn't it?'

Ena stared. The headline sent her back in time. *'Gateshead football team lost in deadly Western Front battle.'* The article provided background information about the working-class town in the North East of England, where the soldiers who died made up the local football team. Like the communities who lost whole streets of men who signed up together, Gateshead lost its footballers. The words blurred in front of Ena's eyes as she read about the harrowing battle the poor men faced. The article said just one man from the team survived. Ena traced the name with her finger. Jack Todd. Her breath came in quick bursts as she learnt the fate of Jack's friends. She could hear Miss Quick's voice but not her words. Something tugged at her. She blinked hard and looked at Jack's name in the newspaper. A connection. Not with where she lived; Pipewellgate was never home. With him. He was pulling her back. She stood up and pushed the chair away.

'I'm sorry Miss Quick, I have to go.'

Ena ran to Capstone Road. Rachel looked up when Ena shouted her name.

'Whatever is it?'

Ena struggled to catch her breath. Rachel manoeuvred her into a chair and waited.

'I need to go back to Gateshead.'

Rachel arched her eyebrows.

'What? Why? What about your job and your flat?'

'None of that matters now. I need to go back.'

'Wasn't your life awful there?'

'Yes, but there's someone I need to look for.'

Rachel's eyes were wide. 'Who?'

'A boy I used to know. Jack Todd.'

Ena told Rachel about the newspaper article, saying Jack was one of only two friends she had before coming to Bournemouth. 'He helped to save me, Rachel. I have to go back; however painful the memories are.' In her flat later, she re-read Donovan's letters. He encouraged her to live. To find Jack, or someone else who made her happy. To find the pretty village she dreamt of and her house with a garden. He told her to live well and live free, to make sure there was a point to the madness of the war. He said to do it for him and for those who would not return. She started packing.

Vernon

The man in the wheelchair laughed when Vernon moved his face into the sunshine. 'Is that better, soldier?' The man laughed again and waved a useless, damaged arm towards the sun. Vernon started coming to Endell Street a few times a week after his brother died. He wanted to make himself useful and he knew some of the men had no other visitors. He and his mother cared for Albert in the best way they could, but the war had already taken him from them. One night Albert went to sleep and didn't wake up. On his first visit to Endell Street after Albert died, he left his name and address with one of the VADs, to be passed on to the woman with the piercing blue eyes. He wasn't sure why, but something about her nagged at him. He hoped she would call at the house but she hadn't. Sitting with the man in the courtyard, he considered his future, wondering if it was time to go back to sea. As a Merchant Seaman with the Royal Navy, he was proud to have made a valuable contribution to the war. But before the war, he enjoyed his job as a ship's steward. His last voyage before the war changed that. He survived being on board *Titanic* but saw things no man should ever see. Back home, Vernon opened his bedside drawer and pulled out a newspaper article. He had read Harold Bride's account of events so many times, he knew the junior wireless operator's words by heart.

'Before I was rescued, I stared out at the water from the overturned raft. I saw the body of my friend, Jack Philips, clinging to debris from the sunken ship. I learnt later he died from exposure. People should know he stayed on board and continued to send passenger messages for as long as he possibly could, risking his own life in doing so. After being rescued and boarding the Carpathia, I was sent to the hospital wing because both of my feet were broken. I was there for ten hours, then I heard the wireless operators in the communication room were having problems. They were overwhelmed by the frantic and traumatising messages going back and forth. I offered to help. On crutches and with the help of a nurse, I hobbled up to the communication room, sat in a chair, and did not stop working until we reached the shore. The press didn't waste any time trying to make headlines. They were constantly sending messages to the Carpathia, asking for anything they could print in their papers. I ignored them and continued to send messages on behalf of the surviving families on board Titanic. When I was safely able to walk on land in New York City, I gave my testimony to a reporter from The New York Times. At the end of my story, I explained I still had over 100 messages left to send from the survivors. I wanted nothing more than to keep working, but the ambulance was insisting on taking me to a hospital. I apologise to those families.'

Vernon returned the article to his bedside drawer. He placed it on top of two letters. Letters from someone else who survived being on board *Titanic*. Letters from a woman with the same piercing blue eyes as the woman at Endell Street.

Ivy

Ivy stared at her new front door. She felt the weight of the shiny new key in her hand. She took a deep breath and unlocked the door. Her lip trembled when she called his name. 'George?' Her voice echoed around the empty room. She locked the door and tried the handle then turned around and leant against the door. She kicked off her shoes and walked around her Garrick Street flat, touching walls and furniture, reminding herself how it felt to be safe. Grace had arranged for the flat to be cleaned in Ivy's absence and had stocked her larder, ready for her return. Ivy chased the ghost of George away during her time in Bournemouth and now she intended to start living again. She slept like a baby. The next day, she visited the hairdresser. When she left the salon, her auburn curls were tamed into a short, fashionable style. She went to Selfridges and bought new shoes, gloves, a hat and a handbag.

Back home, she started ridding the flat of every trace of George. She emptied drawers, cupboards and bags. She collected anything with any sort of connection to him and disposed of it. She wished she could dispose of him, once and for all, but she knew Walter had given her good advice. She could wait. But in the meantime she was going to enjoy life. As she transferred items from her old handbag to the new, dark green leather one she bought in Selfridges, she stopped. It was the piece of paper Victoria gave her when she was discharged from Endell Street. She unfolded the small note. Vernon Revill of 5, North Road, Highgate. She frowned. She was sure she didn't know this man, why did he leave his name and address for her? Was he another conman? Another Squadron Leader George Scott-Smith? She stared at the note for a long time before folding it again and slipping it into her new handbag.

The following week, Ivy went to Endell Street to see Victoria. Walking through Hyde Park, Victoria asked her if she had ever contacted the man who left his address for her. Ivy shook her head. 'No. I have no idea who he is and I don't want to risk meeting another George!' Victoria laughed. 'I think you're safe with Vernon, Ivy. I'm convinced he's the only thing keeping some of our poor chaps alive. He has endless patience and spends hours wheeling them around, talking to the worst of them, men who get no other visitors, men who can't reply. He's the bright light in an otherwise incredibly dark place for those men.'

Later, Ivy mulled over her conversation with Victoria. Vernon sounded harmless enough and she trusted her friend's opinion. She decided. Tomorrow she would go to North Road in Highgate and see what Mr Vernon Revill wanted with her. The next day, she lost her nerve. What was she doing, thinking about visiting a complete stranger? Hadn't she learnt her lesson with George? Why hadn't she asked Victoria to come with her? She shook herself; Victoria painted a very favourable picture of Vernon and if she didn't do this now, she never would.

A little later, she raised her hand and knocked on the door of number 5, North Road. She heard a man shout from inside. 'I'll get it, mother', then the door opened. Ivy and Vernon stared at each other. She didn't remember him and she stepped back, thinking she should leave. He continued to stare and she turned to walk away.

'No, don't go. Please don't go.'

Ivy turned back. 'Who are you? Why did you leave your address with Victoria and ask her to give it to me?'

Vernon nodded and raised his hands. 'I know, it must seem very strange considering we don't know each other.'

Ivy waited. Vernon continued. 'It's just, I think we might know someone in common.'

Ivy raised her eyebrows. 'Who might that be?'

Vernon opened the door and stood to one side. 'Please, would you come in? I need to show you something.'

Against her better judgement, Ivy walked past Vernon into the house. Vernon was the epitome of good manners; he asked Ivy to sit down and offered to make her a cup of tea. He introduced her to his mother, Irene, whom Ivy saw carried the all-too-familiar look of loss. Ivy sipped her tea. Suddenly, Vernon stood up. 'I'll go and get the letters.' Ivy's hands shook as she tried to put her cup and saucer down without spilling her tea. 'What letters?' But Vernon had left the room. Irene smiled at Ivy as they waited for him to return. The letters were yellowed with time and Vernon handled them with the utmost care. 'I met her on RMS *Titanic*. It was your eyes. You and she, you have the same eyes.' Vernon held a letter out towards Ivy and the room swayed as she took it. It was dated the 1st of May, 1912.

'*Dear Vernon,*

Thank you again for your help on that darkest of nights. Seeing you on the Carpathia was the sweetest moment in the middle of a nightmare. I do hope you made it safely back home and found your mother in good health. I am writing this letter from the Paradise Theatre on Broadway in New York City. This was mine and Peggy's intended destination and my heart breaks to be here without her. We had such plans! Marv (the director) and the rest of the production company are finding it difficult without our star, and I suspect the show will not run for long. Then, who knows? I may come back to London. I cannot think of that awful night without seeing Bella's face. I hope I did the best I could for her, although I'll never know. I see the faces, the grotesque grey faces in the water, in my dreams. I hope you are faring better and I thank you again for your kindness.

Your friend, Miss Mona Leighton.'

Ivy looked up. She had so many questions but before she could speak, her tears started. Irene handed her a handkerchief. When her sobs subsided, Vernon spoke. 'Who is she to you?' Ivy smiled. 'She's my younger sister.' Then she shouted. 'My sister is alive!' She turned to Vernon. 'You said letters. Plural.' Vernon nodded. 'Yes, she sent me two letters. Here's the other one.' Ivy took the second letter and started to read. This one was dated the 26th of September 1913.

'*Dear Vernon,*

I hope this letter finds you and your mother well. I wanted to write again to let you know I decided to continue with the journey Peggy and I talked about, albeit on my own. Peggy had heard about a theatre in Australia, called the Tivoli. She was very keen to go. Now I am here, I feel so far away but perhaps I will make this my new home. The sun is shining anyway. Vernon, I hope this does not trouble you but I feel the need to set down my recollections of that night, to someone who was there and will hopefully understand. If my words upset you, please rip this letter up and throw it away.'

Ivy stopped reading and looked at Vernon. He nodded. 'It was something I hadn't wanted to think about, but it helped me, reading her words.' Ivy returned to her sister's letter.

'*I remember the quiet, as if the disaster had silenced the rest of the world. I watched a thin blue line in the sky. It looked as though an artist had painted a line between the clouds. How could the line remain so serene amidst the chaos below? I tried to concentrate on the blue line then I tried to rouse Bella but she had lost consciousness. Someone shouted we should go back and look for people in the water, but the officer in charge was fearful the boat would be swamped. We didn't go back. You may remember the day you took me to the gift shop and I asked you about steerage conditions on Titanic. You must have wondered at the reason for my question. Suffice to say, I felt it was where I truly belonged, not in first-class. In the lifeboat with Bella, I pictured the fiddle players and the dancing and I prayed*' *for the people in that part of the ship. I knew they were the least likely to have made it to safety.*

At night, when I lie down to try and sleep, I cannot shift from my mind the sound of people drowning. Their gasps and screams. Then silence. I see the yellow carnations, given to men boarding at Southampton, hundreds of them, floating on the icy ocean. After hours of horror, I imagined a moment of calm. The ocean was a patchwork of ice, some small like stepping stones, others monstrous and deadly. The night was still, apart from our frozen breath and muted voices. I stroked Bella's hair, thinking how angry she would be that it was matted with filth and debris. Eventually, the sun climbed above the slate-flat sea and streaked the sky with rose. Carpathia came and I heard one lifeboat had gone back but it was too late for those in the water. And then I saw your friendly face but Bella was gone and I could do nothing to help her. I heard 706 were saved and 1534 perished that night, many of them poor souls trapped in steerage.'

The letter ended there. Ivy fired questions at Vernon. 'There is no signature, why didn't she sign it? Did she come to London? Who is Bella? Where is my sister now?' Vernon shook his head. 'I'm so sorry. That's all I know.'

Back at Garrick Street, Ivy paced back and forth. Vernon had given her the letters and she read them, over and over again. She knew her sister survived *Titanic* but little more. She didn't know where she was now. After a sleepless night, Ivy called Grace. She told her about Vernon and the letters from Mona and said she didn't know what to do. Grace arrived within the hour and Ivy showed her the letters. Grace shook her head. 'Well at least you know she's still alive.' Ivy sighed. 'Only that she was alive in 1913, eight years ago. Anything could have happened to her since then.' Grace nodded. Before she left, Grace said she would ask Walter to see if his private detective could discover Mona's whereabouts. 'You never know; he found her once before in New York City!' Ivy laughed sadly. 'Yes, and by the time we got there, she'd gone again!' Grace moved towards the door then turned back. She pulled a newspaper from her handbag and gave it to Ivy. 'It's the latest edition of 'The Stage'. I thought you might be ready to go back to work, darling.'

After Grace had gone, Ivy flicked through the newspaper. Was she ready to go back to performing? She wasn't sure but turned the pages anyway. She hadn't read the weekly newspaper for years, and after a while she started looking at the articles with more interest. The publication contained news, reviews, features and recruitment advertising, directed at people working in the theatre and other performing arts. As she read, she started to think Grace was right and she should look for something suitable. She licked her finger to turn the next page then stopped. She went cold when a name jumped out at her. Mona Leighton. There was a section in the newspaper called 'The Letter Box'. Theatrical performers could ask for their name to be listed as looking for work and send a stamped, addressed envelope to the address provided. Letters about opportunities would then be sent to them. Ivy picked up the telephone to call Grace. Perhaps with this information, Walter's private detective would be able to track Mona down.

Mona

Mona left the theatre by the stage door. She sauntered along the street, thinking the audition had gone well. She hoped to be offered the part but if not, thought she would leave London and go back to working in repertory theatre, perhaps in a pretty sea-side town. She was growing tired of city life. She became aware of footsteps close behind and quickened her step. It was like New York City all over again, when she had been watched and followed by a private detective. Suddenly, she stopped. She was older now and after everything she had been through, she refused to be intimidated. She turned and faced the man.

'What do you want?'

'Miss Mona Leighton?'

'Who wants to know?'

The man looked at the piece of paper in his hand. 'Your sister, Ivy.'

Ivy

Ivy wasn't surprised by Ena's reaction when she told her about Mona. Mona had let Ena down throughout her life and Ivy didn't expect her niece to welcome her with open arms. But when she told Vernon the news, he was delighted. Ivy asked if they could meet at his house for their reunion. Vernon hesitated; he thought the sisters should be alone for their first meeting. Ivy insisted, saying it was because of him Mona had been found.

When Ivy arrived at North Road on the day of the reunion, Vernon was waiting at the door. He ushered her inside, saying his mother was making tea and sandwiches. Ivy smiled, there was something comforting about the Revill's family life. She bit her lip, remembering the last time she waited for Mona, in the Lyons Cafe on Shaftesbury Avenue. She was convinced her sister wouldn't turn up.

'She'll be here.' It was as if Vernon had read her mind. Ivy heard a knock on the front door and she ran. Her sister stood on the doorstep; older, thinner, but still her sister. Mona's soft brown curls had been straightened and cut into a short, sleek style. Ivy noticed Mona's eyes. They still shone brightly with the same piercing blue as her own, but dark shadows told Ivy her sister had suffered in the time they were apart. Mona smiled and Ivy pulled her inside. The sisters embraced as if they never wanted to let each other go. Vernon appeared in the doorway to the living room and Mona started to cry. Ivy watched them take each other's hands. She could only imagine the horrors they had endured on *Titanic* but she would be forever grateful they both survived. Ivy asked Mona when she had returned to London and there it was, her sister's mask.

'I'm not sure, a few years ago.'

'And where are you living?'

'Oh you know, here and there.'

Ivy laughed, thinking her sister would always live her life 'here and there'.

'I did a pantomime at the women's war hospital, what's it called?'

Ivy stared; something tugged at her memory. 'Endell Street. When were you there?'

Mona tutted. 'Oh I don't know, Ivy. A few years ago. It was during the war.'

Ivy remembered. 'I heard you. I saw you, well the flash of your dress. Elizabeth Robins invited you, didn't she?'

Mona's mouth fell open. 'Yes, how did you…?'

Ivy explained her connection to Endell Street then Vernon told Mona about his brother. Ivy shook her head. 'To think, we could have all been there at the same time. This reunion could have happened years ago.'

It was dark by the time Ivy and Mona left North Road. They had told each other their stories; everything that had happened, good and bad, over the last nine years. Mona took Ivy's arm as they walked. 'Let's not be apart for that long ever again.' Ivy nodded, wondering how long it would be before her sister disappeared.

Chapter 38

1922
Ena

Ena stepped off the train at Newcastle Central Station. The cold air caught the back of her throat and she shivered. She pulled her coat tighter and walked out of the station, turning in the direction of the Swing Bridge. She stood at the Newcastle side of the bridge. The day she and Nancy planned to run away, they arranged to meet where Ena was standing now. Nancy didn't turn up. Ena shook her head, it was a pointless plan, to go to London and find her mother. Over the years her mother had proved she didn't always want to be found. Their recent reunion was a disappointment. Mona asked Ena how she was and what she was doing with her life, but Ena watched her fidget and look out of the window. It was like having a conversation with a stranger. They parted with no promise to meet up again. Ena knew Aunt Ivy was delighted to have her sister back in her life, but she wondered how long it would last. Mona stayed in London and Ena knew she and Aunt Ivy met up a number of times. But Ena was counting the days until her mother disappeared again. She found it easier to accept her mother would never be part of her life. She sighed and walked across the bridge to Gateshead. On the other side of the river, she saw the Fry's Cocoa sign. She smiled, the smell of cocoa always reminded her of her grandmother, now it reminded her of Ma Leaman too.

She headed towards Pipewellgate, where she lived with Lizzie. She tutted. She hadn't lived there, she existed. But she survived. And she was returning without hatred or anger. The war years had proved they all needed to live while they could. She squinted at the familiar skyline; something was different. The dark bulk of the workhouse had always hidden everything beyond, but now the long rows of terraced streets were clearly visible. She could see the streets because the workhouse was gone. She passed the Globe Hotel. Lizzie spent more time in there than at home, drinking herself into a stupor and mixing with the worst men of the area. Ena waited outside the Globe in all weathers; freezing, starving and longing to be part of a loving home. Broken shutters covered the windows and Ena looked around, expecting to see Lizzie slouched outside the rundown watering-hole. She glanced over the road to South Street Infants School. On her first day, her threadbare dress set her apart. Lizzie refused to buy her new shoes. Instead, she cut holes in Ena's old shoes; her toes stuck out at the front and her feet were permanently freezing. She tried to ignore the taunts from other children and her gnawing hunger pains at dinner time. The good thing about school was meeting Nancy and Jack. Without them, she wouldn't have survived. She stopped walking, her feet had brought her to Jack's uncle's house on Cross Street. She didn't know if Jack still lived there but she knocked and waited, her heart thumping against her ribcage.

Jack opened the door and the years fell away. Ena looked at the handsome young man her childhood friend had become. Tall and muscular, Jack's familiar smile spread across his face and his eyes sparkled when he shouted to his uncle John. 'You'll never guess who's here!' Jack held the door open and Ena stepped inside. Jack's uncle was exactly how she remembered, only older. He repeated his story about Ena's grandmother pushing her around in her pram. 'She was proper proud of you, pet.' His words warmed Ena, knowing early in her life she was loved and wanted. Ena told them everything that had happened to her aunt and said her mother, like a will-o'-the-wisp, appeared in London after surviving RMS *Titanic*. John laughed, 'your ma, she'll outlive aal of us!' The men said they understood why Ena changed her name and Jack's uncle reached for her hand.

'Divvent blame ye, pet.' She talked about her experience of the war, losing Uncle Bertie and Donovan. Jack said nothing about his experience and she didn't ask.

'What about Lizzie? Do you know where she is?' Jack and his uncle exchanged a glance and Ena steeled herself for bad news, she expected Lizzie to have drunk herself to death by now.

'She's at Cobden Terrace.'

Ena stared. 'And how is she?'

Jack stood up. 'Howay.'

Ena pulled her coat on and followed Jack outside. When she reached him, their eyes met and he smiled. Jack stopped outside the first house on Cobden Terrace. Ena raised her eyebrows; it was a distinct improvement on Pipewellgate. Jack knocked and they waited. Ena heard shuffling and keys rattling then the door opened a fraction.

'Whe are ye?'

Ena stared at the old woman. Jack moved closer to the door and shouted. 'It's Jack Todd, John's nephew.'

'Whe's behind ye?'

Jack turned and Ena gave a quick nod of her head. 'It's all right, Jack.' He stepped back and for the first time in ten years, Ena faced Lizzie. The woman's rheumy eyes narrowed. 'Whe are ye?' Ena knew her new name would mean nothing to Lizzie. 'It's me, Evie Brown.' Ena shuddered at the sound of her old name. The woman shuffled forward, her back hunched, and peered at her. 'Na, divvent knaa ye.' Jack started speaking but Ena stopped him. She shook her head. She looked at Lizzie. Her cheek bones, visible beneath yellowing, paper-thin skin and her grey, wispy hair, told Ena Lizzie hadn't changed. The older woman's hands shook as she pulled a dirty shawl around her shoulders. She closed the door and stumbled past them without another word. Back at Cross Street, Jack's uncle told her what had happened to Lizzie, according to local gossip.

'Just before the start of the war, Lizzie's mother died. Do you remember her? Agatha Brown, she was your mother's aunt.'

Ena shook her head. 'No, I never met her. But I know she was to blame for Aunt Ivy being sent to Northumberland to work as a scullery maid and for sending me to…' Ena stopped. 'For sending me away.' John nodded.

'When she died, Lizzie's elder sister Mary came to make the funeral arrangements. Mary was the apple of her mother's eye and as different from Lizzie as it is possible to be. It was Mary and her husband who moved Lizzie from Pipewellgate to Cobden Terrace. Mary tried to persuade Lizzie to take the abstinence pledge. Rumour has it Lizzie's taste for alcohol started because her mother used whatever came to hand to pacify her when she was a baby. Agatha did anything she could to keep her younger daughter quiet and make her sleep, including using spirit laced with laudanum to sedate her. Mary stayed with Lizzie after the funeral and for a while, people said Lizzie was keeping away from the drink. Once Mary left, Lizzie was straight back to the Globe and her old habits. During the war, neighbours tried to help her but Lizzie is her own worst enemy.'

John said Ena could stay at Cross Street for as long as she wanted. Later, after they had eaten, Ena and Jack talked. About everything but the war. Jack told her he worked at the Cooperative Wholesale Society Flour Mill on the banks of the river.

'What do you do there?'

Jack looked at her and smiled. 'I'm a General Clerk.'

'What does it involve?'

Jack explained he kept records of grain in and flour out, making sure the books balanced. Ena told him about her book-keeping work during the war and her job with Reeves Solicitors.

'You could do that kind of work here, at the flour mill. If you decide to stay.'

Ena looked at Jack. In his eyes she saw she was home. On the train back to Bournemouth, she wrote to Aunt Ivy. She also wrote to the Cooperative Wholesale Society Flour Mill. She gave notice at Reeves and on her flat. Aunt Ivy travelled to Bournemouth for a farewell celebration. Unsurprisingly Ena's mother wasn't there, but everyone else came to wish her well. Ena looked at the family and friends around her, with Aunt Ivy by her side. She wrote in her diary later, *'we are all finding a way towards some sort of peace'*.

A few months later, Ena was working at the flour mill and living in a small flat above the Lyons Tea Shop on Bottle Bank, just a short walk from Jack's uncle's house. After work one day, Jack said he wanted to take Ena somewhere. She smiled up at him, remembering their childhood walks to the People's Park. 'Where are we going?' Jack smiled and touched the side of his nose. 'You'll see. It's a bit of a walk.' Ena linked her arm through Jack's and started walking. Their walk took them through lush green fields and past little villages. Ena smiled, she had known there were better parts of Gateshead, better homes than the one she was forced to endure as a girl, but she had never seen them. Until now. When they reached the top of Carrs Bank, Jack stopped. 'We're here.'

Ena looked around. In the field to her right stood a magnificent beech tree. Two brown horses grazed under the tree, oblivious to her and Jack. 'Where is here? What is this place, Jack?'

Jack looked down at her and smiled. 'Someone at work mentioned it, Ena. She called it '*the village on the hill*' and it sounded like the place you've talked about.'

Ena covered her mouth with her hands and shook her head. Her words were a whisper. 'You listened to me.'

Jack took her hands. 'Of course I did. Now let's see if this village matches the picture you've had in your mind for so long.'

The first thing to strike Ena about Whickham was how green it was. Fields and trees stretched as far as her eyes could see. They walked through Chase Park where the trees continued, along with rows of bushes and flowers. Statuesque oaks ran in a line from an old windmill. Jack stopped walking and turned to her. 'At one time, the villagers will have milled their own grain into flour to make bread.' They walked to the end of the park then retraced their steps, wanting to see as much of the village as possible. They left the park and walked along the street running through the middle of the village. Front Street. Ena pointed at a building on the opposite side of the street and they crossed the road to take a closer look. To Ena, Whickham Parochial School appeared welcoming and not at all intimidating. Jack pointed at the roof of the school, where a stone turret, or as Jack said, a bellcote, housed the school bell. Ena shuddered, remembering the bell at South Street booming out from its tower. To her, this village felt different. Friendly. A little way along from the school was St Mary's Church. A wide expanse of green lay in front of the church and Ena pictured the village green being the perfect place for children from the school to play.

'Look at the shops, Jack. That one is a baker's and there, look! It's the Whickham branch of the Swalwell Cooperative Society, the sign says the shop sells teas, coffees and cocoa.' Jack looked at the buildings then turned to Ena. 'It's nice here, isn't it?' Ena nodded and they continued walking. At the end of Front Street, they turned left into Fellside Road. To their right were rows of terraced streets, leading, Jack said, to a pit. 'I know a little about coal mining, Ena.' Ena looked up, eager to hear more. 'Coal mining is important here because Whickham and the surrounding areas are rich in good quality coal. Wagonways and railways criss-cross the villages, on their way down to the staithes on the river. The coal is loaded onto ships and sent all over the world.' Ena nodded, impressed by Jack's knowledge. A little way up Fellside Road, Jack stopped. He pointed to a sign at the top of a steep road. 'This is it, the street the woman at work mentioned. West Street.'

Over the coming months, Ena and Jack continued walking up to Whickham after work. At the very bottom of West Street, they found the perfect house. With gardens to the front and back they quickly agreed on a name for it. Littlecroft. At work one day, Ena found Jack sitting outside the back of the flour mill, hunched over a writing pad. She moved closer. 'What are you drawing, Jack?' He turned the pad towards her and smiled. 'It's the garden I pictured when we saw the house at the bottom of West Street. When we saw Littlecroft.' Ena looked over Jack's shoulder. The garden was in an H shape and Ena saw Jack had already sectioned the garden off into vegetables, flowers and lawn, bordered on all sides by bushes and trees. He had written the names of certain vegetables in the top half of the H; turnips, potatoes, cauliflower and some berries; strawberries, raspberries and currants. In the bottom half of the H, the flowers included roses and pansies.

'I can see myself sitting looking at that garden, Jack, while I read.'

Jack looked up at Ena. His girl who came back. He knelt down in front of her. 'Ena Leighton, will you do me the honour of becoming my wife?'

Ena laughed and pulled Jack to his feet. 'Yes, I will!'

They stood outside the flour mill, arms around each other. Ena's eyes followed the bends of the river, back in the direction of Pipewellgate, where she had known such misery. She thought about the people in her life; people she had learnt things from, good and bad. That night, she turned to a new page in her notebook and wrote, *'The Village on the Hill'*. Underneath she wrote one word.

'Home.'

THE END

AUTHOR'S NOTE

Writing a story within the context of key historical events, I was keenly aware of getting my facts right. I also kept reminding myself that I was writing a fictional account of the ways my characters were affected by these events. As a history lover, I could have carried on reading about RMS *Titanic*, World War One and the Spanish Flu and never finished writing *The Village on the Hill*, but finish it I did and I hope readers enjoy it.

I read many accounts of *Titanic's* disastrous fate, the horrors of the 1914 – 1918 conflict and the now-frighteningly familiar Spanish Flu pandemic of 1918. Those I drew on most extensively in telling my story were: Sam Halpern's beautifully detailed *Titanic Chronology* which first appeared in *Samuel Halpern, et al., Report Into the Loss of the SS Titanic – A Centennial Reappraisal, The History Press, 2011*; Wendy Moore's marvellous *Endell Street: The Women Who Ran Britain's Trailblazing Military Hospital, Atlantic Books, 2020*; and Laura Spinney's fascinating *Pale Rider: The Spanish Flu of 1918 and How it Changed the World, Vintage Digital, 2017*.

I took some artistic licence in my descriptions of *Titanic's* orchestra and the accommodation, decorations and facilities on board, but I retained other key features such as the fate of the Grand Staircase and the number of lifeboats. Ena's school in Bournemouth is fictional but I based it on descriptions of two Bournemouth schools from the time, moving it closer to Lansdowne Road and Capstone Road to enable Ena and Rachel to walk to school.

Any apparent errors or misinterpretations are mine and mine alone.

The Village On The Hill is Annie Doyle's second novel. The story follows some of the characters from Annie's debut novel *The Cocoa Girls,* based on her nana's life and inspired by long-hidden family secrets, uncovered when Annie undertook some family history research.
Annie lives in Gateshead and is currently working on her third novel, *The Good Neighbour.*
Contact Annie on Facebook Twitter or Instagram.

Photo by ValeriejaiPhotos